Juno Rushdan is the aw
action-packed romantic
edge of your seat. She w
strong heroines fighting for their lives
happily-ever-afters. As a veteran air force intelligence officer, she uses her background supporting Special Forces to craft realistic stories that make you sweat and swoon. Juno currently lives in the DC area with her patient husband, two rambunctious kids and a spoiled rescue dog. To receive a FREE book from Juno, sign up for her newsletter at junorushdan.com/mailing-list. Also be sure to follow Juno on BookBub for the latest on sales at bit.ly/BookBubJuno

Beth Cornelison began working in public relations before pursuing her love of writing romance. She has won numerous honours for her work, including a nomination for the RWA *RITA*® Award for *The Christmas Stranger*. She enjoys featuring her cats (or friends' pets) in her stories and always has another book in the pipeline! She currently lives in Louisiana with her husband, one son and three spoiled cats. Contact her via her website, bethcornelison.com

Also by Juno Rushdan

Rogue Christmas Operation
Hostile Pursuit
Witness Security Breach
High-Priority Asset
Innocent Hostage
Unsuspecting Target
Tracing a Kidnapper

Also by Beth Cornelison

Rancher's Deadly Reunion
Rancher's High-Stakes Rescue
Rancher's Covert Christmas
Rancher's Hostage Rescue
In the Rancher's Protection
Colton 911: Deadly Texas Reunion
The Return of Connor Mansfield
Protecting Her Royal Baby
The Mansfield Rescue

ALASKAN CHRISTMAS ESCAPE

JUNO RUSHDAN

COLTON 911: SECRET ALIBI

BETH CORNELISON

MILLS & BOON

First Published in Great Britain 2021
by Mills & Boon, an imprint of HarperCollins*Publishers* Ltd
1 London Bridge Street, London, SE1 9GF

www.harpercollins.co.uk

HarperCollins*Publishers*
1st Floor, Watermarque Building,
Ringsend Road, Dublin 4, Ireland

Special thanks and acknowledgement are given to Beth Cornelison for her contribution to the *Colton 911: Chicago* series.

ISBN: 978-0-263-28362-4

1121

This book is produced from independently certified FSC™ paper to ensure responsible forest management.

For more information visit: www.harpercollins.co.uk/green

Printed and Bound in Spain using 100% Renewable electricity at CPI Black Print, Barcelona

ALASKAN CHRISTMAS ESCAPE

JUNO RUSHDAN

This is for my little ones, K. and A.

Thank you for your patience and for being my biggest cheerleaders.

Chapter One

You're a fugitive, Zenobia Hanley reminded herself. Getting in any deeper with this man, regardless of how amazing he was, would only end in disaster. Might even get him killed.

"Thanks for the wonderful meal," she said, washing the last plate and handing it to John.

"All I did was cook the roast." Drying the dish, he smiled, a charming flash of white teeth that never failed to make her heart flutter. "You made everything else, and it was excellent as usual." His grin grew wider and that flutter inside her spread deeper.

Taking the wineglass from her hand, he brushed his fingers across hers. Their gazes caught and held. His grass-green eyes sparkled in the warm firelight of the room.

Zee struggled to keep her thoughts silent, but they leaked out like the water running through her fingers. "We should do this again tomorrow."

His smile faltered. He turned, putting the dishes away. "Two days in a row?" He gave a low whistle. "When we started this arrangement, you made it clear that once a week, for a game of chess, was more than enough. I've respected that."

Chess had turned into lunch. Lunches into dinners.

"I was being careful," she admitted. "A city girl, alone,

in the remote wilderness. I didn't want to give you the wrong impression." To show any hint of weakness, no vulnerability, especially to a man who had a coiled readiness to him, reflexes honed to a razor-sharp edge. "That was before we became friends and I got to know you." Now she was confident he was one of the good guys. Even though he had secrets and a past, too. None of which he wanted to discuss any more than she did. "It's the holidays. Besides, we see each other three or four days a week as is."

"While trading, my goods for yours. A shared cup of coffee in between. Fishing when the weather is good. Not this."

Something inside her sank. Their time together was starting to change. Evolve. Their get-togethers felt less casual and more romantic each time. That wasn't healthy for either of them.

"You're right." She dried her hands on a towel. "Sorry for suggesting we break a rule I set." But she liked *this.* She liked *him. A lot.* Despite her best intentions, she'd grown to rely on John, for far more than game meet and chopped firewood. "Let's forget it."

Grabbing her coat from the back of a chair, she turned to leave, which was for the best.

"Don't misunderstand me." John put a hand on her shoulder, turning her around. He stared at her, really studying her, as if what he was about to say next mattered. "It is the holidays." He dropped his hand. "I'd love to do this tomorrow. I'll make venison stew. How about we do it at your place?"

She had changed the boundaries, and now he was testing to see how far they could be stretched. She slipped on her parka. "Is it okay if we hang out here again?"

Being able to make a graceful exit whenever she needed was important. No hurt feelings. No pressure.

His brow furrowed as he raked a hand through his shaggy light brown hair. "Why don't we ever spend time inside your house?"

She shrugged. "Your place is cozier." She glanced around at his framed photos of family and friends hung on the walls and at the hand-stitched quilt that his mother had made for him draped on the back of the sofa.

John was shrewd and if he spent enough time in her place, he'd eventually notice that she lived like a ghost. Not a hint of anything personal in the space. Her cabin was a sterile showroom that would make him uneasy after a few hours. Cause him to ask questions.

There were countless reasons why they didn't need to hang out in her cabin.

"Okay." He flashed an easy grin. "But come the New Year, we should shake things up."

She'd worry about that next year. "Let's make a whole day out of it. Begin with scones or maple pecan sticky buns."

"I love those fancy biscuits, but I want the sticky buns."

"Fresh rosemary bread to go with the stew. For dessert, I can make apple pie."

"My mouth is watering already, but you're spoiling me."

"I'm doing no such thing. You hunt and chop the wood. I go into town for essentials you can't forage, and I ply you with all the home-baked goods you can handle. That's our deal."

Fishing was as far as she was willing to go to become a wilderness woman while John wasn't much for baking and avoided going into Fairbanks at all costs.

"At the irresistible rate you're going, I don't know if I'll be able to keep my willpower in check and my waistline from expanding." John put a hand to his taut belly that was in no danger of getting flabby anytime soon.

"You have nothing to worry about." Zee patted his chest without thinking, and he covered her hand with his, holding her palm there. The isolation, the great expanse of wilderness got to her sometimes, had her craving the barest physical contact. So, she allowed herself to enjoy the hard contours beneath his turtleneck as he tensed and leaned into her touch. He had a heavily muscled frame. Up close he was imposing, in a sexy way. "You look great."

Warmth from the hearth curled around them. The soft amber glow played over his features. The term *ruggedly handsome* didn't do this man justice.

But she had made a horrible mistake once in getting involved with the wrong guy. A gross error in judgment that haunted her to this day, making her doubt whether a *normal* relationship was possible.

John was different, on a cellular level, from the monster who had hurt her, but it didn't change the fact that she was on the run. Her situation alone made any relationship impossible.

Stop courting disaster. "It's late." Already after eleven.

She lowered her hand and put on her gloves. John followed her to the door.

Smiling down at her, he took the wool cap hanging from her pocket and tugged it over her curls that she'd corralled into a ponytail. As he lowered his hands, he grazed her ears and cheeks. The contact was light and brief, and more than enough to make her breath catch and belly tighten.

"I can walk you home," he said, his voice gravelly and low.

"No need." Her place was less than a quarter mile cutting through the woods on foot. Not to mention she had the loaded Beretta she carried everywhere in her coat pocket. In Alaska, it was odd if you weren't always armed. One of the reasons she'd chosen to hide out up here. "It's snowing again. I remember the weather makes your leg ache."

He dropped his gaze and stepped back. "My leg only aches when rain and trouble are coming." His tone turned flat and dry. "For some reason, the snow doesn't bother me too much." He cracked the door open, letting in a bitter December breeze. "I'll see you tomorrow. I'm looking forward to it. To the sticky buns. You're an amazing cook."

Zee's heart shriveled like a dried prune and she knew it wouldn't plump back up until she saw John's smile again. "You're too kind," she said, equally flat, regretting that she'd chosen a humdrum word for the most captivating man she'd ever met.

He pulled up her faux-fur-lined hood over her head. "If you need me for anything, just give me a holler on the radio."

"Sure." She kept her two-way radio on her nightstand within easy reach. "Good night." She felt like a hug—a platonic one; some simple gesture was in order, but she stuffed her hands in her pockets, curling her fingers around the hilt of her gun instead.

"'Night, Zee," he said with a tip of his head.

She hurried out, and when she glanced back, the door was closed.

Bracing against the brutal slap of the cold, she ran down the porch steps and trotted through the snow, taking the same path she followed several times a week.

Had the comment about his leg triggered the abrupt goodbye? She simply hadn't wanted him to go to the trouble of walking her home in this snow.

When had showing consideration become a faux pas?

She'd gleaned he was ex-military from the way he carried himself and fluidly used military jargon and guessed that it wasn't his choice to leave the service. He never talked about it. Or how he had injured his leg. He had an easy, self-assured gait and no hint of a limp unless he'd been sitting for a long time. Even then it disappeared after a minute or two and he was a good runner. Though she suspected the act brought him some discomfort. One night after too much wine, he'd made a comment about his disability check and she'd put the pieces together.

But like John, she had too much respect to pry. There was also the fact that asking questions invited the tables to turn. Her answers would only expose him to unnecessary trouble.

On her porch, she stomped most of the snow off her boots. She hurried inside, then shut the door behind her. The knifelike chill that had settled in her bones started to drain as she soaked in the festive glow of the Christmas lights that she'd strung up in the living room.

She longed to be with her family. How she missed them. All of them.

Peeling off her coat, she removed her gun from the pocket. She tossed the parka onto a chair and slipped the weapon into the back of her waistband.

In the kitchen, she got a drink of water to combat having too much wine with dinner.

Her gaze fell to her laptop on the table and she cursed her talent. Her gift.

Hacking wasn't something she did, it was who she was, and it posed the biggest danger to her, but it might be the only way to clear her name. She'd give anything to have her life restored.

Her entire team had been forced to flee. Zee might be able prove their innocence if given the chance. Already she'd risked everything by digging where she shouldn't. She'd found important breadcrumbs. Now she had to follow the trail and see where it led.

She trudged into her bedroom and plopped down on her bed. Glancing at the handheld radio on her nightstand, she contemplated calling John. Have him come over and make her forget about her troubles. In a different universe, she would, but in this one, she was a fugitive who needed to be ready to run at a moment's notice.

If she slept with John, gave him her heart and then had to bolt later, she'd be tempted to say goodbye and offer some brief explanation. Not simply disappear without a word. The time it'd take, two minutes, ten, to say farewell could mean the difference between life and death.

RYKER RUDIN WASN'T a patient man, but it was more efficient to wait for his team to round up all the civilians on the premises before he got down to the business of killing.

Give his spiel once and then the first bullet would have the biggest impact. This boiled down to professional expediency.

The back outer door of the hackerspace opened, letting in an Arctic gust of late-night air that tasted of pine. His man, Delta Three—code names only on a mission—hauled in the last person here tonight. Officially the 24/7 lab was a community space for like-minded people with common interests such as computers, technology and digital art.

Unofficially, it was a space for hackers. The name was a bit on the nose in his opinion.

Delta Three shoved the sobbing woman who had made a run for it down to the floor. With her palms raised, she crouched beside the others, all trembling together in a huddle.

Ryker, known as Delta Prime for this CIA assignment, crossed his legs and swung the muzzle of the gun toward the group.

The five technophiles shrank back, cowering as if a bullet might fly at any second.

It could.

Eyeing them one by one, Ryker withdrew the sound suppressor from the pocket of his leather trench coat and attached it to the threaded barrel. "Whether or not I kill you is your choice. Tell me what I need to know and I won't shoot you. I'm looking for a woman. Zenobia Hanley," he said, and a knee-jerk spike of lust tangled inextricably with the ever-constant rage flowing through his veins.

A flurry of memories flashed like lightning. Holding her in bed, their sweat-covered bodies pressed close. The look in her eyes, once filled with affection for him. Her unthinkable betrayal that had left him gutted. Furious.

Ryker swallowed the bitter taste in his mouth. "Light brown complexion, brown eyes, long, dark curly hair. Slim build. Hers is not a face you'd soon forget." Maybe never regardless how hard you tried. He gestured to Delta Seven to show her picture. "I need to know how often she's been here and where I can find her. She may be going by a different name. Might prefer to be called Zee."

The twentysomething blond guy lowered his head and squeezed his eyes shut, jaw clenching before he was shown the picture. He was the one they needed. Blondie knew her.

Ryker stood and stalked closer. Aimed his weapon at the woman who had been brought in last. "Someone better start talking, or I start shooting."

One. Two. Three. He pulled the trigger. A single bullet spat from the end of the long black barrel, and the woman collapsed. The others screamed and sniveled, clutching one another as if there were safety in numbers. There wasn't.

Ryker stepped in front of the next person. Lowered the muzzle to his forehead.

"Wait!" Blondie said. "Please, stop. She goes by Zee.

No last name. She was in here earlier and yesterday, too. Over the past nine months or so, she comes in every two or three weeks. Except for this month. She started coming in several times a week."

"Why the change?" Ryker asked.

"I think she was close to finding something big. But she was scared to dig. Afraid to stay online too long for any given period."

Fear was a survival instinct, and when heeded, it kept you alive. Her fear had been justified. She had dug too deep for too long.

The CIA had caught her yesterday and unleashed Ryker's team for cleanup—a palatable euphemism for assassination. He wouldn't rest until he reclaimed what she'd stolen from him.

Then he would kill her. Slowly. Brutally. Preferably with his bare hands. His vengeance had been a long time coming. "Does she ever come in with anyone or only on her own?"

"Always alone."

"Where can I find her?"

"I don't know." Blondie shrugged. "I swear."

Ryker pulled the trigger, executing a redhead.

"Please!" Blondie raised his palms. "Don't do this. She'll be back in a few days. Just stick around and wait."

What a brilliant idea. His team could cram into the local hotel and roast marshmallows while twiddling their thumbs.

"We're on a tight schedule." Ryker clasped his wrist in front of him and tapped the sound suppressor against his leg. "She may not have told you the name of the town she lives in, but I assure you she's given you enough information to help us zero in on her residence." Zee was a natural chatter, made friends wherever she went. Being on the run, separated from the rest of her old team, she would be inclined to strike up conversations with regular faces. "She lives in a town with no internet, correct?"

Blondie nodded. "Yes, yes. That's why she comes here."

She didn't want the constant temptation of being able to get online. Smart. "How long is the drive for her?"

"Uh, an hour in the summer. With snow it takes her longer. Last time, she mentioned maybe an hour and a half."

"Does she own or rent?"

"She rents, I think. A small cabin."

"Did she ever mention a particular route she takes, the 2 or 3?"

"I don't know," Blondie cried. "Please."

They always became whiny, falling back on useless entreaties. Ryker lowered to a knee and cupped the man's face in his leather-gloved hand. "Shh. Calm down. Think. Route 2 or 3."

Blondie sucked in a shaky breath. "She complained about the late plow of a road once. The 2, I believe. Yeah, that was it."

"That puts her north of Fairbanks," Ryker said to his team, and Delta Ten continued inputting all the information in their shared database with the agency. Their designated intelligence analyst was working this in real time. They would collate the data, scan rental records, date of occupancy, owners who accepted cash on a month-to-month basis, and cross-reference it with roads and terrain to pinpoint the needle in the haystack. The more data the better. "What does she drive?"

"A silver pickup. Old. Ford."

Good. A vehicle parked outside a residence was useful when verifying the location on satellite imagery.

"Did she ever mention a view where she lives?"

"It's Alaska—everyone has a view."

Ryker sighed. "A particular mountain. A lake. River. Campground. Forest."

"Yeah. A neighbor taught her to fish. She's in walking distance to a large pond or a lake and a river. The Chatanika."

Fishing? Zee wasn't an outdoorsy woman but perhaps being forced to live in the boondocks to stay off the CIA's radar inspired changes. "Name of the neighbor?"

"John something or other. A disabled vet. Helpful guy."

One look at Zee would turn an uncooperative curmudgeon into an accommodating fool. Ryker bet the man had been helpful indeed.

Delta Ten nodded. "We've got her location."

Faster than Ryker had expected. Then again, the area was sparsely populated, even more so outside the city, and rentals on the outskirts were bound to be limited.

"Are you going to kill me?" Blondie asked.

"No, I won't." Ryker patted his cheek. "I'm a man of my word." He was, and hope had been necessary to elicit honest answers. But none of the technophiles would survive. Once his team was finished, the place would be torched. "Delta Fifteen will kill you." Four pips in rapid succession followed, and the hackers slumped over, dead. "We'll hit her location at 0200," Ryker said to his entire team over comms, preferring to wait until the wee hours. "Catch the target while she's sleeping. You're free to wound her. I don't care how badly, so long as it's not fatal. I want to look that traitor in the eyes right before I kill her. So she knows that it was me."

"I'M LOOKING FORWARD to the sticky buns," John Lowry muttered under his breath.

You should've kissed her, you idiot.

Sticky buns?

John had sat in front of the fire for hours, replaying the evening, and he was still berating himself.

Zee was wicked smart, cool in a cosmopolitan way that screamed she didn't belong out in the Last Frontier, and one hell of a chess player. A real knockout, too, way out of his league.

Runner's physique. Smooth skin the color of wet sand. A Cupid's-bow mouth. Almond-shaped eyes. Her hair was stunning, especially when she left it loose and wild. He'd never seen anything like it. A magnificent mass of dark spiral curls that he ached to wrap his fingers around and feel spread across his bare chest, sliding over his belly.

Maybe he should traipse down to her house and knock on the door. She might open it wearing her nightgown and a smile, those curls loose around her shoulders. Take his hand and lead him to her bedroom.

He glanced at the clock. Two in the morning. She'd be more likely to open the door with a loaded gun and a scowl and rightfully so.

Growling in frustration, he picked up the silly romance novel Zee had given him as a lark, which he'd been stupid enough to read, and tossed it into the fire.

Zee was wary, her guard always up. Everything she had told him tonight about being more comfortable around him had made sense.

The Alaskan wilderness held extra dangers for women. Not long after moving here he'd learned that this state had the highest rate of rape in the country. Getting to know him and discover he was a decent guy had probably been a delicate balancing act for her. One he respected. Still, he sensed there was a deeper reason behind the boundaries she'd created. She was running, hiding, the same as him.

His demons were personal. There was something inside him that he couldn't switch off, something restless, bred by the military and capable of ugly things for the right reasons. But Uncle Sam no longer wanted him. Had stripped him of his purpose and put him out to pasture.

Forty years old, retired and miserable.

Loneliness was bad, but Zee kept him from reflecting on the misery. The only time he felt alive, happy, these days was when he was with her. In her absence, he was aware of the gaping hole in his life.

He believed her demons were of a physical nature. The giveaway was the perimeter intruder alarms she had set up in the woods around the vicinity of her place. Shortly after she'd moved in, he'd spotted them mounted to the trees. He suspected she might be out here taking such precautions because of an acrimonious breakup. Maybe she had an ex stalking her.

John looked at the mini decorated Christmas tree she had given him to spruce up his place for the holidays. He smiled, though his chest ached.

He didn't want to ruin what was real with her for what might be possible. Yes, he wanted to hold her, make love to her until they were both sated, share the things on his mind that he kept bottled up. Which was bananas since they hadn't even hugged much less kissed.

And what woman in her prime wanted a broken man like him anyway? A washed-up vet, almost ten years her senior, booted from the service for a bum leg and PTSD.

He wanted Zee in his life in any capacity, even if it was only platonic.

A cold shower was what he needed. Though it was a temporary fix. Come tomorrow, one look at her, one hair-flip over her shoulder, one whiff of her skin—coconut and flowers, she smelled like a vacation destination he never wanted to leave—one lick of her tongue across her lips, and he would be a hot mess of a man yearning for something he couldn't have.

John stood, stretching out his stiff right leg. A brutal throb ran from his thigh through his knee to the tibia—the particular ache that forecasted rain.

Or trouble.

A shower and sleep would do him good. Tackle the next day with a clear head. He'd take a long walk before she came over so he could keep up his streak of not needing his medication.

Stretching, he crossed the room and then stopped.

Instinct kicked in before his ears caught the sound. The telltale *whomp-whomp-whomp* was quiet. Too quiet to be military. Or search and rescue. After eighteen years in Special Forces and three living out in the Alaskan wilderness, he knew the difference. If music had been playing or he had been asleep, he would have missed the sound entirely.

That *whomp-whomp* was getting louder, resonating in his soul.

He snatched his down jacket from the hook, stepped out onto his porch and searched the night sky. Clouds obscured the aurora borealis that would otherwise be visible. He took a deep breath, scanning carefully, and waited. The hair on the back of his neck stood on end and it had nothing to do with the crisp, frigid air vibrating around him.

Where is it? Where is it? Where—

Ah, there it is. At his three o'clock.

A black helicopter cut through the sky.

His heart thudded as the chopper took a position over the woods, where it hovered in the scant moonlight. From the outline of the unmarked helicopter, it didn't look like law enforcement. Possibly foreign. He couldn't be sure, but it was unusual.

Four ropes dropped, dangling from the aircraft.

His brain recoiled, yet what he was seeing registered. This was a covert operation. But there was something very wrong about it that gnawed at him.

In his gut, all the way down to the ache in his leg, he sensed this was bad.

Men in tactical gear rappelled down each rope. Close to Zee's place. So close they wouldn't trigger the perimeter alarms she had put up farther out.

Ice water rushed in John's veins. *Zee.*

The four men touched the ground. Red laser sights popped on. Then four more rappelled from the helicopter.

Ah, hell.

Lights came down the main road. Two vehicles stopped and killed their headlights. Once again near Zee's. The ice water in his veins froze solid. How many of them were there?

They weren't SWAT, not police nor FBI. Of that he was certain. He didn't know who they were, but he did know that they were a strike team of some kind, heading for Zee.

His heart was hammering now. A warning chill rippled down his spine, telling him not to stand by and let whatever was happening simply unfold. It was instinctual, and he'd always trusted his instincts.

He had to get to her, which meant going through them, but there was no way he'd make it to Zee in time before those men reached her place.

Chapter Two

"Zee."

She roused at the sound of John's voice calling her name. Rolling over, she reached for him, but only found a cold, empty side of the bed.

Groaning, she opened her eyes. *No John.* She was alone and dreaming about him again.

"Zee!" His voice was low and harsh with urgency.

She jackknifed up in her bed and grabbed the walkie-talkie. "What's wrong, John? Are you okay?"

"They're coming for you. Closing in fast. Hot and heavy. Get out of the house. Now. Go west."

A fist of ice clenched in her gut. Why hadn't her alarms gone off?

She dropped the radio. Tugged on her jeans and boots. Whipped off her nightgown, trading it for the cashmere sweater that she'd taken off last night. She snatched the gun from the nightstand.

Her gaze cut over her coat on a chair in the living room, to the kitchen. Her laptop was in there. Traces of *everything* she'd looked up were still on the hard drive.

Movement outside her window seized her attention. Her eyes strained to see into the murky shadows.

She spotted the dark silhouettes of two men, coming

up onto her porch. Red laser sights from their automatic weapons sliced through the air.

Damn it. There was no time.

She ducked low and bolted for her closet. Inside on the floor was a door she had installed. Not an easy task and one that had taken her days to get it right. She lifted the door without making a sound thanks to the WD-40 she used on the hinges every other week planning for this very eventuality.

Preparation drove her to stay in peak physical condition. Hours of training every single day. Running with a thirty-pound pack on her back, double what she might have to haul for real. Push-ups, sit-ups, pull-ups, burpees. Krav Maga classes in Fairbanks to stay sharp. She had to be ready in case this happened.

The front door squeaked open and the floorboards she'd deliberately loosened creaked under the heavy footfalls, revealing the enemy's location with every step.

Closing the door behind her, she ducked down into the crawl space.

She counted as she crept on her hands and knees through the dark, hollow area between the ground and the floor of the cabin. Once she reached ten, she stretched out her right hand and her fingers closed around her emergency go bag—a duffel made of laminated, high-density nylon that was impenetrable to nature's assaults and contained everything she needed to run.

The boards above her groaned as dust fell, clogging the air. She held her breath rather than dare risk a cough or sneeze that would give away her position.

From the sounds overhead, four men were in the house now, searching the rooms.

Zee unzipped her go bag and ran through the protocol she had rehearsed numerous times blindfolded, anticipating a real scenario would require her to do it at night in the pitch-black dark. She threw on the bulletproof vest that had zippered sides instead of noisy Velcro. On one hip, she attached the holster with her telescopic baton. On the other, she hooked the specially designed holster that held a suppressed 9mm.

She dumped the Beretta inside the bag and made a quick sightless check by hand of the rest of her gear.

Grabbing the *create-a-distraction* device, she tugged on a streamlined coat, thankful she'd packed one to blend in with the snow. She pocketed the device, dropped to her belly and slipped her arms through the straps of the duffel that weighed exactly fifteen pounds, wearing the bag like a backpack.

"Prime, this is Delta Two. The target isn't here," a man said from inside the house. "But the bed is still warm, and we found a laptop."

Damn. How sloppy of her not to scrub the computer clean earlier before dashing off to John's. She had been so excited to see him for dinner, but at the very least, she should've brought the laptop into the bedroom like she did most nights.

Rule number one on the run—no margin for error. She had broken it, messing up big time. Such a stupid mistake that could cost her what she cared about most in the world.

Zee waited to hear a response from Prime, but didn't, so the reply must have been given over their comms.

That meant whoever was leading this Delta kill team was out in the woods somewhere.

"Understood," Delta Two said.

Furniture was tipped over clunking to the floor. They were looking for her escape door to follow her tracks.

Zee low crawled to the west exit of her hidey-hole and pulled the wood cutout in toward her since the snow on the other side was pressed against the foundation. She burrowed out with her bare hands, wishing she had packed spare gloves, and peeked both ways.

Men wearing night-vision goggles were searching the woods. Multiple red beams swept all around. The combination of their NVGs and laser sights gave them every advantage, not including the sheer number of them.

She steadied her breath, bracing herself, and waited for the right moment to move. The device in one hand and her suppressed weapon in the other. Her field of view was limited with threats lurking beyond her vantage point.

Now this was instinct. Prey trying to escape predator.

Another long, deep breath, silencing the whisper of fear, oxygenating her blood and stoking her adrenaline to a pure white heat. When her opening came, she scurried from under the house, scrambled up the mound of snow and bolted for the forest.

Bullets bit into the trees behind her. She kept running, her head low, zigzagging to avoid getting shot, but she never slowed.

Grasping hold of the device in her pocket, she pressed the remote trigger. Explosives she had rigged under the cabin detonated.

The explosion shook the earth, ripping the front door off its hinges and knocking anyone close by off their feet as the house went up in a fireball. Fragments of wood and stone blew a good fifty feet into the air, pelting the surrounding ground.

The blast would have killed anyone inside, and the pandemonium would buy her a few precious seconds. If she was lucky, they hadn't had a chance to get the laptop out. She prayed that was the case.

She pressed on, headed west, like John had told her to go, toward his house. Slim chance the CIA kill team had been tuned in to the two-way frequency since they were dialed into their own comms.

Still, danger would follow her for certain. She didn't want to put John at risk. But his cabin sat on a hill at an advantage. Also, he had spotted the team inbound and had warned her. He had some idea of what was out in these woods stalking her.

Don't think.

Keep moving.

Breathe.

Run.

A twig snapped on her left.

She spun in a crouch toward the sound, gun at the ready. Squeezed the trigger.

The first bullet struck her pursuer in the shoulder, throwing off his aim. On a bended knee, she stabilized her gun hand with a two-hand hold, exhaled and fired.

A clean head shot.

Before she could fully stand and pivot, someone struck her in a football tackle from the side, taking her down to the cold ground.

He was big and heavy. Another one from the tactical team.

She raised her gun, angling for a shot around his body armor and going for his neck. But he seized her wrist and pinned her with his body weight, squeezing the air from her chest. She dug her heels in the snow and bucked her hips up, struggling to move him. To shift the slab of muscle a few inches, giving her the latitude to throw a knee to his groin.

He bore down harder, not allowing her the slightest chance to maneuver.

In this wrestling match, he outweighed and outmuscled her.

There was no contest. Were their orders to kill her on sight, or torture her first for information about the whereabouts of the remaining members of Team Topaz?

No matter what, she'd never talk. She'd fight to the death to protect those she loved. Delta could go to hell, and she'd take out as many of them as she could right along with her.

He slammed her wrist against the forest floor, trying to get her to drop her weapon. She tightened her grasp. Two rounds went off, hit a tree.

If he disarmed her, it was game over and she was as good as dead.

She relaxed her arms, but not the hand clenched around her gun, and stopped struggling, pretending to relent. He rotated as if preparing to stand and she launched her knee up between his legs with all her might.

His breath hissed out, his eyes rolled up into the back of his head, his whole body tensed from the excruciating pain only a man could understand. She slammed the heel of her palm up into his nose, thrusting him to the side. Scrambling to her feet, she came face-to-face with another one from Delta. He already had her locked in his sights, finger on the trigger.

Zee's stomach bottomed out. Every muscle clenched, a blade of fear slicing through the adrenaline, chilling her heart.

There was nothing she could do.

Someone swept up behind the man with the lightning speed of a shadow.

John. He threw a kick to the back of the guy's knee, bringing him down, and flipped off the tactical helmet and then struck him across the skull with a gun, knocking the guy out cold.

She exhaled with momentary relief and ran to John.

They locked eyes for a suspended instant as he took her hand, his fingers closing around hers. Something gave way under the strain and washed over her. A startling sense that everything would be okay if they were together.

"What's going on?" John whispered. "Who are these men? Are you in trouble with the law?"

"They aren't law enforcement and I'm no criminal. I promise you." Her gaze fell and she saw it.

A red laser dot on his chest.

Zee lunged in front of John, putting herself between him and the bullet.

The first slug that struck her chest hit her harder than a punch, stealing her breath. The tremendous impact of the second twisted her sideways and dropped her like a sack of potatoes.

It hurt like hell. Shockwaves of pain coursed through her stunned body, her vision blurred, her mind reeling. She wanted to move, to fight, but she could barely breathe.

A tear leaked from her eye as sounds of a struggle filled her ears. She had to get up. To help John. The gun was still in her hand, but she couldn't wiggle a finger.

Quick, brutal blows resounded, fists pummeling flesh. Then there was the crunch of bone snapping.

Her heart quivered.

Not John. Please! Not because of me.

A body hit the ground beside her with a thud. Black tactical gear. It was the man who she'd kneed in the groin.

John rushed to her, lowered to her side and dragged her onto his lap. He unzipped her coat and ran his hands over her, inspecting her body for wounds. He squeezed his eyes shut, a half smile spreading across his mouth. "The vest caught the bullets." He hugged her. "You're going to be okay."

Her chest loosened enough from the viselike grip of

agony for her to suck in a breath. She swallowed. Her throat felt swollen.

"Up," she whispered, her voice rough. "Help me up." She needed to be on her feet.

They had to move. There were too many men on the Delta team.

John grabbed the dead man's silenced weapon and something else from his utility belt before he hauled her up. "Eight fast-roped in. I don't know how many more came in by vehicle."

Were there a dozen of them tracking her? More? Why had they sent such a large team?

Leaning her against a tree, John gave her a second to catch her breath while he scanned the area.

"Come on," he said, taking two steps, and froze. "They're making a beeline toward my house." He gestured at the hill. "Head north. Around the lake to Asa's place." He was referring to one of the neighbors that didn't live too far away.

She shook her head. "I can't endanger anyone else."

"Go to the tree stand he uses for hunting. I'll make sure none of these bastards sneak up on your *six*," he said, using military jargon for *your back*, "and I'll meet you there."

"No, John." What was he thinking? He had no idea who these men were, what kind of hell she was up against. "You can't. It's too dangerous for you."

"Go." Ignoring her warning, he took off, darting around trees and disappeared like he was ready for full-on battle.

With the woods swarming with a large CIA hit squad, that was precisely what was going on tonight. Battle.

She grappled with the idea of following him for the longest second of her life. Four key things she had learned about John were that he knew how to handle himself in a melee, never made a rash decision, never bit off more than he could chew and always demonstrated good judgment. Always.

Trusting him was best under the circumstances despite her concerns, because the truth of the matter was there wasn't time to dissuade him otherwise.

Shoving off the tree, she hurried toward the lake. She doggedly pushed ahead, gritting her teeth through the pangs in her chest. With the woods around her quiet, she tried to keep her sound signature to a minimum as she moved. Her heart pounded against her temples steady as a metronome while she cursed herself for getting John roped up in this deadly business. If anything happened to him, she'd never forgive herself.

At the perimeter, staying hidden in the tree line, she noticed a man from Delta team closing in from the north, sweeping the area headed in her direction. Her first instinct was to crouch down and wait for him to pass by and then take him out, but his attention swung her way and he spotted her.

Damn NVGs.

The man stiffened and leaped into action.

Full panic rolled through Zee. Going east wasn't an option. Most of the kill team were out that way and if she headed back in the direction from which she'd come, it would only endanger John more. Doubling back was a mistake.

That left her with one choice.

To go *across* the lake.

Gunfire split a branch not ten inches from her face, leaving her no chance to back out. She rallied and dashed forward.

John had warned her to stay off the lake in the winter. Even though it looked frozen solid, it wasn't meant to

She swung her weapon at his head, but too late. It was like the jaws of hell opened as the ice gave way.

"Zee!" She heard her name as she grasped at the slippery terrain, not finding any purchase. "Hold on!" John's voice was drawing closer, but he was still too far away.

Hurry, John.

The broken surface tipped, and the operative was sucked toward the black watery hole.

The man flailed wildly, trying desperately to grab hold of something, anything to stop his descent into the icy water. At the last second, he snatched on to her ankle, his fingers biting into her skin. She cried out as he dragged her along with him into the frigid depths.

Chapter Three

No!

Paralyzing horror tore through John at the sight of Zee being dragged into the water. At the sound of her bloodcurdling scream. He'd witnessed the all-too-brief struggle and watched in impotent fear as that coward had held fast to her leg in desperation and yanked her into the dark lake.

John ran like a man possessed, sliding as he went across the ice, moving as fast as he could with his bad leg and the slippery surface. He ignored the stabbing pain slicing down his right thigh, shooting to his shin. Moving on autopilot, he gave no thought to hauling enough air into his lungs, only to driving his body forward. Harder. Faster.

No time. There wasn't a moment to spare. With the combined weight of the man and the duffel on her back, she didn't stand a chance on her own. She was drowning, every air sac stretched to the limit ready to burst, fighting for her life under the water.

He had to get her. To save her. She wasn't going to die.

Not on his watch.

The surface of the lake was solid beneath him, but the closer he drew to the hole, fissures and growing slits spread, allowing water to rise. He didn't dare approach any farther upright or would risk becoming a victim himself.

He dropped to his belly and rolled the rest of the way, to distribute his body weight over a larger surface area, making the ice less likely to break more.

Nearing the edge of the hole, as close as he could get without the entire plane that he was on falling through, he prepared to shed his coat and dive in after her.

But Zee popped out of the water, gulping in oxygen. Her arms flailed as she still managed to hold on to her gun. She must've somehow shed the grasp of that man, shooting him, or kicking him loose.

Either way, she was downright amazing.

She went back under. For one excruciating moment his heart stopped. Then she bobbed up to the surface again. This time she swam to the edge of the hole and used her elbows to lift herself partially out of the water. Without a doubt she was strong, but the weight of her wet clothes and the pack would make it impossible for her to hoist herself out.

John unfastened his belt buckle and slid the leather strap free from his jeans. He tossed her the buckle end.

Zee caught the metal piece, sputtering up lake water, gasping for air. Still clutching her gun.

"Kick your legs. Try to get your whole body horizontal." John pulled her out as she kicked, holding on to the belt buckle. The muscles in his arms and back burned from the strain at the awkward angle. He tugged harder, dragging her from the watery hole and clear from the edge to safety.

Lying on her stomach, she rested, panting, and heaving up water.

More men in tactical gear, wearing NVGs and carrying suppressed weapons with laser sights, burst from the tree line and rushed out onto the ice.

They just kept coming, worse than a pack of insurgents with human resources to burn.

John took Zee by the elbow, ushering her on their knees along the ice farther away from the hole. Taking the duffel from her back, he helped her stand.

Without protest, she rushed for the shore. He shoved his hand in his coat pocket and withdrew the one item that he'd taken from the dead man's utility belt.

A fragmentation grenade.

He pulled the pin, cocked back his arm, and lobbed the explosive device high and far in the air. Without waiting for the explosion, he whirled and took off.

Once Zee reached the shore and made her way to a tree, he glanced back. The grenade hit the ice and skidded, sliding toward the assault team.

The men caught sight of it. They skittered, their arms windmilling, their boots sliding, trying frantically to alter their course. They did a sharp one-eighty in the opposite direction. But not all of them would make it.

John groaned through the pain in his leg, forced to hop and slow his pace. He set foot on land and looked back as the earsplitting sound erupted.

Boom!

Ice shattered, shooting up into the air in shards. The rest of the surface groaned and collapsed like a chain of dominoes falling. Two men yelped, the solid terrain beneath them dissolving, and they plummeted into the ice-cold water.

A secondary blast echoed in John's head as memories reared up, eclipsing him as if it were happening all over again.

Dust clogged the hot air. Rubble fell around his team. Shrapnel shredded his leg. The pain. The pain was un-

bearable. Immense pressure bore down on his chest. Debris had him pinned. But Dawes and Thomas were down.

"John!" The sound of his name pulled him from the flashback.

Frozen in place a second, he glanced around, dazed, reorienting himself. Snow-covered trees and the lake came into focus in a slow, sickening whirl.

Alaska. Not Syria.

Zee. They needed to run, to go. Now.

Across the lake, there was someone watching them.

One man wearing a trench coat over his black tactical gear, no NVGs, no helmet, stood on the shoreline with his hands in his pockets. Rather than showing a shred of concern for his drowning men or casting a glance at the ones who had survived the close call, he stared at John and Zee. Not as though he was in shock, but as if he had all the time in the world, and this was merely intermission.

It was the first time John had felt a twinge of fear facing an enemy. Or maybe it was only a symptom of his PTSD.

"John!" Zee called again.

He turned and rushed to her. She was bent over with hands on her knees, struggling to catch her breath.

"I called you five times," she said. "Did you hear me?"

Five?

Holy hell. He must've lost total awareness of what was happening around him. That was dangerous. That could get them both killed.

"I heard you." He put an arm around her and helped her through the woods, out of sight from the man in the trench coat. Their breath crystallized on the air in great white puffs as they hauled themselves through the snow. "Those men are going to come around the lake on foot." What was left of them anyway. "Change of plans. We're going to Old Man Bill's cabin."

"What?" She stared at him, shaking her head. "You told me never to go across his property. Isn't he crazy? Aren't there traps in the surrounding woods?"

"Old Man Bill is surly, not certifiable. But there are foothold traps and dangerous snares." To help him catch animals, not to hurt passersby who Bill felt should not be on his property to begin with. For that reason, there were numerous bright yellow no trespassing signs posted to the trees so no one would miss the warning. "The trick is to go from one tree with a sign to the next. I'll guide you since I know where his traps are, but I need to cover our trail in the snow as we go so those men don't track us. Move as quickly as you can. It'll be hard, but you've got to push yourself." After taking off his coat, he draped it around her. He estimated she'd be able to hustle for five to ten minutes before hypothermia and frostbite set in, overriding the adrenaline, and slowed her down.

Sweat slicked his brow and coated his back from all the exertion. Without a jacket he wouldn't last long either. The wind slashed right through his damp clothes. Already he could feel his body temperature dropping.

Shivering and dripping wet, she nodded, her teeth chattering from the cold.

He ached to get her warm. "Let's move out. Double time if you can."

They cut through the trees at a quick pace and when they reached the border of Old Man Bill's property, John directed her exactly how to move through the woods while he used a fallen pine bough to cover their tracks. The snow had picked up. A good thing on one hand. It would make it more difficult for the assault team to trail them. But the flip side of that was the snow and wind added to the misery of their tough trek up to the house, wearing them thin. It was so cold that John's lungs hurt every time he took a breath.

By the time they made it to Old Man Bill's cabin, Zee was in bad shape. Her lips were turning blue and the shiver had turned into an uncontrollable shake. He could only imagine what her feet were like, throbbing with fire until they went numb.

Shrugging the duffel from his shoulder, he dropped beside Bill's truck—a beater with a camper shell. John sat her down on top of the waterproof bag and leaned her against one of the tires. Tugging off his gloves, he looked her over more closely. Her eyelids looked heavy and her breathing was shallow.

"Stay with me. Okay?" He pulled one of his gloves on her hand, which was a block of ice, and had to pry the gun—a 9mm with an attached sound suppressor—from her other hand long enough to slip the second glove on. He gave her his knit hat as well to conserve her body heat, making sure to cover her ears. "Keep your eyes open and stay with me until I can get you warm." The sooner the better. They were only a hundred miles from the Arctic circle, and he estimated it was below zero tonight. The Alaskan elements were nothing to trifle with.

"We c-c-can't stay here."

"I know. Too close to the action. Trouble will soon close in." He rubbed his hands up and down her arms. "I'll get Bill to loan us his truck and get you out of here."

She nodded. "Cops. Have Bill…c-call cops." She wrapped her arms around her midsection, tremors racking through her, teeth chattering. "Their prime w-w-will hate—" she swallowed hard "—the interference."

Prime? What did that mean?

After the man in the woods had opened fire, shooting Zee twice without identifying himself, he was certain those guys weren't any kind of law enforcement. And if that assault team didn't want the cops, then that confirmed they weren't FBI or NSA. They could still be CIA, operating illegally on American soil. Or mercenaries. Or both.

"I'm sure the state troopers are already headed out to what's left of your house," he said, then he understood what she meant. The authorities would be out in droves, but in the wrong place. "You want Bill to have the police on this side of the lake." Where the assault team was headed.

She nodded, and in her eyes, he could see she was starting to fade.

"We could go to the police station," he said.

"They'll c-come for me." She shook her head. "Cops w-will die. Please, n-no."

Brutal men were hunting her, she was out here fighting for her life and she was worried about cops getting in the crosshairs?

Anger burned in his gut at thinking about how close she had come to death. "Wait here." He stood, stretching through the fiery ache coiling in his leg. John limped up to Bill's door, feeling the strain of the evening in every fiber of his being, and knocked. Before his neighbor opened up and thrust a gun in John's face, he identified himself. "Bill, it's John Lowry. From across the lake. I need assistance." After waiting a minute, he banged with his fist, repeating his words.

The porch light came on and the door cracked open. Bill peeked through over the chain on the door. He was close to ninety and had long white hair and a bushy white beard. "What in the hell, John? Do you have any idea what time it is?"

"Kill the light."

"Huh? What?"

"The light will attract unwanted attention." John crossed his arms, unable to fight off a shiver. "Kill it."

Bill's lips pinched and his mouth twisted like he was sucking on a lemon, but he turned off the bright porch light. "What do you want?"

"To borrow your truck for a few hours. Day at the most. Please don't ask questions I can't answer."

"Nope." Bill slammed the door.

Damn it. John listened for footfalls moving away. There were none. "I'll give you a hundred bucks." No response. "One thousand, Bill. It's an emergency. Life or death. If I didn't need your help, you know I wouldn't ask."

The chain slid off with a clink and the door opened again. Bill stood holding a shotgun in the crook of his elbow. "Let me see the money."

"I don't have it on me, but I'm good for it." The door swung to close, but John shoved his boot across the threshold, stopping it. "I give you my word as a man of honor."

"Honor won't put food on my table or bourbon in my gut. Know what I'm saying?"

John looked at his watch. His gaze fell across the stainless-steel case, the black ceramic bezel, the strap made from sturdy canvas sail. He unfastened it and took off the watch. "This is a Blancpain Fifty Fathoms. It's worth seven grand. More than your ride. I get it back when you get your truck and the cash. Deal?" He handed over his most prized possession. Not that he cared about luxury items, but his SEAL team had all chipped in for this parting gift, the officers coughing up more than the enlisted. The inscription meant more to him than the watch itself.

"I can't tell the difference between a blank pan and any other froufrou watch." Bill snatched the priceless timepiece from his hand and inspected it. "It sure does look expensive. All right. I believe you. But in the back of the truck,

I've got wood I chopped down out at Salcha," he said, referring to the salvage woodlot. "I want it all returned."

John restrained a sigh. "No problem."

"And for you to unload it for me?" Bill asked, and John nodded, willing to help his elderly neighbor with the task under any circumstances. "The keys are in the truck. In the visor."

"One more thing. Call the police. Tell them you saw suspicious men in the woods. Tactical gear and laser sights. Not a word to anyone about me." He was glad he'd had the foresight to keep Zee hidden on the other side of the truck. The less Bill knew, the better. "Got it?"

He didn't expect much pushback from Bill or questions for that matter. People out here tended to mind their own business.

Bill eyed him long and hard. Then he gave a two-finger salute. "Tallyho." The door slammed shut.

John hurried down the steps to the truck.

Scanning the area for movement, he opened the driver's door. The woods were quiet, and the coast was clear. For now. But not for much longer.

They needed to get on the road before that assault team was in the chopper and searching from the sky. At this hour, they'd be easy to spot. With any luck, those boys still had boots on the ground and were combing the area on foot.

John slipped his hands under Zee's arms, hauled her up and got her into the truck. Grabbing hold of the bag, he glanced around once more, his gaze searching for any sign of a threat before he climbed in and set the duffel in the back on top the firewood.

Flipping down the visor, he found the keys as they plopped into his palm. He cranked the engine, keeping the headlights off, and turned on the heat. "It'll take a minute to warm up."

He swung out onto the road, following it until they hit Elliott Highway, which was part of Route 2. On the main road, he turned on the headlights to avoid getting pulled over by the state troopers.

Once the heater got going, he put it on full blast to chase away the cold. Little good it seemed to do. Zee was shaking harder and slipping faster.

"You hanging in there?" he asked, his own tremors setting in from the exposed cold with his clothing damp from sweat.

"Y-yeah."

"Sing something. It'll help your mind focus. Keep you alert." It would also cue him in to the state of her condition, whether she was improving or worsening. "Pick anything. Though I'm partial to country."

She gave a shallow half laugh as her mouth quirked. Through her rattling teeth, she started singing.

He had expected her to pick a pop song, but the lyrics to "The Ants Go Marching" spilled from her lips. The choice of a nursery rhyme was surprising.

Not as shocking as the covert op that had unraveled in his backyard or how this entire time she hadn't let go of her gun. She clung to the weapon like a lifeline. The practiced way someone of his ilk would, knowing that a gun was as essential to survival as food and shelter.

In so many ways, he would've sworn that he knew Zee. What made her tick, made her smile, made her angry. Her favorite color and dessert. That she valued hard work. Never tried to skate by on her sensational looks. All about her childhood growing up feeling like she didn't belong in Breezy Point—what Zee had described as the least diverse and most insular right-wing area in New York City—with a Black democrat mom and a republican Irish dad. How she came from a family of cops and was a patriot who understood that sometimes self-sacrifice for the greater good was necessary.

John could distinguish her laugh from a hundred others blindfolded.

But he didn't even know her last name. Or the real reason she was hiding out in Alaska. She had first introduced herself as Zoey—*just call me Zee*—like she was Cher, Madonna, Beyoncé. He'd thought it cute at the time. Then those perimeter alarms went up. That combined with her initial hesitancy to be around him for long periods of time, especially alone together indoors—and when they were, she had always been armed—had him chalking it up to a lunatic ex. Women moved and changed their identities to get away from an abusive ex-husband far more than they should have to.

She had seemed to need a friend who could keep his distance and not push. So he'd been that for her.

Who are you, Zee? What are you hiding and what kind of trouble are you in? How deep does it go?

He'd get answers, one way or another. No more evasion. No more secrets permissible. But now wasn't the time to grill her. Once she was safe and warm, he'd demand the truth.

Zee's lyrics began to slow and slur. "H-h-hurrah," she sang barely above a whisper, "…hur…" Her head lolled to the side as she slumped down in the seat and the gun slipped from hand, clattering to the foot well.

John slammed on the accelerator, gunning the engine. "Zee!" He shook her. "Wake up. Don't fall asleep."

They weren't far. He cut off the highway, turning down the road toward the campground, the rear end of the truck fishtailing.

No CCTV in the vicinity to give away their position and there were public recreational cabins. They were located along trails and near remote lakes in backcountry areas such as this. State park staff did their best to keep the cabins tidy between uses. You were supposed to reserve one, but he doubted anybody would be out here this close to Christmas.

Two miles down the road he came to a cabin. No vehicles were parked nearby, and no one went hiking this time of year.

He cut the engine and eyed her bag. Whatever was in it, he was certain there'd be critical provisions. Snatching the duffel, he hurried from the truck inside the cabin for a quick once-over. It was empty. A simple single room in decent condition. He dropped the bag and hightailed it back to the truck.

Opening her door, he caught her before she fell out. He pushed her wet hair from her face, took her gun and scooped her into his arms. With his bad leg, he kicked the door closed, balancing on his good one. Despite his injury, perhaps because of it, he worked on maintaining the honed strength of his body, particularly in the muscles that supported his knees, with weight-bearing exercises. His diligent efforts paid off, enabling him to hustle up the steps, carrying her, and whisk her inside without faltering.

She was so cold and wet. The feel of her body sent a chill shooting down his spine.

He set her down on the wood floor. Took a quick inventory of her bag for something to help them. Bundles of cash—at least twenty thousand, prepaid VISA cards, sleeping bag, MREs—meals ready to eat. Change of clothes, passport and IDs for a Zadie Hall and Zoey Howard, which he doubted either was her real name, medical kit, firestarter packets, laptop, burner phone *and* a sat phone. Not something you see every day.

The cabin had a wood-burning stove and getting Zee

warm was his number-one priority. He dashed back to the truck and grabbed some logs. Bill wouldn't miss a few pieces. Then again, he might, but the money his neighbor was going to receive was more than adequate compensation.

John made swift work of building a fire that would last a few hours and rolled out a Hyperion sleeping bag. A solid choice, it was ultralightweight and extremely warm, but the fastest way to raise her body temperature was skin on skin.

She might be livid enough to slap him later, but at least she'd be alive to do it, and that was the only thing that mattered to him. Zee living to see another day.

Taking a deep breath, he started with her boots and worked his way up. John had imagined undressing her a hundred times, but never under such dire circumstances. Thinking about it, the fantasy had entailed them taking off each other's clothes. A mutual act of consent and desire. Welcomed affection.

Not like this.

Averting his eyes, he treated her as he would any battle brother, sister in arms, who needed him. He laid her in the sleeping bag close to the fire and covered her. With his back to her, he stripped down to his birthday suit, desperate to drive away the terrible cold in his own limbs.

Quickly, he strung a nylon cord he found in her bag and hung their clothes near the fire.

He grabbed the gun, keeping it close, and climbed in alongside her. Her skin was cold and clammy, her body stiff.

What was the protocol? Roll her away from him with her back to his front? But if he put his arms around her, he might accidentally touch an intimate body part.

There wasn't enough room in the sleeping bag for them to lie back-to-back.

This was a KISS situation. *Keep it simple, stupid.*

Staying as they were, front to front with her back to the fire, he brought his body closer, zipped them up in the down-filled cocoon, and curled his arms around her.

John had full control over his mind and in turn over his body. In truth, he refused to allow himself to enjoy being close to her beyond the much-needed heat they generated together. With the cold and exhaustion dampening any appreciation for the moment, it wasn't too hard.

But he feared warming up and falling asleep for two reasons.

First, they might be found, caught off guard.

Second, if he allowed his mind to relax, his body would follow, relinquishing control to Mother Nature. The last thing he wanted was for her to come to and find his lower appendage standing at attention while he slept.

There was only one thing he could do. Even though his leg was hurting, and he was in bad need of shut-eye, he vowed not to sleep.

After a few minutes, her head inclined forward, resting on his chest, and she nestled against him. They both stopped shaking not long after, settling into the sleeping bag. Relief trickled through his heart. Hypothermia and shock would not take her from him tonight. A little bloom of contentment unfolded inside him as he held her tighter.

With rest, she would be all right. And that brought him more comfort and peace of mind than eight hours of sleep ever would.

Chapter Four

Zee jerked awake, her sluggish mind swimming, her fists clenched ready to fight, her heavy eyelids refusing to lift. What happened? Where was she? Where was Delta team?

"Shh." A soothing male voice in her ear. "I've got you. I won't let anything happen to you. I swear it."

John.

If she was with John, she was safe. She relaxed into the soft warmth of skin against skin.

Gentle fingers pushed hair from her face and tested the pulse at her throat. Strong arms surrounded her, enfolding her in sublime heat. Zee pressed her face to his bare chest. Inhaled the scent of testosterone and fire smoke. She curled an arm around his waist, tucked a leg between his and let the undertow of exhaustion pull her back to sleep.

Sometime later—an hour, several, she didn't know—she opened her eyes to the smell of coffee. She was in a cabin. In a sleeping bag, alone and naked.

Memories rushed back on a tide of fear in her foggy brain, ticking up her heartbeat. The assault on her cabin. The explosion. John's help in the woods. Taking two bullets to protect him, which explained the soreness in her chest.

The lake. Getting dragged into the icy water.

Utter terror. She had thrashed and had fought. Shot the man holding her and had kicked and kicked until she was free of his grasp. Pain, searing and hot, had cut through her chest. But she had to reach the surface. Swam through the darkness, pushed against the cold and the heaviness of the duffel on her back, her wet clothes. Then air. And John had pulled her out of the water.

Lightheaded, soaked, freezing they had made it to Bill's house. Then she didn't remember much else.

Except for John. The sound of his voice as he had spoken to her. Snuggled beside him, as close together as a man and woman could be without having sex. The steady thrum of his heartbeat. The precious warmth of his skin against hers. The intimate feel of him. *All of him.* Chiseled muscle of his chest. Sculpted abdomen. Hair on his hard thighs and between his legs. The length of him pressed to her belly.

A different kind of heat slid through her. The kind that had her aching to have him back in the sleeping bag with her.

"John?" She pushed up on her forearm and a wave of dizziness slowed her.

"Take it easy." He knelt in front of her, fully dressed, and helped her sit up while keeping her covered.

"What time is it?" Her internal clock was kaput and in December, they got less than four hours of daylight, starting around eleven.

"About eight in the morning. Here." He handed her coffee in one of the collapsible mugs from her duffel. "I was able to heat some water on the stove in the small titanium pot you packed. Good thing you had water-purifying tablets. You thought of pretty much everything, though a foil blanket and hand warmers would've been good. I didn't eat the MRE. I saved it for you, but I did have some of the coffee."

She took the mug and sipped. Bitter warmth slid down her throat to her stomach, spreading through her. "You should eat. There are a thousand calories in one of those meals. Just save me the cheese and crackers." She had two more MREs and could share one.

He gave her a lopsided grin and heart skipped a beat.

Lifting his hand to her face, he brushed her jaw with his knuckles, sending a tingle from her cheek to her toes. Time came to a halt as they stayed like that. There was nothing but the two of them for a moment. His green eyes held hers and his face softened as the air backed up in her lungs.

She liked the way he looked at her and she loved the way he made her feel.

At ease. Safe.

Yes, both of those beautiful things just looking in his eyes.

"I guess I'll address the elephant in the room," he said, lowering his gaze and hand. "Sorry I undressed you without your permission. You were unconscious and hypothermic. You could've died. I didn't take advantage of the situation in any manner." He spoke in a rush, as if he were nervous, but she'd never seen John nervous.

She believed him. The circumstances had been grave. They both could've died. Most men would've ogled, some might've copped a feel, others could've done worse, but John was not most men.

"It was to preserve body heat only," he continued, "and keep you alive. Nothing inappropriate happened. Promise. I just couldn't let—"

Unable to stop herself, she slipped a hand around the nape of his neck, sliding her fingers in his hair, and brought his mouth to hers. She had wanted to know, wanted to feel him. Taste him. For so long.

His arms went around her as his warm firm lips moved over hers, brushing, seeking, and she moaned at the feel of his hot tongue. He held her close and tight, like he had craved this, too.

The kiss sizzled through her, slow and sensuous, drowning her in sensation. Heat slid through her, racing under her skin. She leaned in to him, her body igniting under the edgy delight.

She wanted more. To haul him down to the sleeping bag, strip off his clothes and make love to him, right here in this austere cabin on the wooden floor.

But she'd endangered him far too much already, and she refused to drag him in to her mess any deeper.

A sudden, heartrending thought occurred to her. This beautiful, toe-curling kiss was their first. And it had to be their last.

The only way to protect him was to let him go.

Ignoring the hot throb between her legs and the achy tension coiling low in her belly, she tore her mouth away with a knot forming in her chest. "Thank you, for helping me. For saving my life."

Their gazes met. It was almost as if she saw straight into his soul, and the powerful sense of connection to him was overwhelming.

"You're welcome." He moved in to kiss her again, but she pulled back.

A deep ache bled into a deeper longing and if it had only been physical between them, she would've given in.

Lowering her head, she said, "I'm grateful, John. But that's all." A horrible lie, but a necessary one. "The kiss was a gesture of appreciation to show you that undressing me was no big deal between good friends."

He sank back on his heels and the expression dawning on his face sent a pang shooting through her chest. "Oh. I thought..."

"You should go," she said, swallowing a scream of yearning and sorrow and anger.

"Go?"

"Can you pass me my clothes?" She shifted, putting her back to him. "I need to get dressed."

"Right." He handed her the clothes that he had hung up near the stove. "Your boots should be good to go. I removed the soles and put heated rocks inside them, so they'd dry quickly. I'll wait outside while you dress, then we can talk."

"There's nothing to discuss. When I said you should go, I meant you should leave."

"Leave? What are you talking about?"

She unzipped the sleeping bag to climb out.

Averting his gaze, he spun around and faced the door.

She stabbed her legs into her jeans and yanked them up over her hips. It wasn't until her socks and sweater were on that she realized she'd been in such a rush last night that she'd forgotten underwear. There was some in her duffel, but no time for it now. She had to rip off this Band-Aid between her and John. Send him on his way.

"I'm talking about how you need to let a sense of self-preservation override chivalry and take off," she said.

"Take off? What about you?"

She tugged on warm boots and laced them up. Neat trick with the rocks. "Why do you keep repeating everything I say?"

Sighing, he scrubbed a hand over his face. "Are you dressed?"

She considered lying, but she couldn't pretend she was naked for the duration of this conversation. Perhaps she should have delayed putting on clothes. "I am."

He whirled around. The confusion on his face had been replaced with a grimace. "What's your real name?"

She hesitated.

"Don't lie to me," he warned. "If you do, I'll know."

"Zenobia. Hanley."

"Zenobia," he repeated as if trying it out on his tongue. "Why are those men after you? Who are they? FBI? NSA black ops? The mob? I would've guessed CIA since I've worked with enough of those guys to know how they move, but they can't operate on American soil."

"Stop asking questions."

"I deserve answers." He crossed his arms over his chest. "I've earned the right. Start talking."

She drew in a shaky breath. "The answers will only get you killed."

"So be it."

Incredible. This man would not back down. "I'm not a criminal, but I am on the run."

"Good start. Go on."

"The rest is classified."

He put his hands on his hips, standing his ground. "Then give me the redacted version."

She growled in frustration. He was stubborn as a mule. The nature of her trouble *was* classified and telling him too much would open Pandora's box in his life. She was a former CIA operative, trained to withstand interrogation, but he wasn't going to accept her stonewalling. Fierce determination blazed in his steely eyes.

The heat of his stare was scorching, and inside this operative's skin, the woman was melting. She had to tell him something. A nugget of truth, small enough for him to swallow and large enough to scare him off.

"You're a movie buff," she said. "Did you ever see *The Warriors*?"

He folded his arms again, his eyes narrowing, and his jaw clenched. "No."

"They were a mixed-race street gang in 1970s New York

City. They were blamed for a murder they didn't commit. Caught uptown in enemy territory, they had to make their way back home to Coney Island with all the other gangs gunning for them. So they ran. Or rather they fought and ran. Until they could prove their innocence. My former team—think of us as the Warriors. Only we did kill someone, under orders, but it turned out to be the wrong person. The op was bad from the beginning. I couldn't put my finger on it, but I didn't have a good feeling about that one and then everything went sideways. Before we could get answers from our handler, all the other gangs came for us. Anyone we get close to is in danger. Understand?"

Oddly, John nodded as if he understood completely. He paced the length of the cabin, rubbing his chin. Digesting that nugget of truth.

"They don't know who you are. Yet," she said. "Let's keep it that way. You need to leave."

"How do you think they found you?" he asked, still moving from one end of the room to the other.

"On my recent trips to Fairbanks, I started digging around to find evidence to clear our names. Breached their database. I was careful, but I must've stayed online too long that last time. Hackers, we leave behind virtual fingerprints in an intrusion—a preference for a particular type of tool or action, typos in a command line, the nature of the activity itself. Everything can be masked with enough caution and preparation, except for the last item." The nature of the activity. No one else would hack into the specific CIA database she had breached, and certainly not into the file labeled Topaz. "I guess I didn't get out of the system before an alarm had been tripped or an analyst had noticed."

He stopped and looked up at her; his eyes were unreadable, but he didn't appear the slightest bit daunted. "Have you seen *The Godfather*?"

She wasn't sure where he was going with this, but she didn't think she'd like it. "Who hasn't?"

"You have to go to the mattresses," he said matter-of-factly.

Now she was the one confused. "I understand the phrase means go to war."

"But do you know why they call it that?"

"They never explained the mattresses part in the movie."

"It's because the mob family had to move out of their home and hole up someplace where no one could find them and all their soldiers. But they had to do it quickly, so that they could get the jump on the rival family. They had places stashed around the city with the mattresses on the floor. And that's where they would make their stand until they nailed the boss of the rival family. You're not at war right now, you're on the run," he said, and it was as though she was seeing him clearly for the first time—a battle-hardened warrior unafraid to rush back into the fray. "You need to stop running and make a stand. But you need men. You need me." He flashed that grin at her and tucked his tongue in his cheek.

How in the hell had he turned this around?

He was too smart for his own good.

"No," she said, waving her hands to emphasize her point. "You need to get out of here." She stabbed a finger in his direction.

He stared down at her, rooted firmly in place. "I'm not going anywhere without you," he said, his tone adamant.

"But you are. Please, leave."

"Some of those men were headed in the direction of my place last night. They probably already know who I am."

"They have no reason to come after you unless you're with me, but it's best that you don't go home for a few days."

Concern etched his face, but she suspected that none of it was for himself.

"The Warriors, did they win in the end?" he asked.

"Yeah. They did."

"How?" He leaned against the wall, his expression intense, his full attention lasered on her. "Did they do it alone while scattered, or together working as a team?"

Zee folded her arms and gritted her teeth at how he was twisting things around on her. "I can't turn to the rest of my team." They were all in hiding, supposedly off the grid, and she didn't know where.

Glancing at her duffel bag, she thought about the SAT phone inside. It was meant for a one-time, dire-straits call to her former team leader Hunter Wright. But using the phone now wouldn't solve her immediate problem.

"All the more reason you need me. You can't do this alone," John said, and she hated the bite of truth in his words. "I take it you're going to try to get out of Alaska. Head back to the lower forty-eight."

She looked at him with an annoyed frown over the fact that he was right. "What makes you think that?"

"You hate it up here in the freezing wilderness. You'll want to go someplace you can navigate easier on your own."

He was half right.

John lifted a brow, pleased with himself. "I can help you get out of Alaska under the radar. Fast."

The one thing she didn't have was an impromptu exit strategy out of this state that was two and a half times the size of Texas. Her original plan had been to lie low in a state park if a team had ever showed up to take her out. But that was before she'd left her laptop behind. With the area crawling with operatives and not knowing if they had her computer, she had to get to Seattle before that assault team figured out why she would head there.

Time was of the essence and she had no clue what her next move was.

Thanks to John having done a brilliant job illustrating why she needed him, her annoyance with him ballooned; all the while her fear of him getting hurt or worse on her behalf swelled in her chest, making it hard to breathe.

He wouldn't listen to reason, so she used a different tactic.

She stormed across the room to the door and flung it open. "Take off for a week. Go on a vacation. Enjoy your retirement."

His eyes flashed, their bright green color turning a hard malachite, and he looked as though he'd been slapped. "Enjoy my retirement? Is that a sick joke?"

Whoa. That had struck a nerve. One that she hadn't anticipated.

Zee was stunned by his reaction. John was—well, she had no idea how old he was exactly. Somewhere between forty and fifty, she guessed. Not that he looked that old. In fact, he was strong and vital, might not even be forty yet. It was the way he carried himself, with a seen-it-all manner, and spoke about things. Like a wise, old soul.

But she hadn't meant senior-citizen type of retirement.

John marched up to her and slammed the door shut. "You're facing a formidable force and you're not going to win this war by yourself."

She had serious skills cultivated over the years, but she was far from being an army of one.

Through the havoc of her feelings, she said, "I'm just trying to survive the battle for now." She blew out a heavy breath. "You've already gotten in too deep and for that,

I'm sorry." More than he would ever know. "But it's not too late for you. Go home."

"I have nothing waiting for me back home, and I've got nothing left to lose…besides you."

Her heart clenched violently. What was he saying? What did it mean?

He cupped her face in both of his hands. His thumbs stroked her cheeks in a tender, sweeping caress that made her chest ache. "I want to protect you, Zee." His unwavering gaze was an anchor weighing down her heart. "Let me."

Want. She shivered at the word, the chill running both hot and cold. After what he'd already gone through last night, he still wanted to protect her.

"You have your life, John. I'd like you to keep it." When he looked at her like that, touched her, it was hard to think. Impossible to refuse him anything. *Please, please, go.* Otherwise, she was going to have to do something awful. Say something to hurt him, to save him. She would hate herself for it, but if it meant he'd never become collateral damage, then the pain would be worth it. "Now, stay the hell away from me."

Doing the exact opposite, John edged closer, bringing them chest to chest, and rubbed her arms. "Listen to me and stop being so stubborn," he said, his smooth, deep voice dipping in a way that curled in her belly. "Let me help you."

It was all too much and took everything in her not to lean against his solid frame, absorb his warmth, accept his help, rely on his comfort.

John was steadfast, reliable and she needed his help. So much was at stake, not just her own life, and she wanted him at her side, as more than a hired gun or a friend.

But what would it cost him?

No, this wasn't fair to him. He deserved better than getting further embroiled in her trouble.

Zee turned her back to him. If she looked him in the eye, she wouldn't be able to go through with it and force him to leave. An emotional attack was the logical choice.

He stepped up behind her and curled his hands around her shoulders, sending a tingle across her nerves that almost stopped her. Almost.

"I don't need you," she said. "Don't want you around." Her eyes stung as she tried to breathe. "You were great, doing my hunting and chopping my firewood, but beyond that what good are you to me? I don't want the dead weight of a disabled retiree slowing me down. I already took two bullets for you." Was that her voice cracking? She needed to hold it together, stay firm and lie to John for his own sake. She drew in a sharp breath against a pain more shocking than she wanted it to be. "I can find some other sucker to get me out of Alaska."

The security of his warm hands slipped away from her arms. The heavy thud of boots stomped across the room. Keys jangled. The door opened and slammed closed.

The world went watery, but she refused to let the tears welling in her eyes fall as her heart broke into pieces.

Chapter Five

Speeding away from the cabin headed down the snow-covered road, John cursed himself for a fool.

Damn her, and damn himself for letting her breach the wall he'd built up over the past three years and for getting so caught up in her that he couldn't think straight.

His brain was twisted into such a pretzel that when she had kissed him, he had actually thought it had been real. That it had meant to her what it had to him.

A heck of a lot more than a mere gesture between good friends.

The word *friends* had slapped his heart as though she'd let loose a taut rubber band against it.

Last night, the intimacy of lying beside her had been staggering. Their breaths mingled, with him smelling the heat of her skin, feeling the solid thumps of her heart beating.

Before his injury and his discharge from the service, women had been easy come, easy go. No risk of an emotional connection. No one worth holding on to. The mission had always been his top priority. The SEAL teams came first, and he had given them everything he had. He'd seen too many broken relationships with his battle brothers to put any real effort into one.

What would've been the point? A bitter divorce? Loss

of half his military pension? Kids who didn't understand why he had to drop everything and leave whenever the call came and ended up hating him for it?

But with Zee, when they spent time together, he didn't feel alone. Not once in his life could he say that about any other woman. Slowly, he had let her into his heart, had shown her his vulnerabilities, and in turn had given her the power to eviscerate him with a few choice words.

The muscles in John's shoulders bunched and tightened like cords of thick rope that had swollen and shrunken. He was shaking with anger. Not only for the things she'd said to him, but also for what she was going through and for not being able to convince her to put him to good use instead of putting him out to pasture, the same as the military.

His abrupt discharge from the service had been less jarring than the way she'd booted him from the cabin. He couldn't remember ever being so angry—most of all at himself.

He was the biggest idiot. Had risked his life for her last night and had been prepared to do it again, to put it all on the line for her, a woman whose real name he had just learned.

He believed her story about her op going wrong and needing to prove her innocence. Whatever system she'd breached, his guess was the CIA's, it had scared someone enough to send a large team of commandos to eliminate one woman. He had experienced firsthand precisely what she was up against, the magnitude of her problem, but it would take a little more than that to scare him off.

One of those operators had gotten the drop on him and Zee had saved his life. When she'd lunged in front of him and taken those bullets, it had been like all the oxygen had been sucked out of the atmosphere and then he'd flown into a rage and killed the man who had shot her.

They had saved each other, working together. As a team.

But she'd never spoken to him the way she had in the cabin, not in the nine months they'd known each other. He didn't think she was capable of such…flagrant disrespect. Of wounding him so viciously.

Disabled retiree!

The deep blow of those two words had struck him even harder than *friends*. Putting an end to the discussion.

What more could he have said to her?

Technically, he was disabled according to Veterans Affairs with a ninety percent combined rating for his leg and PTSD. And yes, technically, he was retired from the military. But it was *the way* she had said it.

The same way he felt at times, sitting cooped up in his cabin with his memories for company, like he was useless. Worthless.

Except when he was with her, especially last night. He had been his old self. A little slower, but no less effective.

How dare she speak to him in that manner after everything he'd done for her?

Not that she owed him anything for the help he'd freely given, other than the respect he had earned.

Her cruel words rang in his head, taunting him. *Sucker. Disabled. Retiree.* The sting burned through him all over again.

He'd show her who was a disabled retiree. It wasn't him. He was still a force to be reckoned with.

John stomped on the brakes, slapped the steering wheel and cranked it, whipping the truck around.

Galvanized by what she thought of him, he raced back to the cabin and threw the truck in Park with the engine running. It took him less than ten seconds to clear the vehicle and burst through the door.

Zee whirled around, those gorgeous brown eyes narrowing for a fight, the gun in her hand pointed at his head. As always, the sight of her gave him a quick inner jolt, the sheer beauty of her stealing his breath. Her face should be captured in an oil painting. It would rival the *Mona Lisa*, or the *Girl with a Pearl Earring* and he'd call it *Goddess with a Gun*.

She had a face that men would kill for.

Hell, he already had and might very well again.

Zee lowered the weapon. "What on earth are you doing back here?"

A part of him was asking himself the same question, but in his gut, he knew this was where he needed to be. His internal compass had never led him astray.

"I may be disabled but I'm not an invalid," John said, coolly, despite the fact he was livid. He had never raised his voice to her and never would. "I was forced into retirement but there's still plenty of fight left in me. You did take two bullets for me and by the way don't ever do that again. But I'm the one who warned you about the strike team approaching."

"And I appreciate the heads-up, but—"

"Nope." He raised a hand to silence her as he cut her off. "I'm not finished speaking." It required every bit of his strength to keep his voice even. "I stopped one of those men from apprehending you in the woods. Prevented you from drowning by dragging you out of the freezing lake. Kept that team from following you. Brought you to safety and I made sure you didn't die from hypothermia while remaining a perfect gentleman." Which had nearly been an impossible feat. He was learning that he could do what was required when it came to her. Even set aside his anger and bruised feelings to do the right thing. "In short, you would be dead if not for me. Why don't you tally up the scorecard before you start hurling any more insults?"

Her mouth dropped open as she rocked back on her heels.

"You may not want my help, but you need it." He charged inside, grabbed her duffel with one hand and Zee's elbow with the other, fully aware this woman knew how to handle herself and if given the chance could very well take him down in a few moves. "That's a fact, plain and simple. You're too smart not to see that."

As he hauled her and the bag to the truck, his words sank in. She was too smart. He recalled how she always managed to beat him at chess, strategized, willing to sacrifice her queen and any other player. It was foolish of her not to use him, and she was no fool.

So, why had she discarded him faster than a used tissue?

"When you were sleeping this morning," he said, "I swore to protect you. Not to let anything happen to you. That's a promise I intend to keep whether you like it or not." He opened the passenger's door, steered her inside to sit, dumped the bag on her lap and closed the door.

Hustling around the front of the truck, he decided then and there not to be dissuaded by anything ugly she might say. He'd get her out of Alaska and settled someplace safe. Where he wouldn't worry about her, wondering if she was dead or alive. Regardless of whether she only saw him as a friend and had no real feelings for him, it didn't change the fact that he had a heart full for her.

If anything happened to her when he had the power to prevent it, it would wreck him. The kind of devastation one didn't get over.

He hopped in the truck.

She stared at him in wide-eyed disbelief.

"I let you draw the line between us, Zee, and now I'm moving it," he said. "You can poke holes in me if you want, try to turn me into Swiss cheese to see how much I can take, and we can waste time arguing, all of which would only work in that assault team's favor. I suggest instead you tell me where you want to go, I'll help you get there, ensure you're safe and off their radar. Then since you want me gone so badly, I'll walk away like you want. No strings attached. Just tell me where you want to go."

Imposing his will on others wasn't his usual style. Taking this approach with her sickened him, but her plan was suicidal. He simply couldn't abide it.

The fire in her eyes dimmed as her rigid posture relaxed in acquiescence, and a tingle of relief loosened the fist clenching his heart.

She clutched the bag to her heaving chest. "Seattle," she said, her voice low and soft.

John tensed. *A large city.*

Reflexively, he checked his coat pockets, but he knew he'd left his meds back at the cabin. Going to Fairbanks was a struggle for him while medicated and Seattle had more than twenty times the size of that population. The last time he had taken his pills was…two days ago since he'd felt good. No, better than good, great. Sometimes he skipped whole days because his routine was working. Every day he'd been taking long, strenuous walks when the sun was up for endorphins, and he'd been spending loads more time with Zee, which had always been a pleasure, alleviating any stress. But now he was forty-eight hours without any medication in his system and the pressure was going to continue to build.

You'll be fine. You just need some sleep.

Zee shifted toward the window and dabbed at the corners of her eyes like she was the aggrieved party. "I need to get there today. As soon as possible. Then we can go our separate ways, and you stay away from me."

The word *need* struck him along with the urgency to make it happen. He ruled out driving there and flying commercial, but he had an idea that might take some finagling to work.

He put the truck in Drive and hit the accelerator. Tamping down his emotions, he buried them deep in the same manner he used to before he went on an op.

"John, tell me exactly what you used to do in the military that gives you the unflappable confidence to help me."

It wasn't confidence and it wasn't chivalry and certainly wasn't unflappable. He was crazy about her. Another fact that was cut-and-dried. But he would spill the details of his professional background as she demanded.

"I'll explain on the way to Bill's," he said, planning not to hold anything back from her. Not so much to impress her, although he wouldn't mind if that was a byproduct, but to remind himself what he was capable of and who he was deep down at his core. "We'll need him to drop us off somewhere." And since John wouldn't be back in twenty-four hours, he didn't want to give the old guy an excuse to keep his watch.

Chapter Six

Six men down and nothing to show for it. Ryker clenched his jaw, wanting to tear something or someone apart. State troopers had fanned out in the woods surrounding the lake, putting a premature end to Delta team's search.

Ryker didn't have a single lead on where Zenobia was now.

It seemed so long ago when he had first approached Zee and asked her out while she was living in Germany. The most challenging aspect of cultivating a relationship with her had been pretending to be a normal person. Killing had always been easy for him. Making conversation with a beautiful young woman, coming on strong without being overly aggressive had been much harder. To pull it off, he had imagined himself a magician playing a shell game. Instead of hiding an object and shuffling around cups, the trick had been to keep her from seeing the true nature of his character.

He had been very good at it. For a while. And for as long as he had maintained that psychoemotional sleight of hand they had enjoyed their time together. If only he hadn't gotten complacent and given up the charade. Had figured out how to juggle being Jekyll for her and Hyde the rest of the time without her ever knowing the truth.

If he had, where would they be today?

Delta Two entered from the adjoining room.

"What have you found?" Ryker asked his second-in-command.

They had rented two connecting rooms at the inn on Eielson Air Force Base, twenty-five minutes from Fairbanks, where they were regrouping while the helicopter was refueled.

"We combed through the neighbor's place. The man helping her is John Lowry. He's a retired master chief special warfare operator. Was assigned to SEAL Team Two."

Ryker stiffened, the tidbit giving him pause for a moment, but it made sense. The man who had gotten Zee out of the lake and thrown the grenade was a skilled operator. Ryker had recognized that immediately. But a SEAL?

"I got you the unredacted file on him." Two handed over the tablet to Ryker. "A real die-hard hotshot. Knows how to dig in for a fight. More medals than me and Five combined. There's nothing this guy hasn't done. Direct action raids. Rounding up and eliminating high-value targets. Sensitive-site exploitation to collect information. Thrown himself in harm's way to protect his guys. Been a prisoner of war and tortured."

"Was he also single-handedly responsible for killing Osama bin Laden?" Ryker asked sarcastically.

"That was SEAL Team Six," his guy said, and Ryker rolled his eyes. "But Lowry is still impressive. We'll need to take extra precautions."

Ryker tuned out his second-in-command gushing over Lowry. As he read the former SEAL's résumé, his blood pressure skyrocketed and all he saw was red.

For years, Ryker had been itching to hurt Zee the way she had hurt him. To make her pay for her betrayal. Finally, the CIA had cut her loose, depriving her of their protection. She was on the run, without her team or Hunter Wright to fall back on for assistance—*his for the taking*—and she had somehow managed to ingratiate herself to the one man in the local area who was a fire-seasoned killing machine.

He burned with raw hatred for that ungrateful, lucky bitch. Surely she was sleeping with the former SEAL, had exerted her witchlike wiles on him and seduced him into helping her. Images flashed through his head of Zenobia curled up in bed with this man, Lowry. Touching him. Kissing him. Making love to him.

Ryker growled his frustration. He flipped over the table, smashed the tablet under his foot and swept everything from the dresser to the floor.

Two eased back, clearing out into the next room with the others.

Giving one last howl of rage, a veritable blood cry, he expelled the pressure building in his chest. Lowry deserved to die for getting close to her, sleeping with her. They both did and would know his wrath as soon as he found them.

Ryker went to the mirror. Slicked back his blond hair that had fallen out of place. He held on to the fury simmering just below the surface and to the rush of adrenaline, funneling it for fuel. This was a dirty little secret: there was nothing like the hunt, the throes of war, unadulterated contempt to make him feel alive.

Invigorated, he took a deep breath, straightened and strode into the adjoining room. Looking around at his men, he dared any of them to say a word about his momentary outburst.

Gazes avoided his, heads lowered, mouths twitched, but there was silence. He had worked with this group long enough for them to know better.

"John Lowry," Ryker said through clenched teeth, "is just a man. Not a legend, and soon, he'll be nothing more than collateral damage. But if anyone glorifies him again,

I will cut out that man's tongue." He put his hand on the hilt of the Ka-Bar knife holstered on his hip to drive his point home.

Heads nodded.

"Sir," Two said, using judicious caution. "You didn't allow me to finish. Lowry was injured in an explosion that messed up his right leg, and he also has PTSD after being tortured and losing two men who got him out. We found meds in his cabin. Prescriptions he'll need but doesn't have. If we take precautions, he won't be a problem."

Won't be?

Did he need to buy Two a clue? John Lowry already was a problem. Zee had gotten away because of him. That was huge.

Ryker wanted Zee terrified and alone, looking over her shoulder, friendless, penniless, with no one to turn to, and when he finally had his hands wrapped around her throat, the last thing he wanted was to hear her beg for mercy that wouldn't be given. "If you're wrong and Lowry *continues* to be a problem, you'll pay for underestimating him."

A muscle ticked in Two's jaw, but he nodded.

An idea occurred to Ryker. "Tell our analyst back at headquarters to set up an alert for any prescription refills for Lowry."

"Will do." Two took out his phone and made the call.

"Prime," Seven said. "We're just now getting to her laptop. She has a ton of pictures. Taken from a live feed."

"Of what?" Ryker asked.

"Not what, sir," Seven said, shaking his head. "Who."

Ryker's pulse quickened as he hurried to the laptop that was opened in front of Seven on a desk. He pushed back the screen, leaned over and took a look.

"It's a little girl," Seven said. "I think she might have a daughter."

Ryker stared at the child. About ten years old. Long hair similar to Zee's but looser curls. Brown eyes. Skin that was closer to tan than brown. *It's her.* "Where were these pictures taken?"

"From a live feed, sir," Seven said.

A blood vessel throbbed in Ryker's temple. Was he surrounded by incompetence? "I heard you the first time. I need a location."

"I don't know, but I'm working on it. I sent the photos to our analyst and I'm going to try to extract what metadata that I can."

In the pictures, she was wearing a uniform, plaid skirt and white button-down shirt, sitting beside another child dressed the same. "It's a school," Ryker said.

But Zee wouldn't leave her with relatives, then she'd never see the child. After what happened in Germany, her father barely spoke to her. He was a cop. Her uncles were cops. She came from a long line of police officers. They would sooner turn her in than give her safe harbor or let her see her daughter as a fugitive on the run. If the girl was on her own, Zee would go for the child before disappearing again.

"A boarding school," Ryker added, "maybe one where kids can stay over Christmas break and summers. Check the west coast first, including Canada. The Midwest, too. Start with international schools that cater to kids from abroad and Christian schools. We find her," he said, pointing at the image of the child on the screen, "we'll find the target."

Knowing what alias she used to register the kid would also prove useful.

Eleven chuckled. "Then we'll have the ultimate leverage. I can't believe she was stupid enough to have a child in this business. Once we get that kid, that'll open up some interesting possibilities," he said, cracking his knuckles. "I guarantee the mom will give herself up in a heartbeat to spare her daughter any pain. She'll be such easy prey she'll come to us."

Standing upright, Ryker swung his arm, rotating his whole body to put real power behind it, and slapped the man backhanded.

Eleven staggered, his bell ringing nicely, and pressed a palm to his cheek. "What the hell?"

Ryker glared around the room at the men. "That kid…is *my* kid. If anyone lays an unauthorized hand on my daughter, I will chop it off."

"Jeez, all right," Eleven said. "We didn't know. Usually, it's no holds barred to get the target."

Ryker had a reputation that preceded him for getting the job done, whatever the job was, no matter what line had to be crossed. No matter how despicable the act. It was a reputation he enjoyed living up to.

"You neglected to brief us on this *detail*," Two said.

There hadn't been a need for them to be told. Ryker knew the child wouldn't be with her. Zee would do everything in her power not to expose their daughter to any danger, which meant keeping Olivia far away.

No one posed a bigger threat to the child than Zee did while the CIA was after her.

Ryker had claimed Olivia as his daughter in his heart a million times, but never publicly until now. Not because he hadn't wanted his little girl. *Oh, no,* he had wanted the child from the moment he had first tried to get Zee pregnant.

But that bitch had stripped him of paternity rights, with the Agency's help, and pretended as if he no longer existed.

He stared at the photo of Olivia. She was beautiful. Meant to be the light of his life.

Zee had stolen his kid from him. Had thrown the engagement ring in his face and refused to give them a chance to be a real family. Had deprived him of the simple joy of hearing his daughter say his name, call him *Daddy*. Had denied him the ability to be a part of Olivia's life and upbringing. Had him cast out of Langley as a respected operative, given one choice—lead cleanup teams from black sites, making the Agency's problems disappear, or lose his pension.

What kind of callous woman did that?

A heartless harpy who didn't deserve Olivia. And Zee thought he was the monster.

She had earned the hellfire that he was going to rain down upon her.

He used to keep tabs on her from afar and had abided by the CIA's leash on him, but if he had ever seen Zee with another man—someone playing daddy to Ryker's child—he would have broken the accord and broken her neck. Consequences be damned. He would've gone on the run, faced jail time, lost his daughter for good before he ever allowed Zee to replace him.

His patience and restraint were about to pay off. The tables had turned in his favor. He had no idea what her team had done wrong. All he knew was they had made a colossal mistake by becoming traitors and he was going to make the most of this golden opportunity. Show her that he indeed still existed.

Two stepped forward, looking reluctant to speak his mind. "Does the Company know that this is personal for you, sir?"

"Of course they do," Ryker said. "Why do you think they chose me for this assignment?" No one wanted Zee dead more than he did. Smiling, he looked back at the pictures on the screen, at his daughter. His flesh and blood.

He would mold her in his image and teach her to hate the woman who had kept them apart. For once, his hollow soul didn't feel empty. He was filled with righteous purpose. "This is now our top priority. We need to find my daughter and get to her first."

Chapter Seven

"Thanks again for driving us, Bill," John said.

Rubbing his wrist, he was ready to have his watch back, but his neighbor had refused to return it until their new arrangement was done.

The ride in the truck was tense and quiet. Minutes felt like hours in the strained silence. Unasked questions hung in the air: Bill's regarding Zee and what was going on, John's about why Zee needed to go to Seattle of all places, Zee's about the details surrounding his accident that had forced him out of the SEALs.

He was grateful she hadn't broached the subject. Talking about it would only dredge up ugly things he'd rather not reflect on and would only reinforce how she viewed him, as disabled.

"Sure," Bill said, casting a wary glance at Zee and the duct tape covering the bullet holes in her coat. "No problem since you're paying me."

John didn't think Bill had anything personal against her. The old guy was simply ornery with everyone. It had taken a year and a half for Bill to stop giving John a suspicious side-eye and to hold a conversation with him that lasted longer than two minutes and consisted of more words than grunts.

People out in these parts were helpful. The remote wilderness fostered a supportive community. No sticky-nosed gossip hounds getting in your business, but that also meant folks tended to look the other way during domestic disputes or when something sordid happened.

Finally, Bill pulled up to the front gate of Eielson Air Force Base and stopped the truck under the awning beside the guardhouse.

John leaned over and handed the guard his retired military ID, which was required to get them through the gate, but everyone had to show identification. Bill passed the guard his driver's license and Zee flashed her fake passport.

"All right." The guard handed everything back and waved them through.

"We're headed there," John said to Bill, pointing to the airfield. "Drop us at the passenger terminal."

Bill followed the signs, taking them to the terminal and then parking out front. "Where are you two headed?"

John smirked at the old man's curiosity getting the better of him. "The lower forty-eight," he said.

"I figured as much." Bill quirked an eyebrow. "I meant where?"

"Doesn't matter." John took the money, one thousand and two hundred dollars—a surcharge for the lift to the air force base and the logs—that he'd gotten from Zee and handed it to his neighbor. "Can I have my watch back?"

Bill touched the timepiece affectionately before unstrapping it. "This blank pan was starting to grow on me." He offered it with a frown.

Pleased to have his watch back, John glanced at the inscription.

T.O.T.S. Always.

He smiled on the inside and then he strapped it on.

John and Zee hopped out. Giving a wave of thanks to Bill, they headed into the passenger terminal.

"What does T.O.T.S. stand for?" she asked.

He shouldn't have been surprised at her perception, but she never ceased to amaze him. "Tip of the spear. The guys never wanted me to forget who I am." A special warfare operator. Now and forever.

"Why are we here?" She looked around the terminal.

There were only a handful of folks in uniform and civvies, some walking around, others seated.

"Their database is completely separate from the FAA's. That assault team," he said, lowering his voice, "or should I say the CIA, won't think to check military passenger manifests."

She didn't confirm or deny whether he was right about the CIA part. "I'd pat you on the back for this clever idea since there are no metal detectors, which also simplifies things, but they're never going to let me on a flight."

Air Mobility Command had a strict policy regarding passengers. Space available only for active duty, reservists, retirees and dependents—spouses and kids—no ordinary civilians. Even then a seat wasn't guaranteed. But if he could get them both on board this idea was a no-brainer. As long as they declared their firearms to passenger service agents, their weapons could be transported as checked luggage. And it was free. The only thing you had to pay for was an in-flight meal if you wanted one.

The trick was getting her a seat on the aircraft.

"Let me worry about that," he said, carrying her bag. "Just play along with however I decide to handle it."

"Okay."

They went up to the terminal counter.

"Good morning, sir," an affable staff sergeant said. The

man had kind eyes and a genuine smile. "What can I do for you?"

After three years, it still felt odd to hear *good morning* when it was dark as night outside at ten.

"Morning," John said. "You guys have regular flights to Lewis-McChord, don't you?" It was a joint army and air force base near Tacoma, Washington, forty to fifty miles south of Seattle.

"Sure do," the sergeant said. "Several times a week. Our last flight before Christmas is actually today. Leaves in an hour."

John gave Zee an optimistic grin which was met with a skeptical frown. "Do you happen to have two seats available?" he asked.

The sergeant checked, looking down at the computer and typing on the keyboard.

John glanced around, making sure nobody else was within immediate earshot and then gave the staff sergeant a once-over, sizing him up in anticipation of the forthcoming problem. A bribe wouldn't work on this Dudley-Do-Right. Getting irate and taking the poor customer service approach only worked in the civilian world. The customer wasn't always right when it came to the military. But John noticed his wedding ring and hoped a sentimental appeal might work.

"You're in luck," the staff sergeant said. "We have plenty of room, sir. Most folks have already taken off for the holidays."

Even better. John's grin at Zee widened and her grimace deepened. She must have forgotten the part about playing along.

The staff sergeant looked up. "I just need to see some identification."

John put his ID down, took the passport from Zee and slid it across on the counter.

"Ma'am, I'm going to need to see your CAC," the sergeant said, referring to the Common Access Card issued to everyone affiliated with the military.

Zee's gaze slid to John. "She doesn't have one," he said.

The staff sergeant glanced between them. "Uh, I'm afraid I can't issue her a ticket. She's not authorized to fly with her CAC, sir."

Zee's expression turned to one that screamed *I told you so.*

John handed her the duffel. "Sweetheart, would you mind taking a seat over there." He hiked his chin at the waiting area and then leaned over to whisper in her ear. "In a minute, when the sergeant looks at you, flash him a hopeful smile." He gave her a peck on the cheek.

"Okay, *darling.* Whatever you say." She strode off to the seats.

John turned back to the airman, noting his name tag. "Staff Sergeant Torres, I need your help here."

"There's nothing I can do, sir. It's against regulations for her to fly."

"Do you remember what it was like falling in love and proposing to your wife?"

Torres sighed as his face softened. "Yeah, I do." He tried to bite back a smile and failed.

"I gave the Navy SEALs my best years. Do you know what I have to show for it besides this," he said, tapping the face of his wristwatch, "and a bum leg…?"

"No."

"Her." John hiked a thumb over his shoulder and then followed the staff sergeant's gaze.

Zee flashed a tempered smile, equal parts innocent and sexy, and his heart moved in his chest.

None of it was real, he reminded himself.

He spun back to the officer. "I want to spend the rest

of my life with that woman. I blew my savings on an engagement ring." He patted the upper pocket of his coat. "And sprung for a fancy suite in Seattle. I'm planning to pop the question at the top of the Space Needle overlooking the city on Christmas Eve."

"Sounds sweet, sir. She'll brag to her friends about that forever. I wish I could've afforded something that lavish for my wife."

"That's just it—I'm so crazy in love, I wasn't thinking straight. I spent so much money on the ring and hotel I can't afford to fly us commercial. Come on, Staff Sergeant Torres. She's going to be my wife," he said, his voice dipping softer. "Practically my dependent already. If I don't pull this off, I think she'll dump me."

Taking a deep breath, Torres lowered his gaze. He chewed on his bottom lip, debating.

"My hotel reservation was a special and it's nonrefundable, man," John pleaded. "Just this once, in the spirit of Christmas, for the sake of true love, will you make an exception?"

Torres looked around. "All right. The flight is empty anyway. In the system, I'll list her as your spouse."

"Thanks, buddy."

"We don't get many SEALs through here. I'm honored to help."

"What kind of bird are we flying on?"

"C-130."

Slow and noisy, not very comfortable, but you could stretch out and sleep if there were enough empty sidewall seats. The toilets didn't offer much privacy, basically a porta potty behind a screen. But the plane was reliable, they were getting on it and that was sufficient.

It would be his first time on one since his discharge.

The airman printed up the boarding passes and handed

them over. "Boarding starts in half an hour. You two made it just in time." Torres leaned forward. "Good luck with the proposal."

"You're a lifesaver. Truly." John thanked him again and crossed the space, sitting down beside Zee.

"Well?" she asked.

He handed her a boarding pass.

"How did you manage this?"

"I gave him a sob story about us being in love," John said, tension seeping through him, "and how I was going to pop the question to you at the top of the Space Needle." He pulled his gaze from her and stared at the floor. All of it was a crock. The reality wasn't the least bit rosy. "The staff sergeant bought it hook, line and sinker." Torres was as big of a sucker as John was apparently. "Nothing to it."

Zee took his face in both of her hands and then she was kissing him, and her mouth was... *God*, her mouth was sweet and too good at what it was doing—a hard, slow, thorough kiss that made his insides leap and spark to life.

Again, a sense of familiarity stole in, as if he'd known her all his life or would for the rest.

She twined her arms around his neck in a tight hug and pressed her cheek to his. Over the rush of his heartbeat thrumming in his ears, he heard her say, "I had to make it look good. He's watching us." She eased back and smiled at John, brightly, falsely.

He looked at the ticket counter.

Torres beamed and gave him a thumbs-up.

John forced a grin and a nod in return at the airman, feeling like a fool for believing, even for a split second, that the kiss and that accompanying feeling had been real.

"The lip-lock wasn't necessary," he snapped at her, holding that stupid grin on his face in case the staff sergeant was still watching. "I wish you hadn't done it."

She should *not* have kissed him because the last thing he should be thinking about after the incident in the cabin was kissing her again and that's exactly what he was doing. Thinking about pulling her into his arms and kissing her a whole hell of a lot more with no regard for onlookers.

It was only hormones, he told himself, a ridiculous spike of testosterone, a normal male reaction to a sexy woman brought on by his past three years of celibacy.

Zee gave a one-shoulder shrug. "The guy looked like he was expecting to see fireworks or something. You told me to play along."

Now she gets it.

"I'm sorry," she continued. "Obviously it was a big mistake. It didn't mean anything. The kiss was only for show."

Any more displays of inconsequential affection and he might lose his mind. "Wow. You. Are. Good. All this time, everything between us has been one big lie. You've just been acting, haven't you?" He scrubbed his palms over his thighs, his flesh beginning to itch beneath his skin.

"Our friendship is real." She put a hand on his shoulder. "It has been from the start."

He didn't want to think about the start: her knocking on his door to literally borrow a cup of sugar and offering to pay him back with a home-baked pie. He didn't want to think about all the little things in between that had saved him from his self-imposed solitude: games of chess, fishing, playing cards, fireside chats over a glass of wine, trading chopped firewood for cinnamon rolls and butterscotch blondies and muffins. He definitely didn't want to think about how this was going to end.

Raking his hair back, he jumped to his feet, needing to move, needing to breathe. Why was it so stuffy in there? "I'm going to grab a coffee—you want something?"

She stood in front of him. "I'll go get it. You take a seat."

Rolling his eyes, he tugged at the collar of his turtleneck. "Enough coddling me—I'm capable of getting us something to drink."

"I know you are." Zee put her hand on his chest. "It's just—"

"Just what? Huh?"

"You're tired, John." She slid her hand up to his cheek. "You get cranky when you're tired."

Or when he'd been under too much stress without taking his meds.

John had considered swinging by his place on the way to Bill's to grab his medication. The odds were low that the assault team was watching his cabin, but it wasn't a chance worth taking. Missing two days' worth of doses and the lack of sleep was a bad combination.

"All right." He sat. "I'm sorry."

"Don't worry about it." She ran her hand through his hair and kissed his forehead.

All for show, of course, and if that staff sergeant's gaze hadn't been focused on them, he would've swatted her hand away and wiped the feel of her lips from his brow.

"I'll get us some food," she said. "You need to eat, get your blood sugar up." She walked away.

Restlessness coiled through him, tightening in his limbs. John got up, rolling his shoulders, and strolled to the wall of windows overlooking the aircraft on the apron.

This was how the crippling anxiety started without his meds. Restlessness that swelled into unease that had the potential to cascade into full-blown agitation. Drop him in the middle of a city, lots of people, heavy traffic, a sensory overload of sounds, the crush of pedestrians on the sidewalks…and then the static in his head would kick in—a roar of white noise.

More flashbacks and dissociation were a possibility, too.

Prevention was key, knowing his triggers. Stress. Fatigue. Cities. Explosions. Fights. Large groups of people. Being around his old teammates.

He could prevent one out of seven. Not too bad. He rubbed a hand across the scruff on his jaw, thinking of ways to mitigate his symptoms before they worsened.

Sleep always helped. If he slept on the flight, he might be able to function. Muster through to get Zee someplace safe.

He didn't want to unravel in public. Not in front of her. At times, he hated being this changed man, different than who he'd been for almost two decades. As a SEAL sleep deprivation had often come with the territory, in BUD/S—Basic Underwater Demolition/SEAL—training, out on long missions. Always, he'd coped, had managed to push through. Now fatigue wasn't something he could overcome and conquer.

If he weren't careful, it would conquer him.

Pressing a palm to his forehead, he stared out the window at the C-130 Hercules sitting under the bright lights of the apron. That plane was probably going to be their ride. Off to the side, not too far away, was a helicopter.

Big. Black. The same freaking model as the assault helicopter from last night.

Icy calm stole over him, his heartbeat slowing down. He needed all his senses and wits about him if that strike team was here on Eielson with them.

His gaze flickered up at the movement in the reflection of the window.

One of the Delta operators walked through the terminal. He was wearing all-black utility gear, tactical boots, a sidearm hooked on his hip.

The man strode up to Torres. "When will the helicopter be finished refueling?"

Thankfully he didn't keep his voice down.

"One more aircraft, then yours. About two more hours. Did you need it sooner?"

The guy from the strike team shrugged. "We don't have a destination yet. I needed an update, but would you mind bumping us up? Just in case. If we get a bead on a location, we'll need to move fast, and I don't want it to be my fault if that bird isn't fueled and ready to go."

While the two men continued to chat, John lowered his head, scratching his brow to hide his profile, and beat a path in the direction Zee had gone. He chose to leave the duffel bag behind on a chair. No one would touch it during the few minutes he'd be gone and going back to the seats for the bag might draw unwanted attention.

The pressing matter was that Zee might pop up at any minute, completely unaware that danger had waltzed in, and he didn't want that operator spotting her. Then all hell would break loose and their exit out of Alaska would be a bust.

Picking up his pace slightly—he didn't want to appear to be in a rush—he headed for the lone coffee shop. She was at the far end of the counter, waiting for an order that was probably for him. She loved her coffee black with no sugar, and he tolerated the same, but he loved a good cappuccino. Whenever she went into town for him, she'd always pick one up.

The barista handed Zee two cups with lids and a bag as he entered. "Black coffee, decaf cappuccino, and I heated those sandwiches for you."

Decaf?

She caught the look on his face. "What's wrong?"

"They're here on base. One from Delta is at the ticket counter."

"Damn it," she said, her voice thin with shock, almost so soundless that she had practically mouthed the words.

"He didn't see me." Sheer dumb luck that the guy from Delta hadn't spotted her either on his way in. The man had passed right by the coffee shop.

John ushered her to the back corner of the café where there was a bathroom. He checked the door. It was unoccupied and they ducked inside. Maintaining a crack in the door, he kept an eye on the main corridor so he could see when the operative left.

"He was asking about the refuel time on their helicopter," John said.

"It should've occurred to me that they might come here. Sometimes the Agency will use bases as way stations for lodging and fuel, especially in remote locations such as this. Clearance goes through in a snap. No one asks questions and everyone will stay out of their way."

He glanced at her. "So this is the CIA?" When she hesitated, he said, "I'm in this. For better or worse." Immediately he regretted the poor choice of words. "You know what I mean. I think we've established I have a need to know and I can be trusted."

"Yes, it's the CIA."

He shifted his gaze back to the corridor.

"It was never about not trusting you," she said. "The less you know, the better. To keep you safe."

"Yeah, yeah." The operative strolled past and out the front doors, none the wiser. "It's clear. He's gone."

"Did he say where they're headed?" she asked.

He shook his head. "No, he had no idea. They don't have a location yet, which means they don't know where you are or where you're going."

Relief shone in her gaze and she sagged against the wall. "Good. Let's hope they keep spinning their wheels. What do we do in the meantime?"

"Thirty minutes until we board. I think it's safe for us

to wait in the terminal. Doubtful they'll be back before we leave, but I suggest putting your hair up as a precaution." She had striking curls that were distinctive and noticeable. "And I'll scrounge up a ball cap for myself."

She set the things in her hands down on the bathroom counter. Looking in the mirror, she gathered her lush curls into a bundle and twisted the hair into a topknot that held its form without the help of pins or an elastic band.

"You need to eat." She handed him one of the cups and the bag as they left the bathroom.

His stomach rumbled with hunger. Starving, he peeked in the bag. It smelled good. The sandwich would be perfect. A decent helping of healthy carbs and protein would make him feel better.

Looking him over, she pressed a palm to his forehead.

He swatted away her warm hand that time. "Stop it." At the sharpness in his voice, he realized he was beginning to prickle in defensiveness and needed to take it down a notch.

"Are you going to be okay?"

"Sure." The response was automatic. After it came out of his mouth, he took stock of his condition. The truth was he was embarrassed by the timing of this, that *this* was an issue for him at all. He should tell her, wanted to explain what was happening to him, but it felt like weakness. Deep down he knew it was biochemical. Something had gotten scrambled in his brain after he'd been tortured and with the explosion during the escape that had killed two of his guys and messed up his leg. Still, it felt like weakness. "I can't believe you got me decaf," he said, wanting to change the subject.

"You need sleep on the flight." She circled right back to the topic he sought to avoid. "You're on edge, wound up too tight."

She had no idea, and he prayed that his condition wouldn't worsen to the point that she found out. But he feared that he wouldn't get better unless he got his medication.

"It'll pass," he said. "I'll be fine once I eat and get some rest."

Watching him intently, she nodded, but doubt gleamed in her eyes. "I hope so."

Chapter Eight

By the time they reached the passenger terminal at Joint Base Lewis-McChord, John wasn't looking any better and was far from being himself. He was ghostly pale, not just ashen, but a sickly pallor. Of greater concern to Zee was that he wouldn't make eye contact with her.

During the five-hour flight, he had stretched out across almost four seats and tried to rest. But it wasn't the deep REM sleep that he needed. Maybe it had been the adrenaline, maybe it had been the deafening roar of the engine, or the uncomfortable seats that had kept him tossing every five minutes.

Whatever the issue, Zee was worried about him. "You got me out of Alaska and to Tacoma. This is above and beyond," she said. "Whatever vow you made to me I release you from it."

John took off his ball cap and wiped his sweat-covered brow with the back of his hand. "This isn't Seattle and you're still not safe." He hoisted her duffel bag on his shoulder and walked away from her going to the ticket counter.

Arguing with him was pointless. She was learning that the hard way. Once John had set his mind to something, he saw it through to the end.

She only wanted to keep everyone she cared about safe.

At the terminal counter, John made arrangements for a ride with the airman on duty.

The airman ordered a Lyft, using base mode in the app. It ensured the driver who was matched would have access to get through the front gate because they already had a CAC. As their destination, she gave the address of a coffee shop one block from her true objective, and she used her prepaid VISA card to cover the fare.

They waited for their driver, Peter, in the vestibule. Estimated time of arrival was twenty-two minutes.

Once the car arrived, they climbed into the sedan. It was an older Hyundai. Silver. She saw it had over 130,000 miles.

"Hey, Peter, we need to go to more than one destination," she said, thinking long-term.

His brows drew together. "Only one location was entered and paid for on the app."

"Yep, and I'm willing to pay you five thousand more, in cash, to give us your car."

Both John and Peter stared at her.

"I need this car to get to the base for my day job and for my side hustle at night." The kid was about twenty years old.

She unzipped her bag and pulled out the cash. "I'm guessing this beater is worth two grand. Four tops." She offered the money. "That means you make a profit." The car wouldn't stand out, would blend in, and if he was using it to cart people around, she figured it was well maintained and reliable, too.

"Are you for real?" Peter asked.

"Yes. I am."

Peter clenched the steering wheel. "I don't know."

John hit the button on the door with a trembling hand,

sending the window buzzing down. He stuck his head outside and took deep breaths.

What was wrong with him? Was he coming down with something?

Zee pulled out an extra bundle of cash. "Ten grand. You can buy another car, take a vacation and have money in your pocket for a nice holiday season."

"I think she wants you to retire," John said.

At least he hadn't lost his sense of humor. She'd take what she could get. "My final offer, Peter. Take it or I'll find someone else who will."

"Yeah, yeah, all right." Peter snatched the money. "I'll take it."

"Do you need us to drop you someplace close by?" she offered.

"Nah, I live on base in the barracks." He jumped out, keeping the driver's door open, and thumbed through the money.

Zee left John in the back along with the duffel bag and slipped in behind the wheel.

"Have a merry Christmas and a happy New Year!" Peter waved as Zee pulled off.

John tipped his head back on the seat with the window down, letting in the frigid air. He wasn't okay, so she wasn't going to ask a question that had an obvious answer.

"Did you sleep at all on the flight?" she asked.

"No. The engine was too loud. The noise was a trigger that made it worse."

"Made what worse?"

Shutting his eyes, he pinched the bridge of his nose. "Nothing."

He wanted her to trust him with her secrets and rely on him for support, but he wasn't willing to do the same in return.

This wasn't going to work.

"What do you need, John?" Food hadn't helped, and he definitely needed something. "What can I get you?"

"I'm fine."

But he wasn't. She only wanted to help him, to protect him, and he wouldn't let her.

The one-hour ride was awkward with both of them keeping secrets. He probably thought his reason was as justified as hers. She knew how dangerous secrets could be.

Her ex had lied to her from day one about everything. Had used manipulation and coercion to keep her close. She vowed never to go through that again.

There were similarities between Ryker and John. Two sides of the same coin. She'd be a blind fool not to acknowledge it, but the fundamental differences between them far outweighed anything they had in common.

Whatever John was hiding, she sensed it was related to his military service and to the reason he was no longer in the navy. That was the one touchy subject for him that he had difficulty sharing.

If they were going to stick this out together, then she'd push for them both to put all their cards on the table. But that wasn't part of her plan.

Nothing had changed. The only way for John to be safe was if he were far away from her. And she was set on making that a reality.

She parked the car at the front entrance of the sprawling campus of the all-girls Emerald City Academy for grades three through twelve.

John lifted his head from the backseat like he had a sixth sense that they'd reached their destination and opened his eyes. "What are we doing here?" Sitting up, he looked around. "Is this a school?"

"Wait here." She turned off the ignition and pocketed

the keys. "Better yet, take what cash you need from the bag and lie low in a hotel for a week or so. Okay?" If she trusted him with her life, she could trust him with her money. "You've done more than enough to help me. I'm grateful. *Please* believe me."

One day, she'd send him a letter expressing not only the depths of her gratitude but also her true feelings for him. For now, he needed to go.

He leaned forward, putting a hand on the back of her seat. "Zee, think of me as a boomerang. You can throw me away, really put your arm into it if it makes you feel any better, but I'll just come right back. Until you're safe." His gaze bounced around, avoiding hers, and flicked up to the rearview mirror. "And that's not here in the middle of Seattle with only God knows how many CCTV cameras for Delta to tap into and locate you via face recognition."

It wasn't lost on her that when thrown properly, boomerangs were lethal weapons. "By the time they get here, I'll be long gone."

"They're already here."

She stiffened. "What are you talking about?"

"In the rearview mirror, I spotted three black SUVs, large enough to hold a baker's dozen of those Delta boys, headed toward the west side of the school. Could be coincidence, but my gut is telling me that it's not."

That meant Delta team had recovered her laptop and were probably in the process of doing a deep dive into her hard drive, extracting any data that might be useful.

She shoved the thought aside. For now, thinking about the hard drive was a distraction. She had a far more pressing problem.

On the west end of the school was the seldom-used entrance for VIPs. It was probably the easiest access point for them to breach discreetly.

How had she missed their arrival?

She glanced in the rearview mirror, but of course there was nothing to see. The one bright spot in this was that regardless of what was going on with John, he was cognizant and competent, and she hoped still physically capable.

"Why are we here?" he asked.

"I'm not answering that question and I'm not letting you go inside that school with me unless you tell me what's wrong with you. Tick, tock, John." She was moving out in five seconds, with or without him.

"I don't have my meds." He squeezed his eyes shut. "For my PTSD." The agony in his voice sounded like it was choking him.

It was all she could do not to hold him close and hug until her arms ached, then find a way to get him his medication. But there was no time. She had to move. "Can you handle going in there?"

His eyes flew open. "Yes," he said without a second of hesitation, his gaze holding hers *finally*.

"Come on."

They alighted from the car and made a beeline for the entrance.

"What do you take?" she asked.

"Sertraline, fifty milligrams twice a day. Most days anyway."

The front doors were locked per protocol. She waved at the camera so someone inside would buzz them in.

"How many doses have you missed?" she asked.

"I'm going on five. If I were in the woods, with peace and quiet, sticking to my routine, it wouldn't be a problem. That's how I can go a few days at a time without it."

Oh, John. He was in pain and it was her fault. His suffering made her heart hurt.

She wanted him to go back to the car, wait for her there,

but he'd only take offense, and she'd done too much damage already. "You should've told me. I would've understood."

It bothered her, deep down in a way she barely comprehended, that he hadn't trusted her enough to confide something so important. She'd thought them closer than this. The only secrets she'd kept from John were those to protect him or Olivia. This was different.

The buzzer rang, the lock disengaged and she opened the door.

"Are you going to make me ask you again?" he pressed, his tone implying he wouldn't drop it until he got an answer.

Since he had shared, something that seemed difficult for him to admit, it was time for her to do likewise. "We're here to get my daughter," she said, walking into the building.

John stumbled across the threshold behind her, and she realized it wasn't because of his leg injury. Any shock he was feeling was to be expected.

"Are you angry with me?" she wondered. "For not telling you about her. I thought it was the best way to keep her safe." It was never to be dishonest with John or hide the fact that she had a daughter. Her number-one role in life, the thing she was most proud of was being a mother.

John shook his head. "Ditto."

"What does that mean?"

"You should've told me. I would've understood."

And in that moment, she fell a little harder for John. "Olivia means everything to me. There's nothing in this world that's more important to me than her."

"We'll get her." He put a hand on her shoulder. "I might look like I'm in rough shape, but I won't let you down." His voice was ironclad with determination.

Nodding, she had every confidence that John would follow through on his pledge.

In the front office, she signed in at the desk. “Hi, I’m Zoey Howard, here to pick up my daughter, Olivia, for the holiday break.”

“Certainly.” An elderly woman got up from a desk that was situated farther back in the room and came to the front. “May I see some—”

Zee showed her one of her fake IDs.

“Oh, you’re prepared for the drill.” The older woman, a short plump gray-haired lady, put on her glasses and took a look. “What class is she assigned to?”

“She is in the sixth grade, Ms. Colvin’s homeroom.”

Her daughter was a Christmas baby and would turn eleven in two days. To bypass the rule in Virginia that children had to be five before September 30 to be eligible for kindergarten, Zee had put Olivia in private school. When they went on the run, her little girl had to take an entrance exam for the Emerald City Academy. Olivia had scored remarkably high. Turned out that her daughter was gifted and was able to skip the fifth grade.

The principal of the academy had worried that putting Olivia in the sixth grade at such a young age might negatively impact her social and emotional development, but Zee saw it as an extra layer of protection.

Anyone trying to find her daughter would be looking for a little girl in the fifth grade. Not the sixth.

The woman looked Olivia up in the computer. “It says here that you weren’t going to pick her up for the winter break.”

“Change of plans.” She’d wanted nothing more than to spend the one day a year with her daughter that they had dubbed a double holiday, Olivia’s birthday and Christmas rolled into one—*Olivmas*. The one day the CIA would triple their efforts looking for her because emotion might lure her out of hiding and to her daughter. Zee had worried about getting spotted on CCTV in an airport, hotel, on the streets of Seattle, and exposing her daughter to unnecessary danger. But look at them now. Danger was breaking in through the west gate. "I was able to take time off from work and so was my fiancé." She gestured to John.

He smiled and nodded, looking like he might pass out at any minute.

"Okay," the woman said, not seeming to notice John's sickly appearance. "I made a note in the system. I'll call for her." She reached for the public address system that they used to announce a parent's arrival and to send for the children.

This was the preferred method Zee had used two previous times. It limited her exposure on the school's security feeds and she didn't have to interact with anyone else inside the building. But advertising her arrival and broadcasting that Olivia could be intercepted on her way to the front office was the last thing she needed.

"No." Zee's sharp tone elicited a raised brow from the woman. "I want to surprise her. We'll go get her. And one more thing. I saw some suspicious men lurking on the west side of the school," Zee said. "They looked like they were up to no good. I'd feel a heck of a lot better as I'm sure every parent of a child here would, if you called the police. Right away. Tell them it's an emergency."

"I could've sworn at least one had a gun," John said. "I'd hate to think that they were here to kidnap a child."

Alarm streaked across the woman's face. "Oh, dear."

Zee began ushering John out the office door and into the corridor of the school.

The woman picked up the phone. "Thank you for telling me. I will also get our security team on it."

Police would have a difficult time facing off against Delta. School security guards wouldn't stand a chance.

Getting Olivia out of there as quickly as possible might be the only way to save innocent lives.

AS THE GUARD's radio squawked, Ryker squeezed the trigger, putting a bullet in his forehead. The man was dead before he crumpled to the ground.

"According to the online schedule," Two said, "the fifth graders have dinner at this time."

"Everyone, move out to the cafeteria," Ryker said. "Except for Two, Eleven and Five. Find her room and check there as a precaution." Not everyone ate at the same pace and some probably preferred to eat in their rooms. He wanted all bases covered in any eventuality. "Pack a bag with some of her stuff, too. Essentials." He didn't want the hassle of the kid needing something while he was still focused on finding and terminating Zee. "No one is to hurt my kid. And try not to kill any others." That last part seemed like something a father should say, but Ryker didn't feel any repugnance over some other child getting caught in the crossfire. He felt absolutely nothing besides the desire to claim his daughter like a conqueror and lay waste to Zenobia, leaving her as nothing more than scorched earth.

His men nodded and dispersed, following the order.

Ryker led the main team to the cafeteria. They crossed the spacious open-air courtyard, a quadrangle that the school was built around. He imagined Olivia sitting outside on a bench in pleasant weather, reading a book, giggling with her friends, kicking around a ball. This was a posh school. Expensive. A beautiful place for people to dump their offspring. Must have taken all of Zee's savings. Probably offered one of the best educations.

Once Zee was dead, he'd put his daughter in one similar on the East Coast. All girls, too, with no boys as a distraction. Someplace safe where Olivia would be watched over while he was away on assignments, taking lives and crossing out names on the CIA's hit list.

Their time together might be limited, but he would ensure it'd be precious, cherished. Fun. Enough to train her, shape her and teach her to be loyal to him above all else.

He would sow the necessary seeds and reap her unconditional love.

That was how he'd give Olivia Jekyll, so that she never saw Hyde.

ZEE HAD MILES of hallway to navigate before they made it to the third floor of the dormitory that housed the fifth and sixth graders. Zee raced down the corridor with John at her side, their footfalls not making a sound. Unlike the rest of the school, the halls in the dorm were carpeted.

Olivia kept to a strict schedule that Zee had memorized. Her daughter always read in her room before dinner for at least thirty minutes.

Kids were assigned rooms based on their grade and last name. She glanced at the name tags along the way, stopping at the one at the end of the hall that read: Hoffman, Madison. Howard, Olivia.

She knocked then twisted the knob and flung open the door.

A startled brunette with braided pigtails, sitting cross-legged on top of her bed, looked up from a book she was reading. It was Olivia's best friend, Madison.

Zee's gaze swept across the large room, to the second empty bed and over to the sitting area with two desks.

Where was Olivia?

Zee looked back at the girl. "Hi, Madison." She stepped inside and John followed her, sticking close to her heels.

"I'm Olivia's mom. Where is she?" Zee hoped for a bit a luck that her daughter was only down the hall in the bathroom.

"Hi, Mrs. Howard." Madison set her book to the side. Pushing her glasses up the bridge of her nose, she climbed down from the bed and proffered her hand. "It's so nice to finally meet you. She talks about you all the time," Madison said, shaking Zee's hand. "It was great of you to give her permission to come home with me for Hanukkah since my parents were back in the country. We had so much fun together. It was awesome to have a friend to hang out with at home for once."

"She told me how much she enjoyed it, too." Zee tamped back her rising panic over her daughter's whereabouts. "It was nice of you to invite her." A kindness that Zee had appreciated, unable to spend quality time with her daughter herself. Zee was aware that the friendship had become a lifeline for both girls. "Madison, we're in a bit of a rush. Where's Olivia? I really need to get her so we can go," she said, grabbing her daughter's coat from a hook.

"You're taking her?" Disappointment and surprise washed over Madison's face. "We thought we'd be together for the winter break. We had the whole thing planned." Her shoulders slumped. "Now I've got to spend it alone?"

Ripping Olivia away from the sanctuary of EC Academy and destroying the little sense of normalcy that she'd found wasn't what Zee wanted. Her daughter didn't deserve this upheaval in her young life. But it was unavoidable.

"Madison," Zee said, pointedly, while trying to keep her anxiety out of her tone. She didn't want to scare her. "Where is Olivia? It's important I find her right now."

The little girl sighed. "She was hungry and decided

to go to the cafeteria early for dinner with the elementary kids."

The response sent fear spiraling through Zee as her stomach went hollow.

CLEARLY MARKED SIGNS guided Ryker and his team down the halls and around the bends. The temperature in the building was perfect like everything else one would expect from a place like this. Not too hot, not too cool. Even the air was faintly scented with lemon.

He took out one more guard along the way, a double tap to the chest. By the time his team was finished, there would be quite a mess of bodies to clean up.

They pushed open the double doors to the cafeteria and swept inside. The girls were all chatting and eating in clusters like normal kids would, not paying attention to anything around them.

Then one child noticed Ryker and his team, followed by another and another. A hush fell over the dining hall as gazes swung their way. The screams came next, like fingernails on a chalkboard.

"We're not here to hurt anyone!" Ryker said, lowering his gun. He waved at his men to also lower their weapons. The sooner he got the frenzy under control the easier this would be.

The kids in the cafeteria ranged from eight years old to ten, possibly eleven. There weren't many of them. Maybe seventy at most. But after a cursory glance, he didn't spot Olivia.

"Point out the fifth graders and we'll leave," Ryker said. His thinking was that birds of a feather flocked together. Or rather those in the same grade would congregate.

One lone finger pointed to tables at the far side of the

cafeteria, and others were quick to confirm where he'd find his daughter.

He strode to the other side of the dining hall as the girls cowered, keeping their heads bent. Walking in between tables, he looked them over, one by one.

There!

At the last table, he spotted a girl with long dark hair, her head hung with her chin to her chest. Her spiral curls shrouded her face like a curtain.

A euphoric jolt of victory zinged through him. "Olivia!" He ran over to her, put his hand on her shoulder and spun her around.

The terrified face that looked up at him wasn't his daughter's.

Chapter Nine

At the sound of footsteps in the hall, Zee whirled around as a shadow fell over the doorway. Her heart leaped into her throat. Men had silently crept up on them as a result of the carpet.

John lunged across the threshold shoving them back.

"Get down!" Zee instructed the little girl, and Madison dove for the floor.

A third man fired into the room, narrowly missing Zee and shooting a desk. Dropping her daughter's things, she snatched her baton from the holster and extended it with the flick of her wrist.

She threw a boot heel into the man's gut, kicking him into the hall to avoid Madison getting hit by any stray shots. Whipping the baton up, she struck the man's firing arm, sending it into the air and knocking the gun loose from his grip. Then she went for his head and kept swinging until he dropped and stopped moving.

John had disarmed two men, shot one and coldcocked the other. Sweat beaded on his face like he had just sprinted a four-minute mile and rolled down his temples as a tremor ran through him. But he was steady on his feet and his reflexes were sharp.

Zee knelt beside the man she'd bludgeoned into unconsciousness and grabbed his earpiece. Putting on the

Bluetooth comms device, she needed to stay abreast of Delta team's movements in the school and whether or not they'd found Olivia.

No way in hell they were leaving the premises with her daughter. She'd tear them all to pieces first.

Standing, she spun toward movement in the hallway.

Olivia. Her daughter stood five doors down, wide-eyed and frozen, holding a to-go container.

Zee dashed down the hall, whisked her daughter into her arms and hugged her close to her chest. *Thank God.* Olivia was safe and in her embrace.

"Mom?" Olivia's arms wrapped around her neck. "What are you doing here? What's going on?"

"I'll explain later. We have to go." Hugging her little girl tighter, her heart overflowing with relief, Zee stroked Olivia's hair that was up in a ponytail and kissed the top of her head.

Never wanting to let her go, Zee forced herself to break the embrace. She held her daughter at arm's length and looked her over from head to toe.

"Go?" Olivia asked. "Where?"

"Mockingjay," Zee said, using the code to tell her daughter everything she needed to know in the moment with a single word: they had to run, time was pressing, their lives were in danger. Olivia loved *The Hunger Games* series of books and Zee knew that she'd never forget what it meant. Other than keeping her daughter safe, preparing her for whatever might come was the next best thing she could do.

Olivia went rigid and pulled away from her. All questions and confusion drained from her expression. "I have to get my go bag." She turned and rushed down the hall to her room.

Zee was right behind her, worried that goodbyes with Madison would slow them down.

Olivia grabbed her coat from the floor, throwing it on as she passed Madison, who stood in the middle of the room, agape, her face pale and stark with horror. Olivia snatched a backpack from her closet and shoved the wrapped Olivmas present that Zee had sent her inside the bag.

Her daughter hurried up to her roommate and threw her arms around her in a hug. "I'll miss you, Madison. You're the best friend I've ever had." Then Olivia let her go and walked out of the room without a glance back.

Zee was proud that her daughter was so strong and brave, but it saddened her even more that Olivia had to be this tough at such a young age. It wasn't right.

She took her daughter's free hand since she was still holding the to-go container and the three of them ran to the stairwell.

"This is Prime," a familiar voice said in Zee's ear over Delta's comms, and she tripped down two steps as her heart seized. No, it couldn't be him. *Dear God, please, not him.* "My daughter isn't in the cafeteria. Delta Two, you better have her. Report."

Blistering shock seared through her. Hot nausea boiled in her throat.

No, no, no. "Ryker," she muttered to herself.

"WHO'S RYKER?" JOHN ASKED, wondering why they had stopped moving. Static hadn't started blaring in his head, yet, but once the white noise kicked in, he didn't know how much good he'd be and would prefer to make tracks before that happened.

Zee stood frozen, looking shaken as if she'd seen a ghost. "We have to get out of here."

His sentiments exactly.

They hustled down to the main floor and ran along the corridor, leaving the dormitory section. Scrambling around the bend, they hurried down the hall toward the entrance and passed a wall of windows that overlooked the open-air quad at the heart of the school.

Zee's attention whipped outside as she slowed.

John followed her line of sight. Across the way, on the other side of the courtyard in the parallel section of the school, was Delta team.

One man caught sight of them as well and slowed to a stop. Mr. Trench Coat.

There wasn't a door leading to the quad in the hallway they were in. The rest of Delta took off down the corridor, no doubt headed their way.

But Trench Coat just stood there for a second, the same way he had at the lake. Back then, John had thought the man was being cavalier about the situation. Now he suspected it was something else entirely and far worse.

Trench Coat raised his weapon and opened fire, shooting out the windows in his own hallway. He leaped over the sill past the shards jutting around the frame. Firing more rounds, he bounded across the courtyard.

Zee lowered Olivia's head, shielding her as she also ducked. The windows in their corridor shattered under the continued gunfire. Bullets hammered into the inside wall opposite of where they were positioned as Olivia gave a startled cry.

John threw his arms around both of them and made a beeline for the entrance.

"Zenobia!" a man called out, and John guessed it was Trench Coat. "Zee!" Her name echoed with rage in the corridor. "Give her to me and I'll kill you quickly!"

Police rushed inside the building and down the hall from the entrance, weapons drawn.

The woman from the front desk was behind the four officers and beckoned to them. "Mrs. Howard, come this way."

"Those crazy men are shooting," Zee said, pointing back behind her. "You have to hurry."

John stole a glance over his shoulder as Delta team rounded the corner, joining up with Trench Coat who had just jumped into the corridor.

"Freeze!" one cop said. "Drop your weapons and put—"

The *pip pip* of suppressed gunfire whispered in the air. A series of rapid bangs rang out as the officers returned fire.

"Zenobia!" Trench Coat said.

The older gray-haired woman yelped and scurried into the main office.

John put Zee and Olivia in front of him, using his body to shield them from the incoming barrage. They bulled through the doors into the vestibule and shoved through the next set outside.

Hustling down the steps, he checked their surroundings. Two squad cars with flashing lights were parked out front. Sirens sounded in the distance drawing closer.

There was no sign of Delta team. It looked all clear, but that wouldn't last for too long. The cops would slow Delta down, not stop them.

They ran to the beater Hyundai and hopped in.

Zee peeled off, tires screeching, and whipped into traffic, cutting off another car that blared its horn. The strident sound slashed through John's head, and he rubbed at his temples.

"Stay down low," she said to her daughter.

The girl slid down in the backseat, without any questions asked and not a single whimper, as though this were routine.

Taking sharp turns and blowing the speed limit as much as traffic allowed, Zee drove like she knew where she was going.

"Where are we headed?" he asked. The tremble in his hand had gotten so bad that he crossed his arms to keep her from seeing it.

"A motel. In Issaquah. There's limited CCTV in the area. I know what exit to take so they won't be able to track us. We stayed there when I was first getting Olivia settled into the school."

He cracked the window, letting in fresh air, but didn't roll it all the way down because he didn't want the kid to catch a chill in the back.

After he checked the mirrors and was certain that they weren't being followed, he closed his eyes. Focused on taking steady deep breaths.

In the airport at Eielson, he'd been on edge, the first prickle of anxiety starting to get to him, but the plane ride, with the roar of the C-130 engine, brought everything back to him in a rush. Kept the most horrific parts of what he'd been through playing on a loop inside his head.

How he was able to function without having a complete meltdown was any wonder. Back at the school when he had taken down two operatives, instinct, training and efficiency gained from many years of practice had coalesced into action for him.

But the pressure was mounting. In his head. In his chest.

John breathed in slowly through his nose, feeling his stomach expand as he inhaled. Concentrated on filling up his lungs with air. Released the breath through his mouth. Opening his eyes, he looked around and went through the rest of the grounding technique that helped him stave off flashbacks and dissociation.

One, I see the glove box. Two, I see the freeway. Three, I see a minivan. Four, I see Christmas lights. Five, I see Zee.

So beautiful.

Closing his eyes, he strained to go through the next part.

One, I hear the hiss of the car's tires on the wet asphalt. Two, I hear the wind rushing in through the window. Three, I hear "Santa Claus Is Coming to Town" playing on the radio. Four, I hear the crinkle of polystyrene foam. Five, I hear Zee drumming her fingers on the steering wheel.

It all came back to Zee. Goddess with a baton.

At the motel, she parked away from the check-in office and kept the engine running, the radio on. "I'll be right back." She pulled on a wool hat, covering her hair, and yanked her hood up over her head.

The door slammed and she was gone. He glanced around the dark motel parking lot. It wasn't the best neighborhood he'd been in, but it wasn't the worst either. About half the rooms appeared occupied.

In the backseat, Olivia was quiet, still slouched down, her fingers digging into the to-go container, causing it to squeak every now and again. The sound grated on his ears, making his nerves flare and his limbs twitch. But he could only imagine the riot of emotions going through the girl. For someone so young, she displayed impressive cool under pressure. Olivia had a backbone of steel, just like her mom.

Gritting his teeth, he clenched his fingers and decided to run through another grounding technique.

Two minutes later, Zee hopped back in. She pulled off and drove to a part of the lot that offered three different exits and parked in front of a room. "Let's go."

The three of them got out, with John grabbing the duffel bag from the back and hitching it onto his shoulder.

Zee unlocked the door. Flipping on the lights, she ushered them into suite that had a semiprivate bedroom and small separate sitting area. He presumed the sofa pulled out into an extra bed.

After locking the door, Zee took him by the arm over to a corner. "I have to run an errand. It'll take me an hour. Two at most."

"What's the errand? I'll go."

"No, you need to rest. Will you be okay here, alone with her?"

He wasn't quite sure what she was asking. "With my PTSD attacks I don't get violent or destructive if that's what you're worried about," he said, sounding somewhat more insulted than he wanted to let on.

Some guys from the cognitive therapy group he'd gone through at Veterans Affairs had vicious episodes on occasion, making them a danger to themselves and those around them. John prided himself on not having that type of issue.

"I trust you with my daughter," she said with unwavering confidence. "I know she'll be safe with you. I asked if you'd be okay with her. You've been under a lot of stress."

Understanding what she meant, he exhaled with relief. "I'll be fine." More like he'd hold it together for as long as necessary. "What if you get into trouble out there?" He wouldn't be able to help her.

Zee's gaze bounced to her daughter and then back to him. "I doubt that I will. On the off chance that I do, there's a letter in Olivia's go bag. My parents' address is on the envelope. Take her there."

Surprise rocked through him. She really had planned for the worst. "What about you?"

"Nothing is going to happen. I'll be back." She pressed a palm to his chest. "Two hours tops." She crossed the room and went to Olivia. The girl had taken a seat on the sofa and looked as if she was awaiting instructions. "Honey, I have to go out, just for a little bit. My friend John is going to stay with you. He'll make sure nothing happens to you while I'm gone. When I get back, we'll talk."

She kissed her daughter's forehead, gave John one last, long look and slipped out of the room.

John put the chain on, not that it would stop someone from getting in. He sat on the floor, with his back to a dresser and his legs blocking the door as an added precaution. If he suffered a flashback or entered a dissociative trance, he didn't want to chance one of those Delta boys busting in without him being aware.

As difficult as the past twenty-four hours had been for him, it had given him a renewed sense of purpose. Serving his country had been the only career he'd ever considered. Joining Special Forces had been a calling. He'd thought for sure that he'd be a lifer.

Then he'd been captured, tortured, permanently injured, changing his destiny.

But it had also led him to Zee. To saving this little girl. He couldn't dismiss how once again he felt *called* to serve.

Taking off his coat, he kept it within easy reach. The gun he'd taken from one of the men was concealed in the pocket.

"Are you all right?" Olivia asked.

"Yeah, kiddo. I'll be fine. I'm only tired."

"You look sick."

That, too. "I'm tired and a bit under the weather, but it's nothing to concern you."

"You need chicken soup. It'll make you feel better." She took off her jacket and set her backpack down. "Is it okay if I turn on the TV?"

"Sure. My head hurts, so if you could watch a show that's not too noisy, I'd appreciate it."

She switched on the television and scrolled through the channels. Once she'd picked something, he heard her moving around the room. Then she came over, sat next to him and handed him a bottle of water.

"I put on a nature show. It's about the migration of birds. I turned the TV in case you wanted to watch it with me."

A swarm of swallows dipped across the blue sky on the television screen. "Thanks," he said, for the water and the overall consideration.

She opened her to-go container. "Do you want some?" She held the box out to him. Roasted chicken, mashed potatoes and green beans were inside.

Suddenly, he was famished. "I'm good." His stomach rumbled, betraying him.

"Are you sure? I can hear your stomach growling." Her voice was soft as cotton. "I have enough to share."

As she offered the food to him once more, he met her gaze. She resembled her mother. Same almond-shaped brown eyes. Her hair was a little longer and the mass of brown curls had natural blond highlights. The genuine smile she gave him was tentative.

It reminded him of the first time he'd met Zee. Same smile. Kind mixed with a bit of apprehension.

"You eat up." He opened the bottle of water and chugged the whole thing, hoping it would quiet his rumbling belly.

She dug into her food, and his shoulders relaxed.

"Can we play twenty questions?" she asked.

His head was killing him, and he'd rather sit quietly, but he said, "Sure. If you want."

"How do you know my mom?"

"Uh, we were neighbors."

"Where did she live?"

"I don't think this is how the game goes."

Her smile this time was less wary. "It is the way I play it." She was clever, too, like her mom.

"Alaska," he said, realizing there were probably lots of things she was curious to know. But he was surprised this was what she'd asked. "About an hour outside of Fairbanks."

"That's north of Anchorage, right?"

"Yep."

"Describe it to me. What it looked like. What the air smelled like. The air smells different here than it did in Virginia."

Somehow, this little girl got him talking. The conversation eased the tension bubbling in the back of his brain, helping him to focus intently and stay grounded. All good things.

Before he knew it, a key was shoved in the lock and the door opened, catching on the chain. "John," Zee said.

"Right here." He climbed to his feet and let her in.

Zee walked through the room carrying shopping bags. After setting everything down, she roped Olivia into a big hug and kissed her cheeks and forehead like she couldn't get enough of her. "Hungry?"

"No, I ate the food from the school."

Zee fished out pajamas from the bag and gave them to her daughter. "Go run a bath," she said, opening a container and then dumped two gummy pills into Olivia's palm. "I'll be there in a sec and we'll chat."

Olivia nodded and disappeared into the bathroom. Behind the closed door the water ran.

Sitting beside John on the sofa, Zee dug back into the bags. She whipped out a bottle of prescription medication and handed it to him.

Sertraline—fifty milligrams. Prescribed to Zoey Howard.

"How did you get this?" he wondered.

"There's a hospital about fifteen minutes away. I went to the emergency room. Told the doctor I was on vacation visiting family and forgot my meds for my anxiety disorder. He prescribed five days' worth. I convinced him to bump it up from three, enough to get me through the holidays until I go back home."

She was brilliant. He was so thankful, he could kiss her, but he knew well enough not to.

John popped the lid off and swallowed one dry.

She opened his hand and shook four of those gummies into his palm. Double what she'd given Olivia.

"What is it?"

"Melatonin." She showed him the label on the container. "It'll help you rest but won't make you drowsy when you wake. Trust me."

It was the same stuff his body made. He desperately needed sleep, but he was still a bit wired, and he did trust her. He threw them in his mouth and chewed the fruity gummies.

"And there's this." She gave him a brown paper bag. "Chicken soup, a couple of soft baked rolls and a large salad. There's also a grilled chicken sandwich."

Danger was circling them, and she'd gone out of her way—left her daughter who she hadn't seen in months, who had a ton of questions and must be scared, confused—just to take care of him.

Emotion swamped him, backing up in his chest.

"Eat." She patted his leg and stood, grabbing two of the shopping bags. "I'm going to talk with Olivia."

He cleared his throat. "I told her about Alaska. She asked. I hope that was okay."

She nodded. "I've never told her where I was, thinking it was safer for her, but she's been curious. Now that I can't go back there, it's fine." She walked toward the bathroom.

"Hey" he said, and she stopped, throwing him a glance over her shoulder. "Thanks, Zee." He held up the bag of food and the meds.

Her mouth lifted and the smile was worth a thousand of anyone else's, the look in her eyes he could only describe as affection. She had seen him sweating, frustrated, angry, in the throes of a panic attack. At his worst. No matter how he had been, it never seemed to faze her, other than her showing concern. She always looked at him exactly the same way. Without pity. Only fondness.

Even though he wished it were more than that, he'd take it.

"No problem," she said. "You would've done the same for me. That's what friends are for."

Friends. The word still cut like a dagger in his chest.

Was he a selfish, greedy jerk for feeling this way?

She knocked on the bathroom door, waited for the go-ahead and slipped inside with her daughter.

John took off his boots, scarfed down his food and sucked back another bottle of water. By the time he was done, and his anxiety medicine was kicking in, the ladies emerged from the bathroom that was right next to the bedroom area.

Olivia wore rainbow, doughnut, sunshine pajamas that seemed a stark contrast to their situation. Zee had her arm wrapped around her daughter's shoulder and got her into bed under the covers. "John, why don't you take a hot shower and change your clothes before you go to sleep."

The idea was more than appealing. "I don't have anything to change into."

"I bought you some things. It's all in the bathroom."

One surprise after another with her.

In the bathroom on the counter, he found a cheap men's travel case. The kind you could pick up at any drugstore.

Inside there were shaving cream, a razor, deodorant, toothpaste, toothbrush, all the essentials. Zee was used to seeing him clean-shaven. As a SEAL, he'd sported a beard for years, which helped him to blend in while in countries where American servicemen might not be welcome. Once he was discharged, he figured it was time for a fresh, new look.

On top of the closed toilet seat were new clothes, neatly folded. She'd gotten something called the Mission Jean. High-tech pants that were water-resistant, provided four-way stretch and had classic jean styling. There was a pull-over sweater with thermal insulation and a performance T-shirt to wear underneath. Boxer briefs. Socks. There was also a pair of sweats. She'd thought of everything.

On the other side of the door, it was quiet enough for him to overhear them talking.

"Are you going to stop stalling and tell me now, Mom?"

"Tell you what, honey?"

"Who is that man?"

"John? He's a friend of mine."

"Like Hunter, Gage and Dean?"

A lot of names. How many men did she have in her life?

Zee gave a soft chuckle. "Those guys are family. Think of them as uncles. John is different. He's…special to me."

"Do you work with him?" Olivia asked.

"No, honey. He was in the military. John is a war hero."

"Wow, really?"

Well, he hadn't described himself as such and neglected to tell Zee about any awards or commendations he'd received. What did any of it mean in the great scheme of things?

"I think so," Zee said. "He would never admit it because he's too humble, but the one thing I know for certain is that he's my hero. Our hero. He's a good person, the best kind, and we can trust him to help us. Okay?"

"Okay, Mom. I like him. He's nice."

His heart stuttered as John smiled to himself. On a deeply personal level, it was important to him what Olivia thought of him. But he was also painfully aware that neither Zee nor her daughter would be in his life for much longer.

He turned on the faucet to shave and give them privacy. Eavesdropping wasn't something he normally did, and he wouldn't make it a new habit.

A shave and shower made him feel like a new man. The medication had a lot to do with it, as well as the hot water sluicing down his body, and getting clean. Worked wonders. He tried on all the clothes but opted to sleep in the sweats for comfort. Probably why she had bought them, thinking the same.

No woman had ever shopped for him before. Dressing in the clothes that Zee had picked out for him was intimate. Nice. He even enjoyed the scent of the bodywash she'd chosen, sandalwood. It had a woodsy warmth. This was something he could get used to, but he shoved the thought aside along with the feeling, tamping them deep down.

John switched off the bathroom light and eased the door open, trying not to make any noise in case the little girl was asleep.

Zee was singing a song about a honey bunny while massaging a pressure point on Olivia's forehead.

John crept out of the bathroom. His gaze met Zee's and he gestured that he was going to the sofa.

"I'll be over in a minute," Zee whispered.

He was surprised to see that she had pulled out the sofa for him. Then again, doing so after Olivia fell asleep might wake her. One additional lovely touch he noted, a rubber wedge-shaped stopper was under the motel door. Ten times better than a flimsy chain.

Zee did think of everything.

Sitting on the bed, he leaned against the back of the sofa and stretched out his legs. His injury didn't ache, which was a good sign. They might have a spot of peace tonight.

Once the singing stopped, the lamp beside the king-size bed was switched off, and Zee came into the sitting area.

"Is she asleep?" he asked.

"Soon, I hope," she said, keeping her voice low. She sat on the edge of the pullout next to his legs and folded her hands in her lap.

"I need the full story. Unredacted. Start with Ryker. Who is he?"

"He's the devil." She flicked a glance at Olivia and lowered her head. "I can't get into details, give you what you want, the unredacted truth. Not while she's in earshot. Always assume a tween is listening even if they look sound asleep."

"I know a safe place where we can go tomorrow. An old friend. Former SEAL." Being around him could be a potential trigger, bringing John to seven out of seven strikes, but now he had his meds. "We can talk there and sort out your next step."

Zee hesitated, and the uncertainty in her face niggled at him.

"She changes everything," he whispered, gesturing to the child across the room. "Please, let me do that much for you."

Another long moment of deliberation. "Okay," she said with a nod. "You're right." She met his gaze and all he wanted was to hold her, assure her that he'd do his best to keep them both safe. "Get some sleep."

As she stood, a horrible thought struck him and he

grabbed her hand, stopping her. "You won't take off in the middle of the night with the kid, will you? Disappear on me?" That wasn't the reason she'd given him the melatonin, was it?

She frowned and squeezed his fingers. "No, I won't."

"You give me your word? We'll talk someplace safe before you make any big, life-altering decisions."

A sad smile ghosted her lips. "Not everyone is as honorable as you. A lot of people would break their word."

"Not you. Not with me." He had to believe that at least their friendship was real and if it was, then she would keep her word.

"I wouldn't do that to you, John. I'll tell you everything before I make any big decisions." She squeezed his hand tighter. "I owe you that much. More. I give you my word."

Chapter Ten

Two was lucky he was dead. Otherwise, Ryker would've killed him. Which would have been bad for morale. Whenever he killed someone from his own team the others invariably considered going AWOL.

According to the others, John Lowry had fired the fatal shot.

Ironic.

Bet Two thought Lowry was a problem now as he burned in hell.

More men dead and another dead end. They'd learned of Zee's Zoey Howard alias. But by the time they'd connected it to the prescription filled for sertraline, they'd gotten to the pharmacy too late.

"Did you pick up anything on CCTV that might indicate where the target is?" Ryker asked, taking off his leather coat and tossing it on a chair in the room at the Rainier Inn on the Lewis-McChord joint base.

"The analyst at Langley lost them once they exited I-90. Couldn't find anything useful after that. If they're holed up in a hotel somewhere, they must be using cash or fake IDs."

Damn it. He'd been so close to getting his hands on his daughter and putting a bullet in Zee he'd tasted victory in his mouth. Now they were in the wind. With Lowry.

The former SEAL had thrown his arms around Ryker's

child and his woman. Deep down, he would always think of Zenobia as his, though he'd preferred her young, naive and easy to keep under his thumb. The image of Lowry ushering them out the doors of the academy, facilitating their escape, filled his mind. Dominated everything.

A slow-burning fury coursed in Ryker's veins. But he had to be careful. When it came to Zee, he often let his rage and lust cloud his thinking.

All he had to do was keep his head clear and use the resources at his disposal. Then he'd find her and his daughter. Lowry, too. "We need to extract all the data on her laptop and have it analyzed."

"Seven started the process," Fifteen said, "but he didn't get a chance to finish because we pinpointed the location of the girl and dropped everything to get to her first."

Little good it had done them. If only he had wounded Zee or Lowry at the very least, then it might have been worth the sacrifice of manpower.

Now Seven was dead, too. Killed by the police at the academy. His men were dropping like flies. Given enough time, they could be replaced with more hired guns from the contracted security firm, but the clock was ticking and the loss of his one techie hurt.

"This isn't my specialty, sir, but I'm doing my best." Fifteen clacked away at the keyboard.

"Unfortunately, your best isn't good enough," Ryker said, stating a fact. "Contact our Langley analyst and give them whatever information they need to patch into this laptop and take control of it. They can do the extraction remotely." An expert touch was required to handle this. "I want to know precisely what Zenobia was interested in and looking at besides my daughter. She didn't breach the CIA database for nothing. If she found anything valuable, she'd do something with the information. I need to know what, who, why and where. Then we can figure out her next step."

"How do you know she won't just lie low until she finds a new safe house?" Three asked.

That would be too easy. Instead of playing it safe, Zee preferred to play with fire. Only Ryker wanted to be the one to burn her. "Because I know her too well. She waited months to access the database. According to that dead geek at the hackerspace, she'd found something big. Important to her. Whatever it is, she won't drop it. If she uncovered a loose thread, she'll be compelled to pull it."

Chapter Eleven

A tendril of doubt snaked through Zee.

This is not a mistake. At least that was what she told herself as they drove past the welcome to Montana sign.

They'd gotten an early start, hitting the road at four in the morning after having breakfast at the IHOP down the street. As they had sat in the vinyl booth, the three of them together, eating eggs and sausage and stacks of pancakes, it had felt normal and for five minutes she'd forgotten they were on the run.

With Olivia in the backseat of the car, it was impossible for her and John to discuss the things weighing on either of their minds.

She still couldn't believe that Ryker was leading the Delta team.

He'd told her… *The CIA can't protect you forever. One day, I'll make you regret leaving me.*

She rubbed her arms at the sudden chill that had pebbled her skin.

No matter how this ended, she would never regret getting free of him or keeping Olivia away from that monster.

If he wanted her daughter, he'd have to kill Zee first. But that was the reason he was out there tracking her, wasn't it? To put a bullet in her head.

Out of all the twisted psychos the Agency could have

sent. Why had they picked him? Someone who would take pleasure in her death.

This was personal. For both of them.

Zee didn't know what to do. Which choice was wrong? Which was right?

Her daughter was the most important thing, but Zee's decisions also affected John and the rest of Team Topaz. The situation was too big, too monumental to screw it up.

Taking a day to catch her breath at John's friend's place and talking it over with John was a good call. It wasn't a mistake.

But if that was true, then why didn't she believe it? Why did she have a knot twisting in her stomach that in making this choice, there would be repercussions? Something bad was going to happen.

"Are you okay?" John asked, glancing at her.

She forced a smile. "Yeah."

His mouth twitched like he didn't believe her.

"I'm worried," she admitted and glanced back at Olivia, who was reading a book. Zee could never read in a car. It always gave her motion sickness. "Your friend doesn't know we're coming. On Christmas Eve no less." John didn't have his cell phone and didn't have his friend's number memorized. "There are people who wouldn't take kindly to unexpected visitors turning up on their doorstep, two of which are strangers, looking for a place to crash. Correction, hide out from dangerous people."

"Mike isn't *people*. He's..." John shrugged. "Mike. He won't turn us away."

"How can you be sure?" With Delta team out there, time was working against them and she couldn't begin to think about her next step until Olivia was someplace safe. She needed John's idea to pan out.

"We were swim buddies in BUD/S training. Any idea what that is?" John asked.

"I watched a miniseries about the Navy SEAL training course," she said. Looked grueling.

"You were a Navy SEAL?" Olivia looked up from the pages, setting the book down in her lap.

"Yep, kiddo. But once a SEAL, always a SEAL."

"Okay, so he was your swim buddy. So what?" Zee asked.

"In BUD/S, your swim buddy has to be within three feet of you at all times for six months. Two Is One. One Is None. I'm talking everywhere, during an evolution, the ocean, chow hall, running an errand, in the head."

"What's the head?" Olivia asked.

John cleared his throat. "The bathroom. Sorry about that."

"So you mean," Olivia said, "you two were together in the shower and even when doing private stuff?"

"We were very close in BUD/S. Leaving your swim buddy was a serious no-no. Your teammate, your team is everything. No man left behind. Ever. Dead or alive. But it took both of us about four or five months to internalize the deeper message."

Olivia leaned forward, completely engrossed at this point. "Which was?"

"SEALs are unprotected and vulnerable if we're caught alone in an operation." He cast Zee a glance and she knew this message was also for her. "By working in pairs in training it taught us that we would always be better protected and more likely to succeed in our goals." His gaze shifted back to the road. "We made it through Hell Week together. In some regards, it's the hardest part of training."

"Why?" Olivia asked. "What's so hard about it?"

"The pace is relentless. Downright brutal. Five days

and five nights solid with a maximum total of four hours of sleep while doing obstacle courses, beach runs, surf drills, night swims, log PT."

Olivia's eyes were wide with interest. "What's log PT?"

"That's when you do physical training, in boots, long pants and T-shirts, while carrying a telephone pole," he said, eliciting a *sheesh* from Olivia that Zee echoed in her head. "We had to hold it up over heads and do sprints, squats, whatever we were told."

"Sounds excruciating," Zee said. Her training with the CIA to work in the field as a member of Team Topaz had been tough but paled in comparison.

"I've been through worse." His tone was casual, light, masking painful, dark things that she longed for him to share with her when they were in private. "Anyway, we'd made it through Hell Week. We were in the third phase of training and had just finished a two-mile swim that had a seventy-five-minute cutoff. Mike had failed. By seconds."

Olivia grimaced. "Oh, no."

"Who are you telling?" John chuckled. "I had to do the darn thing over with him. Right then and there."

"Did he pass the second time?" Olivia asked before Zee could.

"Yes."

Her daughter exhaled in relief.

"But then we had the next evolution. We had to run an obstacle course."

Zee turned to John. "Without proper rest first?"

He nodded. "That was BUD/S. So, Mike was throwing a fit, feeling sorry for himself. I could see him starting to go down the spiral of self-doubt. He'd already decided in his head that he was going to be too tired to make it. So I pulled him to the side and do you know what I told him?"

"What?" Zee and Olivia asked in unison.

"I said, man, if I asked any yahoo in town to do what you just accomplished, swimming those two miles twice, do you think they would've done it? Think they would've passed at all? You passed and you're feeling sorry for yourself because you're completely wiped? This is the wrong place for sympathy. Because I was right there with you. I'm going to run that obstacle course at your side. Don't wallow, man. Relish it. Relish the fact that you rose to the occasion doing something that ninety-five percent of the global population would run from, much less try. Relish the fact that you won a battle that most people lose—the battle with themselves. I told him, man, we got this. And he passed."

"Because you helped him," Olivia said with a bright smile. "Was that the moment when you understood the point of having a swim buddy?"

"It sure was. We both did. By the end of BUD/S we could finish each other's sentences and almost shared a brain." He chuckled. "We each know that we can count on the other when we need them most. That's how I'm sure he'll help us."

John knew how to deliver a speech and tell a story. She'd give him that. He truly was compelling, even to Olivia. "Fine. I'm convinced Mike will help us, but is he married?"

He frowned. "Yeah. He's on his third wife. Enola Littlewolf."

Zee folded her arms. "How do you know that she'll let us in?"

"All right, you've got me there. But Mike is persuasive and she's awesome. I met her at their wedding right before I moved to Alaska."

If Mike was anything like John, Enola was probably wrapped around his finger.

Zee's heart fluttered at the thought of being in a relationship with John, and how there would be nothing that she wouldn't do for him. Squeezing her thighs together, she pushed the thought aside.

Thanks to light traffic they pulled up sooner than she expected in front of the two-story house that sat on a large plot of land and offered sweeping views of rolling hills, evergreens and mountains.

The house was decked out for the holidays with a ton of string lights, wreaths hung on every window; several lanterns were around the door and an animated Santa sleigh and reindeer sat in the front yard.

"Wait here." John hopped out of the car, climbed up the front porch and knocked.

He looked great in the new clothes she'd bought him. Stylish. They flattered his body, those long legs and all that sexy muscle.

Zee cracked the window, figuring with luck that she might be able to overhear the conversation.

"What are we going to do if they don't let us stay?" Olivia asked.

Zee had no clue. She'd probably have to abandon the idea of following up on her lead and investigating further into what went wrong on her team's mission. Doing it with her daughter in tow wasn't a possibility.

"We'll figure it out, honey. I don't want you to worry about it."

The front door opened. A guy just as big as John stepped out. Six-three. A solid two hundred pounds. A tighter, cleaner haircut. Black curly hair.

The two men hugged, and it was evident that Mike was thrilled to see him, but Zee couldn't hear a word exchanged.

When Mike gestured for him to enter, John hiked his thumb back at the car. His friend glanced over and nodded at John's explanation. The smile fell from Mike's face as he shut the front door and stepped out onto the porch.

She had to trust John's judgment. Surely he would let his friend know about the possibility of danger following them, but hopefully, he'd limit the details and neglect to mention the CIA at all.

"Hooyah!" Mike said, slapping John on the back.

John turned to the car, flashing a grin that made her belly tighten, and waved them over.

"See, Mom. John was right."

He'd already managed to turn her daughter into his cheerleader in less than twenty-four hours. *Impressive.*

But Zee noticed that Mike hadn't gone into the house and cleared it with his new wife. She swallowed the comment, not wanting to tempt fate.

She rolled up the window, shut off the engine and they grabbed their bags.

On the porch, John took the duffel from her. "Mike Cutler, this is Zee and her daughter, Olivia."

Smiling, she was pleased that John hadn't offered her surname. A good indication he'd only shared the necessary details with his friend.

"Pleasure to meet you." Mike gave her a double handshake with his left cupping the back of her right. "Olivia, I'd say you were about my daughter's age. Let me guess, eleven?"

Olivia grinned. "I'll be eleven tomorrow."

"Oh," Mike said, beaming. "A Christmas birthday. That's pretty special."

"We call it Olivmas," her daughter said.

Mike touched his nose. "That's clever. I love it. Come in." He opened the door wide.

As they walked into the house, the smell of eucalyptus and sugar cookies hit them. It was warm and comfy and loud. Kids ranging in age from eleven to, she guessed, twenty were running around all over the place.

A soaring Christmas tree that hit the ten-foot ceiling engulfed a corner. Wrapped gifts with red bows were piled underneath it.

Mike closed the door. "We're a blended family. Enola's got three boys from her previous marriage. I've got two boys from my first. Another boy and girl from my second. Amanda is the youngest. She'll be happy to have another girl around, Olivia. I can assure you of that. The kids are with our exes on Thanksgiving and we both have them together for Christmas. So, it's a crazy full house. But you're more than welcome to stay. After lunch, we're heading into town for the winter carnival. We do it every Christmas Eve. It's a ton of fun."

Two boys on the sofa playing video games started roughhousing and overturned the coffee table.

"Knock it off!" Mike said. "And clean up that mess."

"Yes, sir," the two said in unison.

"Amanda!" Mike called out.

A girl with curly dark hair who favored Mike came to the top of the stairs. "What?"

"Don't *what* me," Mike said.

Amanda frowned. "Yes, sir, what can I do for you, oh mighty one?"

"That's better." Mike put a hand to Olivia's back and pushed her forward. "This is Olivia. This is her mom, Mrs...." He glanced between her and John. "Is it Lowry? You've been best man at all three of my weddings—if you got hitched without me there, man—"

"Just call me Zee. Let's keep it casual."

"And say hi to your uncle John," Mike said.

Amanda waved. "Hey, Uncle John. Hi, Zee."

"Make Olivia feel welcomed. She's sharing your room

since there's no place else. John and Zee will bunk in the attic."

John stiffened, making her wonder what the attic was like. A dusty space with no drywall and exposed insulation?

Safe shelter was all that mattered to her, and if Olivia had a bed to share, then Zee would be fine on the floor.

"Cool," Amanda said. "Come on up, Olivia. We'll hang in my room until lunch."

Olivia looked back at Zee for the okay.

"Go have fun."

Olivia took off up the stairs, hauling her backpack.

"Where's Enola?" John asked, glancing around.

"In the kitchen." Mike flashed a tight smile. "Let me show you the attic first." He hurried to the stairs. "Get you settled in. Don't worry, Zee, it's cozy up there."

They climbed two flights of stairs, passed a small hallway bathroom, and he opened the door, letting Zee and John in first.

A window on the far wall let in natural light. In front of it was a full-size bed with a nightstand to the side. Was the bed even a full? It looked more like an oversize twin, large enough for a teenage boy to fit comfortably. Alone.

A surge of alarm rippled through her.

"You two will have your privacy away from everyone," Mike said, easily. "You stayed up here during the wedding, didn't you, John?"

"About us sharing," John said, his cheeks turning redder than strawberries, "this one room—"

Zee put a hand on his forearm. "It'll be just fine." If they handled a sleeping bag, surely this would be nothing, but even at the slight touch on his arm sexual awareness simmered between them, and she stepped away, dropping her hand. It would be easier, if John wasn't quite so hot, say hideous as a troll, or stupid. Stupid wasn't attractive. Neither was mean, and he wasn't that either. In fact, he was ridiculously good-looking, wise, funny, brave, patient, resourceful—everything she'd ever wanted in a man. *Damn near perfect.* "Thank you so much for letting us stay. Considering the circumstances."

"Think nothing of it," Mike said. "John's my brother in every sense but blood. Whatever you two need is yours. I'm happy to help."

"I'd love to meet Enola," she said.

"Plenty of time for that. Get cleaned up. Catch your breath. Give me a chance to grease the wheels with her. Then come down to the kitchen. Be sure not to mention the words *fugitive* or *dangerous*. When it comes to discussing specifics, less is more, but I'll do my best to prevent the question mill from running wild."

The shooting at the school would make the news and be splashed across social media, but names wouldn't be given, and pictures of students wouldn't be shown. The CIA would do what they could to clean up the stories and filter information.

"Lunch is going to be soon. I can't wait to get the kids out of the house and to the carnival, so they can burn off some energy." Mike gave them an exasperated look, then he was out of the room and shutting the door.

John set the duffel bag down. "I can sleep on one of the sofas downstairs. I'm sure no one will mind. You don't have to be cooped up in here with me."

"If we can share a sleeping bag without clothes, I think we can handle a bed with us both fully dressed." They were two mature adults capable of controlling themselves.

Turning, she looked away from the bed to John and her confidence faltered.

A flash of disappointment, maybe even hurt, crossed

his face when he closed his eyes, as if to block her words. It only lasted a heartbeat.

Then John stepped closer, right up to her, and she wrestled the reflex to back away. Looming over her, he stilled, his face turning deadpan, making him suddenly appear as placid as she struggled to feel. On an inhale, she took in a lungful of sandalwood spice and the luscious base note that was pure John.

The scintillating proximity to him had her heart and body warring with her mind. Never had she felt such a powerful craving for anyone or anything in her life. She didn't want to desire someone the way she wanted him.

Maybe when it came to falling for someone, choice wasn't a factor.

Cupping her jaw, he tilted her head back. His gaze searched hers before landing on her mouth. Every cell filled with the impulse to touch him, to kiss him. The way she was drawn to this man felt like fate and resisting it went against the laws of nature.

He slid a finger behind her earlobe, and her answering bone-deep shiver sent tingles to her thighs.

"Whatever you want, *buddy*," he said.

The little word dissolved, leaving behind a bitter sting.

It was so silly. Buddy, friend, none of it should faze her since she was the one who had erected this platonic wall between them.

Part of her wondered what the point was of pretending any longer. No matter how much she pushed him away, tried to protect him, he kept inserting himself between her and danger, rushing to her side to help her without asking for anything in return. He was the most selfless, big-hearted man she knew.

A lump of frustration formed in her throat as she looked up at him.

Dropping his hand, he went to the door. "I'm going for a walk." His voice was gravelly with heat, so rough it scored her like sandpaper. "I need to stretch my legs. Get some air." And he was gone.

She considered running after him, stopping him, but there was so much he didn't know about her. Things in her past that could change how he felt, how he looked at her.

It was complicated and messy. At the heart of it was Ryker. Thinking about what she'd gone through with him filled her with such shame. The fact that she had fallen for Ryker in the beginning…what did that say about her judgment?

But she wouldn't let her embarrassment over her past mistakes stop her from telling John the truth. She owed him nothing less.

Maybe he would understand. She loved the way he saw the world. How he appreciated complexity, and even in ugly things he could find beauty.

After composing herself, she checked her appearance in the bathroom mirror. The shower in the hall bath was small and the sloping ceiling was so low John would probably have to hunch over inside. She finger-combed her curls into submission and dabbed on lip gloss.

On the way to the kitchen, she smiled at the kids she passed, and they acknowledged her with a head nod or wave.

The two oldest ones were clearly Mike's. Tall and strapping with curly dark hair. He must have been around their age, maybe a little older when he had them.

At the threshold of the kitchen, she spotted Mike. He was standing behind a dark-haired woman who was in front of the stove. His arms were wrapped around her waist. He whispered in her ear and kissed her neck.

The woman giggled. "Stop it, Mike. I already said it's fine."

A persuasive sweet talker who could bend his woman to his will.

As Mike kissed her again, pressing his pelvis to her behind, Zee considering backing away to give them privacy, but Mike glanced over his shoulder, spotting her.

He waved her in with a wide grin, stepped to the side, and looked at his wife. "Hey, babe, this is Zee."

Enola spun around from the stove and wiped her hands on dish towel. "Hi, I'm Enola. It's so nice to meet you."

Zee extended her hand, but Enola gave her a big hug instead. It was warm and genuine and much appreciated.

Enola was a pretty woman with voluptuous curves and a smile like sunshine that immediately put Zee at ease. Her hair was straight and black, falling to her waist in a glossy sheet.

"What can I do to help?" Zee looked around the kitchen at the feast that was being prepared.

"Oh, nothing." Enola waved a dismissive hand. "I've got it under control."

Never one to shy away from pitching in when there was work to be done, Zee went to the sink and washed her hands. "Tell me what to do. I insist. Carve the turkey? Mash those boiled potatoes? Slice the ham?"

Enola grinned, the gratefulness in her eyes unmistakable while Mike leaned against the counter drinking a bottle of beer with a hand on his hip.

"All of the above," Enola said. "Please." She opened the oven and took out macaroni and cheese and put green beans in a serving dish.

Mike tipped the bottle back, taking another swig of beer. "Oh, John said not to wait for him to eat lunch. After that car ride, he needs a long walk to stretch out the kinks."

A sharp pang twisted through her chest. He needed a long walk away from her.

"I will leave you lovely ladies to it." Mike disappeared into the next room and yelled at the boys.

"Men," Enola muttered under her breath. "Useless in the kitchen, right?"

Perhaps Mike was, but John was a great cook. He enjoyed whipping up meals, elevating tasty improvisation into an art form. Which probably explained why he wasn't much for baking. That was more of a science.

"Well, I'm happy to help," Zee said, deciding it was better not to comment. She picked up the carving knife that was next to the turkey and got to work.

Enola started frosting a cake. "I heard we have a birthday tomorrow."

"Olivia is turning eleven."

"Does she like yellow cake with chocolate frosting?"

"Loves it." Olivia had never been a picky eater, but she wasn't partial to lemon-flavored sweets.

"Always a winner, am I right? Unless some kid has a food allergy. They're all allergic to something these days. Nuts. Gluten. Dairy. Fresh air." She sighed. "I was thinking we could save this cake for tomorrow since I've got cookies and pies. I could add some sprinkles to the top of the cake and put her name on it. We've got candles tucked away in a drawer somewhere."

Tears stung Zee's eyes at Enola's kindness. "That's really sweet of you."

Emotions welled in her chest. Remorse over the deadly situation she'd dragged Olivia and John into. Fear that Ryker would get his hands on her daughter. Guilt for robbing her little girl of normalcy and stability, forcing her to grow up far too fast. Regret over hurting John by pushing him away when all she wanted was to pull him closer. To love him.

And it hit her like a lightning bolt.

I love John.

The timing was all wrong. Disastrous.

Doubts, concerns, worries—stacked up in a long list of reasons why they shouldn't be together.

Professionally, she took risks all the time and convinced others to step into that dark void of the unknown with her, all while suppressing what she needed on a personal level. But she was so tired of denying that she needed John. That she cared for him. Loved him. As much more than a friend.

A tear leaked from her eye and she sniffled.

Enola came to her side, handing her a tissue. "It's just a cake. No trouble at all. It was already baked, and I was going to ice it anyway."

"But it'll mean the world to Olivia." A stranger thought of a birthday cake for her daughter while Zee was plotting how to get evidence that might prove the innocence of her team. What kind of life was she giving Olivia? "And I appreciate it. Thank you." She dabbed at her eyes. "I feel like such a bad mother." The absolute worst. She hadn't even thought of buying cupcakes from a gas station convenience store.

Enola glanced around like she had a secret to share before opening a cabinet above the wall oven. She pushed some stuff around, pulled out a bottle of Lillet Rose, and poured a couple of ounces of the aperitif into two glasses over rocks, topped it with seltzer.

"It's five o'clock somewhere." She handed Zee a glass. "The only mother who has never felt like a failure or that she wasn't getting it quite right at some point was Mother Teresa." They both laughed. "If any woman ever tells you different, she's a liar. Take comfort in that." She rubbed Zee's back and clinked their glasses together. "Cheers."

Zee sipped the bittersweet drink that tasted of berries and orange blossoms. Enola's pep talk relieved a bit of the pressure that had been simmering inside her chest.

"Are you guys going to join us for the winter carnival?" Enola added milk and butter to the potatoes.

"John and I have some important things to discuss."

"No need to say another word. How about after lunch, we take Olivia with us. Mike always makes the kids buddy up whenever we go somewhere. Even at the mall. Two Is One, One Is None," Enola said, imitating him, and Zee smiled, understanding the significance. "I'm sure she and Amanda will be glued at the hip, but I'll keep a close eye on her so you won't need to worry. It's a lot of fun. I guarantee she'll enjoy herself."

Mike and Enola were a godsend. A holiday activity with kids around her own age was exactly what Olivia needed. A healthy distraction, a slice of normal.

Zee could use a bit of that herself. "That'd be great and I'll take care of cleaning up the dishes."

"You don't have to do that. You're our guest."

"I insist. That way you guys can get going sooner, which I think Mike would prefer."

"We both would." Enola took another sip of her drink.

Coming here had been a good decision. Not a mistake. Once again, John was right.

Chapter Twelve

The long walk across the property had done John good, allowed him the distance to get his head straight. Zee had him spinning in circles, on the verge of his control snapping and being completely destroyed. He despised the sensation.

On his way back, he'd caught sight of Mike's GMC Yukon XL heading out down the road. The vehicle looked packed to the brim. He wondered if Zee had been in the car, or if she was waiting for him back at the house to talk through her situation. Come up with a way forward.

She was all about business and maintaining the lines in the sand. Of course, she'd be at the house. Looking lovelier and more tempting than ever. Ready to discuss a plan.

But he was going to be hands-off with her this time. Just touching Zee's jaw earlier in the attic had been too much. He had silently commanded his heart to keep beating, his lungs to continue pumping air. Knowing what her naked body felt like against his, those spectacular curves—warm, silky skin and toned limbs, yet, with a woman's softness—was miles beyond anything his self-control could deal with again sleeping in a bed next to her. Clothes or no clothes.

Entering the house, he removed his coat.

"I'm in the kitchen," Zee called out when he let the door slam shut.

He walked through the living room and down the hall.

Zee was cleaning the kitchen, loading the dishwasher and wiping down counters with all the precision and focus she applied to everything else.

He drank in the sight of her with such extreme pleasure that his blood pressure shot so high he could actually hear it rushing in his ears.

"Hi." She glanced back at him over her shoulder. Heartbreakingly beautiful. Then she flashed one of those tentative smiles, sweet vulnerability in her eyes, and it hit him in the solar plexus, knocking the air from his lungs. "I made a plate for you and put it in the microwave. Are you hungry?" Her slightly husky voice, the softness of it, stroked over him, making his gut clench.

"Starved." He went to the microwave and grabbed the food. "Thanks."

Sitting down at the table with his back to her, he dug into the meal. She'd prepared his plate exactly as he would've done for himself. A mix of white- and dark-meat turkey, one slice of ham, mashed potatoes sans gravy, a little mac and cheese and lots of veggies. No sweet potatoes smothered in marshmallows.

It pleased and pained him that she knew him so well.

"Everyone left a little while ago," she said. "They all piled into the SUV and somehow seemed to fit. Olivia made fast friends with Amanda."

"Of course, she did. She's like you."

Behind him, he heard her movements stop. Felt her gaze on the back of his neck.

"I'll take that as a compliment," she said in a low, unsure voice.

"You should. It was meant as one." He stuffed his mouth full of more food, happy to have a home-cooked meal after the past two days. "I gave it some thought and it's best if

I use the sleeping bag. I can put it out on the floor at the foot of the bed." There was just enough room to make it work. "Gives you some space in the bed and keeps me from being in anyone's way downstairs."

The best thing was to keep his distance from her. Sharing a bed would only complicate matters, especially when he needed to stay on his toes to make sure she didn't get any deeper under his skin.

"John… I thought…it wouldn't be a problem for us to share the bed. Do you really think this is necessary?"

He'd finally found a woman he wanted to give himself to, entirely, and he had the misfortune of her not wanting him in return. She was a constant source of temptation for him and he was at his breaking point of resistance.

"Yes. It's necessary." For the sake of his sanity if nothing else. He finished his food and took the plate to the sink.

"Fine," she said with a sharp note of determination that made him sigh. "But I'll take the sleeping bag. You can have the bed."

What was this new game she wanted to play?

She sucked in a deep breath, standing there like she was waiting for a response from him.

But everything he wanted to say, everything he needed to tell her, got stuck in his throat. He didn't want to argue, try to convince her, he simply wanted her. Even though it struck him as wrong to desire more than friendship, and the truth was, they were friends. Best friends.

Why couldn't that be enough for him?

Zee marched out of the kitchen and he heard her footsteps ascending the stairs.

He put the plate in the dishwasher, thinking everything over, questions burning through his head that begged for answers.

Friendship wasn't enough because from the moment

they'd first met there had been an instant flare of attraction. At least on his part. But all those hours they'd spent in his house, all the lunches, dinners, lingering looks, stolen touches, long conversations late into the night enticed him to believe she might be interested, too.

Still, he'd put his desires and expectations in check until she had kissed him in that cabin.

The kiss had not only filled his head with possibilities that burned straight through him, tightening in his groin, but also the way she'd kissed him had been flirty, fiery. Filthy.

Not the least bit friendly.

The genie was out of the bottle and there was no way to put it back in.

Leaving the kitchen, he strode through the house and took the stairs two at a time up to the attic.

She was on her knees rolling out the sleeping bag at the foot of the bed. "If you think this is best, then this is the way it's going to work. It's my sleeping bag and your friend's house after all."

He stepped inside the room and closed the door. "Let's forget about what's *best* for a minute, or what's right or wrong, and discuss what's real."

Her gaze flew up to his as she sat back on her heels. "What do you mean?"

"You know everything of importance about me while you've still got all these secrets. Are you going to be honest with me? Answer everything that I ask truthfully?"

"Yes." Nodding, she climbed to her feet. "I promised that I would. Whatever you want to know, ask me."

"The kiss." Actually, kisses. The cabin and the airport. "Did it mean more to you or was it really only a gesture of friendship?"

Looking him in the eye, she backed away, putting distance between them, and his heart sank. He'd committed to helping her and he'd follow through, but it hurt to think that things were only platonic for her. He understood of course. Would respect her feelings.

The wall stopped her retreat. "After everything that's transpired, your need for the unredacted truth, and that's your first question?"

"Yep." He folded his arms.

She looked downright flustered. "Why that one above all the others?"

Because it would frame every other answer that came from her mouth. "Humor me, please. I need to know the truth."

Rolling her shoulders as if bracing herself, she met his gaze. "It was more. Much more for me."

Her response only sparked other questions for him.

Not understanding, he sought to close the gap between them and strode toward her.

But she sidestepped his touch.

"Are you afraid of me?" he asked. "Afraid of how I'll react about something?"

"No, I'm not afraid of you. But how can I even think about being close to you, the way I want," she said in a voice that shook slightly, "when there are so many things that you need to know about me." With a grimace, she lowered her head. "I need to put all my cards on the table before you come any closer. Because once I do. You might want to walk out that door."

There was nothing that she could say that would make him turn his back on her. Nothing. Didn't she realize that by now?

"Put them on the table. I'm listening."

She chewed her bottom lip and he saw fear in her eyes.

"You can tell me anything," he said. "No matter how

bad. No matter how ugly." His gut twisted hard when she started to tremble.

"You asked me a question in the motel," she said, "that I couldn't answer at the time with Olivia nearby."

He thought for moment. So much had happened. "About Ryker? Who is he?"

She squeezed her eyes shut. "The biggest mistake of my life, who gave me the greatest gift."

John shook his head. "I don't understand."

Looking at him, Zee took another deep breath, letting it out slowly through her mouth. "I told you about my childhood."

"Breezy Point." Insulated. Right wing. How she felt like she didn't quite fit in. "Yeah."

"I rebelled. A lot. I was a constant headache for my dad and source of concern for my mom. In high school, I fell in love with computers and coding. When I went to MIT," she said, referring to the Massachusetts Institute of Technology, "my dad was so relieved, he thought he didn't have to worry about me anymore, that I was on track. Focused. The summer before I was set to complete my degree, I received an encrypted invitation from a hacktivist group in Germany, to come and check them out. I did and got caught up in their cause. They did good things, Robin Hood style, and some not so good things." She ran her fingers back through her hair. "Then I met Ryker. Ryker Rudin."

"In Germany?" he asked.

"Yes." She blew out a heavy breath. "At the time, I didn't know he was CIA and working me to be an asset. He came across as the ultimate bad boy, someone my father would loathe. Fit right in with my rebel-with-a-cause profile. He was charismatic, charming, flattering, and seduced me. Rather easily, thinking back on it. They'd profiled me and told him who he needed to be, how to act, to get close to me. He used me to take the group down and then threatened to have me arrested unless I went to work for the CIA," she said, covering part of her face with one hand, like she was ashamed.

"A common tactic the CIA and FBI use to recruit specialized talent. Not the seduction part, but the rest."

"That wasn't all. Ryker added a caveat to the deal that I had to remain his girlfriend. He claimed it was so the Agency could keep an eye on me at all times and that it was the only way he would endorse me for a position with the CIA instead of having me arrested."

A flash of white-hot anger spiked through him. "He couldn't do that. No one would give him the power, the authority to coerce you like that."

"I know that now. But at the time, I was only nineteen, hadn't the first clue about the CIA's inner workings. I was terrified to go to prison, and the thought of my father never speaking to me again was…" Her voice trailed off as she shook her head.

"How much older was he when this happened?"

"Fifteen years."

It sickened John. To think of a thirty-year-old with someone forty-five didn't seem like a big deal. But at nineteen, she had been too young. Too innocent. Still a teenager.

"Like a naive idiot, I agreed," she said. "I accepted his deal."

He edged closer and this time she didn't move away. "How long were you with him?"

"Two years. Three months. Nine days. At first, our relationship in Virginia had been the way it'd been in Germany and I thought it might be okay. I wanted to believe his words instead of trusting my feelings that there was something wrong with him. But then, slowly, the real Ryker came out. More and more the charming facade fell, and I saw him for the monster that he is. A sociopath, incapable of love." A shudder ripped through her. "It was a nightmare. I honestly thought if I had tried to leave him, he would've killed me and made it look like an accident. He was very good at that. Killing and making it look like a mishap." She hugged herself and rubbed her arms. "*Everything* was on his terms, his way. Even sex. He manipulated me from the very beginning and every day that I was with him." Tears welled in her eyes. "Getting pregnant with Olivia was the biggest deception of all."

Every muscle in John's body locked down as he connected the dots.

Trench Coat—the maniac at the school—was Olivia's father?

Chapter Thirteen

Shock rocked through John, but he didn't let it show as he took another step closer to Zee. "How did Ryker deceive you?"

"I found out that he had been poking holes in the condoms and switched my birth control pills for sugar pills."

"What?" He reeled back horrified, unable to hide his emotions. "What kind of man would do that?" His voice had risen two octaves.

"The despicable, selfish, manipulative kind. Like Ryker Rudin." She wrung her hands and shook her head. "When I was five months pregnant, he proposed. After I refused him, said no, he admitted the truth about the condoms and my pills. Told me that now we would be linked together forever. No matter what. He actually thought, in his twisted head, that once the baby was born, I would forgive him." A tear leaked from the corner of her eye. "I love Olivia and she's the best blessing I could ask for, but what he did to me was…"

He brought her into his arms and held her. "Reprehensible. Unforgivable."

She nodded against his chest. "Hunter Wright, he's my team leader, former anyway. The CIA wanted him to put together a unit to focus on taking out sensitive high-value targets."

"An elimination team, like Delta?" He turned, sitting them both down on the bed.

"Not quite. There are two kinds of teams that work for the Agency. Those like mine are given specialized missions. Agency-acknowledged targets. We limit collateral damage and ensure the assignment never gets traced back to them. When we succeed, we're celebrated in the halls at Langley. Given monetary bonuses for a job well done and a lot of leeway when we're at home. Teams like Delta, they clean up problems. They live and work in the shadows. Operate on American soil as well as abroad. They're expendable. Sometimes they do heinous things to get the job done. Nobody wants to see them or hear about them. The Agency just wants the problem to be gone."

He caressed her face and wiped her tears with his thumbs. "So, Hunter agreed to put together a unit and picked you."

"Exactly. The team was code-named Topaz. He handpicked every member. He saw I was talented and thought that with the right training I would be exceptional in the field. I had turned him down several times before, but when I had learned what Ryker had done, I went to Hunter. Swallowed my shame and spilled my guts, told him everything and agreed to be on his team, if he could get me away from Ryker and protect my child." She curled her arms around her stomach.

John wrapped an arm around her and pulled her close. She felt good pressed up next to him. She smelled good, too, always, but he hated seeing her upset. "How did Hunter respond?"

"Hunter was furious. He found Ryker, and they got into a fight, right in the middle of the cafeteria. Came to blows and drew blood. Afterward, Hunter took me to the director of operations. Spelled out what needed to happen. The director had always hated Ryker, thought he was scum, and agreed. Ryker was sent to work in the shadows, far from Langley where I'd never have to see him, leading cleanup teams. They made it clear to him that if he came near me, my child, or if I so much as got a paper cut that wasn't mission-related, they were going to take care of him."

Reining in his fury over Ryker, John put a supportive hand to her back, processing everything she'd told him. "Until things went sideways for your team."

She propped her elbow on her thigh and pressed her palm to her forehead. "We're good people. We were following orders. I don't know what went wrong."

"Tell me about the mission."

She pinched her lips in a grim line.

"They've seen my face," he said. "There was CCTV all over the school. I'm sure they know my name by now. I'm already in this. Neck-deep."

Pain and tears lingered in her eyes. "I'm so sorry. I never meant to involve you in any of this."

"Don't be sorry. I'm not." He wanted to kiss her, to confess how deeply he felt for her. "Tell me about the mission."

"Do you know who Khayr Faraj is?"

The name had his hardwired instincts snapping to high alert. "Definitely. He's an extremist, a terrorist, with a great deal of power. His number of followers grows each day. He recruits American citizens to carry out attacks in the United States. Pretty soon he'll be a bigger threat than Abu Bakr al-Baghdadi and Osama bin Laden combined. SEALs tried to take him out a couple of times. Hard to do when there are no pictures of him. Only a description. A distinctive birthmark on his cheek, if I recall correctly."

"We were ordered to eliminate Faraj in the mountains of Afghanistan, at a meeting he was supposed to have with his financial backer. A corrupt Afghan official who was secretly funding him."

"Sounds like an op I would've loved to sink my teeth into. I know a bunch of warfare operators who'd say the same."

"We were eager to take him out, too," she said. "Normally, we assess the situation and decide how to best achieve the objective. The strange part about this mission was that we were instructed to use explosives and take out everyone at the meeting. We thought we had been successful. A man with a birthmark on his cheek matching the description we had been given was there, but it turns out that it wasn't Faraj."

"Then who did you kill?"

"A tribal leader who was meeting with the corrupt Afghan official. Neither was a sanctioned target on his own. The official would have been acceptable collateral damage since the meeting with Faraj and exchange of money would've proven his guilt. Without that proof it spelled big trouble with an ally."

Errors of that magnitude weren't common. "How did the mistake happen?"

"I wish I knew. We were in the dark. Still are."

"What did your handler say?" Teams like hers always had a CIA point person.

"We never got a chance to ask. Barely made it out of Afghanistan. Our planned extraction was compromised. A cleanup team ambushed us. They had been waiting. We weren't sure if they were CIA or if someone else had sent them. But Hunter was prepared, as always, and had a contingency ready."

A leader was supposed to take care of his people. The more John heard about Hunter Wright, the more he liked the man.

"We made it back stateside by hiding out for weeks in a shipping container on a freighter. Tight quarters for the four of us, but we made do, toughed it out. Hunter tried to meet up with our CIA handler, but everything went to hell in a handbasket. Instead of Kelly Russell turning up at the meet the way she was supposed to, another cleanup team of mercenaries did. It was a shoot first never ask questions type of debacle. They had no interest in apprehending us and taking us in alive. That's when we knew without a doubt that the CIA wanted to eliminate us. We had to split up and go our separate ways. Stay under the radar."

"How are you all going to clear your names, scattered and on the run?"

She shook her head. "I'm not sure. But I found something a couple of days ago, hacking into the CIA's database."

"Is that how they found you? Because you went nosing around where you shouldn't have?"

"Guilty as charged," she said with a nod. "We were set up, and I can't let this go. Finding the truth is the only way I can have a life with Olivia. She doesn't deserve this."

He took her hand in his. "Neither do you." Falsely accused and on the run with her life in shambles. There was also the complication of her ex, Olivia's father, spearheading the team after Zee.

"I found a lead." There was hesitancy in her eyes.

"But?"

She got up, crossed the room and unzipped her bag, pulling out the sat phone. "I can reach Hunter on this. A one-time, dire-straits call. When he picks up he'll say *parachute*. I have to respond with *rip cord*."

"A security challenge-response authentication?"

"Yes, then I'll receive coordinates and instructions that

will eventually get me to him. I have a choice. Leave now. Or follow the lead first. Find out what I can."

John wanted Zee and Olivia to be safe. No matter what. But ultimately, the only way for them to remain safe was for her team to clear their names. "What's the lead?"

"I discovered that right after we were set up, the Agency fired David Bertrand."

"Why is that important?" he wondered.

"Bertrand worked in a support capacity on our last operation. I think he knew something."

"Do you know where he is?"

"He disappeared. I haven't been able to find a trace of him anywhere, but I don't think he's dead. I think he's hiding. He had a fiancée. I was able to locate her. Luisa Morales. From footage I saw of her on CCTV, she looked happy. Not like she was grieving."

"You think they're together?"

"They were so in love. If they're not together, she's the best shot at finding him."

"Where is she?"

"Idaho Falls."

"That's less than a three-hour drive." Felt like providence to him. "We'll go today."

"There's something else. I need to access the internet, but away from here. I left something behind in the CIA's database. A zero-day virus."

"What's that?"

"A Trojan horse program I designed to exploit a software security flaw. It's called zero-day because the CIA has zero chance of plugging the hole. The malware will gather everything related to Team Topaz and anything Bertrand had worked on. I'm positive there's something there. But once I go back into the system to get it—"

"They'll find you."

She nodded.

He rubbed a hand across his jaw. It was a big risk, but it might reap an even bigger reward if it provided information that her team could use to clear their names.

"Olivia will be safe here," he said. "You can access the internet in Idaho Falls. I think we have to take the chance."

But there was still something else he needed to know.

Chapter Fourteen

"Put the analyst on speaker," Ryker said for efficiency. Everyone in the room would be clued in and on the same page.

Only three of his men were present. The rest were taking downtime: sleeping, eating, whatever tickled their fancy so long as it was being done in one of the rooms at the Rainier Inn.

"Delta India here," a female voice said over the encrypted secure line. India was the designation given to the intelligence analyst tasked with field support from Langley. "Ninety percent of the files the target accessed in the home database were in the Topaz folder. But I can't say for certain what she was looking for. Nothing was downloaded."

"Talk to me about the other ten percent," Ryker said.

"She tried to backtrack through the last files that David Bertrand accessed."

"What do you mean tried?"

"She must have realized that she was in danger of getting caught if she stayed online much longer. She started the process but didn't have time to complete it."

Every detail India gave him he lined up in his head like dominoes, waiting for the right piece to start the chain reaction and knock them all down. "Who is Bertrand?"

"A former analyst. He provided support to her team several times, including their last mission."

The plot thickens. "Where is he?"

"We have no idea. He was fired shortly after Team Topaz was disavowed and a kill order on them was authorized," she said. "He's gone underground. There's no trace of him. Something else you should know. As of 2100 last night, a kill order was issued on Bertrand."

The man had been fired and no one cared diddly-squat about him until Zenobia started sniffing around, digging into him. Now there's a kill order out on him. *Curious.*

Zee would love to know that. It meant whatever thread she found was the right one. Too bad for her, Ryker had no interest in helping her, only killing her and retrieving his daughter.

"What did you find in the dive on her laptop? Was she trying to locate Bertrand?" Ryker asked.

"There wasn't a single query on Bertrand on the computer, but that doesn't mean she didn't try to find him. It looks as if she performed routine scrubs on the hard drive, erasing it every few days. A painstaking precaution. Probably conducted within hours of accessing the internet in the event her place was raided and her laptop seized. She may have tried searching for Bertrand before. There's no way of knowing. But you got lucky that she didn't wipe the hard drive clean the last time."

Luck came in two varieties. The good kind and the bad. At the moment, Ryker wasn't feeling fortunate. The pictures on her laptop had led him to his daughter, only to lose Olivia and confirm that Lowry was still helping Zee.

"Tell me something fortuitous," Ryker demanded. "Or at the very least, useful."

"The target probably hit a dead end trying to locate

Bertrand. I did find other queries. She was doing a deep dive into Luisa Morales."

The name didn't ring a bell from the case file he'd been given. "Who is that?"

"Bertrand's fiancée."

This was the piece he'd been waiting for. "Do you have a location for Morales?"

"Idaho Falls. She relocated there after Bertrand was fired."

"Find out exactly where in the city. As much info on her as you can. Contact me when you have it. We'll be en route. You have until we touch down to give me what I need."

"Yes, sir," she said, and he heard typing. "From your current location, your flight time will be approximately four hours."

"Then you have four hours. Don't disappoint me. Also, tell the Agency that I'll handle the kill order on Bertrand." He disconnected after India acknowledged, and turned to his men. "Get the others ready. We leave in twenty minutes."

Chapter Fifteen

There had been so many instances when John had been alone in his house in Alaska, had relaxed his mind, let it wander, and his thoughts had rolled in free-floating directions that invariably, sooner or later, turned to Zee.

Consistent happenstance alone should have made him realize the depths of his feelings for her, but he'd always dismissed it. Had made excuses not to dwell, not to feed it energy. Each time they had gotten together for chess or a meal he'd been a bit dazed, stupefied to inaction.

Sitting beside her in Mike's attic was no different than those other times.

She put a hand on his leg and looked up at him. "You've been incredible. Thank you for helping me get to Olivia before Delta team did. I couldn't have done any of this without you."

All his thoughts and feelings spun and coalesced. Looking at her, he felt connected not only to his past but also to his future, as if he were standing at a crossroads in his life and seeing all the possibilities of his actions played out for him, here and now.

He had to make a tremendous decision. One he knew would determine which road he went down. "I've got to ask because I need to know—why did you kick me out back at the cabin, say those awful things to me?"

"I'm sorry." Her eyes teared up again. "I didn't want to hurt you, but I didn't want you getting hurt either. I'm toxic, radioactive, and I don't want you to die because you're standing too close to me."

He cupped her cheek, and she pressed her face against his palm. "I understand the trouble you're in and I'm choosing to stand with you. All you have to do is let me."

"But the thought of anything happening to you," she said, shaking her head as tears fell. "It just guts me. Then there's Olivia. Sometimes I think that I should send her to live with my parents. Give her the stability she needs. They'd love her, hug her every day, watch over her, make sure that she has a cake on her birthday."

"I can't tell you what to do, but I know you'd miss her. And what happens once you do clear your name? Will they just give her back?"

"No. They'd fight me in court. I know it. But what if I *don't* clear my name?"

"What if Ryker found out that Olivia was with your parents? There'd be nothing to stop him from snatching her. Your parents won't be able to keep her safe from him."

Shutting her eyes, she trembled against him.

"Do you really want to know what I think?" he asked.

She looked up at him and caressed his cheek. "Yes."

"We question Bertrand. See what he knows. Get everything you can from him. Then you'll need to contact Hunter. Remember, the Warriors didn't do it alone."

She twined her arms around his neck and hugged him.

"I also think you should take Olivia." He pressed his cheek to hers.

"John," she whispered, the word trembling as her body did the same, the shiver running through him, as well. "I'm afraid for Olivia and for you."

But not for herself. Did she have any idea how amazing she was?

He pulled back, needing to see her. When their eyes met, his decision was made. No doubt. No stupefaction. "I love you, Zee. Your fight is my fight, and I haven't lost one yet. I can help you keep Olivia safe. As long as we're together, I don't want you to be afraid."

She put her forehead to his and sobbed quietly. "You love me?" she asked as if it couldn't possibly be true, but underlying her disbelief, he heard fear.

"I do. I love you." He cradled her head and stroked her hair. "Don't. Please don't cry, sweetheart." There was nothing quite so astonishing and terrifying to him as this strong woman with a backbone of steel in tears.

"You could have your pick of women if you wanted." She sobbed. "It would be so much easier for you with someone else. Have a nice quiet life."

He'd tried nice and quiet in Alaska for three years and hated every second of it until he'd found her. "I don't want easy. I don't need safe. I want complicated." The more difficult and complex, the better. Hell, give him impossible, if it meant that his life still had purpose. "I need you."

They were perfect for each other, if only she could see it. Feel the certainty that was like a fist in his gut telling him that they were meant to be.

"I wish you didn't love me." She drew in a shuddering breath. "You tell me not to be afraid, but I'm worried that I'll get you ki—"

He drew her to him and kissed the word from her lips, swallowing the bad luck without letting her put it in the air. But the electricity of that instant connection was exhilarating, like jumping off a cliff. Like being in free fall before you hit the ground.

"John." She eased back.

He wondered if he had messed up completely. Misread her, misread everything. Wanting his help and wanting him might not be one and the same.

"I love you," she whispered, her breath fanning his lips. "And I've wanted you so much, for so long that I dream about you sometimes."

A riot of emotions exploded in his chest from relief to rapture. It was as if he'd won the lottery.

Instead of taxes, he'd have to deal with Ryker and Delta team, but as long as Zee loved him in return, he was a winner.

"Tell me about your dreams." He hoped they were sweet and sexy. Naughty but all good.

"I'd rather show you." She leaned in and brushed her mouth over his.

His blood caught on fire, and he kissed her. It wasn't soft or exploratory. No, this was about total possession. The mutual kind, where they claimed each other.

She lay back on the bed, bringing him down with her, settling his hips between her spread legs. Her tongue curling against his and the unreserved sensuality in the way she'd sucked on it, the press of her body to his, eager and responsive, lured him in, driving him wild like no other. Knocked him so crazy that the need to be inside her was like the beat of a drum pounding through him.

Cupping her buttocks, he lifted her hips, drawing her closer so that his erection was nestled in the soft notch of her legs. He rubbed her back and forth against him, groaning aloud at the exquisite pressure.

He ran a hand down the swell of her breast, stroking the hourglass of her curves, lower, playing over her hip bone. Lower still into her pants, between her thighs, and he slipped one finger, then two inside her, and she gasped.

All he could do was revel in the slick softness between

her legs and feel the wet heat of her. "I can't believe how ready you are for me." He pressed his thumb to that sensitive bundle of nerves and her body arched and trembled while her lips clung to his and she caressed every inch of him as she rocked against his hand.

The last time he'd wanted a woman so much had been… never. Not even as a teenager with raging hormones. His desire for her went deeper than the physical. Zee was everything that he had been waiting for and needed in his life.

But he didn't want her to make an impulsive decision. He wanted to be the love of her life. Not a one-hit wonder that she'd regret.

Because once they were together, one time wouldn't be enough for him. He'd need days. Weeks. Years with her. He was completely hooked.

"Are you sure?" he asked, giving her a chance to reconsider. "I don't have protection." The need to make that as clear as his desire was important. Doubly so after what she'd been through with that psycho. "I got a clean bill of health from the service and haven't been with anyone since, but if you want me to stop, I will."

She took his face in both her hands and held his gaze. "I'm one hundred percent certain, and healthy and covered on birth control." She kissed him. Then she pulled off both layers of tops over his head and started to undo his belt. "I want you, John. Right. Now."

He'd never heard sweeter words.

DESIRE RUSHED THROUGH HER like a high-speed train as John peeled her clothes from her body and kissed her all over.

It had been three years since she'd been on a date, and that had ended after one cup of coffee and a handshake. Kisses and sex had been reserved for her fantasies. Ryker had been the last man she'd been with. Perhaps that was odd, made her weird, but she could never get comfortable with anyone. Always felt watched. Stalked, even though Ryker hadn't been around. There was also the fear that a potential boyfriend might one day turn into another monster.

The hassle and the risk weren't worth it. Not with Olivia to think of. Zee had never even noticed her lack of a sex life or wished to change that until John.

Running her hands over the patchwork of scars on his torso, she knew the healed pucker marks of bullet wounds, the severe lines of old knife cuts. There were other blemishes, too, that she couldn't begin to guess at. His body was a map of violence survived, and it made her want to love him even more.

Her body cradled his now, instinctively welcoming him. She let out a greedy sound, not even thinking they might be getting too deep, too fast. There was only need. Hunger for this man that she was tired of denying.

As his fingers slid into her again, he held her wrists above her head with his other hand. Stared down at her face and watched every feeling she couldn't hide with such raw intensity that it brought her closer to the brink. She moved her mouth up to taste him, but he kept his lips just out of reach, his fingers stroking, teasing...sensual torture that made her writhe beneath him and had her begging him not to stop.

It wasn't enough. Not even close. But she was seconds from reaching that sweet peak. Shudders overtook her and she cried out.

His head dipped then, swiftly catching her mouth and swallowing her cries of pleasure. His tongue slicked over hers in total possession. He made a guttural sound in his throat, kissing her deeper.

She hadn't known it could be like this. That kissing could be intoxicating. Addictive.

"You're so beautiful," he rasped, his deep voice rippling through her. "But when you climax, you're drop-dead gorgeous."

John kissed a path down her body, featherlight, and crouched between her thighs, using his big shoulders to push her legs wider apart. Then his mouth latched on to her and she bucked at the intense sensations that bombarded her from his lips and the deep swipe of his tongue. Waves of pleasure rolled through her body.

No man had gone down on her since college. Ryker hadn't been interested in giving, only receiving and taking.

Grabbing the back of John's head, she urged him closer. The pressure built inside her, twisting deeper than before. Her toes curled. Her legs locked, muscle shaking. Everything in her tightened and squeezed, pleasure centering where his mouth was on her, his tongue laving, bringing her so much ecstasy it verged on agony. She moaned, screamed, coming apart in a loud, embarrassing way, and she was grateful the house was empty.

In a heartbeat, he was poised over her, forearms braced down on the bed on either side of her head. A corner of his mouth kicked up in a self-satisfied grin right before he was drinking the last sounds of her release from her lips.

She needed him inside her. After unzipping his pants, she helped him get them off. Along the way, she appreciated the landscape of his body. Taut, muscular chest. Sculpted arms. Ridged abdomen. A thin happy trail that led to his arousal.

Her inner muscles clenched at a stab of apprehension.

"It's been a long time for me." Eleven years. "And you're…" She glanced down at him. *Too big.* "Well-endowed."

He palmed between her thighs and she arched up from the bed. "I'll go slow, but trust me, I belong here."

Shifting their bodies, he changed position so quickly and with such remarkable strength, putting her on top. Giving her full control of everything. She settled on top of him, straddling his hips. Taking him in her hand and guiding him where they both wanted him to be, she lowered herself slowly down on him.

They both gasped as he entered her.

He growled, "You're tight." Clutching her hips, he threw back his head against the bed. "You feel so good."

Everything melted and softened inside her at knowing she brought him pleasure.

She rocked her pelvis, bringing him deeper. They found an easy, steady rhythm. Feeling sexy and empowered, utterly alive, she bucked her hips, loving the fact that finally she was with John.

Suddenly, he rolled, flipping their bodies, bringing her beneath him. "Is this okay?" he rasped.

She smiled. "Better than okay."

He went slowly as he promised, but from the strained look on his face she could only imagine how much self-control it took on his part. Running her hands over his body, she kissed him and encouraged him with her touch to go deeper, faster, harder, if he wanted. Her inner muscles loosened, stretching for him and she trusted him not to hurt her.

This was what lovemaking should be. Connection. Trust. Not holding anything back.

The brush of his mouth sent waves of sensation vibrating along every nerve ending. She clutched his shoulders, her fingers curling into the lean muscles of his body. The texture and taste of his mouth, his hot tongue as necessary as air as it stroked against hers. The feel of all that muscle pressing down on her with him buried deep inside was completely devastating.

Her body ached and hummed. He felt so good it was frightening. She never wanted this to end. He was close, his body tensing, going faster, powering deep and providing friction in all that right places that surprisingly brought her to the edge again, too.

With one last deep thrust, he grunted through his release, holding her tight, and she followed, spiraling to the other side along with him.

She'd read articles about how women could be multi-orgasmic but had never believed it before. Not until him.

Panting, chest heaving, he pulled her close so that she lay snuggled against his side with her hand on his chest, her thigh on his. He put his palm on hers and threaded their fingers.

This was real. John was in her arms. He'd listened to all her secrets without judgment and had chosen to stand by her, to love her. She hugged him tighter, languid. Happy and hopeful.

"One minute." He shifted up and away, slipping out of the bed.

She heard the tap go on in the bathroom. A few seconds later he returned, the bed depressing as he sat. He trailed a hand across her hip, down her thigh and hitched her leg. Gently, he cleaned between her thighs with a warm washcloth.

The intimate gesture was so unbelievably sweet and thoughtful, it made her chest ache with love.

"We should leave soon, for Idaho Falls," he said.

"Can I get two more minutes with you first?" It had been so long since she'd been held. She missed the simple act of cuddling. "I like the feel of your arms around me."

He leaned back against the headboard, resettling her

between his legs and tugging her into the cradle of his arms to rest against him. She put her cheek to his chest, curling an arm around his waist while he wrapped her in a warm embrace.

"I can do better than two. How about ten." He scooped her hair away and pressed his mouth to the side of her neck. "When we get back, I'll hold you all night."

"You might not have much choice in this tiny bed."

He chuckled and the deep rumble vibrated through her, soothing her in a way she hadn't expected. She'd never felt more at peace, oddly enough.

It made her wonder if they were in the eye of the storm. But one never knew when the eye would pass and then the scariest, nastiest, gnarliest part would follow.

She clung tighter to John.

"There's something I never told you," he said in a low voice, stroking her arm.

"What's that?"

"The day you knocked on my door, introduced yourself to borrow a cup of sugar and sidled up to me—"

"I did *not* sidle up to you."

Another deep chuckle from him—a sound she adored so much. "Yeah, you did, and I didn't mind one bit."

She preferred to think of it as facilitating friendship with a pie. After he'd opened his door and she'd seen *him*, touched him, that's when she'd decided to ask for the cup of sugar. He never even knew she had to use the entire cup for the one pie that she had baked for him.

"Was it my stunning good looks or charming personality?" he asked.

"I'll admit you're very easy on the eyes." She ran her nose up his neck and kissed along his jaw. "And your personality is not only charming but also compelling. But I immediately felt comfortable around you. Safe. I never worried that you'd drug my food and do something untoward to me."

She'd also been intrigued by him and attracted to him. Drawn. Something about his intense green eyes and that palpable aura of power and strength that pulled her to him, like an iron to lodestone.

Not that she had a predilection for big strong men who could easily overpower her. When it came to guys, she hadn't known what cup of tea she'd enjoy, only that she'd been thirsty for a long time.

He stroked her hair. "What I never told you was that after we met and I saw how gorgeous you were, I was worried for you. So I made my rounds to the guys in the area that I knew and told them that you had moved in."

"I was trying to keep a low profile and you told people about me?" She hit his leg playfully.

"Have you looked in the mirror? You can't keep a low profile even in the wilderness. Trust me, they would've noticed you on their own. I told them that you were my new neighbor *in shouting distance* of me," he said, and she glanced up at him, "and that if anyone messed with you, they messed with me." He gave her one of those smiles, and her heart moved in her chest.

No wonder he'd insisted that she have the two-way radio handy when they weren't together. That was the reason she'd kept it on the nightstand while she slept. "You did that for me? Even though we weren't dating?"

"Sure. Like I said, I was worried. It made me feel better that you carried a gun everywhere and had those perimeter alarms."

Leave it to a former Navy SEAL to notice everything.

"Don't get me wrong," he continued, "I secretly hoped you were interested in more than playing chess with me and swapping goods, but that's not why I was looking out for you. It was just the right thing to do."

There were a lot of jerks in the world and a few psychos like Ryker, but thank goodness there were men of integrity such as John. He truly was the best.

John held her a little longer, their ten minutes flying by, feeling like two, but it was best for them to get a move on. He left a note for Mike and Enola, explaining they had an important errand to run, that they'd return late, and jotted down the number to Zee's burner phone in case of an emergency. Before she knew it, they were in the car and on the road.

"What's the plan?" he asked.

"Luisa's father is a minister, and he has a church in Idaho Falls. I'm sure they'll have a Christmas Eve service. We should start there."

Chapter Sixteen

John drove through Idaho Falls, getting his bearings in the city while they found the church. The house of worship's parking lot was full and the streets adjacent to the building were lined with cars, indicating a packed house for the Christmas Eve service. Two streets down from the church, he found a spot to park in front of Cup of Joe.

Zee thought the local coffee shop or public library would offer the best chance for her to use free Wi-Fi in the vicinity of the building. But they didn't have a direct line of sight on the church from the library.

Here they could keep an eye out for Luisa while allowing Zee to hack into the CIA's database one last time and download the information her malware collated.

Her fingers flew across the keyboard as she sat in the passenger seat working on her spare laptop from the duffel bag. "I'm in," she said.

That meant the clock was officially ticking on how long they could stay in Idaho Falls before Delta or some other team showed up. He didn't know how much time they had, but he figured at least two to three hours. Delta team was already mobilized but they didn't know where Zee was. Once they found out, it would take them time to travel. With any luck, they were in Seattle trying to figure out their next step.

John climbed out of the car and went into Cup of Joe. Every chunky armchair was occupied, and holiday music flowed from the speakers.

He ordered a black coffee for Zee and a cappuccino for himself. "Hey, do you have any idea how long the Christmas Eve service at the church lasts?" he asked the barista.

"Less than an hour. We expect to have a full house in here in about twenty minutes. Folks always stop in after the service."

"Thanks." He sipped the cappuccino and moaned with the delight.

Stopping by the car, he set Zee's coffee in the cup holder for her since she was typing away furiously on the laptop and then he crossed the street to hit a store that had caught his eye. The bell at the top of the door rang as he entered the toy store.

They had things arranged in age-appropriate groups. It took him a couple of minutes to decide on Dungeons & Dragons Adventure Begins and a pink instant camera for Olivia. In the age of cell phones and selfies, the kid probably didn't know what a Polaroid was. He took the items to the register. One gift for her birthday. One for Christmas. He didn't think it was fair to deny her an extra present because they fell on the same day.

From the front of the store, he could see the church. The doors were closed, and the street was quiet. He used his debit card since the CIA would know that they were there within minutes if they didn't already.

Service was still ongoing two blocks down, so he made one more stop at a bath shop. An explosion of fragrances bombarded him as he crossed the threshold. Since Zee enjoyed a good, long soak in a tub, he headed for the bath oils. Not that she'd get to use it anytime soon, but she would appreciate the gesture. A tropical scented oil reminded him of her. She always smelled like a luscious mix of coconut and flowers. *Everywhere.* From her hair to between her thighs.

The sooner they found Luisa and hopefully David Bertrand the sooner he could get Zee back to Mike's attic, strip off her clothes and curl up in bed with her. The idea of making love to her again was more than a little appealing, but he'd be fine with holding her, too. He simply wanted to be close to her, as close as possible.

Never had he understood how his buddies could walk down the aisle and pledge to love one person for the rest of their days. Then again, Mike had done it three times. But John could see hitching himself to Zee. One woman. Forever.

Because she was the right one.

The thought was probably premature, but he'd keep it to himself.

As he crossed the street back to the car, the old injury in his leg ached something fierce. He hoped it meant they were in for a rainy Christmas, but he knew better.

Trouble was coming.

He dumped the bags in the back of the sedan as Zee pulled a thumb drive from the computer's port and powered off the laptop.

"It's done. I hope it was worth it." She glanced at the backseat. "What is all of that?"

"Christmas gift for you. Olivmas gifts for the kiddo."

"You're making me look bad."

"Impossible. You could never look bad. You're too beautiful." *Just as much on the inside as the outside.* He leaned over and kissed her, a quick, warm press of his lips against hers.

"Your gift is in ashes. It was back in my cabin."

"What was it?"

"A backgammon set with a leather case."

That would've been perfect. "It's the thought that counts."

She rubbed his thigh and he smiled at the way she touched him. Intimate. Possessive.

He finished his cappuccino and then checked the ammo on the gun with the attached sound suppressor that he'd lifted from one of the Delta team guys at the academy. Almost a full clip, two bullets missing. He had pumped the slugs into a member of their team.

Zee had her gun and baton, both holstered.

They didn't expect any problems from Luisa Morales or David Bertrand in the event they found him, but preparation for the unknown never hurt anyone.

"What do Morales and Bertrand look like?" John asked.

"Luisa is thin, delicate-looking. Light-colored hair. Big brown eyes. Full lips. In every picture or shot of her on CCTV, she's in full makeup with a bold lip color. That's the way I remember her. Always fashionable. David has salt-and-pepper hair, he's on the trim side, fair complexion, average height. Maybe five-ten. Nothing distinctive about him beside a little limp like one leg is shorter than the other."

"Have you ever seen her with a guy here in Idaho Falls?"

"I've only observed her for a limited time, and she was always on her own or with her parents, I think. But it's the holidays. People get sentimental. Sloppy."

John couldn't help but think of him and Zee. They had gotten sentimental, going so far as to confess their true feelings and make love for the first time—something he'd replayed in his head during the three-hour drive, but hopefully they hadn't been sloppy in a way that would come back to bite them.

Finally, the church doors opened. The congregation

poured out onto the sidewalk. People were holding lit white candles, chatting and giving hugs goodbye.

Zee perked up in her seat, putting the coffee down in a cup holder.

"Do you see her?" John asked.

Staring through the windshield, Zee scanned the crowd. John started the car and repositioned closer, parking in front of a fire hydrant.

It wasn't until the crowd thinned and most of the congregation had traipsed off that Zee said, "There she is. Light gray coat with a furry collar."

The woman stood out in a crowd. Her hair was pulled back in a tight bun and she wore an elegant wool pillbox hat that matched her coat. She had her arm linked with a man's. He was dressed in a dark suit. Dark wool overcoat. Mousy-brown hair.

"He doesn't match Bertrand's description." When Zee didn't respond, he said, "Maybe she moved on. Found someone else out here."

"Maybe. But I remember this one time, after a particularly difficult mission that David had been a part of, Hunter had a barbecue at his town house. David had brought Luisa. She was all over him and not in some contrived, fake way. It was a genuine handsy-feely thing where she was calling him *pookie* all night, ad nauseam, and David had looked like he'd crawl over broken glass for her. Do absolutely anything to keep that woman. Perhaps he'd be willing to gain weight and dye his hair, too."

John understood that feeling all too well. He was willing to do anything to be with Zee, to help her keep Olivia safe, especially from a maniac like Ryker.

Zee pulled her hair up into a ponytail and twirled it into a bun, securing it with an elastic band. Tugging on a cable-knit wool hat, she covered her head and slipped on black gloves. "I'm going to get a closer look. If they hop in a car, follow slowly and I'll get back in."

He put a hand on her forearm, stopping her. "Let me hoof it. You get behind the wheel."

"John, I used to do this as my job for the CIA. I didn't always sit behind a computer. They trained me well. Hunter chose me because as a woman, I can blend in where men can't. Or because he knew that a man would look at me and see a pretty face instead of a deadly weapon. No one will perceive me as a threat. I'll be fine." She jumped out of the car.

No one but Bertrand, he would've told her if she'd given him the chance.

She was forgetting that the analyst knew precisely what she was capable of. If the man with Luisa was indeed Bertrand in disguise and he got a glimpse of Zee, he would be gone faster than spit in the wind, and then they would be back at square one.

Gritting his teeth, John kept the engine running and watched.

Zee hurried down the sidewalk, crossed the street and disappeared in the throng of the congregation.

Luisa hugged the minister and the woman beside him, presumably her mother. With air kisses and one last wave, she took the arm of the man next to her and the two proceeded down the street.

The man in the dark suit strode with a slight yet distinctive limp. A positive sign, but not definitive confirmation as he had hoped. The couple passed the church's parking lot and continued strolling.

They were either parked farther away or in walking distance of their destination.

Zee wasn't far behind them, but she wasn't close enough to be easily spotted either. Head down, she moved like a shadow, gently winding past others in a manner that made the gaggle of evening parishioners seem oblivious.

John threw the car in Drive, pulled out from the space and rolled down the road.

Three blocks down, Zee crossed the street in front of the car. He stopped and let her in.

“I think they might be going home,” she said. “The church owns a large plot of land not far from here. They recently started a rent-to-own program for mobile homes to bring in income.”

“They run a trailer park,” he said.

“Apparently. Luisa is renting to own. She has been since she relocated here.”

“The boyfriend lives with her?” he asked.

Zee shrugged. “I don’t know. This is the first I’ve seen of him.”

“What do you think of the limp? It’s not quite what you described.”

As they crept down the street in the car, Zee’s gaze was glued to the couple.

“If that is Bertrand,” she said, “the limp has changed. Improved.”

Which wasn’t possible. But what were the odds of her dating two men in a row with limps?

Not high.

“Maybe he’s wearing a lift in his shoe to compensate for the limp,” she said. “To lessen it. Hide it.”

That was an explanation John could buy into. “Yeah, maybe.”

The couple turned left into the mobile home park. There weren’t any other vehicles parked alongside the road in front of the community and he didn’t want their sedan to stand out.

“Do you know which trailer she lives in?” he asked.

"I know the number, 221. But not exactly where it's located in there."

John threw the car in Reverse and parked on the rear side of the mobile park in the shadow of a Dumpster and some trees as a precaution. They got out of the car and darted across the street to the brick wall that enclosed the park.

"Give me your foot. I'll boost you." He cupped his hands, forming a stirrup.

She shoved her foot into the supportive grip. He hoisted her up, and she caught hold of the top of the six-foot wall and lifted herself over. John hopped up easily and climbed over, but he was careful to land with most of his weight on his good leg.

They skirted around a couple of trash bins and hurried along the center path through the park, which was paved. She searched the numbers on the sides of the homes while he stayed sharp and on the lookout for any nosy neighbors who might spot them.

Zee took a sharp turn to the right, leading him deeper into the community. Ducking down near a trailer, she waved at him to take a knee and pointed. "That one is Luisa's."

There were two windows on the front side. He guessed the living area in the middle and the bedroom at the far left.

The lights were on in the center of the trailer, the living room.

"How do you want to play this?" he asked Zee.

"I knock on the door and see what happens."

A bold proposition that might give better results than snooping through the window or breaking in. Either way they needed to talk to the couple inside.

"Okay," he said, glancing around. "I've got your back."

He drew his weapon. Not knowing what they were

walking into, he figured it best to be prepared and have no need to use the gun than be unprepared and filled with regrets.

Staying crouched low, they moved forward to the trailer marked 221.

As Zee climbed the front steps, he noticed a flurry of movement inside through the window. She knocked, and they both waited.

The door swung open inward, and Zee pushed her way inside the trailer without waiting for an invitation or wasting valuable time trying to convince the woman to let them in.

Luisa gasped and stumbled back, disappearing in the trailer.

John scanned the surrounding area before crossing the threshold to make sure no one snuck up behind them. A force of habit he couldn't break. He closed the door and locked it.

"Oh, my God!" Luisa's palms were raised in the air like this was a stickup.

The man in the suit stood in the kitchen holding a shotgun.

Zee lifted her hands, showing that they were empty, but John trained his weapon on the man with the twelve-gauge in his hands.

"I know you," Luisa said, recognition dawning on her face.

Zee nodded. "We met once at a barbecue in Virginia. You were with David."

"Yeah, I remember," Luisa said. "Baby?" She turned and looked over her shoulder back at the man.

"David?" Zee inched forward. "Is that you?"

"Zenobia." The man tilted his head to the side, staring at her. "What are you doing here?"

"Just to talk," she said. "To ask you a few questions. Then we'll leave. I promise," she said, waving at John to put his weapon down.

But he wasn't going to lower the gun until the other man did.

David's gaze bounced between them. His shoulders relaxed, and he plopped down in a chair at the table in the kitchen, setting the shotgun on the wooden surface.

The room buzzed with tension. John stayed on high alert, keeping his gun close to his chest but lowering the muzzle.

"How did you find me?" David asked.

"I didn't. I found Luisa. Figured you two might be together."

David lowered his head and sighed.

"I'm sorry." Luisa went to his side. "I should've done a better job of covering my tracks."

"I learned that you were fired after what happened," Zee said. "I came to see what you might know. We need your help."

His gaze shifted to John. "Who is he?"

"A friend," she said, but this time the word didn't burn his gut. "Someone I trust with my life. He's one of the good guys—I assure you."

"I'm not sure there are any good guys anymore." David ripped off his drab brown wig, revealing salt-and-pepper hair. He took off his suit jacket, unbuttoned his shirt and removed the top piece of a fat suit. "I'm not as savvy and creative as you guys, able to transform into a different person like something from *Mission Impossible*, but I was flying under the radar and undiscovered until you came here. What do you want?"

"You were fired," Zee said. "Right after our last mission." She stepped deeper into the trailer, crossing in front of the one of the windows.

John grabbed her arm and pulled her back. He hated these flimsy trailers. The lightness that made mobile homes easily transportable also meant they weren't as sturdy as a standard house. He felt vulnerable pinned in place inside this tin can. Every window was a point of further exposure.

He sure as hell wasn't going to let either of them stand in front of windows, announcing their presence.

Faces couldn't be seen from the drawn sheer curtains, but anyone watching would be able to tell that someone was standing there. If more than two people were seen moving around inside, it might signal a change of pattern, that something was off.

"What did you find that made you disappear and go underground?" Zee asked.

"I don't want any trouble." David gave a grave shake of his head, his gaze hardening. "I just want to live my life, marry Luisa, have a couple of kids."

A sad smile tugged at Luisa's lips. "Oh, pookie."

"None of us want trouble." Zee sighed at him. "My daughter, Olivia, turns eleven tomorrow. All I want is peace and quiet, but I can't give her a safe, stable home unless I can figure out what went wrong on my team's last mission. I think you know what it is. Please, I'm begging you. Tell me."

"I've stayed safe this long," David said, standing up and walking closer, "because I've kept my mouth shut and haven't caused any trouble. The minute I start talking to you, all that changes. I may as well flush my life here down the toilet. It might be selfish, but I'm not ready to do that."

"You're already talking to her," John said, holding tight to Zee's arm. "And they know it." Or they would soon enough. That's how the CIA worked. "Her kid was almost taken yesterday. She could've been killed. They both could've been."

"Taken?" David's hands trembled. "Wait, there's a team tracking you and you came here? What in the hell is wrong with you?"

"They know Luisa is here," Zee said. "This location is blown for you. That's the other reason we're here, to warn you. A team will eventually show up on your doorstep. You need to leave tonight."

"What?" Luisa said.

"Go pack our things," David told her.

"But what about Mom and Dad? We can't leave them behind."

"We'll discuss it in the car after we're packed."

Luisa nodded and ran to the bedroom. David opened a cabinet in the kitchen and pulled out a coffee canister. He flipped off the lid, grabbed a roll of money and shoved it into his pocket.

"Please, help me, David," Zee said. "Help all of us. Hunter. Dean. Gage. Olivia. My team was set up and I think you know it."

David rubbed a hand across his forehead, down over his face, and grabbed hold of his chin. "I did find something."

"No, don't say anything," Luisa said from the bedroom. "We talked about this. You're not obligated to endanger yourself any further. You did what you could, you tried, but you don't owe them anything."

"What did you try to do?" Zee asked, but he didn't respond. "You'll have to keep running just like us until we clear our names."

David walked out of the kitchen and strode into the living room. "I found discrepancies in the mission, after it was all said and done."

"What kind of discrepancies?" John asked.

"The description of Khayr Faraj's birthmark for one. Turns out that it's shaped like a tree on his left cheek. But in the file, it was—"

"Shaped like an apple on his right cheek," Zee said, cutting him off.

David nodded. "Someone changed it. Other things were different, too. When the mission was first input into the system, it had the usual parameters, where the team decides how to execute the objective. But it had been altered later to specify the target should be eliminated in a bombing."

"Was there anything else that you can remember?" Zee asked. "Any other discrepancies?"

This was taking too long. John didn't like lingering someplace that wasn't safe, but the one thing in their favor was they had a healthy lead on Delta team. They should be able to put plenty of miles between themselves and this trailer by the time danger came a calling.

"No," David said, mouth thinned, "but that was enough to lead me to believe that they never wanted you to kill Faraj in the first place. I think the Afghan official Ashref Saleh was the intended target all along."

"The Afghans are our allies," John said.

"He would never be considered a sanctioned target," Zee said, shaking her head. "Only as collateral damage after he handed over the money to Faraj proving his complicity."

"Yet, he never handed over any money to Faraj because Faraj wasn't at the meeting and your team still ended up killing Saleh anyway."

John's throat went dry. "Because someone wanted her team to believe that the tribal leader with a slightly different birthmark was Faraj."

"I think so. It'd looked to me like you were set up."

David walked around the small living room as he spoke. "I couldn't find any evidence that the Afghan official was corrupt or funding terrorism. I have no idea where those mission details came from, other than from someone's imagination. That someone wanted Ashref Saleh dead and used Team Topaz to do it."

She stepped forward and John hauled her back again. They needed to wrap this up and get out of there.

"But who would do it?" Zee asked.

David shrugged. "I don't know who is responsible."

Zee exhaled a shaky breath. "What about the proof of the discrepancies? Do you have copies?"

"Copies? Are you kidding me?" David asked. "If I had copies, I'm sure I would've been killed instead of fired."

"Who fired you?" John wondered. "Did you show anyone what you found?"

"Someone must have been monitoring my online activity. I started digging around—shortly thereafter, I was locked out of the system and escorted out of the building by security with no explanation. I had a bad feeling. Knew better than to make waves about it and disappeared."

"I don't understand why anyone would believe that we killed Ashref Saleh for no reason without giving us a chance to explain ourselves?"

"Everyone believed it because of the money," David said.

Zee grimaced. "What money?"

Luisa hurried to David's side, carrying a suitcase, and putting a comforting arm around his shoulder. "You've said too much already. We agreed to stay out of this. To protect ourselves."

"She found me." David's manner shifted. "She's asking. She needs to know. They all do." David looked at Zee.

"There are four offshore accounts in the Cayman Islands. One in each of your names with balances of 500,000 dollars."

Holy hell. John whistled. *Two million dollars.*

Staring at David with her face contorted in shock, Zee said unsteadily, "What? But we were never paid off."

David frowned at her. "Try telling that to the Agency and anyone who will listen. That's why the kill order was approved without an investigation."

"But we never took any money." Zee's voice grew agitated. "It must still be sitting there."

"That doesn't prove you weren't paid off," David said. "Only that you didn't get a chance to enjoy the money because the CIA found out about it before you could and froze the accounts."

Zee cradled her head in her hands, her mouth gaped in disbelief.

Red beams of laser sights slashed into the room, painting spots on David and Luisa. A chill rushed down John's spine like the icy fingers of a wraith. He yelled for the couple to duck, but he was slow. *Too slow.*

Gunfire shattered the windows, pumping lead into David and Luisa.

John lunged, bringing Zee down to the floor. She covered her head, her body jumping in reaction to the startling barrage of bullets. A cold sweat broke out on his neck.

Luisa and David were both dead. There was nothing that could be done for them now.

His gaze darted around the trailer in search of some means of escape. John had to get Zee out of there before Delta stormed in.

Chapter Seventeen

They were dead. Because of her.

Zee stared at Luisa and David, regretting that she came there. But how did Delta vector in on this location so quickly?

They couldn't have already been in Idaho unless…

Her laptop. She'd left traces of her deep dive into Luisa on the hard drive. Led them straight here.

"Listen to me," John said in her ear over the gunfire. "We have to get out of here."

"How?"

"I have an idea. We need to crawl to the kitchen. Find anything combustible and put it in the microwave."

"What?" He wanted to create a bomb?

"Trust me. Move."

They crawled through the trailer as Delta team riddled the mobile home with bullets.

In the kitchen, Zee grabbed two cans of nonstick cooking spray and any aerosol cleaning supplies from under the kitchen sink that she could find.

John snatched the shotgun from the table and began pumping holes into the laminate floor.

She threw the aerosol sprays into the microwave.

Put under enough pressure and heated to the point that they'd burst would turn the canisters into a weapon.

"Set it for five minutes."

Doing as he told her, she turned the microwave on, essentially activating a powerful improvised explosive device.

He kicked at the holes he made in the floor with the shotgun, enlarging them. The thin laminate and layer of plywood beneath gave way easily under his boot heel until the hole was large enough for them fit through.

The metal inside the microwave sparked and crackled within seconds. That thing was going to explode in less than five minutes.

He got her down through the opening first and quickly followed.

They scrambled through the underbelly beneath the home. The gunfire died down, stopping altogether, but they quickened their pace.

The homemade bomb was going to blow and when it did, they needed to be clear of the blast.

John kicked out the lattice board that skirted the bottom of the home. The noise be damned. They had to move. She shimmied through the hole and he was right behind her.

They took off running toward the rear of the trailer park as the windows on the mobile home shattered, sending a hail of glass and shrapnel toward the parking lot.

Gunshots rang out behind them.

They both sprinted for the brick wall at the back of the community, weaving around trailers to prevent anyone from a getting a direct shot at them.

At the wall, she climbed on top of one of the trash bins to help her over. With a running start, John hopped up, grabbing the top of the wall and swung over to the other side. But when he touched the ground, a grunt escaped his mouth and he limped forward.

He must've landed wrong.

"Go to the car," she said. "Get it started. I'll cover you."

Men were going to be hot on their tails and John's injury was going to slow them down. This made the most sense.

He clenched his jaw, either in pain or protest or both. But there was no time to argue.

She took aim at the top of the wall. Sure enough, the head of a Delta operative popped up as the man began climbing. She squeezed the trigger, sending him back over from where he came.

John took off, made it to the car. The engine cranked down the street. Tires screeched forward and the vehicle stopped behind her. "Come on. Get in."

Zee spun around, lowering her weapon. John had opened the back door for her.

As she dove inside, a hot spike of fire tore through her flesh.

RYKER STOOD ON the roof of a trailer that was adjacent to the rear wall. Squeezing the trigger, he fired two more bullets as the silver sedan squealed down the street and careened around the corner.

Damn. He hadn't even gotten the license plate.

He might not have stopped them and couldn't track the car, but he had shot Zee. Of that he was certain. It wasn't fatal. She didn't deserve a quick death and his daughter wasn't in the car.

Ryker needed to find Olivia before he killed that woman.

They had stashed his daughter somewhere.

But Zee would never leave Olivia alone. Especially not in a motel. The child would be with someone Zee trusted. Not that she knew anyone in this part of the country.

His thoughts churned. Maybe she had enough faith in her lover to leave Olivia with someone that Lowry trusted.

The door of the trailer he stood on opened. "Is someone up on my—"

Ryker aimed and pulled the trigger silencing the older man. Taking out his encrypted cell, he pushed the button, calling India on speed dial.

"Where you successful?" India asked.

"Bertrand has been eliminated. I'm still in pursuit of the main target. Compile a list of all of John Lowry's known associates. I need the names and addresses of any within a four-to-eight-hour drive of Idaho Falls. At the top of the list, I want to see those closest within the shortest drive of this location."

"Yes, sir. I'm on it."

LOOKING IN THE REARVIEW, John exhaled in relief. "I don't think we're being followed. It should be safe to hit the interstate."

Zee hissed in pain.

"What's wrong?" he asked.

"When it's possible, we need to pull over."

"Why?"

Zee's agonized gaze snapped up to the rearview mirror, and there was such pain in her face that it stole his breath. "I was hit."

His nerves wound tight as a metal spring. "How bad is it?"

She dug in her duffel, pulled out a cloth and pressed it to her left arm. "I'll live." Her voice was gritty as sandpaper. "The wound can wait until we're out of Idaho Falls. It's superficial," she said, but he doubted that she'd only been grazed.

It was best not to stop in the city. Better to get a few exits down on the interstate. His warrior goddess was putting logic ahead of medical care. He admired her strength more than she'd ever know.

John hit I-15 heading north and sped down the highway. Getting pulled over for exceeding the speed limit was a possibility, but he was willing to risk it. He spotted a sign for a rest stop ten miles away and pushed the accelerator past ninety until they'd reached it. If the car hadn't started rattling, he would've tried going even faster.

Parking far away from any other vehicles, he picked a well-lit spot under a lamppost. By the time he'd climbed into the backseat beside her, she'd slipped off her coat and had the tools that he needed from the medical kit waiting for him.

"You should've let me cover you instead." He cut up the sleeve of her top and peeled the fabric away from the wound. "You could've run to the car faster and we would've been out of there sooner."

"Hindsight is twenty-twenty. But that might have gone another way, too. If Ryker was the one who shot me," she said, looking down at her arm, "then he would've killed you. Not wounded you. Whereas he wants me to suffer before I die."

He cleaned her arm. "What are you saying, lucky you?"

She gave him a tight smile.

"There's an exit wound." No need to extract a bullet.

"See. Lucky."

If she weren't bleeding and in extreme pain—he was talking hell-on-fire kind of misery—he would've taken a second to kiss her.

They were both lucky. Unlike David and Luisa.

Instinct had kept John away from the windows and in turn kept Zee out of the line of fire in the trailer. He wished he could've saved David and Luisa, too. Ryker and that team of ruthless killers he was leading had no compunction about murdering innocent, unarmed people. They destroyed everything in their path, leaving a trail of carnage behind them.

One day, karma would come for them.

"When we get back to the house, maybe I should make the call to Hunter," she said. "Leave tonight."

"What about Olivmas? Maybe wait until tomorrow. Let her enjoy the day first. Cake. Presents. That sort of thing."

He tore open a package of Combat Gauze. The dressing was pretreated with a powerful hemostatic agent and would stop arterial and venous bleeding in seconds. He put a piece on the entry and exit wounds and applied continuous pressure for a few minutes.

"Do you want to come with us?" she asked, not making eye contact when in his mind this topic had already been resolved. "I don't know where we'll be headed and if you'd prefer to stay, I'd understand. Just because we slept together and have feelings for each other doesn't mean there's a commitment here. I don't have any expectations."

For him, he was all in with big expectations, but the declaration felt a little profound, possibly too heavy-handed after what she'd said. "Wherever you two go, I want to go. If you'll have me."

"I'll take you, John." She caressed his face. "With pleasure. I just didn't want you to feel pressured. Obligated. I wanted you to have an out."

"Trust me—I don't want *out*." All. In.

Once the bleeding looked controlled, he wrapped her arm with fresh Combat Gauze and moved her to the front of the car.

He started the vehicle and drove to the interstate. "I don't know what I would've done if that bullet had hit a vital organ. I finally got you to admit how you feel about me. I can't lose you."

She put her hand on his leg and rubbed his thigh in that way he was starting to love. "Ditto, big guy."

Chapter Eighteen

"Michael Cutler," India said in Ryker's ear. "He's the only known associate within a thousand miles of Idaho Falls. Most of the people Lowry knows are in Coronado, California, or Virginia Beach. Cutler is originally from Montana and has a house there. The drive to Bertrand's could be down in less than three hours from his place."

"Their association?" Ryker asked.

"They've been close friends for twenty years. They went through BUD/S training together and served on the SEAL teams together. Numerous missions. Lowry acted as best man to Cutler three times."

He was the one. Zee would be at ease leaving Olivia with a SEAL as a protector. Ryker's daughter was at the Cutler residence.

"Give me an address and ETA," he said, referring to an estimated time of arrival. "Research the property. I need the best place to land and the most efficient way to cut the power before we breach the house."

"Regarding the power, sir, do you care if surrounding homes or the nearby town is affected?"

Was she for real?

"Do you know who I am?" Sometimes the analysts weren't aware of their true identities or their reputations.

"Yes, sir."

"Then you already have your answer."

Chapter Nineteen

The pain was excruciating, but Zee refused to complain or take anything for the discomfort beyond acetaminophen. She didn't want anything that would make her loopy.

With her coat draped over her shoulders, she trudged up the porch steps of Mike's house. John was beside her, carrying the duffel bag and his shopping bags. He was walking a little better, but she could tell that his leg was still bothering him.

The house was aglow with Christmas lights. Inside it looked as if most of the lights were on even though it was almost eleven.

Teenagers.

John opened the front door and they strolled inside. He locked it, put on the chain.

The oldest boys were on the sofa playing a shoot 'em up video game.

Mike and Enola were in the den dancing together in front of the fireplace.

"Hey," the boys said, both turning to look at them and their smiles fell.

Zee imagined how she must've looked to them. A torn sleeve on her sweater. Gauze wrapped around her biceps. Bullet hole in the arm of coat. Blood stains.

"Are you okay?" the tallest boy asked, standing. Actually, he was a young man with a deep voice and looked strong enough to bench-press her weight with ease.

"Yeah, Tanner," John said. "She's fine. You guys go back to playing."

The alarm in Tanner's voice must have caught Mike's attention. Seconds later he was leaving Enola's side and coming into the living room. He looked her over and glanced at John.

"Why don't you go to the bedroom," John said to her. "I'll be up in a minute."

"Okay." She headed for the stairs as the two men spoke in hushed tones off to the side.

For a minute, she considered stopping by Amanda's room to check on Olivia and let her know that she was back, but after the reactions of the others to her appearance, she thought better of it.

She decided that she would wait until after midnight. The kids seemed as if they'd be up late and that way she could be the first to wish her daughter a happy birthday.

In the attic bedroom, she shrugged off her coat and sat.

John hurried up, shutting the door behind him. "It's all good," he said, answering her unspoken question. "Olivia had a great time at the winter carnival. I told Mike about the gunshot wound. A few details. He understood and told the boys not to say anything to Enola."

"I hate putting him in that position, where he's lying, omitting important things, to his wife."

"Mike is handling the situation the way he thinks is best and I happen to agree with him."

That told her a lot about John. Omission was okay in his book if he thought he was protecting someone he cared about.

He sat beside her. "Want any assistance getting out of those clothes?"

"Sure." She didn't need his help, but she wasn't opposed to accepting it.

They stripped, with him doing most of the work and then climbed into the bed beneath the covers. He switched on the radio that was on the nightstand. Soft instrumental music filled the room.

He pulled her into his arms and held her close. Dragged his knuckles across her hips. Let his fingers dance over legs and stomach. Cupped her breasts, feeling the weight of them in his palms. None of it was overtly sexual to make her think that this was foreplay, though she suspected he wouldn't turn her down if she suggested they make love. The way he touched her was tentative but intimate, like he was exploring new terrain that he'd laid claim to.

For a long time, they stayed that way, with him holding her, caressing her while she thought about all the little and big things that Mike hadn't shared with Enola. Things that John had thought it best to keep from her. Things Zee hadn't objected to because she'd been desperate for shelter.

"I need you to promise me something," she whispered.

"Anything. What is it?"

She sat up and looked at him. "Promise me that you'll never lie to me or omit sharing scary, dangerous things because you think it's best or that you're protecting me or whatever it is you guys tell yourselves. If we're together, then I need complete honesty."

His mouth hitched in a wry grin. "If you can promise the same in return, consider it done. But the second you break your word I'll go back to doing what I think is best."

"I can't believe you think I'll be the first to renege on this deal."

His smile deepened and she melted inside. "We'll see."

The music stopped.

Zee sat up and checked the radio, adjusting the volume and station. The clock face was dark.

Odd.

She glanced out the window behind the bed. The lights at the closest neighbor's house blinked out, followed by a wave of darkness spreading across the nearest town.

A firm, cold pressure ballooned in the bottom of her chest under her ribs. "John, something is wrong."

Turning toward the window, he looked at the sudden sea of darkness. "Get dressed."

They rushed around the room, throwing on their clothes and shoes. She slipped on her bulletproof vest before donning her sweater.

Zee peered out the window.

Men swarmed from the tree line, wearing NVGs and holding automatic weapons with red laser sights. They stalked across the property drawing closer to the house.

Her stomach bottomed out. "They're here."

Somehow Ryker had tracked them to the house. To this sanctuary filled with children.

Anger sliced her down the middle. She wanted Ryker's blood before he had a chance to hurt anyone else.

"Stay in the attic," John said. "Mike and I will handle this."

"There are children here," she snapped. Not only hers, but Mike and Enola's, as well.

"I know. We'll make sure nothing happens to them."

"I'm injured, but I'm not an *invalid*," she said, and the word had him stiffening. "Ryker wants me. They all do. I'm the target, the mission objective. I'll go out there, draw their attention by not using a silencer on my gun and lead them away. Ryker will follow. Some of the others will, too. Take out the rest who get into the house. Then come to the woods and help me. I'll run in that direction." She pointed out the window.

John's eyes drilled into her. "Hell, no! Over my dead body."

"We don't have time for this. That pack of cold-blooded killers is coming. And I'm not staying in this room."

He swore under his breath. Silence fell for a heartbeat, its presence suffocating. "I'm not going to talk you out of this, am I?" he asked.

"No. But no matter what happens, don't let Ryker get Olivia." She'd sacrifice her life for her daughter without a second thought.

"Mike has a rifle with a scope. I'm a good shot. Wait for me. I'll tell him what's happening, make sure the kids are hidden and get the rifle. Then you make a break for the woods. I'll pick off every bastard that chases you. Wait for me." John dashed for the door and hurried down the stairs.

Zee turned to the window.

Delta team was closing in. Any minute they would breach the house.

Dread pooled in her belly. The weight of it all pressed down on her. Not just the hours of running and fighting and battling to stay alive, but there was an ache in her soul. The consequence of all the choices she had made and the deaths she was responsible for. At the forefront of her mind were David and Luisa. They only wanted to stay safe, be happy, love one another.

No one else could die because of her. No one.

She had to do whatever was necessary to not only protect Olivia, but also the other children in the house, as well as John and Mike and Enola.

Unscrewing the sound suppressor, she took a deep breath. She tossed the silencer on the bed and pulled on her gloves.

She opened the window and looked around for a way to climb down.

To the side of the window ledge was a PVC pipe. If the pain in her arm wasn't unbearable, she could make it without falling.

"THE STRIKE TEAM I told you about," John said, standing in the living room, "they're here."

Emotion flashed across Mike's face. Alarm. Rage. Resolve. "They came to the wrong house."

"They've got NVGs. Is your generator up and running?"

"Yeah," Mike said. "I'm tracking what you're thinking."

Light this place up bright enough for Santa to see from the North Pole and blind those fools, seizing the advantage.

"We've got to hide the kids somewhere safe," John said, "and I need Big Betty." That's what his buddy called his rifle with a scope.

"Mike, what's happening?" Enola asked, coming into the living room.

"No questions right now, babe," Mike said. "Round up the kids. Fast. Take everyone down to the cellar." He clapped his hands, and the sound sparked her into action.

Panic widened her eyes, but she ran up the stairs.

"Dad, what do you want us to do?" Tanner asked, standing beside his younger brother who was only a couple of inches shorter.

"Come on." Mike led the way to his office, flipping every light switch up along the way. He unlocked the gun case, pulled out a 9mm for himself, handed each of his sons a shotgun and tossed Big Betty to John. "Boys, help Enola with the kids." Mike threaded a sound suppressor to the barrel of his weapon. "Anyone other than us comes into the cellar, blow them away."

"Yes, sir." The boys took off, leaving the room.

John snatched a box of ammo and dashed out of the office while Mike ran for the back door where the generator was in the yard.

Enola shepherded the frightened kids down to the first floor, shushing them not to ask questions, and led them around the corner to the cellar door.

Olivia cast a glance at John, her face stoic as she hurried with the others.

"It'll be all right," he said to her. Whatever it took, he'd make sure of it.

Tanner and his brother were close behind the kids and shut the cellar door once they were all inside.

On his way back up the stairs, John loaded Big Betty.

Shots outside shattered the silence.

But they hadn't come from the back of the house where Mike had gone. They'd come from the side.

I'll go out there, draw their attention by not using a silencer on my gun and lead them away, Zee had said to him.

No! *What have you done?*

RYKER AND HIS MEN were creeping up onto the porch, preparing to breach the house from different ingress points when four shots rang out.

Raising his fist in the air, he silently told his guys to hold. He backed down the steps and hurried in the direction from where the shots had come.

Zee jumped from the porch and ran, headed for the woods.

"You three with me," Ryker said to some of his men and then looked at the other two. "The rest of you, find my daughter. Kill anyone who gets in your way."

He turned and took off at a mad dash toward the woods. She might have a head start, but he was so much faster. And she had no one to help her.

This was a chase he would savor.

Kicking into a sprint, he ran flat out, his long legs eating up the distance between them. Nothing on earth was going to stop him from catching her. Nothing and no one.

"Zenobia!"

JOHN MADE IT to the second-floor landing as Delta burst in through the front door.

Right on time, the generator switched on, flooding the house in bright light. The men reeled back, trying to adjust their NVGs.

John raised Big Betty and pumped slugs into each of them, taking the two of them down. He waited for more men storm in.

But none came.

Zee.

He raced up the stairs and pain flared from his thigh to his shin. His leg was killing him. He had to hop and use the railing for leverage up the steps, but he blocked out the discomfort and moved as fast as his body would carry him.

In the bedroom, the window was open. A bone-chilling breeze swept through the room. Zee was gone.

He rushed to the window, propped Big Betty up on the edge of the headboard and looked through the scope.

It took him a moment to focus and scan the property.

There!

Zee dashed into the woods. Trench Coat—*Ryker*—disappeared into the tree line seconds after her. Too fast for John to take a shot.

His molten rage bled into an icy calm. Sighting through the scope, John took a deep breath, finger on the trigger, exhaled. Waited.

A Delta operative sprinting toward the woods came

into his crosshairs. He pulled the trigger. A shot rang out and the man dropped.

Another was still running in the same direction.

John aimed and squeezed. That one crumpled to the ground, too.

The third man who had been in pursuit changed his course wildly, heading back to the house, but he was out in the open. Nowhere to hide. Nowhere to run.

One shot and John took him out. He scanned the area.

Once he was sure there was no one else, he bolted for the staircase and rushed down the steps. On the main floor, he hopped over the dead bodies and raced outside. The children would be safe. So would Mike and Enola.

But Zee was out in the woods, injured and alone, with Ryker.

Chapter Twenty

Ignoring the cramping in her side, Zee extended her legs and pumped her arms, running with everything that she had.

Footfalls pounded after her. Getting louder. Gaining. Drawing closer.

She didn't dare look back. It'd only slow her down and she knew what she would see.

Ryker's face. Enraged. Bloodthirsty.

Adrenaline surged through her bloodstream, spurring her on. She darted around a tree, zigzagging to avoid capture, her feet striking the ground faster and faster.

He swore at her. Cursed her. Raved like a lunatic. She could hear his breathing now he was so close. Strong. Steady.

Relentless.

Panic swept through her as her heart raced. Her lungs burned. Her breath punched white into the air. Her legs screamed. Her arm ached with a gut-wrenching agony that would feel like nothing in comparison to what Ryker would do to her if he got his hands on her.

She had to get away. Had to keep going. Had to run faster. But he was closing in on her too quickly. He wouldn't stop until she was dead. Or she killed him first.

The toe of her boot caught, and she lurched forward, her arms flailing, trying to regain her balance.

"Careful," a deep voice said from behind her, "don't fall and break your neck." Powerful arms hooked around her waist, snatching her from the ground.

Her heart seized in her throat.

"I want the pleasure of doing it." His hot breath was in her ear.

Oh, God! No! He had her.

Screaming, she kicked and swung her fists, but only hit air. He knocked her gun from her hand. Not that it mattered. She was out of bullets.

His grip was tight, painful, punishing. Ryker spun them both and threw her to the ground onto her back. He pounced on top of her.

The wind was knocked from her lungs. But that didn't stop her. On pure instinct, her training kicking in, she punched straight out.

Ryker pulled back out of reach. Then he grabbed her by her hair, yanking her head up from the ground and slammed it down, again and again, banging her skull into the hard frozen earth.

Dazed, hurting, she tried to focus on something. Anything. But her vision swam, and her mind was thick from the blows to her head.

Ryker was sputtering vile things, straddling her. His hips had her legs pinned.

She howled in frustration. In a fight, fist to fist, she didn't stand a snowball's chance in hell. A woman's ultimate power came from her lower body, where she was strongest, and a well-aimed kick was her greatest weapon.

And Ryker knew it.

Grabbing the hilt of her baton, she yanked it from the holster on her hip and flicked it out to its full length. As she swung up with her right hand, Ryker snatched her wrist. With his other hand, he seized her throat, pinching her windpipe closed.

She gasped. Involuntarily without thinking, she clawed at his arm bearing down on her throat. But it was no use. He was too strong, and she was in the weakest position possible.

He twisted her wrist a half turn counterclockwise. The pressure and the pain made her open her fingers and drop the baton before he broke the bone.

She would have shrieked in agony if she had been capable of making any sound.

"I gave you everything and you didn't appreciate any of it!" Exertion and rage turned Ryker's face red. "I rescued you from that hacktivist group in Germany. Kept you out of prison. Gave you a career at the CIA. Spared you my darker proclivities in bed because I knew they would scare you. Made you a mother. Gave you a baby. And you repaid me by taking everything from me!" He tightened his hold around her throat. "Instead of despising me, you should have worshipped me!"

Gagging, Zee wheezed for air. Darkness tugged at her consciousness, creeping around the edges of her vision. She couldn't give in to it. She had to fight.

She needed to breathe. *Oh, please, not like this. Not by his hand.* Ryker was killing her.

What would happen to Olivia? Her baby girl. Her precious child. The one good, true thing that came from this evil monster.

Protect her, John.

"Not once did you ever thank me!" Ryker loomed over her, bearing down. "Or show me the gratitude that I deserve. But you will now." He eased up on her throat, slowly, letting go.

She sucked in air and coughed. Her heart throbbed in her chest. The blackness receded.

Then he put a gun to her head.

Click!

The distinctive sound of the hammer being cocked echoed through her brain.

"Keep fighting me and I'll pull the trigger right now," he promised.

Fear thickened her blood. Wrestling against every instinct to protect herself, she stilled.

"Apologize for not loving me. Tell me you're sorry for throwing away our family. Then I want you to beg." He dragged the nose of the weapon from her head, along her throat, down farther. "Beg me for your life." He pushed the muzzle into her gunshot wound.

Squeezing her eyes shut as tears leaked out, she screamed in anguish.

"Start by saying you're sorry. Do it if you want me to treat our daughter well."

She looked at him and bile flooded her throat. Then her gaze drifted to the gun pressed to her injured arm.

But she saw something else, too.

A Ka-Bar knife holstered on his hip.

"I'm sorry," she cried, relaxing her body, spoon-feeding his confidence that he'd already won, and he watched her intently, pleasure gleaming in his sick eyes, his smiling face aglow with triumph that twisted her stomach into a knot. "Sorry for everything I did wrong. But most of all… I'm so, so sorry that I didn't kill you in your sleep."

She drew the knife from the holster and plunged the blade into him and twisted. He dropped the gun, but she'd missed her target, hitting his shoulder.

Quickly, she yanked the serrated blade out and aimed for his black heart.

But Ryker slapped her backhanded, and the Ka-Bar flew from her grip.

Roaring in pain, he reared back and clenched his hand to strike her.

But she launched a fist first to his throat. She bucked her hips, thrusting him off her as he choked and with both feet kicked him farther away. Putting distance between them, she crawled on her butt backward across the ground. She felt around for his gun or her baton.

She had to kill him if it was the last thing she ever did. Ryker had to die. Tonight.

"I'm going to tear you into pieces!" Ryker said, recovering.

Curling her fingers around the hilt of her baton, she braced herself. *Go for his knees, groin, head.*

Ryker charged at her. Growling. Snarling. Teeth bared. Ready to hurt her. To kill her.

Movement rushed in from the side. *John.* He tackled Ryker to the ground.

Zee scurried to a tree and pulled herself up along the trunk.

The two men wrestled, rolling around, throwing punches and kicking each other. She scrambled for Ryker's gun. There was no way that monster was leaving this forest alive.

In a lightning-fast move, John seized Ryker from behind, locking him in a position with the psycho's back to his chest. He snaked an arm around Ryker's throat and wrapped his legs around the man's hips. The struggle only lasted a second longer before John snapped Ryker's neck.

A rush of relief cascaded through her, a dam of terror breaking inside her.

She sobbed, collapsing to her knees. At last, she was free of Ryker Rudin.

John tossed the limp body to the side. Standing, he stumbled to her, dropped to her side and wrapped her in his arms. "The children are safe. The rest of Delta are dead. Are you okay?"

No, no, she wasn't. But… "I will be." She hugged him back, vowing never to let him go.

He lifted her to her feet, throwing his arm around her. Hugging her tight, he kissed her cheeks and her head. He inspected her face and grimaced and kissed her again.

They started making their way back to the house, clinging to each other and slogging along.

"I have to contact Hunter," she said, "and we have to leave before another team shows up. Mike will need to call the cops as soon as we're gone."

"Yeah, okay." He tightened his arm around her. They reached the house and he said, "You do realize you reneged on our deal."

"What? How so?"

"I told you to wait for me," he said, "and you agreed."

"I never agreed. You believed what you wanted."

"You neglected to tell me you weren't waiting and omitted that you'd planned to go out the window. But I'll cut you some slack this one time, and we'll consider it a gray area."

"You know what's not gray?"

"What?"

"How much I love you."

Chapter Twenty-One

Six weeks later...

John walked through the main house on the island off the coast of Venezuela. Hunter Wright's house. It was less than a mile down the beach from the hut that he lived in with Zee and Olivia, and about half a mile away from Gage Graham and Hope Fischer's place.

The island was a slice of paradise. Balmy San Diego weather. In the daytime, seventy-five degrees Fahrenheit and at night the lows dipped into the sixties. Mild breezes. Fresh air, plenty of fish, seafood and produce. A powdery-soft sand beach that he took long walks on every day, most of the time with Zee. His afternoons he spent swimming and helping homeschool Olivia.

He even got on well with the guys from her team and Hope was a nice lady. Best of all, he got to wake up every morning with Zee in his arms, curled up next to him.

Paradise.

Three or four times a week, like this evening, they all gathered for a family-style dinner at Hunter's house.

John entered the dining room, where Olivia was setting the table. "Need any help?"

"No, I've got it," she said, giving him a bright smile.

He pitched in anyway, folding napkins and arranging

them beside the plates. "How did your Mandarin lesson go with Hunter?"

She rattled off something in Chinese and then in English said, "He says I'm a natural."

"Of course you are." The eleven-year-old already spoke Spanish, Zee was teaching her German, and now Mandarin. Her incredible brain was like a giant sponge, soaking in everything and retaining it. Boggled his mind, but he couldn't be any prouder of her. "Since the table is finished, why don't we sit outside and wait for your mom to get back."

Hunter was usually the only one who made trips to the mainland to stock up on supplies, to limit the exposure of the rest of their merry little band, but Zee had insisted on being the one to go today.

"Sure." Olivia led the way with a bounce in her step that brought a smile to his face.

He liked seeing his ladies happy. It made him happy.

"Can we play Dungeons & Dragons tonight?" Olivia asked.

The game was addictive. "I'm up for it. We can see if your mom is interested, but I bet Gage will be in."

They stepped outside onto the wraparound veranda and took a seat side by side on the porch swing.

"What does the air smell like here?" he asked her.

"The ocean and plumeria. I love that flower. I asked Mom if she'd buy me some perfume with that scent while she was on the mainland."

"What did she say?"

Olivia shrugged and pouted. "She'll think about it."

"Well, that's not a no."

"It's not a yes either."

John chuckled. "Hey, I wanted to talk to you about something before your mom gets back."

Olivia tilted her head to the side and looked at him. "About what?"

"I wanted to get your permission."

Perking up with a straight back, she leaned in. "I'm usually the one who has to ask permission."

"Not this time." He took a deep breath. "I want to propose to your mom, but since this concerns the three of us, I thought I should—"

"Yes!" she said with a squeal of delight and threw her arms around his neck, yanked him down in a stranglehold of a hug. "Yes, you have my permission." She let him go and pulled back. "So, would that make you my dad?"

"I'd be honored if you thought of me as such." He already considered her his daughter. "Once I marry your mom, provided she says yes," he said, also knowing they had to clear Zee's name, "I'd like to officially adopt you." Every decision he made centered around Zee and Olivia. His family. He loved them both and would die to protect them.

"I never knew my dad. Mom said he was a bad person who did bad things and that he'd never be in my life. It'll be nice to finally have one." Olivia looked at him and beamed. "Did you already get her a ring?"

"Sure did." He reached into his pocket and took out the ring box. "Do you want to see it?"

"Do birds fly?"

He pulled the ring box back. "Well, now I'm not so sure if I should show it to you since not all birds do fly. Penguins, weka—"

"Ostriches, kiwi, cassowary. Come on, John, it was a figure of speech. Don't hold it against me. I want to see it." She rubbed her palms together, her bright brown eyes gleaming.

"Okay," he said, handing her the black box, "but only because you redeemed yourself."

She flipped up the lid and gasped. "Wow!"

It was a round, brilliant cut solitary diamond. One point seven carats that glinted fire. Perfect for Zee. Hunter had hawked John's watch for him so he could pay for it under the ruse that the watch needed to be repaired.

On the run he didn't have access to his bank account, investments or disability payments, and he didn't want to wait until the situation with Team Topaz was resolved.

He had no idea how long it could take, and he wanted to make Zee his wife and claim Olivia as his daughter, officially, as soon as possible.

Life was too short to delay something this special.

"Do you think she'll say yes?" he asked.

"Oh, I know she will." Olivia closed the lid and handed him the box. "She loves you. And you really love her, too, don't you?"

"I love your mom with all my heart, from the bottom of my soul straight to my gut. My only reason for breathing is to make her happy. I love you, too, and I'd do anything for you both."

"When are you going to ask her?"

"I was thinking tonight. Should I do it at dinner in front of everyone or in private on the beach? What do you think she'd prefer?"

John had already given this considerable thought. Zee loved her teammates. They were family, people who cared for her and would do anything to keep her safe and vice versa. But she valued her privacy, as well. A wedding he could envision in front of everyone, but he suspected Zee would prefer an intimate moment. Just the two of them.

Nothing was set in stone and he wanted Olivia to have a chance to share her opinion. It was important to him to make sure she was a part of the process every step of the way and never felt excluded.

"On the beach at sunset," Olivia said. "Mom will be shocked, and she'll probably cry and wouldn't want anyone else to see. And if she says no that'll spare you any embarrassment."

John's smile fell. Unease churned in his gut. That last part about her rejecting him hadn't crossed his mind. "Do you think she might say no?"

Olivia elbowed his side and giggled. "I'm just messing with you."

He chuckled.

The roar of an outboard motor buzzed in the air drawing both their gazes to the water.

"Mom's back!" Olivia jumped up and ran to the rail of the veranda and waved.

A speedboat with Zee behind the wheel zipped along the water's surface heading in their direction.

John stood, going to stand beside her. "Remember, not a word."

"I'm good at keeping secrets."

Both of his ladies were and didn't he know it.

They strolled down the beach to meet her on the dock and unload any supplies. The sun was low on the horizon, painting the sky red, gold and purple.

Zee's hair was loose and wild, blowing in the wind, her sundress fluttering along with the breeze. She slowed as she got closer and brought the boat alongside the dock. The breeze carried the vessel right in to where it needed to be. She cut the engine on the speedboat as John grabbed a line. He tossed it to her, and she tied up.

Offering his hand, he helped her climb out and up onto the dock. He noticed there were no crates or bags in the boat. Pulling her into his body, he kissed her.

"Did you get it for me, Mom?" Olivia bounced up and down on the balls of her feet with her fingers crossed. "Please tell me you got me perfume."

"Repeat it in Spanish," Zee said.

Olivia sighed and then did as she was instructed. Zee rewarded her with a small roll-on bottle of perfume.

"Gracias." She hugged her mother. "Enjoy the sunset." With a wave, she ran off with the bottle back to the house.

John slipped his arm around Zee's shoulder, tucking her against his side. They left the dock and hit the beach. "Did you have a good trip?" He ran his fingers across her healed gunshot wound, and renewed gratitude that she was alive and well filled him.

"I did."

It was hard to miss the absence of supplies. "Are you going to tell me what you went to the mainland for?"

She opened her bohemian cloth handbag, and John peered inside as she pulled out a medicine bottle.

He spotted a rectangular box with distinctive blue-and-white packaging, Clearblue, in a plastic bag.

She handed him the pills. "The refill will last you a month."

Dropping his arm, he stopped and stared at her. "Sweetheart, could you be pregnant?"

Was it possible?

Well, of course it was. It only took one time and they had enjoyed each other every single night and there had been a few afternoons as well when Olivia was at the main house.

"Oh, gosh no." Zee recoiled. "I'm not. That's not for me, but that is the real reason I went to the mainland. Hope didn't want any of the guys to know, until she knew for certain, so play dumb."

"Okay," he said, sounding relieved, but what he felt was closer to an ache of disappointment.

"The test will confirm what I already know. Hope is pregnant. That's why I also got her these." She showed him a bottle of prenatal vitamins.

"How do you know for sure that she's pregnant?"

"She's two weeks late, suddenly nauseous all the time and her breasts have gotten a little bigger."

Thankfully he hadn't noticed any of that. He wondered if Gage had? Would John if their situations were reversed?

"Are you sure you couldn't be?" John asked.

"Relax, big guy." She put a palm on his chest and rubbed. "I'm positive. After what happened with Ryker," she said, her gaze falling, "I got an IUD. Mine won't need to be replaced until next year. You don't need to worry about me trapping you." She smirked.

"Do you want more kids?" They'd talked about a future together once their names were cleared, discussed money, politics, religion. Had asked each other a thousand questions.

Marriage was about a million different compromises. Things that they'd never think to ask would come up. Life was capable of throwing some wicked sucker punches.

But for some reason this one question hadn't been mentioned.

He didn't even realize he wanted to have a baby with her someday until this moment. What if she didn't want to go through the dirty diapers and lack of sleep all over again?

She wrapped her arms around his waist and pulled them pelvis to pelvis. "I'm open to the possibility. With the right guy. At the right time." She rose on her toes and brushed her nose across his before kissing him. "Do you?" she asked, lowering back to the sand.

"I want to be trapped with you and have babies and

raise Olivia and grow old with you." All of that came out completely wrong.

"John."

He'd started and might as well finish, so he whipped out the ring box.

Zee staggered back, her hand flying to her chest.

Opening the lid, he lowered to his good knee. "I've been with a lot of women," he said, and she frowned at him. Taking a deep breath, he mentally kicked himself and tried again. "What I mean is, you're the only woman that I've ever loved. Just looking at you makes me smile and fills me with a joy I've never known before. You make life worth living. You make me want to be a better man for you and for Olivia. Marry me."

Her jaw dropped as she stared at him. "Are you sure? I'm a package deal with a lot of baggage. I'm a fugitive."

He stood in front of her. "I've never been more certain of anything in my life. I love you and Olivia. I want both of you to be my family. No, you already are my family. I want to make it official, permanent, for the two of you to take my name. And I promise to cherish what we've found together, what we're creating, every day of my life. Marry me, Zenobia."

Tears welled up in her eyes. "Yes, I'll marry you." She leaned in, twining her arms around his neck, tangling her fingers in his hair, and kissed him.

As he soaked in the warmth of her body, the beat of her heart against his chest, the kiss was familiar and new all at once. Like the first time. Like coming home.

This was right. In Alaska, he'd felt a connection to her that he couldn't explain. One that made no sense. But now he understood, she was the other part of him. A kindred spirit. The two of them, make that the three of them, together made all the sense in the world.

"I finally understand why my mom never complained about living in Breezy Point. She used to tell me that it didn't matter if she was in Antarctica or Bed-Stuyvesant. That as long as she was with my dad then that was where she belonged. That's what you are for me, John. You're my shelter and when I'm with you I feel at home. I want to be yours forever."

Happy tears rolled down her cheeks as he slid the ring on her finger. Cupping her face in his hands, he kissed her again and tasted the salt of her tears.

Applause and cheers had them both turning toward the house. Olivia, Hunter, Gage and Hope were all out on the veranda watching them.

With his arm around her shoulder and hers curled around his waist, they strolled up to the house.

"Is your watch really getting repaired or did you have Hunter pawn it to buy my engagement ring?"

He smiled at her. "It's no big deal."

"But it is. I know what it meant to you."

"You mean more. Besides, I know who I am, and I'll never forget it again. I've got T.O.T.S. branded on my heart."

They walked up the steps of the veranda.

"We're getting married!" Olivia said, and everyone laughed.

Congratulations, pats on the back, handshakes, hugs and compliments on the ring were given. Zee and Hope deftly maneuvered down the porch for a moment. Using their bodies to shield their exchange, Zee passed Hope the Clearblue in the plastic bag and the other woman slipped the package into her purse.

The other men seemed none the wiser with their backs turned, but once the ladies rejoined the group, Hunter's gaze bounced between them like he was aware something was up.

Everyone moseyed into the house for dinner and grabbed a seat around the table. There was a spread of grilled fish, octopus, arepas—griddle-fried corn cakes, rice, black beans and loads of vegetables.

Hunter grabbed a bottle of champagne and popped the cork, which made Hope visibly nervous, and poured bubbly in flutes.

Hope pushed her glass away. "None for me, thank you."

"Stomach flu still bothering you?" Hunter asked.

"Yeah." She nodded.

Gage sucked back a glass of champagne and took hers. "If it doesn't clear up in the next day or two, it might be a parasite."

"That's one possibility," Hunter said. "Though I doubt that's what it is."

"Do you think it's something more serious?" Gage asked.

The corner of Hunter's mouth hitched in a half grin. "I think it's something that won't *clear up* anytime soon."

Apparently, Gage and John had been the only clueless ones. John felt bad for Gage. He was the only grown-up at the table who didn't know.

The phone in Hunter's office rang, and a hush fell over the table. It was the first time he'd heard any phone ring since they had arrived on the island.

Hunter got up, putting his napkin down, and hurried to the office. He answered the phone. "Parachute."

"It's Dean," Zee said.

"Does that mean he's in some kind of trouble the way you were?" John asked.

Under the table, she took his hand. "Unfortunately, it does."

Hunter rattled off coordinates and instructions, wished him good luck and hung up. A minute later, he returned to the table and sat. "Dean may be joining us soon, depending on how things shake out for him."

Around the table there were grim faces and crestfallen looks.

"Isn't this a good thing?" John asked. "Your team is stronger together than apart."

"Every teammate who arrives exponentially increases the odds of us being discovered," Hunter said. "If Dean makes it, and I hope that he does, because he's in serious trouble, then I think it might be time to stop hiding and take this fight to Langley's door before they bring it here."

"Yes." John pounded a fist on table, drawing everyone's attention. "We go to the mattresses."

Hunter nodded. "We'll go to war and we won't stop until we clear our names."

Confirmation of everything David Bertrand had shared with them before he died was on Zee's hard drive. But due to the money in the offshore accounts, it wasn't enough evidence to exonerate them. They had to find out who wanted Ashref Saleh dead and why. Then they could track down the proof they needed.

David's death wasn't in vain. Thanks to him, Team Topaz knew what they were looking for and where to start.

Zee squeezed John's hand tighter and glanced across the table at Olivia.

John would figure out a way to keep Olivia out of the crosshairs and make sure she was safe. He leaned into Zee and whispered, "As long as we're together…" Nothing else mattered.

He knew how to endure, and she knew how to fight. Together they were whole. Stronger, better than apart.

She looked at him with pure love in her eyes. "We can get through anything."

* * * * *

COLTON 911: SECRET ALIBI

BETH CORNELISON

Thank you to Kasey Witherington, MEd, LPC, for her assistance as I researched borderline personality disorder and sought to better understand Valerie's mother. Kasey generously answered questions for me and shared further sources for my research.

Any mistakes I have made in portraying the disorder are mine alone.

Prologue

Twelve years ago

Three minutes. Just three minutes.

Good God, who knew three minutes could last so long?

Valerie Yates tried to clear her mind, shift her focus, but waiting had never been her strong suit.

She bent over the paper in front of her and resumed sketching. A face began to take shape in the squarish oval she'd started. Eyes, nose, lips…

Soft, demanding lips. Skilled lips that made her breath catch and her toes curl.

With that unbidden thought, she pressed too hard and the tip of her charcoal pencil snapped off. Huffing her frustration, she leaned back in her desk chair, shook the tension from her hands. Checked the clock.

Seriously? It had only been one minute and fifteen seconds?

She scrubbed a hand down her face and took a deep breath to quell the churning in her gut. The added nervous tension did not help the swirl of nausea that had plagued her lately.

One minute thirty seconds. Halfway.

Groaning, she found her sharpener and fixed the tip of her pencil. Resumed sketching. A smudge with her thumb to soften a line and add shadow, contour. She was drawing Nash again, she realized. Without even considering what she was doing, her fingers, her mind, automatically created the image that filled her thoughts these days. She set down her pencil, closed her eyes and allowed herself to go to those magic nights and stolen moments. To sweaty skin. Adoring hazel eyes. Whispered promises.

Nash Colton. Her first love. Her first lover.

"I wish you didn't have to leave," he'd said morosely that last summer night, two months ago.

"Me, too." Valerie had shifted to her side, pressing her lean, naked body against his. Even at eighteen, he had the taut, muscled body of an athlete. Not gross, bulky muscles like those weight lifters they'd watched on the summer Olympics last year. No, Nash was more… What was that swimmer's name? Michael… Phillips? No, Phelps.

Valerie drew circles on his flat, bare chest and sighed. "I'll come back next summer. And probably at Christmas. My mom was talking about going skiing in Colorado at Christmas, but I'll tell her I want to come back here instead."

"You'd give up skiing in Colorado to see me?" he asked, his tone both surprised and wistful. Grateful. Hopeful. Her heart broke a little for him. She knew how the death of his mother and strained relationship with his father had hurt Nash.

"Of course, I would. I—" She caught herself before she blurted "I love you." Instead she finished with "I think you're special. We have fun together."

He wiggled his eyebrows seductively. "Lots of fun."

She playfully punched his arm. "You know what I mean."

"And how will you explain your preference to come back to Chicago instead of skiing to your parents? Are you ready to tell people about us?"

Val furrowed her brow. "No. We can't tell yet. If my mom ever found out we were…well, whatever this is." She waved her fingers between them. "She'd freak. She probably wouldn't even let me come back to visit Uncle Rick next summer."

"She's really that strict?"

"Yeah."

Nash frowned and folded his arm behind his head. "Has she ever explained why she doesn't want you spending time with my family?"

"Not really. She just says 'Stay away from those Coltons! They're trouble!'"

"Well, I can understand that a little if my father and Uncle Axel are the only Coltons she knows," Nash said, his dark blond eyebrows furrowing, "but has she even met any of the rest of us? We're not so bad."

"It's more than that. I'm pretty sure she got pregnant with me in high school. I mean, all you have to do is the math. So she's worried that I will—" She didn't finish the sentence because it was obvious what her mother was worried she'd do. And because she and Nash had. Recently. More than once.

He flashed an impish grin. "Yeah, well…"

Valerie felt a flush sting her neck and cheeks. "Nash!"

He stroked her face with his fingers. "Don't worry. We've been careful."

Valerie leaned on one elbow and bent her head to kiss him. "I know."

"It's hard, not telling anyone. I really want to tell Damon. He's not just my brother. He's my best friend. And you make me so happy…"

Beaming her own bliss, she framed his face between her hands. "You, too. But…for now, let's not say anything. If my mom found out—" She sighed, knowing how badly that conversation would go and not wanting to risk anything that would push her mother to the edge. To drink. "Maybe next summer—"

A hungry growling sound rumbled from his throat as he captured the back of her head with his free hand and tugged her down for a deep kiss. "I don't think I can wait for next summer, Val. God, I'm going to miss you."

Tears pricked her eyes, and so he wouldn't see her weakness, she kissed him again. Long and hot and full of the love she was scared to put into words.

His hand moved down her spine, cupped her bottom. She scooted on top of him again, her body on fire, and he rocked his hips up, moving—

Ding.

The tiny bell sound of the timer she'd set on her clock yanked Valerie out of her memories. Back to her Ohio bedroom. And the reality that faced her in her en suite bathroom.

"Well," she said, glancing down at the sketch she'd made of Nash, "Time's up. Here goes nothing."

Her knees shook as she crossed her bedroom and approached the bathroom sink. She lifted the washcloth she'd used to cover the plastic stick, as if to hide it from… what? She wasn't sure. So she wouldn't peek early?

Her hand trembled as she lifted the corner of the rag and flipped it aside. Leaned in to read the display.

Positive.

The nausea in her gut surged, and she lost what little breakfast she'd managed this morning. After wiping and rinsing her mouth, then flushing the commode, she sank to the floor with the plastic pregnancy test stick in her hand. What was she going to do? Her mother would kill her. Worse, would her mother retreat into the bottle again? She'd just gotten sober this summer at the clinic. But any little thing could push her to the brink.

A sob rose in Valerie's throat, but she choked it back. She had to be brave, had to figure out what to do next.

"Oh, Nash. I guess we weren't careful enough."

Chapter One

Twelve years later
Late October

"It is flat-out unacceptable to me that your father has access to millions of dollars and hasn't offered one penny of it to help get Jackson back!" Nash Colton raged as he paced tight circles in the kitchen of his cousin's suburban Chicago home. "It's infuriating!"

"Yeah, well," Myles Colton replied from the ladderback chair where he was watching Nash pace, "my dad was cut from the same cloth as your dad, so…you know how that is. They might not be identical twins, but Axel and Erik Colton are exactly alike in all too many ways."

Nash slammed a cabinet door too hard, his frustration boiling over.

"Hey, cool it!" Myles said. "Faith is trying to rest. We haven't gotten any sleep lately, and the stress is wearing on us both."

Nash took a deep breath and scrubbed both hands on his face as he exhaled. "Of course. I'm sorry. I know that anything I'm feeling has got to be a hundred times worse for you."

Myles, whose four-year-old son Jackson had been kidnapped a few days earlier for a ransom of thirty million dollars, balled the hand he'd been resting on the tabletop. "I'm trying to keep it together for Faith's sake. But the waiting, not knowing..."

"I'm sorry," Nash said. "My grumbling isn't helping. I just wish I could *do something*!" He scraped out a chair across from his cousin. "If I could help raise the ransom money—"

Myles angled a skeptical look at him. "You have thirty mil lying around you'd like to donate to the cause?"

"Hardly. Architects in my firm don't make that kind of dough."

"Right. So we have no ransom money. Which means for now we do what Brad Howard, our FBI contact, is telling us. They're working on a plan."

At that moment, Myles's phone sounded with an incoming call. "Speak of the devil..." He lifted the phone to his ear. "You got news?"

Nash signaled to his cousin that he was leaving so that Myles and his FBI contact could work on the plan to bring Jackson home safely and catch the cretin behind the kidnapping and extortion.

He hated not being able to help Myles. He hated even more that the people who *could* potentially do something to make a difference seemed indifferent to Jackson's kidnapping. His father, Erik Colton, and his father's fraternal twin, Axel, received a substantial stipend from the estate of their late father, Dean Colton. They lived well. Very well. But none of that wealth seemed to trickle down to their children. Not that Nash or Myles or any of the younger generation of Coltons wanted the rather tainted money. They all had their own lives and careers. They'd managed to rise above their flawed paternal relationships to become independently successful.

But even if all of his siblings and cousins pooled their resources, they wouldn't come anywhere close to the thirty million that had been demanded for Jackson's safe return. But he knew who did, and Nash found it unconscionable that Axel wouldn't donate any of his sizable wealth to save his grandson.

Nash couldn't let that rest. He dialed Axel's home. The housekeeper answered.

"He's at the racket club, having a tennis lesson as I recall," the maid said. "Is there a message?"

"No. Thanks." Nash disconnected. The racket club. He knew the hoity-toity club the housekeeper meant. "Perhaps this calls for an in-person conversation," Nash said to no one in particular as he headed outside into the late October chill to confront his uncle.

From Myles's front steps, he heard a car door close and glanced up to see who was arriving. And his heart slammed against his ribs.

VALERIE STOPPED IN her tracks, her breath catching when she spotted Nash coming out of Myles and Faith's home. Twelve years of heartache, confusion and anger roiled inside her. Flashes of memory blinked in her mind's eye like a painful slide show—holding Nash, her mother's scornful shouting, sharp abdominal cramps, laughing at Nash's corny jokes, a bittersweet goodbye kiss under the arbor, an incriminating picture. So much history. So much hurt.

Releasing the air she'd snagged in her lungs, she took a couple of slow steps forward. She'd known that eventually she'd run into Nash. Before she'd left Ohio, she weighed that particular risk against her desire to be near Myles and Faith and help the family during the crisis they faced with little Jackson missing. She'd hoped she could minimize her chances of seeing Nash by avoiding large family gatherings and spending the majority of her time at her Uncle Rick's house. Foolish thinking. Nash was woven too tightly into the fabric of the Colton family for her to not run into him.

She gathered the courage to speak to him, to show a modicum of civility and calm, even if her pulse scampered and her thoughts were in a whirlwind.

But then, tightening his mouth, he turned without speaking and marched across Myles's lawn to an Infiniti coupe parked at the curb. He climbed in and sped away, leaving her standing there. Alone. Again.

She couldn't say how long she stood there, staring down the street where Nash had long ago disappeared. And she made a decision. Enough was enough.

Earlier in the month, as she'd driven into Illinois and gotten closer to Chicago, a nervous energy had twisted tighter and tighter inside Valerie. One part of that tension, she knew, was an excitement to be returning to a place where she'd spent happy summers and found a second home with her uncle's stepfamily. She'd loved the warm and welcoming home that sat behind Yates' Yards Plant Nursery, her Uncle Rick and Aunt Vita's business. She'd loved spending hours helping in the nursery's greenhouses, among the beautiful plants and fragrant blossoms. As an only child with a part-time mother who'd let it be known she resented her daughter, Valerie had loved getting to know Vita's family and forming deep bonds of friendship and camaraderie with her Colton "cousins."

Quite simply, over the last twelve years, she'd missed

them. Missed the passion for art she'd shared with Lila, missed the playful teasing of Myles and Aaron, missed the maternal conversations she'd had with Vita and missed her Uncle Rick's dorky dad jokes and made-up excuses to get the extended family together for picnics or outdoor games. Water balloon fights on so-called "wet Wednesdays." Homemade ice cream on National Strawberry Sundae Day. Potluck picnics in his flower garden to honor Red Rose Day. Cheese hors d'oeuvres on the lawn for Moon Viewing Mondays. She smiled to herself remembering all the wonderful, silly times. Good grief, she'd missed those laughter-and-love-filled days when she'd returned to her mother's tumultuous brand of parenting.

But she'd stayed away from Illinois. Because, of all the Coltons she'd met and loved when she'd spent blissful summers in Chicago, one Colton in particular had rooted himself deep in her heart…and shattered her world.

But enough was enough.

She'd sacrificed enough—too much—because of Nash Colton. The time had come to put a few things straight with Nash and reclaim the family that meant so much to her. She didn't want to fear seeing Nash, didn't want to hide from a confrontation with him, didn't want to miss any more family events and celebrations because Nash would be there.

It was time for a reckoning.

WITH EFFORT, NASH shoved aside the image of Valerie, standing on Myles's front lawn, gaping at him with a world of pain in her eyes. He had a mission and needed to focus on his reckoning with Axel.

Nash jogged up the steps of the racket club and paused

at the glass door. Entry was allowed only if you had a membership card to scan. He growled his frustration, but within a few minutes a member in his tennis whites exited and flashed Nash a smile.

Nash nodded a return greeting and caught the door before it closed. He slipped inside and scanned the lobby, orienting himself.

"Can I help you?" a young woman behind the front desk asked.

"Maybe. I'm looking for my uncle, Axel Colton."

The woman sat up straighter, clearly recognizing the name, and she squared her shoulders. If she hadn't been starstruck at the mention of his uncle's name, Nash would have sworn her body language meant she was about to throw him out on his ear. But she flashed a bright smile and said, "Absolutely. Mr. Colton is on the tennis courts, having a lesson." She aimed a finger past the men's locker rooms. "The exit to the courts is just down there."

Nash thanked the desk attendant and made his way through the posh lobby, past a floor-to-ceiling trophy case and a juice bar decked out to look like a tropical beach stand, to the exit. He shielded his eyes from the late October sun and followed the sidewalk to the rows of tennis courts until he found the one where his uncle was flirting with a woman half his age.

Stopping behind the perimeter fence to watch for a moment, Nash observed his uncle's charade as Axel went through the awkward motions of the worst backhand Nash had ever seen. Nash scoffed. He'd played tennis before against his uncle. Axel had won by two points in the last set because of his killer backhand.

The pretty woman with Axel smiled patiently then stepped close and put her arms around his uncle to angle his hand and guide his arm through the correct motion. Axel's expression during the demonstration was pure cat-that-caught-the-canary.

Irritation spiked in Nash. Uncle Axel's grandson had been kidnapped, but he'd taken time to have a fake tennis lesson, the object of which appeared to be tricking his attractive teacher into pressing her ample bosom against Axel as often as possible.

Nash barged through the gate and onto the court without waiting to be invited, then called to the pretty tennis pro, "Did he tell you he was the Bingham Country Club five-oh champion for six years straight in the nineties?"

Both the pro and his uncle turned to face him, clearly startled.

"Nash? What are you doing here?" Axel barked.

He ignored his uncle's question and kept his attention on the blonde pro in the short black tennis skirt and tank top. "His backhand is legendary. In fact, I think he won a tournament here last spring. Or was it the year before? You can check the trophy case in the lobby if you want to see for yourself. Either way, I'm afraid you've been duped, ma'am."

The woman blinked her confusion and divided a look between Axel and Nash. "I'm sorry?"

"Now see here!" Axel huffed. "I—"

"No, he's the one who should be sorry. For wasting your time." Nash stopped a few feet from his uncle and pinned a hard stare on him. "Right, Uncle Axel?"

The older man returned a glower. He waved a dismissive hand and told the young woman, "Take a break, Tiffany. We'll finish after I get rid of my nosy nephew."

The tennis pro gathered a few loose tennis balls and sauntered off the court with a puzzled knit in her brow.

Nash continued to glare disdainfully at Axel, saying nothing as his uncle walked to the players' bench and tossed aside his racket. Axel retrieved a towel and mopped his neck and face before draping it around his neck and facing Nash with his mouth pinched in a grim line. "Well, what do you want? What was so damn important you had to interrupt my lesson?"

"You're unbelievable, old man!"

Axel raised his chin, frowning. "I beg your pardon?"

"Do you even care that Jackson hasn't been found? You're out here farting around with that poor girl, pretending you can't already swing a backhand better than anyone in your age category, while your son and his wife are going through hell!"

Axel stiffened. "I'll thank you to keep your voice down!"

Nash ignored him and shouted, "Everyone in the family is busting their ass to find your grandson or collect the ransom, except you. To you, today's just another day to screw someone over. To lie and cheat and be a selfish prick. You don't care how badly your family is hurting or worried, as long as you get your jollies tricking poor Tiffany into snuggling up next to your sorry hide!"

Axel cast a glance around the other courts, his jaw tight and his hands fisting. "You're making a scene. Do you really want the Colton name sullied again? People will talk!"

"About how you could be so callous regarding your own grandson's safety? I say let them talk! You're a selfish bastard, Uncle Axel. I know you have the money for the ransom. Why haven't you volunteered it yet?"

Axel snorted. "What? You think I have thirty million dollars to pay an extortionist? Do you think I got where

I am in life by buckling under every time someone tried to blackmail me for money?"

Aghast, Nash rocked up on the balls of his feet and down again, flexing his hands at his sides as he tried to rein in his temper. "We're talking about saving your grandson. Jackson is an innocent. He shouldn't suffer because you're too greedy to help get him back."

Axel dismissed his plea with a haughty sniff and tossed the towel aside. "What guarantee do I have that they'll even give the boy back if I did come up with the money? I can't risk losing that much cash!"

"But you *can* risk losing the life of a child? Your grandchild!" Nash gaped at Axel, appalled, outraged—and yet, tragically, not really surprised—at what he was hearing.

Axel huffed loudly, as if terribly put out by being held to account. "Look. I'm sorry that the boy is missing, but I can't be responsible for bailing out every family member that—"

"The boy?" Nash interrupted. "*The boy* has a name. Can you not even bring yourself to say *Jackson*? And he's not just missing, he was *kidnapped*. He's a four-year-old in danger!"

"Enough!" Axel stood and stepped closer to Nash, scowling, jamming his face right in Nash's. Nash was sure the older man had used this gruff and aggressive move to intimidate countless others in his life.

But Nash had a good three-inch height advantage and an equally stubborn glare to rival his uncle's. He was not impressed with the other man's posturing.

"I'm perfectly aware of the situation and the child's relationship to me," Axel growled, his breath smelling of old coffee. "You don't need to thrash me with it over and again. You've said your piece, and I've said mine. Now kindly leave the premises before I call security and have you thrown out." With that, Axel turned, picked up his racket and towel and headed off the court.

"That's it?" Nash called after his retreating uncle. "You're just going to walk away?" Nash muttered a curse under his breath, then shouted louder, to be sure Axel heard him. "You're going to be sorry you walked away, old man! One day soon, you're going to pay for turning your back on your family!"

Nash stood on the tennis court for several long seconds, seething, fighting to get his ragged breathing back under control. How could Axel be so selfish? So disinterested in the well-being of his own family?

No sooner had the rhetorical question filtered through Nash's brain than the not-so-rhetorical answer presented itself boldly and with certainty. *Because he's your father's twin brother.* Erik Colton had been a distant, cold, unsympathetic father to Nash and his younger brother, Damon. In fact, if not for his father's wife, Nicole, Nash would have grown up not knowing what a truly caring and nurturing parent was like. He'd overlooked and tolerated a lot of crappy behavior from his father and uncle in deference to Nicole and his equally kind Aunt Vita. As he often did when he thought of the more senior Colton women, he said a word of thanks to the fates that had brought the loving women and their children into his life.

With a last sigh of frustration, he stalked off the court, encountering Tiffany on his way out. She stared at him with suspicion and a bit of wide-eyed fear. Clearly, she, along with anyone else in the vicinity, had heard a good bit of his argument with Axel.

He shrugged at her. "What? Don't you have family members you want to strangle now and then?"

If possible, Tiffany's eyes grew rounder. "No. I love them all."

Nash grunted and grinned. "Well, consider yourself lucky. We can't all say the same."

He hurried up the sidewalk and through the racket club, nodding to the front desk clerk as he exited. He took a moment in his car to further calm himself before he got on the road. Driving and rage weren't a good mix. Leaning his head back, he closed his eyes and took deep breaths. He should be used to the callous and cold behavior of the Colton patriarchs by now. His father, his uncle and even his grandfather, Dean Colton, had been bastards, to hear his grandmother Carin talk. But then Carin had a chip the size of the Millennium Park Bean on her shoulder concerning Nash's grandfather and much of the rest of his family.

Focus on the positive, he could hear his adoptive mother whisper in his mind. She'd been the bright beacon in his life and his brother's when their real mother died. Nicole knew as well as anyone how screwy Erik and Axel Colton's priorities were, how distant and disappointing they were to their children. But her love and kindness, her encouragement to count their blessings rather than dwell on the broken paternal relationships had made all the difference to Nash, Damon and his cousins.

"Right," Nash said, opening his eyes and cranking his engine. "I have people who care. People I care about." People who needed his love and support. Like Myles and Faith, whose precious son had been taken. That's where he would focus his energy.

A HUM OF purpose and focused energy filled Valerie, as she drove down Lake Shore Drive along the Lake Michigan waterfront. She'd taken a circuitous route to her destination, just so she could cruise the famous, scenic highway. That, and she was stalling.

She may have made up her mind that she had to face her past once and for all, but she'd gotten cold feet halfway across town. She'd taken the detour specifically to practice what she was going to say. One more time. But even with her delaying tactic, her stomach felt like it was being turned inside out. Her hands shook harder as she got closer to the terminus address on her GPS app, and she felt as if she had frayed electric wires for nerve endings.

But no matter how scary or painful this errand was, the time had come. She'd spent too long hiding from her past, had stayed away from people she loved, respected and, frankly, needed in her life. Her own parents had been part-time and uninterested in her at best, and harshly critical and toxic at their worst. Valerie longed for the support and warmth she'd found those cherished summers as a teenager. In order to reclaim her uncle's family and reconnect with her loved ones, she had to deal with the proverbial elephant in the room. So now, when the disembodied voice of her GPS told her to make a right turn into one of the gentrified neighborhoods nestled in the city, she exhaled. And turned.

Soon she was parking in the narrow driveway of a Craftsman bungalow that stirred a bittersweet memory from the dusty corner of her mind.

"Whatcha doing?" seventeen-year-old Valerie had asked eighteen-year-old Nash when she'd found him sketching something on one of Lila's art pads.

"Oh, nothing," he'd said dismissively, trying to hide his work.

But she grabbed it, smoothed out the paper on a table and marveled at the neat, precise lines of the sketch he'd made. A house. A precise, perfectly even drawing of a house with a small floor plan in the top corner.

"This is good. Really good. Whose house is it?"

"No one's. I was just…playing around with ideas." He cast an awkward side-glance at her, and added, "I want to design houses and stuff when I get out of school. Maybe be an architect?"

She gave him her best smile. "You'd be good at that. This is really great."

He took back the paper, encouraged by her praise, then frowned. "It doesn't feel right yet. Something's missing. Maybe a dormer window? An upstairs? But that would mean reworking the first-level floor plan to include stairs."

"I know what it's missing," she said, taking back the paper and retrieving some art supplies from Lila's things. Leaning over the table, she began drawing shrubs and trees and flowers blooming in a flower bed. She added a wreath to the front door and a cat sitting on the steps. She tweaked and blended and shaded until the stark lines of his blueprint came alive with color and depth. Turning it, she said, "Ta-da! Now it's more than a house. It's a home."

Eighteen-year-old Nash's face had warmed, and he'd canted close to kiss her. "Perfect."

Now, more than twelve years later, Nash was living in a bungalow not all that different from the home they'd drawn together. The home she'd dreamed they'd one day share. Before…

She squeezed the steering wheel and sighed. Before life had taken their drawing and ripped it to shreds.

Shoving aside the memory, she climbed the steps to the front porch. After she knocked, she turned to take in the shady street. A woman walked by pushing a stroller while a toddler pedaled along behind her on a tricycle. Val's heart gave a sharp pang.

When no one answered her knock, she raised her fist to knock again, then jolted when something brushed against her leg. She glanced down to find a calico cat rubbing its cheek against her jeans at her calf. She exhaled and pressed a hand to her scuttling heart. "Cat, you scared me. Maybe give a meow to warn a girl next time?"

She reached down to scratch the calico's head, pleased with the idea that Nash owned a cat. That matched the compassion she remembered him having. She straightened as a sleek Infiniti sports coupe pulled in the driveway behind her car and parked.

She held her breath as she watched Nash unfold his tall, trim body from the low seat and scrutinize her car as he passed it.

"Hello, Nash." Valerie stepped out of the shadows of his porch.

His head came up, and his steps faltered when he spotted her. He said nothing for a beat, a hundred emotions playing over his face, as if shuffling through them, deciding which one to keep. When, at last, he spoke, his voice rasped softly from his throat. "Valerie." He approached the steps slowly, eyeing her warily. "Why—? What are you doing here?"

Chapter Two

"Wow. Earlier you walked away. Now you ask why I'm here." She gave a strained laugh. "Is that how you always greet a friend you haven't seen in years?"

He mounted the steps and narrowed his familiar emerald gaze on her. Colton green. So many of his siblings and cousins had the same mercurial green eyes. "Are we friends?" When she didn't answer right away, he added, "Seems to me friends keep in touch. Friends don't cut friends out of their life without explanation."

A shaft of pain arrowed through her heart. "Well, nothing like getting to the crux of things without polite small talk and hospitality." She lifted a corner of her mouth with a weak, tremulous smile. "What would Nicole say?"

The dark shadow that crossed his face sent a quiver to her belly. This was a bad idea. She should go.

But like the wind blowing a puffy cloud on its way, allowing the sun to shine once more, Nash's face brightened a bit, and he flashed a stilted smile. "You're right. My apologies." He moved past her and keyed open the front door. When the calico tried to run inside, he blocked it with his foot. "Nope. Go home, Kitty."

Valerie experienced a pang of disappointment. So

much for the heartwarming image she'd been drawing in her mind's eye. "She's not yours?"

"No. *He* lives two doors down." Standing back, he swept an arm grandly, motioning for Valerie to precede him.

She decided against countering his use of the male pronoun for the cat with the argument that thanks to genetics, calico cats were female. They had enough to discuss without starting with her contradicting him on something so trivial.

"Please, come in. May I get you something to drink?"

Okay. She recognized that he was being a bit patronizing now, but she understood his anger. Until she'd had her say, had a chance to try to correct the wrongs she'd done, she'd give him grace. "No, thank you."

Valerie moved into the living room and turned to face him. Nash chucked his car keys onto a small table in the foyer and marched straight to a bottle of something amber in a decorative glass decanter. He unstoppered the bottle and splashed a small amount in a glass. "Are you sure? I have beer and wine if you don't want scotch."

"No. Nothing. I don't drink."

He bobbed a nod, took a sip. "I see."

She doubted he did understand all the reasons she'd sworn never to drink alcohol, but that point was moot at the moment. Maybe someday she'd explain…

"Then maybe water? Or I think I have orange juice." He took another sip of his drink before setting it down on the wet bar.

She shook her head. "No."

"Food then?"

She sighed. "Nash."

He turned up his palms. "Just trying to be hospitable. How am I doing?"

She gave him a long, silent stare. She imagined that she could hear the tension between them like a hum from a live wire. Finally, after he'd said nothing for several seconds she whispered, "Do you want me to go?"

"I didn't ask you to come."

"I know. But I thought we should talk. I want to explain. To give you some understanding." Tears pricked her eyes as she met his hard stare, then she started for the foyer. "You're right. This was a mistake."

He crossed the room in three long strides and caught her arm. The contact sent a jolt through her. His touch affected her more profoundly than their first kiss had. Because of their convoluted history. Because of the months—no, *years*—she longed for him. Because although she'd mentally prepared herself for confronting him, she hadn't anticipated him touching her. A foolish mistake.

His grip was firm but not rough, and as soon as she stopped, raising her gaze to his, his fingers loosened. But he kept his hand on her wrist. Val knew if he cared to notice, he'd feel the quick, unsteady throb of her pulse there.

"I'm sorry. My foul mood isn't your fault. You caught me at a bad time—"

When she opened her mouth to apologize for her timing, he shook his head. "You didn't know. And you're here now." He drew in and exhaled a breath, on which she smelled the sips of scotch he'd taken. "So say what you came to say."

Steeling herself, she raised her chin. "To start with… I'm sorry. I know my silence hurt you, and…for that, I'm deeply sorry, Nash."

A shudder rolled through him, one she both saw and felt as the hand around her wrist shook slightly. His expression softened, and she saw shadows gathering in his arrestingly green eyes. But then he blinked rapidly, firmed his mouth and released her arm as he strode away from her. He sat heavily on a recliner, but his back remained stiff. She could practically see him pulling his anger and resentment around him like a shield.

She understood the tactic. She'd used her anger toward her mother, toward Nash, toward the unfairness of life as a blanket to protect herself, comfort herself in the early days of their separation. Too much had happened too quickly for her to process it all, so she'd chosen anger as her defense mechanism, to keep herself from shattering.

Clearing the tightness from her throat, she returned to the living room and settled on the edge of the couch across from Nash.

"Okay," he said, gesturing with a flick of his hand. "I'm listening."

THE DOORBELL AT Axel Colton's house chimed, and he started to yell to his housekeeper to answer it before he remembered the staff had all gone home. He was alone. If the door was to be answered, he'd have to do it himself.

He scowled and considered ignoring the summons. He wasn't expecting anyone, didn't want to talk to anyone, was in a pissy mood thanks to Mr. Holier-than-thou Nash reaming him at the club. He'd have to talk to Erik about keeping his nephew in his own lane. What he did with his money was his business and his alone.

The bell sounded again followed by an urgent knock. Axel groaned, set aside his gin and tonic and struggled out of his chair.

"What?" he said ungraciously as he yanked open the door.

His visitor glared at him. "Took you long enough."

"I wasn't expecting anyone. Is there a reason you're here? 'Cause if you plan to tear me a new one or air a bunch of grievances, I'm not interested. Especially not today."

His visitor pushed past him. "Hmph. I bet. I heard that Nash showed up at your club and caused a scene. Threatened you. So the rumors are true?"

Axel slammed the front door and faced the look of disdain and disapproval. "No comment." He was tired of his life being the subject of news reports, gossip and family discussion. The dark look shooting at him said his reply was not what his visitor wanted to hear. "And if you don't like it you can leave."

"We have business to discuss."

"No, we don't. Not tonight. I'm in no mood."

"So because your nephew pissed you off, you're going to shut yourself up in here and suck your thumb? Ignore your responsibilities and commitments to—"

"Shut up! Just shut the hell up or get out of here!"

He could feel the crackle of ice, the chill that filled the room. And he was beyond caring whom he ticked off.

"You're a selfish bastard, you know that?"

"Well, you'd know, wouldn't you?" He turned to retrieve his drink, saw a shadow shift from the corner of his eye.

And something hard and heavy cracked against his skull. Axel staggered. Stunned. Pain exploded in his head, and he slumped to the floor.

"No one talks to me like that! Not even you." His visitor turned and marched toward the door.

And the corners of his vision dimmed. Went black.

NASH WORKED TO keep his expression blank, revealing nothing of the jangling inside him. Of all days for Valerie to show up on his doorstep, why today, when he was already twisted in knots over his confrontation with Axel, worried about Jackson, grieving with Myles and Faith over their missing son? His emotions were raw, and he didn't like starting this potentially explosive conversation with Val when he was already—not vulnerable exactly, but…unprepared.

As if he could ever be ready for rehashing his history with Valerie. Some things were better left in the past. For Nash, Valerie's desertion was one of those things. He'd moved on.

Or so he'd thought, until he'd seen her standing on his porch. Until he'd looked deep into her dark brown eyes and seen real regret looking back at him. And pain.

He could deal with his own heartache and anger over her rejection, but not hers. The idea that Val had lingering hurt, that her disappearing act could have a sad or tragic story behind it…well, that wasn't something Nash thought he could deal with. The mere suggestion that Valerie had scars of her own clawed at his core. Suffocated him.

"The autumn months, after I left here that summer twelve years ago, the last time we—"

Valerie stopped, glanced away, drew a shaky breath. "That fall was the worst time in my life. And thanks to my father's remoteness and my mother's alcoholism and, at the time, undiagnosed mental illness, I'd had some pretty bad times before that."

Nash nodded slowly. "I remember talking about your mother's drinking during those summers when you'd stay with Rick and Vita. Your mother would be in rehab."

"Mmm-hmm. She did several rounds of rehab. None ever stuck."

"What is this about mental illness?"

"I'm getting there." Val tucked a wisp of her light brown hair behind her ear, exposing the delicate skin where the curve of her jaw melded with her throat—a spot he'd traced with his tongue and knew intimately. She flexed the fingers of one hand with her other one, a nervous habit that Nash remembered from their teen years. His heart gave a hard thump of recognition, of nostalgia. A part of him longed to reach for her hand and lace her fingers with his, as he had so many times when they were younger. Instead, he clenched his hands in fists and focused on her story.

"First, I need to explain why that autumn was…my worst by far." Her voice cracked, and she paused to catch her breath. "I wanted to call you, I wanted so badly to hear your voice or even just text you, but then when I heard how you'd moved on without me, I had to deal with that loss, that feeling of betrayal on top of everything else."

Nash sat taller in his chair, confused. *Betrayal? What the—?*

"At first, my mother found ways to block me from talking to you, texting or emailing even, but after I learned the whole truth, I was angry. Hurt. Resentful. And I didn't want to tell you anything. It took me months to forgive you. By then, it felt like water under the bridge, and I didn't think—"

"Whoa, whoa, whoa!" He hadn't planned to interrupt her, despite his confusion. But something deep inside him rebelled. "Forgive me? You had to forgive *me*?"

"Yes. And I did. Well, I thought I had. Forgetting is much harder, and it still hurts sometimes."

Nash scratched his cheek, giving himself time to suppress the righteous indignation that swelled in him. *Hear her out*, a voice in his heart said.

Screw that! You deserve answers! his head countered, and he followed that impulse. "And what was it you had to forgive me for?" He couldn't quell the bitterness that leaked into his tone. "Trusting you with the realities of my own screwed-up parents? Sharing with you my most private hopes for the future? *Loving* you?"

Her brow furrowed over darkening eyes, and her hands clenched in her lap. "Love?" She spat the word at him as if it tasted vile. "How can you talk of loving me when not even two months after I left town you had moved on and had a new girlfriend? One you didn't have to keep secret from your family and were all too pleased to be photographed with."

Nash couldn't decide what startled him more—her venom toward him or her preposterous claim of replacing her. "What the hell are you talking about? I didn't—"

"Don't!" She aimed a finger at him. "Don't insult me by denying it. I saw the picture of you with her. Uncle Rick confirmed that you and that girl had been dating."

He was mentally scrambling to figure out whom she was referring to and what she could have misconstrued while trying not to blow his top. She'd disappeared from his life, broken him with her silence, her lack of communication. And now she wanted to blame *him* for it? To hell with that!

"There wasn't—" He huffed. "Who? Who did Rick say I was dating?"

Val snorted. "Some Lori or Lani or Loni or—"

Click. "Lucy? Lucy Greene?"

She arched an imperious eyebrow. "So you do remember?"

He flopped back in his chair, already exhausted by the conversation, but also relieved to have figured out the source of her confusion. "I took Lucy Greene to some froufrou fall cotillion as a favor to Nicole."

"I know. I saw the pictures. You two looked quite happy together."

Nash gave a bitter laugh. "That's generally what you do in pictures. You'd rather I'd snarled and frowned in the family's photos?"

"You had your arm rather intimately around her."

"Did I? I don't recall. But it seems you studied the pictures pretty closely and read a lot into them."

"Yes, I spent a long time looking at the pictures. They were proof that you'd lied to me. Forgotten me. Betrayed me."

"It was one date! Well…plus a group thing before, so we could meet. Lucy and her mother were new in town, and she didn't have anyone to take her to the dance, so—"

"Did you sleep with her?"

Nash almost choked. "What!"

"Did you sleep with her and get her pregnant, too?"

"No! Geez, Val! I did not 'sleep with her' or 'get her pregnant.'" He mocked her assertion with his tone. "It was one dance, for God's sake!" The accusation was so absurd, spoke so poorly of her opinion of him, that he almost missed the most important word. *Too*.

A numbness crept over him, and he stared stupidly at Val with his heartbeat sounding in his ears.

She brought both of her hands to her face, first pressing them to her mouth, then rubbing her eyes as she heaved a deep sigh. "I'm sorry. That was uncalled for. I told myself I wouldn't do this. I guess I'm still more hurt than I thought. Maybe it's— Sorry." She lowered her hands and raised a beseeching gaze to him. "Can we scratch that last bit and start over. I don't want to argue. I want—" She faltered, tilting her head to the side. "Nash? What? Why are you staring at me like that?"

"Too?" The word sounded strangled, and he cleared his throat. "You said, *too.* Did I sleep with Lucy and get her pregnant…too?"

"I did?"

He nodded slowly.

The color drained from Valerie's face, and he had all the answer he needed. Turning her head away, she whispered, "Oh."

Nash leaned forward in his chair again. A surreal sense of suspended animation engulfed him.

"Val?" he breathed more than spoke.

Trembling and pale, Valerie perched on the edge of the couch like a startled bird ready to take flight. She couldn't seem to meet his gaze for long moments. Finally, she closed her eyes and said quietly, "When I went back to Ohio, after that last summer we were together… I was pregnant." Opening her eyes again, she met his stunned look. "I took a test six weeks after I got home, because I'd been feeling sick to my stomach a lot and had missed my—"

Questions assailed him from so many directions, he didn't know how to process them. He could only stare for painful seconds.

"Nash, say something," she begged while the silence stretched out.

"Why—why didn't you tell me?"

She inhaled and wiped a tear from her cheek. "I wanted to. I was going to, but my mother..."

When she hesitated, he shoved abruptly to his feet, and Val startled.

Nash stalked to the wet bar, where he'd left his scotch, and lifted the drink. He stared into the amber liquid, then slammed down the glass without drinking.

"Why didn't you tell me?"

"I was going to! But my mother found out, and she—" Valerie swiped angrily at the flood of tears that streaked down her face. "She wouldn't let me."

"Excuse me? How could she stop you? It's a simple matter to pick up the phone and call or text or—"

"She took my phone and ripped the cord of the house phone from the wall in a fit of drunken rage."

He scoffed and waved a hand. "So use a friend's phone. Write a letter. Send a damn smoke signal! I had a right to know I was a father!" A chill rolled through him as he spoke the words. A father. He was *a father*?

While that thought buzzed in his brain, Val moved toward him, pleading, explaining. "It wasn't as simple as that. My mother..." She stopped, closed her eyes and started again. "She got pregnant with me when she was eighteen. My father, Rick's brother, isn't my real father. Both my real father and her parents abandoned her when she learned she was pregnant. She was alone when I was born, and she's always hated my real father for ignoring his responsibility. When I told her I was pregnant, she flipped out. She was furious with me for getting myself in the same situation she'd been in. She said she wouldn't let me ruin my chances for a better life the way I had ruined hers." She scoffed bitterly. "That's right. My mother told me I ruined her life. Essentially blamed me for her drinking. For stealing her dreams."

"Yeah, your mom's not a nice lady. We established that years ago," Nash said impatiently. "But let's not brush over the fact that you didn't tell me *I am a father*!"

Valerie stilled, her expression chastened. Releasing a breath slowly, she lowered her eyes to her hands and whispered, "No. You're not."

Chapter Three

Nash thought, in the heat of his anger, he'd heard wrong. He took a moment to replay her words in his head. "I'm not?"

Valerie walked back to the couch and sat down again, not looking at him.

Nash pinched the bridge of his nose, trying to gather his spinning thoughts. What did her last confession mean? Had she cheated on him? Gotten rid of their baby? Had her mother forced her to give away the baby?

"I think you need to explain," he said in a low, growling tone.

Her chin tilted to a haughty angle. "I was trying to when you yelled at me."

He returned to the grouping of his couch and recliners, hovering over her. His whole body was taut, quivering with fury, shock and frustration. "Don't you think I have a right to yell and curse? I can do whatever I feel like when you come into my home and accuse me of betrayal and unfaithfulness and deception! When, now that the truth has come out, you were the one who betrayed and kept secrets, and…hell, maybe you even cheated on me. Huh?"

Her gaze snapped up to his, ablaze with indignation. "What? No! How could you think—?"

"You said you'd gotten pregnant, and now you tell me I wasn't the father. Seems to me—"

"I said you aren't *a* father, not that you weren't *the* father! There's a big difference. Don't twist my words!"

"Gah!" Nash threw up his hands, roaring his frustration as he stomped away. "This is going nowhere. Would you just *tell me* what you're trying to say? Why did you come today? What did you have to tell me after all these years that makes any difference now?"

Val's shoulders drooped. Her whole body seemed to wilt in defeat, and she shook her head. "Maybe none of it does make any difference now. But for years I've avoided coming to Chicago, avoided seeing my family and friends, the place that was once my escape, my happy place, because I was scared of running into you. I was afraid of the pain that would be revived if I saw you. I was afraid of *this* conversation." She pointed at the floor to emphasize her point. "And today I realized I couldn't continue to let my fear rule me, deprive me of things I loved, people I loved. I knew I had to face up to what happened when I was seventeen or I could never really get on with my life." She puffed out a breath and rubbed her arms. "That is why I'm here. I'm trying to put things…if not right, at least out in the open. I don't want to miss out on seeing my uncle and cousins because I'm avoiding you."

Nash shook the tension from his hands. Returned to his recliner. Calmed himself. "Right. Okay. So finish. Explain to me how it is that I'm somehow not a father, when five minutes ago you said I was."

"You're not, because I never had the baby." Her voice was thin, sad.

He narrowed his eyes on her, his mood growing dark again. "Hang on. Are you saying you—?"

"No! I wanted our baby! As scared and confused as I was about being pregnant, as much hell and grief as my mother gave me, I wanted our child! I would have done anything to save it, but I—" She choked on a sob. "I couldn't. I m-miscarried. And it almost killed me."

Nash curled his fingers into the nubby fabric of his recliner and absorbed the revelation. His chest filled with a hollow ache that swelled painfully when he met the grief and regret in Valerie's gaze.

She swiped at her nose, then ducked her head as she dug in her purse for a facial tissue. She dried her eyes and blew her nose while Nash processed everything he was learning. She'd lived a very different reality to what he'd imagined. He'd written a much harsher script in his mind about her coldly dismissing him, ghosting him, having played him for a fool.

The slow, hammering *lub-dub* in his chest, the vise-like constriction stealing his breath and the sour roil of scotch in his gut all called out his unjust conclusions. Yet another voice scratched in his brain, warning him not to forgive too easily. He had too much experience with rejection to trust that one simple conversation could mend all. Valerie's explanation may have cracked his defenses, but until he had proof of her true heart, her loyalty, her intentions, he still needed to be on guard.

She still clutched the crumpled tissue in her hand when she spoke again, her voice still strangled with tears. "I'm not being melodramatic when I say that, either—that it almost killed me. Because the heartbreak of losing the baby, on top of my mother's campaign against you and the report I'd been told that you'd moved on, was only half of the story."

Nash squeezed the armrests harder, bracing himself. "What do you mean?"

"When I miscarried, there were…complications."

Nash tensed. Opened his mouth to ask questions.

But she quickly added, "Long story short, I hemorrhaged because of problems with my post-miscarriage D and C. I lost a lot of blood and needed transfusions. I was very weak, unresponsive for a while. The nurses told me I almost died."

"I DID SOMETHING…REGRETTABLE. And I need you to help me clean up the loose ends."

Simon Wilcox was well into his six-pack when the call came in. "Meaning?"

"Not over the phone. But I'll make it worth your trouble. Never fear."

"Cash. Tonight. I don't take no credit card, you know."

He heard an exasperated sigh. "Fine. Of course. Just… get over to Axel Colton's and take care of things. If you need a fall guy, Nash Colton could use a comeuppance. And he argued with Axel publicly, so it'd be the perfect frame."

"Nash Colton, huh?" Simon rose from his recliner and stretched. "All right. I'm on it."

NASH TOOK A moment to process what Val had said. Complications with the miscarriage? He'd almost lost Valerie for good. To death. Because she'd miscarried his baby. A chill raced through Nash, and he rasped, "My God, Val."

"I don't remember much except waking up in the hospital ICU and learning I'd lost the ba-b-by—" Her voice cracked again, and when she closed her eyes, new tears leaked onto her cheeks. "I'd…l-lost my last tie to you."

Without weighing the ifs, ands or buts, Nash vaulted from the recliner, and as he dropped on the couch, he scooped her onto his lap. Pure instinct and gut-wrenching grief compelled him to wrap her in his arms, as if he could shield her from the tragedy that had already wounded her so deeply.

Without hesitation, she curled against him, draping her arms around his neck and burying her face in his shoulder. Her sobs reverberated in his soul, shook him to his core. "Geez, Val. I wish… Well, a lot of things, but mostly, I wish I'd known what you were going through."

She sniffled and pulled back. "What if you had? What difference would it have made?"

"Well…" Her question had caught him off guard, and after his initial shock, it nudged his ire again. "For one thing, I wouldn't have hated you quite so much for so long."

She made a tiny hiccupping sound and scooted away from him. "You hate me?"

"Hated. Past tense. I had to hate you at first to get over you. Then I just…tried not to think about you. But the underlying hurt was still there."

Val closed her eyes and slumped against the fat sofa cushions. "Oh, man. So much hate and hurt and wasted time. Because I let my mother get in my head."

Nash harbored no illusions about Valerie's mother, but her blame shifting still rankled. It still didn't answer why Val had so easily lost faith in him, denied him the truth about the pregnancy and miscarriage. Her radio silence for years.

"Because she showed you a picture and told you a lie about me?" His tone spoke for his skepticism.

Valerie repositioned herself to fully face him and hugged herself as she spoke, as if trying to hold herself together. "I know I own some responsibility. I can admit that. I let my mother poison me against the Coltons, including you, when I was vulnerable—physically, emotionally and mentally. She was relentless, and I was heartbroken. But I should have known better. I'm sorry."

Poison me against the Coltons. Those words stood out discordantly, like someone striking a gong during a lullaby. He slapped the sofa cushions and grunted. "Again with the Coltons. Why? Why did she hate my family so much? I know my dad and Uncle Axel are no peaches, but Nicole and Vita and my cousins… They don't deserve her disdain. Did Rick say something to your dad?"

She shook her head and flashed an ill-humored smile. "No. It had nothing to do with my dad or his brother. Although Rick marrying Axel's ex was a bitter pill for my mother to swallow."

"Then what? When we were kids you made me keep our relationship a secret because of your mom's ill will toward my family. If her hatred toward the Coltons is the root of what tore the two of us apart, I want to know why." He drilled a finger into the armrest. "Why all the animosity, Valerie?"

Valerie drew a deep breath and held it as she pushed to her feet. She paced over to the floor-to-ceiling window that looked out on his small backyard.

As he waited for her to respond, his phone rang, and he checked the screen reluctantly. He hated to interrupt this discussion when he was finally getting answers, but…

Nicole. Who'd broken her hip recently, and he'd

told her to call night or day if she needed anything. He couldn't *not* answer.

"Sorry, I need to take this." He tapped the answer icon and said, "Hi, Mom. Everything okay?"

Valerie turned and looked out his back window, giving him the illusion of privacy.

"Yes, dear. I'm fine. But I heard through the grapevine that you had a run-in at the racket club with Axel. Care to tell me what that was about?"

He rolled his eyes. "The grapevine? You mean some busybodies from the snobby club wanted juicy gossip."

"Well, your characterization is rather accurate, but my concern for you is genuine."

He didn't doubt that. Nicole had been gracious and warm to him and Damon when their real mother died of an aneurysm when he was eight years old. She'd welcomed the boys into her home and raised them as her own, despite knowing they were the product of one of Erik's affairs. Their parentage wasn't the boys' fault, and they needed maternal love and guidance, she avowed. Damon and Nash loved her with their whole hearts and would move heaven and earth for her.

"I'm fine. Just...frustrated with the a— The old curmudgeon."

"Well, I can only assume you had a good reason for exposing yourself to a dose of Axel's brand of stress and disappointment. I'm here if you need to vent. I'm well versed in his bad behavior and would be a sympathetic ear."

"I know you would. And, thanks, but no. Can I do anything for you? You need groceries picked up?"

"No, thank you, dear. I am enjoying the delights of DoorDash these days. All my favorite restaurant dishes at the tip of my cell-phone finger. I'm having the chicken piccata from my favorite Italian bistro tonight."

"Well, *buon appetito*!" His use of the Italian phrase caught Valerie's attention. After he disconnected the call, he met her querying gaze. "Don't be too impressed. That's one of about five things I can say in Italian."

"Well, then you know three more than I do. *Ciao* and *grazie* are about the extent of my repertoire."

He set his cell phone on the end table beside him, then stretched the muscles in his neck, tipping his head from one side to the other. Nicole's call had given them both a needed break from the tense conversation, and while he still wanted answers, had a hundred questions for her, he was remiss to dive back in. Yet.

Her extended silence echoed his sentiment. She turned back to his window and gazed peacefully out at his fenced backyard, where a pair of cardinals ate from his bird feeder. She rubbed her arms as if cold, though she wore a long, soft-looking sweater over leggings. The pink yarn and cut of the sweater clung to her torso and past her hips, showing off her gentle curves. She'd always been on the thin side, rather flat with a lean boyish shape as a teenager, but the years had been kind enough to soften the bony edges and round out her angular hips. No one could call her voluptuous, but gone was the rangy girl, replaced by a woman with lithe femininity and grace. Like a dancer. Or a lean cat. Or—

She turned and caught him staring, and he blinked, averting his eyes quickly.

"I knew when I came here tonight that this would be a difficult conversation. Contentious." She sighed, walked over and sat back down on the couch, raking her light brown hair from her face with her fingers. "I hadn't realized it would be so exhausting. But deep emotions are exhausting anytime, huh?" Then in a softer voice, "I should know that better than anyone."

He grunted. Nodded. He'd been worn out from his confrontation with Axel, even before he jumped into his tangled history with Valerie. "Yeah. We can put a pin in this and hash the rest out another day."

Her chin jerked up, her eyes widening. "No. That's not what I meant. Now that we're in the weeds… Well, I feel like we need to reach some understanding, finish what we've started."

He rubbed a hand on his belly and cocked an eyebrow. "All right then. But… Nicole's talk of food reminds me I haven't eaten. I'm going to need some fuel if we're going to plow ahead. Mind if I start some dinner while we finish our chat?"

She shook her head. "Not at all. Go ahead."

He stood and started for his kitchen. "Have you eaten?"

She pressed a hand to her stomach. "No. But I'm not really in the mood to eat…if that was an invitation." She chuckled awkwardly. "Way to assume too much, Val."

"That's exactly what I meant. Are you sure? I was thinking I'd mix up something easy like spaghetti and a salad." He opened his refrigerator and started pulling out ingredients. Waving a cucumber toward her, he said, "You were about to explain why your mother hated the Coltons?"

Valerie strolled to his tiny kitchen and propped a hip against the counter. "I only learned the whole truth that autumn, when she discovered I was pregnant. When she dragged out of me that the baby was yours, she went ballistic…which I can see now was a symptom of her illness." She reached for the bag of carrots he'd set on the counter and selected a paring blade from the knife block. "But more on that later."

He aimed his own knife toward the cabinet at her feet. "There should be another cutting board down there." Then, turning over the blade in his own hand, he chuckled wryly, "Are we sure the two of us should be wielding knives while we have this conversation?"

She stilled and cast him a wary look before twitching her lips in a teasing grin. "I'll promise not to stab you, if you'll swear to the same."

He arched an eyebrow, pretending to consider. "Well, okay."

She set to work scraping one of the carrots. "Anyway, all I originally knew, during those summers when I came to visit, was that she'd warned me to stay away from you. She maintained that you Coltons were bad people. That you'd hurt me. That you were liars and cheats and snobby scum, et cetera. She gave me no reasons for her beliefs. She just threatened me and told me to stay far away from you all." She snorted. "Like I could do that all summer while staying with Vita and Rick. You and your Colton cousins and half siblings were always around. And I liked you. All of you. Especially you. Obviously."

"If she hated us, why did she even let you come down for the summer?"

"Let? Heck, she begged me not to leave her to come here. But one of the few good things my dad ever did for me was planning my summers in Chicago. He intervened. Insisted I be allowed to come here. I guess, in his own way, he was protecting me, giving me a chance to experience life with a more normal family. He warned me to be careful not to mention you or other Coltons to her."

Nash angled a glance at her as he dumped diced cucumber in a bowl. "So you just accepted—"

"Let me finish. There's more. Much more."

He motioned with his hand for her to continue.

"Like I said, after Mother found out I was pregnant, she told me the whole sordid story."

Nash stiffened his spine, his gut tensing. A sordid story? Why was he not surprised? Growing up, he'd learned that Coltons attracted drama and scandal like ants to a picnic.

"When my mother was in high school, she and her family lived here in Chicago." She finished cleaning the carrot and laid it on the chopping board to cut. "It's where she met my dad and Rick. And the Coltons. Specifically Axel and Erik." With a short pause, she gave him a side-glance. "They met through the country club they all belonged to. Well, not Rick so much. He had his own friends, but my dad worked there as a bartender. He'd sneak my mom drinks, even though she was underage, because he had a crush on her."

Nash gritted his teeth and fisted his hands, bracing for the bomb, trying to be patient with her story setup.

She must have sensed his impatience, because she bobbed her head once in apology and blurted, "My mom and Erik had a romantic relationship her senior year of high school. It ended badly."

His eyes widened. "Your mother dated my father?"

Chapter Four

Nash wasn't sure what he'd expected to hear, but it certainly wasn't *that*. He swiped a hand over his mouth as he goggled at Valerie, then sputtered, "Are you about to tell me you're my half sister? 'Cause if you are—"

Val gave her head a firm shake, her eyes saying *I know, right*? "No. They dated—if you could call it that—but she wouldn't sleep with him. He was already married by then, but she was crazy about him. Obsessed, really. He knew it, and he pursued her. Tried to seduce her. It fed his ego, I guess, to have a pretty young thing so interested in him. But…she had some warped beliefs about sex, even then. For her it was a tool. A source of power and control. She thought she could string him along by teasing him without ever giving him what he wanted. But he tired of her game. She claims that's why he dumped her. When he started ignoring her, Mother was furious and came up with a twisted scheme to try to win him back." She paused in her carrot chopping and shook her head. "She thought she could make Erik jealous by coming on to one of his friends. Some guy named Jimmy that Erik brought to a country club summer social."

She hesitated and picked up a slice of carrot to nibble distractedly. Then with a sigh, she continued her tale.

"Even at that age—she was barely eighteen—she already had a problem with alcohol. The story she tells is that she slept with Jimmy out of spite, a bad decision made when she was way too drunk to think straight. But Erik didn't bat an eye when she told him, which made her even madder. Then, when Mother discovered she was pregnant, neither Jimmy nor Erik wanted anything to do with her or the baby. Her parents were horrified and kicked her out of the house, cut her off. She was alone. Devastated. All of this, of course fed her BPD."

"BPD?"

She set the knife down and faced him. Nodded. "Borderline personality disorder. We only got an official diagnosis a few years ago."

Nash's brow furrowed. "I…don't know what that is."

Val's shoulders drooped, and she pinched her nose. "It's a mental disorder that manifests in several ways. Extreme emotions, fear of abandonment, delusions and paranoia—"

"Hold up," he said. "Let's finish one topic at a time. Huh?"

"Yeah. Right? I told you it was complicated." She nibbled another carrot slice, then mused, "Where was I?"

"Your mom was pregnant and alone. I assume you were that baby?"

"I was. Remember? I 'ruined her life.'" She wiggled her fingers, making air quotes. "Me…and Erik Colton. She blames your dad for dumping her. Betraying her. Pushing her toward a desperate act with Jimmy." She scooped the sliced carrots into his bowl with the cucumber. "Of course, she also later learned that, in addition to being married, your father had *another* woman on the side, too."

Nausea swamped Nash's gut. Just when he thought his opinion of his father couldn't get any lower… "My mom."

Valerie's eyebrows lifted, her mouth slack for a moment. "Oh, my God. I hadn't put two and two together. I was shocked enough learning why she despised the Coltons—and it is *all* the Coltons she hates. When her family kicked her out, she asked Axel for help, too, thinking he'd be sympathetic. Of course, since the baby wasn't Erik's, wasn't a Colton, he turned down her request for help. Flat. Quite rudely, with plenty of name calling and bad vibes to hear her tell it."

Her comment reminded him of his own attempt to get blood from that particular turnip earlier in the afternoon, and he grumbled, "No surprise. He wouldn't part with a nickel today, even to help his own grandson."

Valerie tipped her head and frowned. "What do you mean?"

He waved a hand. "I saw Axel today. He won't help get Jackson back, but…that's a story for another time. You were saying your mom was alone, and…?"

"Right. Alone. But to hear her tell it, the Coltons, fearing she might try other means to extort money from them, started an underhanded campaign to humiliate her and paint her as unstable and emotionally unwell among their friends at the club." She rinsed her knife at the sink and gave a wry scoff. "Turns out they weren't wrong. Mother is now sober and has doctors and medication helping keep her on a more even keel, but her BPD was untreated back then. Her emotions, perceptions and reactions to people were almost certainly off the charts."

"So she was alcoholic with BPD?" Nash's mind boggled at what that must have been like for Valerie growing up.

She nodded, then added, "Substance abuse is common for people with BPD. They're desperate to numb the emotional pain and anxiety they live with every day. Her biggest fear was abandonment, so imagine how she felt after being kicked out of her parents' house, losing her financial support. All of her friends sort of went 'poof' thanks to the Coltons' influence. Your dad and Axel essentially drove her out of town, branded with a scarlet letter. Only my dad felt sorry for her, offered to marry her. They moved to Ohio together and were married by a justice of the peace three weeks before I was born. But she clung to her bitterness toward the Coltons, would never let it go."

"Fast-forward seventeen years, and she finds out her daughter is pregnant with a Colton's baby…" he said, seeing her situation in a new light.

"Exactly. She could have forgiven me almost anything but that. But knowing I went against her wishes to stay away from you, knowing I was in the same situation she'd been in, because of a Colton… She was merciless. And my dad had pretty well checked out of our lives at that point. Living on the road with his business travel more often than not. He dealt with Mother by avoiding her. So Mother was the only one home when I started miscarrying. I had to tell her the truth about the pregnancy then. I needed a doctor."

Nash blew out a slow exhale. "But you knew I wasn't like my dad. I cared about you. I'd have been there for you!"

"Maybe I know that now. But hindsight is always twenty-twenty. When I was seventeen, in the hospital after losing our baby and so much blood, her words—her venom—changed me. Hers was the only side I was hearing. She'd taken away my means to call you, and when I wrote to you, I got no letters back, despite your promise at the end of the summer that you'd keep in touch."

"No letters?" Nash frowned. He wiped his hands on a towel and pushed the bowl of salad out of his way so he could lean his hip against the counter. "I wrote a bunch of letters when nothing else I'd done got a response. I'd called, texted, emailed—"

"She took my phone away, remember? And she put these ridiculous parental controls on my computer, where she screened my email and internet use for a year, as punishment, after she learned I was pregnant. She said I'd proven I couldn't be trusted with full freedom. Clearly she was screening my mail, too. Both going in and out. I swear I wrote five or six letters before I gave up."

Nash tried to absorb the truths he was hearing. Tried to decide if he believed Valerie or if she was blaming her mother's condition to alleviate her own guilt. He rubbed a hand on his cheek as he processed it all. "So now, your mother is…?" He waved a hand, inviting her to fill in the blank.

Val pulled a face, twisted her mouth in a way that said she was searching for the right word. "Mostly stable, is the best I can say." She took a tomato from the counter and washed it. "She fought me over seeing a psychiatrist, but it's really made a huge difference. The key is keeping her on track, on her meds and attending her AA and therapy sessions. That's where her AA sponsor, Nancy, and I come in. We monitor her and encourage her." She began dicing the tomato. "It's been a long time coming, but she's been sober, in therapy and on the right meds for several years."

"But she—"

She raised a hand to forestall his arguments. "I'm not excusing her previous behavior, but it helps me to know there was a root cause for it. That she isn't a total monster."

"And your dad? Where does he fit in all this now that she's in treatment?"

"He died last spring."

He didn't detect a great deal of sadness in her tone, but still he said, "I'm sorry, Val. I didn't know."

"Thanks." She finished scraping the diced tomatoes into the bowl and rinsed her hands in the sink. "I'm afraid my relationship with my dad is another victim of my mother's illness. Because he avoided Mother, left me alone to deal with her and her hypercritical, unpredictable brand of parenting, and I resented him for years. That's something I'm dealing with in my own counseling sessions."

He rubbed his chin, relieved to hear she had a professional to talk to, to help her deal with her own stresses and issues of caring for her mother. Stepping toward her, he put a hand at her elbow and nodded. "I can relate to a distant father. Erik being who he is, and my mother having been one of his affairs, I knew him in name only for the earliest days of my life."

She turned to face him, her gaze locking on his as she listened.

"I heard her embittered stories about what a jerk Erik was, how he'd done her wrong until the day Damon and I found her dead in her bed from an aneurism."

Valerie gasped. "You found her? You never told me that. How awful for you and Damon!"

"Yeah, that was no fun. As you know, our dad wanted nothing to do with raising us. Thank God Nicole was of a different mind. I owe her so much. She's been the mother Damon and I needed ever since my mom died." He gave a gentle tug, and she came easily into his arms. Lifting a hand to her cheek, he caressed her face with his thumb. "How did you turn out so kind and good with parents like that?"

"Well, Mother had good moments. They may have been few, but…they gave me hope. And, of course, I saw true love and nurturing when I came to stay with Uncle Rick and Vita. Goodness, but I loved being with your family. Nicole and Vita and Rick gave me roots. All of the kids gave me happy memories and something to cling to when Mother had her bad days."

Nash stared into Valerie's dark eyes, and years of resentment seemed to evaporate like the morning mist after sunrise. "So much hurt and misunderstanding. Do you think we can find our way back to each other?"

She exhaled, her breath a soft tickle on his cheek. "Is that what you want?"

He leaned in and pressed a soft kiss to her lips. "Isn't it worth a try?"

"Oh, Nash, I—I don't know." She pulled gently away and pressed a hand to her mouth. Then, raking that hand through her hair, she whispered, "I've spent so many years getting over you. Moving on. It scares me to think of going back, to opening myself to that kind of pain again."

"Yeah, well, it's scary for me, too. I spent most of my life feeling cast aside by one person or another. You, my dad, even my mom when she died. As a kid, I was angry with her for leaving us." He put a hand on her shoulder and turned her to face him again. "Maybe it's stupid to think we can recapture what we had. But I've felt like we had unfinished business for years. Don't we owe it to ourselves to explore whether we had something real or if we were just two kids with raging hormones and idealistic views of love?"

"Is that what you've told yourself all these years? We just had raging hormones and idealism?" Her tone was hurt, and beneath his grasp of her shoulders, he felt her shudder.

"I had to believe something. The evidence, your disappearance and silence, gave that theory credence."

She frowned, hesitated. "If we did rekindle our relationship, what—what would I tell my mother?"

He jerked back as if slapped. "What?" A bitter laugh escaped his throat. "Seriously? After she tore us apart once, do you really care what she thinks?"

Her shoulders squared, and obvious affront swept over her face. "No, of course not. But she's fought hard to get her life on track. She has a job and her days now bear at least a semblance of normalcy after so many years. I have to worry about what hearing I was in a relationship again with you, a Colton, might do to the fragile balance of her mental state."

"So…what? Because your mother might not be able to handle the idea of you with me, you won't even consider the possibility?"

She threw up her hands and shook her head. "I don't know! I haven't thought it through. I never imagined when I came here today that we'd be talking about a reconciliation. I simply thought it was time that you knew the truth and that I exorcized the ghosts that had kept me from the family I love and need in my life."

Nash scrubbed a hand over his face, paced across his kitchen floor and back to her. If he'd learned one thing in his life, it was not to let opportunity pass you by. Life didn't hand you anything. He'd had to work for every bit of love, success and happiness he had today. This house, his education, his job with the architectural firm downtown. If he wanted Valerie, he couldn't let her walk away without a fight.

"Well, while you debate whether our love is worth a chance, consider this…" With a long step toward her, he drew her close and captured her lips with his own.

Chapter Five

Valerie stiffened, stunned by Nash's bold move. Adrenaline pumped through her, spiking her heart rate. But her surprise passed quickly as pleasure swept through her. Her fight-or-flight instinct yielded to a focused attention on the pressure of his mouth on hers, the way his lips commanded compliance, molded to hers, wooed her to respond.

Her body relaxed, and she sank against him, not analyzing the wisdom of what was happening, only following the lead of her desire. She looped her arms around his neck and feathered her fingers through the short blond hair lying against his neck. His touch and his lips were familiar and welcome to her starving soul. She'd been reluctant to date in the years since her miscarriage. Not because she feared getting pregnant again, but because the whole experience of losing the baby, losing Nash and living through her mother's bitterness and scorn had scarred her.

Was she crazy to even consider reigniting the passion and emotions she'd locked away for Nash? Surely doing something so foolish would only open wounds best left scabbed.

"You taste just the way I remember," Nash muttered

as he trailed kisses along her neck. "Like berries and summer sun and a hint of cinnamon."

She canted back and flashed an impish smile. "And you taste like trouble."

He grunted fake indignation.

"Pure temptation and forbidden pleasure. With a hint of scotch."

He wiggled his eyebrows devilishly, and using a deep, mysterious voice, said, "'"Come into my parlor," said the spider to the fly...'"

She pulled a face and shuddered. "Ooo. You'll get nowhere fast with me talking about spiders."

He chuckled. "Oh, right. I remember having to peel you off the ceiling because of a harmless daddy long-legs once."

She arched an eyebrow. "You're still talking about spiders."

"How about...?" He leaned in and took her mouth with his again. "Better?"

"Much." She reciprocated, angling her lips to deepen the kiss and pressing her body more fully along his.

Heat sluiced through her. Sheer lust pulsed to life in her blood, as he stroked his hand down her spine to cup her bottom. He drew her hips closer to his, and she felt his shiver of pleasure as her body found his groin.

His hands hooked behind her legs, and he lifted her, carried her to sit on the counter as he leaned her back and nipped the tendons of her throat. "I want you, Val. I never stopped wanting you."

The husky growl matched the fervor of his searching hands, his hungry lips and his straining muscles. When doubts nudged her brain, she shut them down, allowing a sweet, muzzy oblivion to fill her head as she surrendered to the lead of her heart, the pleasure of his lips guiding hers in an erotic dance.

"Not here. Not like this," she rasped, and he raised his head to meet her gaze with bright eyes. "Take me to bed, Nash. We've never made love in a real bed."

In a back seat, behind Nicole's bushes, in a storage closet and on a blanket under the stars, yes. But never on a bed. His eyes blazed as if he, too, was remembering their youthful liaisons. The reckless passion, hurried joining and awkward fumbling. Rarely did they have time to savor, to cuddle, to explore.

He swallowed hard and scooped her into his arms. "One bed coming up."

THE LAST RAYS of the day's sunlight had been peeking through the blinds when they'd tumbled onto his bed some time ago, but now his room was dark. He angled his head, looking for the spot his phone had ended up as they'd stripped and clothes had been tossed aside without care. He didn't see his pants from where he was lying with Valerie tucked close against him, dozing. Naked. Sated. At least he'd slaked his need with the frantic coupling, followed by long, patient lovemaking that had ended with them napping in each other's embrace.

After several minutes of listening to the soft soughing of her breath, he wiggled out from under her carefully, trying not to disturb her.

"Nash?"

"Oops. Sorry to wake you."

"What time is it?"

"That's what I was just gonna check." He snapped on the bedside lamp, and she groaned and threw her arm over her eyes.

"Do you really need that?"

He found his pants but not his phone. Then he remembered putting it on the coffee table after talking to Nicole…

"Hmm. Phone's in the living room so…still no idea what time it is." He reached for the lamp again, but paused when he saw the curve of her breast at the top edge of the sheet. Without dousing the light, he stretched out next to her and tugged the sheet.

She gasped, lowering her arm to grab the sheet. "Nash! What—?"

"I wanted to look at you. In the light. You're beautiful, you know."

"I—" She clutched the sheet, hesitating, clearly dubious.

"Shy now, huh?" He grinned and, swinging a leg over her hips to straddle her, he slipped his fingers under her arms with a teasing nip.

She yelped and squirmed, laughing. "Nash!"

"Shy and still ticklish. My, my, my…" His tone was playful, as was the narrow-eyed warning look she shot him.

"Nash, so help me if you—"

He tickled her again, and she squealed, kicking her legs and slapping at his hands half-heartedly as she giggled. "Stop! That tickles!"

"That's the point, love." He ducked his head to kiss her, then went for another tickle. The bubbly sound of her laughter tripped down his spine. Filled his soul. He much preferred the effervescent joy to the anger and tears they'd shared earlier that evening. But that was the way his relationship had always been with Val. She awoke in him the full spectrum of emotions, made him feel things he'd worked his whole life to lock away. Which was why she could be dangerous to him, to the carefully ordered life he'd built where only a select few were allowed close to him. Val had been one of them. And he'd gotten burned. So why was he even considering letting her back in?

A loud rumbly gurgle interrupted his thoughts, and he blinked at Val. "Was that your stomach?"

She winced and pulled a sheepish grin. "Not too subtle, huh?"

"Well, we never did get around to eating, and we burned quite a few calories earlier." He climbed off the bed, unembarrassed by his nudity. "I'm peckish myself, and I did promise you dinner, so…"

Valerie sat up, raking her hair back from her face as a frown twisted her mouth. "Thanks, but I should probably head back to Uncle Rick's. He and Vita will worry if I'm very late."

Nash found his pants, and after putting on clean briefs from his drawer, he started dressing. "So text them. Tell them you're having a late dinner with a friend." He poked his arms through his sleeves, then arched an eyebrow. "In fact, tell them you're spending the night."

She paused with only one bra strap up, her face incredulous. "Spend the night?"

He dropped on the bed beside her and cupped the base of her skull with his hand. "Why not? Don't you want to stay? We could make love all night, and I'll even call in sick to work tomorrow if you want. I just got you back, Val. I'm not ready to let you go so soon."

"I don't know. Nash—"

He cut her off with a blazing kiss, pulling no punches

to remind her of the heat and passion that could be theirs if she stayed.

When he broke the kiss, she was breathless and touched her fingers to her mouth. She slanted him a glance. "Feed me first, and we'll play the rest by ear."

He smacked another kiss on her lips, not bothering to hide his cocky grin. "Good enough."

THE NEXT MORNING, in the soft golden light from his window, Nash studied Valerie while she slept, cataloging all the changes the last twelve years had made to her face. Her cheeks were still high and round, hinting at her familiar youthful appearance, but the rest of her face was slimmer, more womanly. He ran a fingertip down her narrow nose, and her dark eyes blinked open.

"Hi," he whispered huskily, overcome with a tangled sense of tenderness and flare of lust. Valerie had always been a blend of soft and sensual to him. Innocence and seduction. So full of contradictions. Mysteries. Magnetism.

Her smile was slow and sleepy. "Good morn—"

A yawn swallowed her words, and he chuckled. "Same to you."

"What time is it?" she asked, turning her head to squint at the room with her elfin nose adorably wrinkled. "I'm blind as a bat until I get my contacts in."

"Early still. No need to rush." He eased closer and tugged her into his arms. With a smirk she couldn't see from her position, he said flatly, "Chocolate is disgusting. People who like chocolate are idiots."

Predictably, he felt her stiffen. "What! Are you kidding me? Chocolate is the best! Where did that even come from?"

"Well, it's just that for all our arguing last night, I had a rather wonderful time making up. So I thought I'd pick a fight now so maybe we could—" he gave her a squeeze and kissed her forehead "—make up again?"

He felt as much as heard the vibration of her laughter against his chest. "And what if I said I agreed that chocolate was nasty?"

He angled away from her, then, mimicking her, said, "What! Are you kidding me? Chocolate is the best!"

She grinned and shook her head at him. "Goofball. As I recall, our post-dinner, completely amicable entertainment was pretty noteworthy, too."

"How about this morning we skip the fighting and get right to the main event?"

"I'd like that." Curving her hand behind his head, she drew him down to her and kissed him. Deeply. He rolled with her, pulling her on top of him, and stroked both of his hands down her bare back to cup her bottom. Heat coiled in his blood and sparked in his veins.

But Valerie ended the kiss abruptly, and her face creased with concern. "Nash, at the risk of starting a real disagreement…"

"Uh-oh."

She slid off him to lie on her side, her head propped on her hand. "There is one thing we need settled."

He made a low growling sound in his throat. "Okay, what?"

"The thing is… I was serious when I said we can't tell anyone about this. About what happened last night. About us."

His stomach swooped, and tension filled his muscles in an instant. "Oh, my God! It's twelve years ago again!" He smacked a hand on the mattress and frowned at her.

"What gives, Val? We're not kids anymore. Why the hell do we have to sneak around this time?"

"Because my mother is—"

"For crying out loud, Val!" He sat up quickly, taking the sheets with him and leaving her to tug the quilt up around her naked breasts. "You're twenty-nine years old! You do not have to answer to your mother or cower from fear of her reprisal anymore."

Giving the sheets a sharp, firm tug, she narrowed a glare on him. "Will you let me finish?"

Nash flexed his fingers and blew out a breath. "Sorry. Go ahead."

"Mother is fragile. I explained that to you last night. In recent months, she'd finally been making progress, taking her medicines, seeing a counselor regularly, attending AA. Then, since Dad's death this spring, she's been on shaky ground. Losing him shook her more than I'd have imagined."

"Okay, so we don't tell your mother. It's not like I had planned to call her up and say, 'Hey, Mrs. Yates, it's that Colton guy you detest. Guess what? I slept with your daughter!'" He tried to keep the exasperation out of his tone, but her expression said he'd failed.

"If your family finds out or if Uncle Rick finds out… *Arrgh...*" She put her forehead against her knees for a moment before looking up at him again. "Word will reach her. I don't know how or who or any of that, but my gut is telling me, she'll find out."

Nash drew a slow breath and swung his legs off the side of the bed. Reining in his composure, he said calmly, "If we decide that this is the beginning of something we want to pursue long-term, she's going to eventually find out, Val. Or were you planning to keep us a secret forever?"

She covered her face with both hands. "Oh, God! I don't know. I don't have a plan. I, for sure, hadn't planned to fall into bed with you last night. Our sleeping together changes everything! It's such a mess."

A prickly sense of defensiveness crawled over his skin. "Are you saying you think it was a mistake? Are these morning-after regrets?"

She dropped her hands and sat up. "No! I don't regret anything."

He remained still, a flat stare pinned on her, and with a pleading look in her eyes, she crawled over to him.

"Nash, I swear to you—" She straddled his lap, the bedcovers falling away so that her nakedness pressed against his. Looping her arms around his neck, she leaned her forehead against his. Her tone was soft and seductive as she whispered, "I regret nothing about last night. Clearly we still have an incredible chemistry together." She punctuated her assertion with a kiss.

His body reacted with the expected rush of blood to his groin, and a crackling energy in his veins. He ran fingers up her spine and savored her breathy sigh as she wiggled closer. "I loved everything about last night, Nash." She kissed him again, then levered back to meet his gaze. "But I'm just not ready to share it with the world yet. Is that so wrong?"

He traced her cheekbone with his thumb and sighed. "Not wrong, just…frustrating. I remember how it was when we were teenagers. How I felt like a thief or something, skulking around to find ways to be alone with you, lying to my family…"

"I'm sorry, Nash. I know it's not a great solution but

I need time to…process. Figure out what to do. What I want. Where we are."

He clenched his teeth, already hating the arrangement. He wanted to talk to Damon or Nicole about what had transpired last night, simply because they knew better than anyone else what he'd gone through after Val left last time. They knew how hard he'd worked to rebuild his life, and he wanted an outside perspective on this strange twist his life had taken. Valerie. Not just back in his life, but in his bed. The chance of a new future before them. And yet, so much painful history still between them.

Sliding his hand to cradle her chin, he nudged her closer, leaned in for a gentle kiss. "All right. I promise."

Her relieved smile broke his heart, but he quashed the rise of pain and pulled her back down on the bed with him, deepening the kiss. When she shivered, he pulled the covers around them, creating a warm nest where they cuddled together, kissing, touching, connecting…

Until the jangling tones of his cell phone, which he'd retrieved from the coffee table after their dinner, broke the quiet of his bedroom.

"Don't answer it," she whispered, clearly as desperate as he was to shut out the rest of the world for a few more minutes, prolong this moment together as long as possible.

Nash huffed a sigh. "I have to. Jackson is still missing, and I promised—"

He moved away from her embrace regretfully, rolling toward his nightstand to check his caller ID, willing to talk to a select few people at the moment, but knowing certain family matters did need his attention. Eventually.

"Myles," he told Val as he touched the screen to

answer the call. And only because his nephew hadn't been found.

"Tell me you have good news," he said by way of greeting.

"I have very good news."

Nash sat upright, his pulse accelerating. He could hear the cheer and relief in his cousin's tone. "Really? What happened? Did you find Jackson?"

Now Val sat up, clutching the sheet to her chest. She watched him with wide, hopeful eyes. *What?* she mouthed.

"Yes, we have Jackson back. Safe. Unharmed." Myles's voice cracked with emotion, and he paused to clear his throat.

"Oh, thank God!" Nash exhaled, feeling as though he'd been holding his breath for weeks, and in place of the air, joy and relief poured in.

"I know it's early, but I knew you'd want to know," Myles said.

"Hell, yeah, I did. I do. I—"

Valerie tugged on his arm, and whispered, "What? What?"

"Jackson's home and safe," he relayed to Val.

"Who are you talking to, man?" Myles asked.

Nash stilled. Scrunched his face in a silent *oops*!

"Uh, no one. Just…saying the good news again out loud 'cause it's just… Whew. I'm so glad. I'm— Did they catch the guy who took him? Did you pay the ransom?"

Was it possible Axel had come around after their acrimonious altercation on the tennis court yesterday and come up with the money? Was that just yesterday?

"No, the guy wasn't caught. Look, Vita wanted us to bring Jackson over there for a while. If you want to join us, I think some of the rest of the family is going to be there, too. We'll update everyone at the same time."

Nash glanced at Val again, knowing they had some unfinished business of their own to discuss. But that discussion would keep. For now. A bridge had been built and as long as no bombshells were dropped to destroy it, they'd made a first big step toward reconciliation. "We'll be there."

"We?"

Nash grimaced again and rolled his eyes. "That, um… was a royal we. *I'll* be there."

Myles half grunted, half laughed. "Whatever. We'll see Your Highness in a few."

Nash disconnected the call and groaned. "I'm not going to live that down anytime soon."

Valerie laughed and kissed his cheek before tossing back the covers and strolling naked across the room to his en suite bathroom. "Thanks for the discretion. For now, do you want to share a shower before we head out?"

Then her phone jangled, as well.

Chapter Six

Despite taking separate cars and using different routes to get to Vita and Rick's home in Evanston, Nash and Valerie arrived at the Yateses' house at the same time.

"So much for our ruse to keep our secret," he murmured, as they walked up the pansy-lined sidewalk to the front steps of the two-story home.

Even with the cool autumn well entrenched, the landscaping around the Yateses' home boasted color and thriving seasonal plants and decor. The abundance of fresh foliage, bright blooms and fragrant blossoms was one of the things Val loved most about her uncle's home. Being surrounded by the beauty of nature, of things growing and scenting the air, inspired and buoyed her spirits even on the most difficult days. Her Aunt Vita kept fresh flowers in every room of their home and replaced fading blooms frequently. Currently, pots of chrysanthemums in shades of rust, crimson and yellow featured prominently in the house, while snapdragon, calendula and pansies populated the family flower beds, as well as Yates' Yards, their plant nursery.

Valerie inhaled the crisp scent of autumn leaves and damp earth as she climbed the steps, invigorated by the clean scents, the morning sunshine…and the sweet ache in her muscles from a night—and morning—of lovemaking. She smiled and sighed happily. Certainly her good mood was boosted by the safe return of little Jackson, but having made positive progress with Nash, having finally unburdened her weighty secret to him, left her feeling infinitely freer, lighter, more upbeat than she had in years.

"Easy, love," Nash said with a droll grin. "I'm glad you are happy and all that, but if you look too pleased with yourself and well-sated, you might raise suspicion."

"Are you saying my smile is so unusual as to be suspect?" She arched an eyebrow and sent him a mock scowl as she reached for the brass doorknob.

"Just sayin'. You're the one who wants to keep our relationship a secret."

The knob in her hand slipped away as someone inside opened the door.

"Oh, a secret! I love a juicy secret. Tell me! What'd I miss?" Lila said as she pulled the door wide.

"Nothing," Val said, with a wave of her hand. "The real question is—" she paused to inhale deeply "—what is that heavenly aroma?"

Lila gave Nash a chaste cheek kiss in greeting and guided them into the front room, where the family was gathering. "Nicole has been baking. Cinnamon scones, chocolate muffins, pumpkin bread. That on top of her breakfast quiche and sausage balls."

Nash furrowed his brow. "But her hip—"

"Is healing just fine, dear," Nicole said from the wingback chair where she was sitting with a walker beside her. "I'm not an invalid, and I need something to keep me busy until the doctor releases me to regular activities again."

Nash moved to greet the woman who'd lovingly and

selflessly stepped in and assumed the role as his mom when his own mother died. "And you're not overdoing it?"

"Using bones helps them heal. That's what my new PT guy says." Nicole reached for Nash's hand and squeezed it. "But thank you for your concern. Besides, I can do most of my cooking sitting down if I gather the ingredients first."

"Lucky for us," Valerie said, bending to give Nicole a gentle hug. "I'm starving, and I haven't forgotten how good your scones are."

"Hey, hey! If it's not *King* Nash, master of the royal we," Myles teased as he entered from the kitchen. Jackson was in his arms, a half-eaten muffin in the four-year-old's hand and on his face.

"King Nash," Jackson repeated, giggling.

Ignoring his cousin's playful jibe, Nash clapped his hands once and opened his arms. "Hey, there's my favorite nephew! You have a hug for me?"

Jackson wiggled free of his father's grasp and trotted across the floor. Nash squatted, wrapped Jackson in a firm embrace, then lifted the boy from the floor as he pretended to steal a bite of the muffin.

The little boy shrieked a laugh and held the muffin high. No one said a word about the large crumbs falling to the floor. What did crumbs matter when they could have lost Jackson for good?

When the doorbell rang, Myles peeled away from the group to answer the door and returned with Nash's fraternal twin, Damon, a dark-haired woman and a little girl with wide brown eyes. When Damon spotted Valerie, he made a beeline toward her. "The prodigal daughter returns! I can't remember the last time I saw you, Val."

"Um, Myles and Faith's wedding."

Damon blinked. "That long ago? Where have you been hiding?"

"Ohio. I, um..." Valerie fumbled but was spared further explanation of her years' absence when the woman with Damon moved closer, and Damon wrapped an arm around her waist.

"Hey, you haven't met Ruby and Maya, the new women in my life."

"Ruby Duarte." Damon's girlfriend offered her hand and a beautiful smile.

Val greeted her and looked to the little girl, who crowded close. "And that must mean you are Maya. Am I right?"

The child smiled shyly and clung to her mother's legs.

"Maya is—" Damon began, just as Nash appeared, crouching in front of Maya.

"Hi, Maya. How are you?" he said and signed at the same time.

The girl's face brightened, and in a flurry of hand motions, she signed something in return.

A bittersweet twang plucked Valerie's heart. Nash was good with kids. He didn't have the awkward falseness that some inexperienced adults had.

He would make a great father someday. And that thought inevitably reminded her of her reasons for having avoided him and this family for so long. The bittersweet ache sharpened, and Val had to shove aside the hurt to keep her expression from revealing too much.

Nash glanced up at Ruby. "Oops. I'm afraid 'Hi. How are you?' is as much as I've learned so far."

"She said she's fine and asked if you wanted to play

hide-and-seek," Ruby said, ruffling her daughter's hair. "I appreciate your effort to learn to communicate with her."

Nash pulled a face. "What? Of course, I'm learning to sign! Would I miss the chance to chat with this little angel? I think not."

Ruby smiled her thanks, then, signing and speaking to Maya, she said, "Let's say hello to Jackson and maybe he'll play with you?"

Valerie dropped to a squat before Maya could sidle away, signing as she said, "After I talk to the adults for a moment, I'll play with you."

Maya looked startled, then glanced at her mother and smiled at Valerie as she nodded.

"There are lots of good things to eat in the kitchen. Are you hungry?" Val said and signed.

The girl's face brightened further, and she nodded again.

When Valerie glanced up at the adults, Ruby's face reflected a pleasant surprise, while Damon and Nash exchanged stunned looks.

"Did you know Val could sign?" Damon asked Nash.

Nash arched an eyebrow. "No. But she's been full of surprises lately."

Valerie shot Nash daggers with her eyes, warning him not to risk exposing any of the intimate secrets they'd shared.

"Has she?" Damon asked.

"Case in point," Nash said. "She's here." He spread his hands. "That's surprise enough, but sign language?" He shifted his attention to Val. "When did you learn sign language?"

"In college. A girl on my hall in the dorm was hearing-impaired. She taught me enough to have basic conversations." Valerie pushed to her feet, smirking. "And curse."

The men guffawed.

Ruby scowled playfully. "Please don't teach bad words to my daughter!" She hitched her thumb toward Nash and his brother. "Or these bozos."

Val winked. "Deal."

"Damon, you bring those lovely ladies over here, dear!" Nicole called, and Damon ushered Ruby and Maya over to greet her.

"Don't worry," Nash said, leaning in close to Valerie's ear. "I promised to keep our relationship on the down low, and I will. No dirty looks needed."

"Hmm." Valerie scanned the room and whispered, "Seems to me if we don't want to raise flags, we shouldn't be hovering with each other all morning."

"True enough." He squared his shoulders and shoved his hands in his pockets as he watched Damon kiss Nicole's cheek. "But that's not a strategy for the long term, so we still need to talk."

Long term. Valerie's breath snagged. Myles's call, before they'd even gotten out of bed this morning, had postponed discussions on that important question. Was there a long term for her and Nash? Was that what she wanted? She didn't know. What she *did* know was that now wasn't the time for such a conversation. "Later. Right now, I'm going to find Uncle Rick for a moment. Apparently he didn't get my text last night that I was staying with a friend. He left a message on my voice mail asking if I was all right. I need to be seen and reassure him I'm fine and not stranded in a ditch somewhere."

"What are you going to tell him?"

"As close to the truth as I can without giving us away.

Last night's missing text could still show up, so I'll stick to the vague line that I was visiting an old friend and was invited to spend the night. Hopefully that's enough to serve my purposes. He doesn't pry or need specifics. Just reassurances I'm safe."

"Right. Well, good luck with that."

Was it her imagination or did his tone darken sarcastically just then? She perceived a slight tensing of his shoulders, a tightening in his jaw.

"Anyway," he added. "Rick's over there with Lila. If you'll excuse me, Myles is motioning for me to come over."

Valerie watched Nash walk away, a strange niggling telling her something had shifted in his mood just then. But why? Although she didn't have any illusions that everything that had transpired over the last twelve years had miraculously been resolved in one conversation yesterday, she'd thought their lovemaking had put them on the right path toward at least a truce. Maybe even reconciliation.

She braced a hand against the wall when the reality of a future with Nash hit her, full throttle. After all the heartache, loneliness and loss, she'd believed that dream was dead.

Whispers of that old pain stirred in her heart. She could never survive losing Nash a second time. She'd have to proceed with caution.

"Val, are you all right?"

Startled from her musings, she glanced up to find Rick studying her with a knit in his brow. "Huh? Oh, um…yeah." She straightened and forced a smile to her face. "I was just…realizing I hadn't had any breakfast, so I think I'll get a bite from the kitchen. But I wanted to talk to you, anyway, so…good timing on your part. Can I get you a plate?"

"I'll go with you." Rick swept his hand toward the kitchen then placed his hand on her upper back as they weaved their way toward the kitchen. "Vita wanted me to take some goodies out to our new hire, Sara, in the nursery. She's watching the register while we celebrate Jackson's return, but I don't want to take advantage of her helpful nature. We didn't hire her to mind the store." He broke his stride and looked at her. "Which reminds me. Would you be interested in sharing your artistic talents to design an advertisement about our holiday plants? Our poinsettias, evergreen wreaths, amaryllises and Christmas cacti will arrive early next week, and Sara is planning a big advertising splash."

Valerie blinked her surprise. In truth, having something productive to do would be a welcome distraction from the unresolved issues with Nash. She liked Sara and the notion of working with her appealed to Val. "Oh, uh…sure. And I wouldn't be stepping on Sara's toes to do the graphic art?"

"Goodness, no. In fact, when she heard of your artistic talent, she suggested we ask for your help. We'll pay you, of course." Rick chuckled and held open the swinging door to the kitchen for her. "I wouldn't presume to ask you to work for free."

Before Valerie could respond, a disturbance behind them, in the corner of the living room, snagged their attention. Then Nash's voice rose over the others, full of shock and tension.

"What! How?"

Rick stilled. "Oh, that doesn't sound good."

NASH GAPED AT Myles in disbelief. "Did you say *dead*?"

Damon and Ruby squeezed in closer, their eyes wide with concern.

"Who's dead? What happened?" Damon asked.

"My father," Myles said grimly.

"Axel's dead? But how? I just saw him—" Nash began, and Myles, his face reflecting shock and strain, raised a hand to quiet him.

A murmur had risen around them, and more family gathered close as someone asked, "Who? What's going on?"

"Everyone, listen up! Can I have the floor, please?" Myles said with the resonance, volume and authority of a lawyer about to make an impassioned closing argument to the court. He cleared his throat and held up his cell phone as if it were exhibit A. "I just had a call from Dad's housekeeper."

"From his housekeeper? Why in the world is she calling you?" Faith asked, making her way closer to her husband.

Again, Myles raised his hand, silently asking for the chance to explain.

"When my father's housekeeper arrived at work today, she found him on the floor of the den. Dead."

Gasps and low mumbles of shock filtered through the room.

"Axel is dead?" Vita asked, her face pale. Rick hurried to his wife's side and wrapped a supporting arm around her.

Myles sent his mother a pained look. "Yes. I don't know much more at this point, but…" He looked at Faith. "I think we should go home. There will be arrangements to be made." He swiped a hand over his face as he grimaced. "God, I'll have to deal with Carin and Erik."

Myles's conflicting emotions played across his face.

Mention of his own father resonated inside Nash, and he considered how tangled his feelings toward Erik were, how complicated and contaminated his relationship with his father was. Myles had to be feeling a bit of the same confusion and mixed emotions. Axel had been an equally poor and distant father to Myles and Lila. Nash was reminded again how Vita and Nicole had been the source of strength, affection and cohesion that kept him, his half siblings and cousins anchored, bound them with love.

Damon moved up beside Nash. "Draw straws to see who calls Dad?"

Nash shook his head. "Nah. I'll do it."

He cut a glance across the room to Valerie. As if she felt his stare, she tore her attention away from Vita and met his gaze. Like the moment he'd seen her on his front porch yesterday, tension closed around his throat. Maybe it was the high emotion of the morning, but a wave of something troubling and foreboding washed through him.

Twelve years ago, she'd assumed the worst about him based on circumstantial evidence from her mother. She'd denied him the right to know about her pregnancy. She'd shut him out. And although she'd explained her side of events, the fact remained that, twelve years ago, she'd dismissed his needs, his feelings and his rights in order to protect herself. She'd easily bought into a lie that allowed her to justify her actions. She'd been hurting, yes. But she'd also not given him a chance to defend himself, to speak the truth, to give her the love and support he'd wanted to give her.

And now? Could he trust her all these years later, after

all the water under the bridge? She still wanted him to keep their relationship a secret. She needed time to "figure some things out." What was there to decide? Did she care about him and believe in him or didn't she?

Acid climbed Nash's throat as his irritation and resentment grew. He'd spent too many years waiting and hoping for his father's love and attention to repeat those mistakes with Valerie. Was it too much to ask for Valerie's unconditional love and faith? He refused to settle for anything less.

She broke eye contact first, turning back to Vita with worry denting her brow.

Nash sighed and pulled out his phone. Enough stalling. He stepped out of the crowded living room to a quiet bedroom down the hall. His father answered with a brusque "What?"

"It's Nash, Dad."

"I know that. I have caller ID. What do you want?"

So much for small talk or a warm greeting. But then, experience had taught him not to expect much from his dad. "You've heard about Uncle Axel, I guess?"

"Of course, I have. Mother called an hour ago with the news. I'm surprised you've heard, though."

Nash rubbed the back of his neck with his free hand. "Damon and I were with Myles and the family when he got the call from the police just now."

"And?"

Nash blinked. And what? "And…so I…thought I'd see if there was anything I could do for you?"

"No. I'm on the way to the hospital now to give a formal identification, then the body will be turned over to the funeral home." Nash heard no real emotion in his father's tone. He might be feeling some grief over losing his brother but was burying it until the unpleasant business at the hospital was finished. Or he could be in shock, the sadness yet to hit home. Or his dad might be more of a distant, unfeeling bastard than Nash had thought.

He sighed. "Want me to come? I could meet you at the hosp—"

"Hell no. The last thing I need is people clamoring around me and getting in the way."

His father's curt response silenced him for a moment, and a familiar river of hurt and rejection spiraled through him. "All right, then. If you change your mind—"

"I won't. The best thing you can do for me is to keep the interfering hordes away."

Nash bit the inside of his cheek to stem his retort criticizing Erik's characterization of the family—especially Axel's children—being a liability to him. They had as much right as anyone to be part of making arrangements for their father's internment. And his estate.

A jolt shot through Nash. "Now that Axel's gone, if Grandmother wins her lawsuit against Dean Colton's estate, you become sole heir to half of the Colton fortune," he mused aloud.

But the line was dead. Of course, his father had hung up on him as soon as he'd delivered his interfering horde dictate. The almighty Colton had said his piece, no further conversation needed. Click. No goodbye needed.

Nash swiped his phone screen to close the phone app while mulling the ramifications of Axel's death. What did it say for his relationship with his father that he could even harbor the notion Erik might be involved with his brother's death? Axel could have had a heart attack or stroke or—

"Need a drink?" Damon said with a wry grin and a

steaming mug extended toward Nash. "It's just coffee, but if you want I can ask Rick for a shot of something stronger to put in it."

Silently, brow furrowed, Nash took the mug and sipped.

"Wow. Did the call with our old man really go that badly?" Damon asked, cocking his head to the side.

Nash waved a dismissive hand. "About as expected. Curt, impatient, he didn't want our *interference*."

"Right. Well, I think Ruby and I are going to take off. Maya's going to need a nap soon, and she's smart enough to pick up on the tension around her without knowing what's happening. That scares her."

"Yeah," Nash replied distractedly. "Damon, do you realize that Axel's death threw a rather sizable wrench in the lawsuit Carin was pushing regarding Dean Colton's will? With Axel gone, Dad becomes the sole heir, to the tune of thirty million dollars."

Damon's body stilled, but Nash could almost see his brother's law enforcement instincts kicking into high gear, the wheels in his brain turning.

After a moment where no words, but plenty of understanding, passed between the brothers, Nash spoke the troubling consensus. "Our dad's got a thirty-million-dollar motive for murder."

Chapter Seven

The celebration of Jackson's safe return ended quickly following the disturbing news of Axel's death. Valerie did her best to help Vita and Rick send off the family with hugs, reassurances and to-go boxes filled with left-over food.

Nash stayed to keep an eye on Nicole, who stayed to keep her dearest friend, Vita, company in the wake of the upsetting news. Of the rest of the family, only Lila and her fiancé Carter stayed behind, purportedly to help Vita clean the kitchen, but Valerie could tell from Lila's expression that she was concerned for Vita's well-being, as well. Divorced or not, learning the father of her children was dead had to be a blow for Vita. Rather, *another* blow on top of the succession of trying and traumatic events that had already plagued the family in recent months.

Lila hovered. Vita swore she was fine. And Valerie busied herself with any task or errand that she thought would lighten the load, alleviate the stress or comfort the family in their shock and distress. Bonus points if the busywork also helped distract her from Nash's presence.

He cornered her in the kitchen at one point and whispered, "Obviously, here and now isn't the time and place to finish our business from last night."

Valerie nodded discretely. "Obviously."

"What if you came over this evening for dinner? I'll cook."

"I feel like I should stay here tonight. For Vita. And because disappearing two nights in a row would be suspicious."

"Then maybe tomorrow?" He lifted a hand to touch her cheek when the swinging door from the dining room opened.

Rick breezed in with another platter of leftover scones and mini muffins. Nash jerked back his hand and jammed it in his pocket.

Valerie sidled away. "Let me put those in storage bags, Rick. They'll keep in the freezer for a while."

"Thanks, Val." Rick smiled at her then sent Nash a curious look. "Myles tells me you talked to Axel yesterday afternoon. Is that right?"

Nash opened his mouth. Closed it. Then, with a furrowed brow, he nodded.

"Did he seem all right to you when you saw him? Did he complain of not feeling well or look sick to you?"

"He was having a tennis lesson with some young thing he was clearly hitting on." Nash arched one eyebrow. "So, no. He didn't seem at all ill. He was pure Axel in his usual form."

Rick frowned. "Hmm. It's amazing how these things can strike out of nowhere. Perfectly fine one day and gone the next."

"So… Axel's death was a health issue? Have you heard something?" Valerie asked.

Rick pursed his lips. "No. I just assumed… I mean, it

could have been a home accident. The only other explanation is foul play, and that—"

"Foul play?" The three turned their glances toward Vita, who stood in the door from the dining room with a stack of plates and dirty napkins in her hands. "I know my ex-husband was difficult and heartless at times, but—"

"Pure speculation. Pointless speculation on our part, darling. Please ignore our thoughtless comments." Rick took the stack of dishes from his wife and set them on the counter. Valerie took over cleaning up those dishes.

"We didn't mean to upset you, Aunt Vita," Nash said.

"Why don't you go sit with Nicole in the living room and let us finish tidying up? Put your feet up and—"

"Rick Yates, I appreciate your concern for me, but I'm fine. I don't need to be coddled or shielded. If there's news about Axel's death, I want to hear it."

Rick nodded as he ushered Vita out of the kitchen. "And you will, love. But there is none now. Come put your feet up…"

Nash returned his gaze to Valerie when her uncle left the room. "Dinner. Tomorrow. My place. Deal?"

Valerie hesitated before answering. Her mother's voice sounded in her head. *The Coltons are a millstone around your neck. They'll drag you down in the mire with them. They're selfish and conniving. Trouble follows them. One day all their sins will catch up to them, and I don't want you to drown in the wake.*

She thought about all the chaos and tragedy that had already plagued the Coltons in recent months. Now Axel was dead. Was her mother right? Was getting involved with Nash a recipe for disaster and heartache? No matter what she decided, she and Nash needed a chance to hash it out. So she nodded and said, "It's a date."

"Myles promised to call when he learned anything," Lila said to her family when Valerie and Nash rejoined the others in the living room.

Nash took a seat in the chair closest to Nicole and reached for her fragile hand. "I can drive you home if you're tired or hurting."

Nicole shook her head stubbornly. "I want to stay." She shot a look to Vita. "If that's all right?"

"Of course. You can help distract me from my fruitless worrying." Vita turned to Valerie. "Val, dear, Rick says he mentioned the winter ad campaign for Yates' Yards to you. Do you think you'll have time to help Sara before you leave town?"

"I will. Definitely. I'd love to help and am already cooking up some ideas. In fact, I'll stop by the nursery and talk with her in a little while."

"Wonderful!" Rick said. "Our first shipment of poin—"

A loud knocking sounded from the front hall, interrupting Rick, followed by the doorbell, and Vita rose to answer the loud summons. From the living room, Valerie heard Vita gasp. "Rick! Lila!"

Hearing the distress in Vita's voice, everyone but Nicole, because of her injured hip, rose and hurried to the front door. The scents of autumn, perfumed with the abundant blooms in the Yateses' flower beds, greeted them as Rick pulled open the storm door.

A woman with a microphone stood on the porch, a bearded man with a large video camera behind her. Seeing the family arrive at the glass storm door, another reporter and cameraman hurried up from the yard, tramping across Vita's pansies, and the reporter shoved a microphone forward.

"Vita Colton, are you aware that Axel Colton was found murdered in his home this morning?" the first woman with a microphone asked.

Nudging Vita aside, Rick opened the door and waved a hand at the news crews. "You're trespassing on private property. Leave now before I call the police. We have no comment."

"And it's Vita *Yates* now," Vita said firmly, her shoulders squared. "I haven't been a Colton in many years." She wagged a finger at one of the cameramen. "You there! In the blue shirt. You're smashing my flowers! Please, be careful!"

Nash and Carter pushed through the door to join Rick in forming a barricade of bodies between the aggressive media and Vita.

"You heard the lady. Get off the flowers and out of the yard. We have nothing to say about Axel's death," Carter said.

"His murder, you mean?" reporter number two asked. The guy looked like he'd just graduated from high school and wore a double-breasted raincoat, red tie and buttoned-up collar, as if he'd Googled the clichéd image of a reporter from old movies and copied it as his uniform.

Beside Valerie, Lila stiffened. "Murder? Why do you say that?"

"Our sources say the police are now treating Axel Colton's death as a murder investigation," the young reporter explained eagerly.

Valerie's gut turned, and dismay bit hard.

"I, uh..." Rick spluttered, while Vita gasped, "Murder?"

"Our source says the word from the crime scene is the likely cause of death is blunt-force trauma to the head."

Irritation peaked in Valerie, seeing the young reporter's overly bright and excited expression as he delivered the news. To him, this was a career-defining story, the family's tragedy be damned.

"That conclusion is pending confirmation from the coroner," the female reporter interjected, signaling for her cameraman to get a closer shot of the family's reaction to the news. "The police haven't yet located the item used to bash Colton on the head and kill him."

Nash scowled at the woman. "A little sensitivity, please."

"Come on, Mom," Lila said, taking Vita's arm and encouraging her to go inside. "Let them handle this."

"Do you know who might want to kill Axel Colton?" the female reporter shouted as Valerie held the door, allowing Lila and Vita to quickly duck back into the house.

"Can you confirm that Axel Colton was embroiled in a contentious legal battle over his father's will?" the second reporter asked before Rick, Carter and Nash could follow Vita and Lila inside.

"Our sources say Nash Colton was one of the last people to see Axel Colton alive and, in fact, threatened his uncle."

Valerie swallowed hard, only narrowly holding in her gasp of shock. She felt Nash tense beside her as he angled a sharp look at the female reporter. "Where did you hear that?"

"Do you have a comment, sir?"

"Have you spoken to Nash Colton this morning, ma'am?" the second reported shouted.

Rick puffed his chest, irritation vibrating from him. "We have no comment. I want you off our property, or we'll call the police to escort you off."

"No need," the bearded cameraman said. "They're already here." He hitched his head toward the yard, where, sure enough, a uniformed officer and what Valerie assumed was a plainclothes detective marched across the grass.

The cameras swung to record the officers' approach, and the plainclothes cop waved his hand at the media personnel. "Enough. You guys, clear out."

"Freedom of the press!" the young reporter said.

"Is yours from the street," the uniformed officer added. "You should know better than encroaching on private property."

The female reporter stood back to allow the police team to climb the stairs, and though they made a show of backing toward the street, Valerie noted they were moving like glaciers, their cameras still focused on the family and the cops.

She inched back toward the entry to the living room with the men close behind her.

Rick closed the front door firmly and heaved a sigh before lifting a wary gaze to the policemen. "Gentlemen, what can we do for you?"

The detective in khakis, a navy sport coat and a blue oxford button-down shirt, open at the throat, introduced himself as Homicide Detective Harry Cartwright. Though his presence was disconcerting, Valerie got a positive vibe from the man. He carried himself with an air of authority and competence, but without any arrogance she could detect. His light brown hair and beard were short and neatly trimmed, and he conscientiously wiped his feet on the welcome mat before heading into the living room. Behind him, the uniformed officer stood stiffly with his hands clasped in front of him.

"Detective," Vita said, her voice unsteady. "That young reporter claims there's evidence Axel was murdered. Please tell me he was wrong. That he was just angling for a sensational story."

Cartwright scowled and muttered, "I don't know how he'd have that information."

Vita's face brightened a bit. "Then it's not true?"

"Sorry, but it's true."

Vita sucked in a sharp breath, and Rick moved quickly to put an arm around her.

The supportive gesture touched Valerie, even as her own stomach swooped. The shocking news settled in her brain like an electric jolt. She glanced to Nash, who met her eyes briefly, his expression stark, before he returned his attention to the detective. How nice it would be to have Nash rush to her side and lend his comfort the way Rick had for Vita. But, by her own decree, he couldn't give away their relationship. A pang of regret twisted around Valerie's heart. If only…

"I meant that information should not have leaked from the department so quickly." Detective Cartwright's low tone cut into her distracted thoughts. "Someone's been talking out of turn." He glanced at the uniformed officer, who mirrored the detective's disgruntled look. Schooling his face, he added, "I'm sorry to interrupt your party with such grim business."

Vita frowned, and her forehead creased with a deep *V*. "Oh, dear. *Party* does sound rather bad under the circumstances, doesn't it? Earlier we were celebrating the fact that our grandson was safely recovered after being kidnapped. The family all wanted to—"

"No need to explain," Cartwright said with a kind

smile for Vita. "Your gathering actually saves us the time of tracking folks down individually."

Vita seemed only mildly pacified by his reassurance. "Well, whatever we can do to help. This family has seen quite enough drama and tragedy lately. We'll be glad to put it all behind us as soon as possible and are here to help the police however we can." She turned awkwardly and waved toward the living room. "Shall we sit down?"

CARTWRIGHT NODDED A genial thank you, but Nash knew the man's intelligent gray-green eyes were taking in every detail, from the family's body language, to the layout of the home, which doors were closed and potentially hiding a suspect or ambush. Cartwright might be polite and friendly, but his instincts and training had him making detailed calculations observations and risk assessments. Finally, he indicated the uniformed officer with a hitch of his head. "This is Officer Moody. He'll be assisting me today."

Nash helped Vita to the couch, where she crumpled in disbelief. His own legs were rather rubbery, and his mind felt numb as he replayed the reporter's announcement. *Axel...murdered?* So he and Damon hadn't been off with their speculation. For once, Nash wished he had been wrong.

Immediately, his thoughts flashed to other recent Colton murders. Axel and Erik's half brothers had been killed earlier in the year. Was there a connection to Ernest and Alfred's deaths? And should he betray his father by mentioning the lawsuit regarding Dean Colton's will to the police? Nash had previously tried to stay on the fringes of his grandmother's lawsuit, but with thirty million dollars at stake, the potential motive for murder couldn't be ignored.

Then another possibility occurred to him. Could his newfound cousins, Dean Colton's legitimate grandchildren, be suspects? They had a great deal to lose if Carin's lawsuit prevailed.

Beside him, Lila tensed, prodding him from his spinning thoughts. Nash raised his head and focused again on what Cartwright was saying.

"One of you might be able to fill in some blanks about where Axel had been and who he'd been with. Routine investigation at this point."

"Before we do," Rick said, "can you tell us first why you suspect Axel was murdered? What's going on?"

When the detective hesitated, Rick touched Lila's shoulder and added, "Lila is Axel's daughter. As next of kin, doesn't she have a right to know what's happening?"

"At this point, no."

"No?" Lila echoed, dumbfounded.

Cartwright twisted his mouth in an apologetic moue. "This is a murder investigation, so the details surrounding your father's death are privileged information."

"So then how—" Carter began then cut himself off. His mouth pressed in a grim line, then, straightening his spine, he said, "Don't worry, Lila. I'll get you answers." He marched out of the living room, and they heard the front door open and close.

Nash leaned forward to glance out the front window and watched as Carter confronted the reporter still loitering on the lawn. Carter's warrior-like size and take-no-prisoners demeanor clearly intimidated the young reporter, and Nash bit the inside of his cheek to stifle a grin.

Cartwright was clearly displeased with Carter's actions, but made no move to stop him.

Nash shifted his gaze to meet Valerie's. Her brown eyes held storm clouds, and she gnawed her bottom lip as she held his stare. But was she worried the truth about their night together would come out, or about the public argument Nash had confessed having with Axel just hours before his uncle was murdered? He wished he could say he knew her well enough to know where her loyalties, her priorities lay.

"Do you think Axel's murder is connected to Jackson being found?" Rick asked the detective as the man pulled out a compact voice recorder. "This morning, Myles mentioned that people connected to his son's kidnapping had connections to known crime rings."

The detective furrowed his brow. "Excuse me? What kidnapping? Catch me up."

"Our grandson was recently kidnapped," Vita explained. *"Axel's grandson,"* she added with emphasis as if to be sure the detective didn't miss that point. "We're all here today because Jackson was found safe last night. But the people behind the kidnapping and an attack on my son Myles are still out there."

Cartwright arched an eyebrow. "Can you tell me about that?"

And she did, summarizing the whole situation with a calm, clear voice. "Brad Howard with the local FBI office took the lead on the case. I can give you his contact information."

Cartwright shook his head. "I know him. Worked a case with him earlier this year. I'll get a recap of the kidnapping case from him later and see if we connect any dots to Axel Colton."

"Goodness," Nicole said with a sigh. "When you consider everything that's happened to this family in recent months, you can build a rather long list of suspects. And God knows Axel must have made a few enemies in his life. He wasn't a pleasant man, and he was known to have had a wandering eye and no problem with bed-hopping." She sent Vita a sympathizing glance.

Cartwright raised a hand. "If you have specific information, names or incidents, known threats, I'll take that information down, but right now I'm more interested in tracing the last few hours of Axel Colton's life. Did any of you speak to him yesterday?"

Nash's gut rolled. He had to be honest, even if it painted him in a bad light.

Before he could speak, Vita said, "I talked with him by phone briefly to update him on the whole kidnapping business. Around three thirty p.m. But only for a minute or so. He seemed in a hurry to get off the phone. Some appointment or something."

"A tennis lesson," Nash clarified. "He was at the racket club."

Officer Moody wrote something down and asked, "You know this how?"

"I went there to talk to him. I interrupted his lesson for our conversation."

"Whatever for, Nash?" When Nicole reached toward him, angling a puzzled look at him, Nash took his adoptive mother's hand and gave it a consoling pat.

"I was trying to convince him to help Myles and Faith fund the ransom for Jackson. By all estimates, he's got more money in the bank than any of us. And as Jackson's grandfather, I saw no reason why he hadn't already pledged the money."

"This was yesterday afternoon?" Moody clarified as he jotted notes.

Nash nodded. "At about four p.m. Maybe four fifteen."

"And he seemed well?"

"Well enough to play tennis and flirt with the tennis pro half his age or younger."

"Did Mr. Colton say if he had any plans for—?" Cartwright began, but a firm knock on the front door interrupted him. Vita hesitated, then stood to answer the door. A moment later Vita returned. A uniformed officer stood with her. "Detective Cartwright?"

Cartwright stood. "What is it, Officer Chatham?"

"A word?"

Chatham and Cartwright excused themselves to the kitchen to confer in private for a moment. As the family waited, Nash felt Valerie's eyes on him and cast a glance her way. Her eyes held the same wary concern they'd had earlier that morning, when she'd begged him to keep her night with him a secret. For the sake of her mother.

While he respected her dogged loyalty to her mother, he wished he could expect even a part of the same allegiance to him. *Please*, her troubled eyes seemed to implore, and the small indentation between her eyes reflected both doubt and worry that cut him. He ducked his head slightly, his gaze locked with hers, trying to silently reassure her. Because, damn it, even if she doubted him, he cared for her, and he was a man of his word. He'd keep faith. But for Valerie's sake. Not for her mother.

The detective returned, bursting through the kitchen door with purposeful strides, Officer Chatham at his heels. "Nash Colton," Detective Cartwright said, drawing both Nash's gaze and Valerie's. "Officer Chatham has brought new information to my attention, as well as a search warrant for your home and car."

"What!" Nash shot up from the couch and gaped at the officer. "On what grounds?"

"At this point the warrant has a narrow scope, based on a tip from an anonymous witness." Officer Chatham produced a document from his clipboard and passed it over to Officer Moody. Valerie crowded in beside Moody, trying to read over his shoulder.

"Anonymous?" Nash scoffed. "This is malarkey."

"If your vehicle's here, we'd like to take a look in it now." Detective Cartwright motioned toward the driveway through the window.

"And what is it you're looking for, Detective?" Nicole asked, her voice reflecting the same deep concern that etched her brow.

"I'm not at liberty to say. Let's just go take a look and see what we find." Detective Cartwright motioned for Nash to come with him. When Valerie and Rick moved to the door to accompany them, the detective held up a hand. "Just Nash. Please wait here."

Valerie sent Nash another worried look, as if wanting to say something, do something, to defend him. As if she wanted to protect him from this ludicrous scrutiny.

He gave her a quick, strained smile, and as he passed her, he whispered, "It'll be okay."

Nash hoped he was right.

NASH STRODE ACROSS the lawn toward his car, wishing he were as sure of a positive outcome as he'd assured Val. An anonymous tip that incriminated him for murder? That didn't sound good. The Colton family seemed to be under attack from outside forces of late. Kidnapping, murder, blackmail. Was he the latest victim of this malevolent crusade? Who could be orchestrating this campaign to destroy his family? His newly discovered cousins? Dean Colton's legitimate children and grands? Maybe. But why?

From his peripheral vision, he noticed the reporters and television cameras scurrying to follow him and the policemen.

"Officer, can you tell us what's happening?"

"Is this man a suspect in Axel Colton's murder?"

Then Carter's voice. "Nash, what's going on?"

Nash glanced toward Lila's fiancé in time to see Office Moody step in Carter's path. "Stay back, sir. This is police business."

"Nash?"

He waved to Carter. "It's all right."

If only he could convince his gut and his brain that everything was fine. Acid churned in his stomach, making it difficult to keep his breakfast down. And an eerie foreboding shrouded his thoughts, a prescience and pessimism born of life experience. He'd had the same strange sense of doom before he'd opened his mother's bedroom door and found her dead of an aneurysm as a kid.

With his key fob, he unlocked his doors.

"We'll start with the trunk, please." After wrangling a pair of latex gloves onto his hands, Detective Cartwright moved to the back end of the Infiniti coupe and waited while Nash hit the right button on the key fob. Nash stalked over to stand beside the detective as Cartwright opened the lid of the trunk…

And found a heavy-looking candlestick inside. The piece was approximately one foot long, sculpted from white marble with waves and flourishes, and decorated with a silver initial. *C*.

Confusion, shock and crushing doom slammed into Nash. He knew instantly that the candlestick had been used to kill Axel. And he was being framed.

"Well, well, well. What have we here?" Cartwright turned to Officer Moody. "Document this, please."

"That is not mine! I have no idea how it got there!" Nash said, knowing he sounded like a cliché, but compelled to at least try to set the record straight. In truth, he knew just how it had gotten there. The anonymous tipster planted it. He said as much as Moody snapped pictures with his cell phone, but, of course, Detective Cartwright was predictably unconvinced.

Moody leaned farther inside the trunk for a better look. "Detective." The uniformed officer pointed to something dark at one end of the foot-long candlestick. "Blood."

"Right." Cartwright faced Nash, his expression flat and stern. "Please turn around and place your hands behind your back."

Adrenaline shot through Nash, and he shook his head. "You've got this wrong. It's a setup! I didn't—"

Officer Moody wasn't having it. He seized one of Nash's arms and tugged it behind his back. "Nash Colton, you're under arrest for the murder of Axel Colton."

As the officer spouted Nash's Miranda rights, Nash angled his head to find Carter, who watched from several feet away with anger and dismay creasing his face.

"Call Myles!" Nash shouted to him. "Tell him to meet me at the police station!"

Carter jerked a nod of understanding and sprinted back toward the house, just as Rick, Lila and Valerie raced from the front door across the yard, shouting, "Stop!" and "Nash!" and "Officer, no!"

Nash's mind spun, and his vision blurred as he was led to the police cruiser. The cacophony of voices—his family protesting, the media buzzing and the police calling for everyone to step back and not interfere—were a surreal backdrop to the thundering of his pulse in his ears.

This was wrong. A mistake. He was being framed.

As the back door of the cruiser was closed, he stared numbly through the window at the crowd of gathered spectators and found the one face he needed most to see—Valerie's.

His lover. His best hope. His alibi.

But given her pleading request that morning to keep their liaison a secret, would she back him up, support his defense?

He honestly didn't know.

Chapter Eight

A shock wave rolled through Valerie when the uniformed officer snapped the handcuffs on Nash and led him to the waiting police car. She sent Uncle Rick a desperate look, her heart thundering with fear and confusion. "What's happening? Why are they arresting Nash?"

She fought the swell of panic that bloomed in her chest and tried to steal her breath.

"I don't know, but I intend to find out," Rick replied, then squared his shoulders and marched across the lawn. Val followed. They ignored the microphones waved in their faces and the questions hurled at them from the media.

Carter already had his phone at his ear. "He needs you to meet him at the police station. They found something in his car trunk and immediately took him into custody." Seeing Val and Rick rush up to him, Carter held up a finger, signaling them to wait while he finished his call. "I didn't see. The cops kept me back, but I heard one of the officers say something about blood."

Valerie gasped, and Rick grabbed her arm when she wobbled.

Blood? Was it possible that more had happened between Nash and Axel in their confrontation than Nash had admitted? Nash had a temper. He held grudges. She knew that from her own arguments with him, but he wasn't violent. Was he? Certainly not with her. And she'd not seen evidence of it ever before.

Her mother's voice from years ago rang in her ears. *Stay away from the Coltons, Valerie! Trouble follows them. One day all their sins will catch up to them, and I don't want you to drown in the wake.*

She gave her head a determined shake, as if she could dislodge the doubts and niggling questions.

"It's all right, Valerie dear." Rick gave her a trembling smile. "We'll straighten this out."

Carter finished his call and turned to them. "That was Myles. He's going to head over to the police station and sort things out."

The rest of the family caught up and gathered around to hear what Carter had to say. As did the media. Carter sent a scowling side-eye to the female reporter who tried to push her way close enough to record what he was telling the family. Placing a hand on Lila's back, he hitched his head toward the house. "Let's go inside."

Before returning to the house, Valerie glanced toward Nash's Infiniti, where Detective Cartwright and Officer Chatham stood guard at the trunk. From the front entrance of Yates' Yards, Sara Sandoval emerged and edged closer to Valerie. The new hire's face was dark with concern, and she clearly assumed the worst. "What in the world is happening?"

Valerie wrapped her arms around herself, fighting the cold that prickled her skin. She knew the chill was as much the shock and dread she felt as the crisp October morning.

"Val?" Rick called, slowing to wait for her to accompany the rest of the family inside.

"Just a minute. I—I'll be right there." She took Sara's hand and pressed it between her own, needing the human connection as much as she wanted to offer the distressed young woman comfort. "The family had bad news this morning."

"Bad news? But I thought Vita told me they'd found Jackson, and he was safe."

Valerie bobbed her head once. "Right. But then we learned that Axel Colton, Myles and Lila's father, was murdered."

Sara's face paled, and she drew a sharp breath. "Axel… is dead?"

Valerie nodded and squeezed Sara's hand harder. "Yeah. A shock for everyone." She inhaled deeply and cast a lingering gaze toward Detective Cartwright. "And they've apparently found something incriminating in Nash's trunk. They just took him to the police station as if he were a common criminal."

She heard a little whimper and turned back to Sara, just as the other woman crumpled to the lawn. "Sara!"

She knelt beside Sara, patting her cheek and calling her name, until Detective Cartwright appeared at her side and nudged her out of the way.

"What happened?" He removed his jacket, balled it up and gently placed it behind Sara's head. He shot the members of the media that hustled closer a scowl and shouted, "Get back!" Then under his breath, he added, "Vultures." He angled a look at Val. "Is she diabetic? Epileptic?"

"I—I don't know. She looked pale after I told her Axel was killed and then next thing I know—" Valerie heard another soft mewl from Sara and shifted her attention to her new friend. “Sara? Are you hurt? Sara?”

Cartwright patted Sara’s cheek lightly and asked, “Are you all right, ma’am?”

Sara opened her eyes slowly, then blinked hard and frowned when she saw Detective Cartwright leaning over her. “What happened?”

“You fainted, ma’am. Do you have a medical condition that might have caused—?”

“No. Nothing like th—” Sara tried to sit up, and her eyelids fluttered.

“Hey, easy there.” Cartwright placed a hand on her arm and eased her back to the ground. “Rest a minute. Did you hit your head? Is your vision blurred?”

Valerie eased back down, eyeing the detective, whose handsome countenance was furrowed with what was obviously genuine concern.

Sara closed her eyes and touched the back of her head, then sighed. “No. I’m not hurt. I just…skipped breakfast. Then when she said…” Her face crumpled again, as if hearing the tragic news of Axel’s murder again. “Oh, wow. I just…”

Cartwright lifted his gaze to Valerie. “Can you get her some water?”

“Sure.” She shoved to her feet and hurried inside Yates’ Yards. She made a beeline to the break room, retrieved a bottle of water from the refrigerator and rushed back out. As she approached the spot where Sara was now sitting up on the grass, she slowed her steps to study the scene. Sara was staring at Cartwright, smiling shyly, and Cartwright was gazing at Sara with a rapt attention and a dazed expression that seemed to shut out the rest of the world. She got an odd sense that she was intruding on a private moment.

The dry leaves crunched under her feet, though, and Cartwright cut his gaze to Val. He stuck his hand out for the bottle of water. "Thanks."

"Really," Sara said, getting her feet under her, "I'm fine now."

Cartwright placed a hand under her elbow and steadied Sara as she stood with a stumble.

Another car with police lights arrived, and Cartwright's ensuing sigh seemed full of regret. "That's the forensic team. I need to go."

Sara stooped to collect the jacket that had pillowed her head and handed it back to the detective. "I'm good. Thank you for your concern."

He gave Sara a half smile, his gray-green eyes lingering on Sara's before he returned to his duties. Sara drew a deep breath and exhaled slowly.

Val stepped closer, ready to catch the woman if she wobbled again. "Okay?"

"Did you see his eyes?" Sara asked, sounding winded.

Val's lips twitched. "They were striking."

"I'll say." Then Sara seemed to remember what had precipitated her faint, and her expression darkened again. "Oh, I'm sorry. You were saying...about Axel. And they arrested Nash for it?"

"So it would seem." Valerie returned her gaze to where the forensics team had removed a heavy-looking candleholder from Nash's trunk and were carefully bagging it as evidence. Even from this distance, she could see that the white marble was stained with blood. With a chilling certainty, she knew she was looking at the murder weapon.

How did it end up in Nash's car? Was it in his car all

night while she'd been making love to Nash? Had he lied to her? Was it possible that before he'd come home yesterday, Nash had killed Axel…by accident?

No. A person didn't hit someone else with a marble candlestick hard enough to kill them by accident. Whoever had hefted that piece had intended to inflict grave harm.

"You know the family better than I do," Sara said. "Do you think Nash could have done it?"

Val fought for a breath. She wanted to defend Nash, wanted to believe that the man who'd so passionately and tenderly made love to her last night couldn't possibly have taken the life of his uncle, even in a fit of rage. But her mother's warning echoed in her head, and the police had found condemning evidence in his trunk. She gripped Sara's hand tighter and wheezed, "I don't know."

VALERIE RETURNED TO the house, where Carter was relaying what he'd learned from the reporter. Vita, Lila and Nicole wore similar masks of horror, and Rick paced the floor, scrubbing a hand over his cheek and through his hair in agitation.

Carter glanced up at Valerie as she entered the room and took a seat beside Vita. "He bled from the head. The guy said he overheard Cartwright tell the uniform at the scene that the cause of death appeared to be blunt-force trauma."

That fit, if the murder weapon was, in fact, the candlestick they'd just removed from Nash's car. Valerie's gut rolled.

"So he hit his head as he fell?" Vita's tone was thin and trembled with both hope and fear.

Carter shook his head. "No. There was nothing close

for him to hit his head on. And…there were signs of a struggle."

Rick muttered a curse under his breath.

Nicole's face was calm but shadowed as she asked quietly, "And they found something in Nash's trunk, didn't they? Something they suspect was used to kill Axel."

"Yeah." Carter grasped Lila's hand and added, "But Myles is already on his way to the police department. He'll get to the bottom of this and bring Nash home, if at all possible."

No one said anything for several tense moments. The grandfather clock in the front hall ticked loudly, marking the seconds and keeping time with the heavy, anxious beats of Val's pulse.

Finally, Carter spoke the terrifying thought that was clearly on everyone's mind, but no one else had dared to give voice. "Someone is out to destroy the Coltons, one horrible act at a time."

Chapter Nine

Once at the police station, Officer Moody escorted Nash to an interrogation room. When he saw the stark room and hard, straight-backed chair, a chill raced through Nash. He was uncuffed and left alone in the room until Detective Cartwright arrived.

"I'm not answering any questions until my lawyer arrives," Nash said as the detective took a seat.

"That's your right, of course." Cartwright folded his arms over his chest as he narrowed his glare on Nash. "Any idea when that will be?"

Nash cast a glance around the Spartan room with the two-way glass mirror on one wall. "Soon, I'd think. But seeing as my lawyer is also the victim's son… Well, Myles is a bit busy today."

"And you don't see the conflict of interest with that? Having Myles Colton as your legal representative?"

"Of course, I see it. Myles will undoubtedly find another attorney to handle my case, but on short notice…" Nash spread his hands. "He'll still see that my rights are protected, and that this railroading doesn't go too far off the tracks."

"Railroading? Is that your way of denying any culpability in Axel Colton's death?"

While he wanted to shout his innocence from the roof of the police station, Nash knew better than to say more before Myles arrived. He'd already said too much. He clamped his mouth shut, pressing his lips in a firm stubborn line.

After a moment of holding Nash's stare, Cartwright unfolded his arms and walked to the door. "All right, then. I'll be back once your attorney arrives."

Nash leaned back in the hard chair. While he waited, impatiently, for Myles, he tried to discern how, *how in hell*, that damn candlestick had gotten in his trunk. Obviously it had been planted, but when? He'd been at home with Valerie from the end of his confrontation with Axel at the tennis courts until he'd headed to Vita's. Perhaps the killer, knowing the family would convene after Jackson was found, had picked his car at random while the family had celebrated inside. Or could—

The interrogation room door opened again and Myles, looking stressed and rumpled, was ushered in by a uniformed officer. Nash shoved to his feet to embrace his cousin.

"What the hell is going on, Nash?" Myles asked. "Carter said they arrested you for Dad's murder. Based on what?"

Nash waved a hand toward another hard, uncomfortable chair and sat back down. "Planted evidence."

"Planted by whom?"

"That is the question of the hour." Nash filled Myles in on the whole series of events, starting with his confrontation with Axel the day before, the detective's arrival at Vita's and the execution of the search warrant.

"I won't ask you to divide your loyalties defending me. But if you can recommend someone—"

Myles raised a hand. "We'll cross that bridge if we must, but I'd rather get these charges against you dismissed."

"I'm listening."

Myles steepled his fingers and tapped them against his mouth as he thought. "If we can prove you weren't the one who put that candleholder in your trunk, this goes away. It's the only thing connecting you to Dad's death at this point."

"So we need a witness who saw someone put the thing in my car."

Myles nodded, his expression still thoughtful. "Or a camera. You have a security video at your house?"

Nash exhaled heavily. "No."

Myles groaned. "What about your neighbors? Any chance they have cameras that would catch any activity at the end of your driveway?"

Nash shrugged. "I've never asked them. My next-door neighbor on the left has a line of evergreens that form a privacy wall of sorts. On the right is an older lady that lives alone. And across the street is a banker and his family."

Myles lifted his phone and tapped the screen. "I'm going to get Damon started talking to your neighbors. Where else have you been in the last eighteen hours?"

"Just Vita and Rick's this morning with everyone else."

"Yates' Yards has security cameras, don't they? Maybe your car will be in frame of their video. I'll have Rick review the feed from this morning ASAP." He clapped a hand on Nash's shoulder. "Keep the faith, cuz. We'll figure this out."

DETECTIVE CARTWRIGHT DIDN'T return for almost an hour. When he did, he set a mug of coffee and a voice recorder on the scarred wooden table. Then, he took a file folder from under his arm, placed it next to his mug and sat down. "Well, gentlemen, shall we begin?"

Nash glanced at Myles, who nodded once. Even though he hadn't killed Axel, Nash's stomach clenched and acid burned a hole at his core. Not knowing who was at the root of the frame job against him and how far it reached left him wary and restless. Were the police involved in this farce? Or some powerful person with the means to sway an investigation? He knew enough from Damon's undercover operations to realize organized crime was alive and well in Chi-Town.

And his best defense rested on an alibi he'd sworn not to reveal. How desperate was Valerie to hide their one-night stand? Would she deny having been with him to serve her own agenda and leave him defenseless?

"Can you tell me the last time you spoke to Axel Colton?" Cartwright asked.

"I saw him yesterday at his racket club." Nash decided his best move was not to play coy. He would be up front about the nature of the interaction, demonstrating he had nothing to hide. "We argued about his unwillingness to help pay the ransom for my nephew Jackson."

Nash exchanged a look with Myles, who frowned but kept silent.

"The little boy that was mentioned earlier at the Yateses'?"

Myles arched an eyebrow. "My son. But he's been located now and returned safely."

Nash sighed and grumbled, "No thanks to his grandfather."

Myles cut a silencing glance to Nash.

Cartwright nodded. "That's what I was told. I'm

glad he's all right." He folded his arms over his chest and rocked his chair onto the back legs. "Do you hold a grudge against Axel for his lack of involvement with Jackson?"

Nash saw the trap and weighed his answer carefully. "I was disappointed in him, yes. Angry, even. But Axel's disinterest in Jackson is no more than I've come to expect from him or his brother Erik, my father. They are both arrogant, spoiled and distant. Neither will ever win father of the year. But Axel's character is something my siblings and I have learned to accept and expect. Yesterday, I shouldn't have been surprised Axel refused to help pay the ransom. He's selfish that way. But I was willing to try to talk sense into him for Jackson's sake. I lost my temper, because I was already on edge and stressed out over the situation. My bad. I admit that. But I didn't kill him."

Myles leaned over and whispered to him, "Keep your answers short and to the point. Don't volunteer information he doesn't ask for."

When Myles settled back in his chair, Cartwright continued. "Would you say you *wanted* to kill him?"

Nash scoffed. "I'm not a murderer, Detective."

"Did you want to kill him?"

Nash gritted his teeth. "No. Not literally."

Cartwright opened the folder he'd brought in with him and shuffled through some papers. "You were overheard by a witness at the racket club shouting, quote, 'You're going to be sorry you walked away, old man,' and that he was going to pay for turning his back on his family."

Nash pinched the bridge of his nose. "Like I said, I was angry. I meant that someday Axel would regret not having made his family a bigger priority in his life."

The detective angled his head. "Regret it how?"

Nash sent Myles a glance, but his cousin said nothing, so he answered, "That he'd realize his family, and not money or status, was what really mattered in life. I was talking about an awareness and sadness he'd have, not a physical retribution from someone."

"Did you tell Tiffany Zimmerman that you wanted to strangle your uncle?"

Nash blinked. "Who?"

Cartwright double-checked his papers. "Tiffany Zimmerman. A tennis pro at the racket club where you confronted Axel Colton."

Raking his hand through his short-cropped hair, Nash recalled the pretty young woman with wide green eyes and his flippant remarks to her. What had he said exactly? "She overheard the argument I had with Axel and looked a little nervous as I left. So—just joking—I asked her something like didn't she ever want to strangle anyone in her family? I didn't mean it literally. I was letting off steam."

Cartwright tapped his thumb on the table and sighed. "Did you threaten to kill Axel Colton, Nash?"

"No! Never!"

"Besides Miss Zimmerman's statement, we have several other accounts from club members that describe you threatening Mr. Colton's life."

Nash's pulse accelerated as he sensed the walls closing in on him. He shook his head vehemently. "No. I never threatened to kill him. I joked about wanting to strangle him because I was frustrated, but I didn't—"

"Where were you between the hours of ten p.m. last night and two a.m. this morning?"

The question struck Nash like a fist in his gut. So here it was. Time to ante up.

How did he prove his innocence without betraying Valerie's request of secrecy? Would she deny being with him to appease her mother? His gut roiled. Surely not. The Valerie he remembered wasn't that cold and selfish. And yet…she'd left him in the dark about her pregnancy. Cut off communication with him for years. Bought her mother's lies without giving him a chance to explain himself. Her previous behavior hadn't exactly earned his trust.

But he'd made a promise to her, and he would keep his word. Surely, evidence that cleared him would come to light soon. It had to.

He flattened his hands on the table and met the detective's stare levelly. "I was at home. I went to bed around eleven. Woke up at nine when Myles called to say Jackson had been found."

"Can anyone corroborate your story?"

"It's not a story. I was at home." Then he added evasively, "I live alone."

"So the answer is no? You have no one to back up your alibi of being at home last night and when you went to bed?"

Nash ground his back teeth together and bounced his heel in agitation. "You could talk to my neighbors. They may have seen my car in the driveway." *And Valerie's*, he thought belatedly.

"We'll talk to your neighbors if we can't verify your alibi any other way. A car in a driveway really isn't proof of anything. You could have called a cab or had a friend pick you up."

Detective Cartwright made some notes and narrowed his gaze on Nash. "Look, Mr. Colton, we're not out to pin this on someone just to make an arrest. We want the person responsible. If you didn't do it, you need to help us prove that."

"I didn't kill my uncle. I was home last night. All night."

"Do you have footage from security camera that would place you arriving home and when you left again?"

"No. I wish I did, because I'd love to know who put that candlestick in my trunk."

Myles cleared his throat, and when Nash glanced at him, he received a warning glare from his cousin. His heart gave a hard thump.

Don't volunteer anything you aren't asked.

"Right. Let's talk about that candlestick," Cartwright said, flipping in his file to a printed copy of one of the photos taken earlier that morning of Nash's trunk.

An earthy curse word filtered through Nash's brain.

"Do you recognize this candlestick?"

"No. I never saw it before this morning."

"How do you explain it being in the back of your car?"

"I can't. But I didn't—" Nash caught the denial on his tongue. Don't volunteer anything… God, he wished he knew what Valerie was telling the police right now. Would she speak up about their night together or let him remain under suspicion?

Cartwright sighed. "Mr. Colton, you understand that, right now, you are the lead suspect in your uncle's death, don't you? First-degree murder? If you have anything else to tell me to clear up this matter, I suggest you share it."

A knock interrupted them, and when the door was cracked open, a female officer with her hair slicked back in a tight bun poked her head in the room. "Sorry to intrude, Detective, but there's a gentleman out here says he has video footage that is relevant to the Axel Colton case."

The detective's brow furrowed. "Tell them I'll speak to them in a—"

"I think we should see the video together, Detective," Myles said. "If the gentleman she mentioned is Damon Colton, he's here with security camera footage that I requested. Footage that can prove Nash didn't put the candlestick in his trunk."

Cartwright held Myles's gaze for long seconds, then let the legs of his chair thump back to the ground. He pushed to his feet and said, "Wait here."

Nash snorted dryly as the detective left the room. "Like they'd let me leave." He rose to his feet and paced the floor, his hands jittery at his sides. "This is a nightmare. Do you think my dad—?" He stopped himself, realizing that Cartwright's voice recorder was still on the table capturing everything he said. And no doubt someone was behind that mirrored glass watching.

"Keep the faith, man. If Damon's here with security footage then—"

The door burst open again, and Cartwright bustled in. With him was Damon, wearing one of his official DEA jackets and clearly using his own connections in law enforcement to gain entry to the interview room. Nash's brother gave him a stern look. "You and I are going to have a talk about the importance of a home security system when you get out of here. You're lucky Cynthia Myer was home." He set a laptop on the wooden table and switched it on. "She was about to leave town to meet her family in Colorado for a wedding." Damon pulled a flash drive from his pocket. "Her husband and kids left Tuesday night, and she was just finishing up a work project before joining them." He plugged the USB drive into a port on the side of the laptop and clicked through a few screens to open a video-viewing program. He selected a file with yesterday's date. Directing his attention to Detective Cartwright, he said, "Security camera footage from Nash's across-the-street neighbor. She's willing to testify to the veracity and authenticity of the tape, that it hasn't been altered. Notice the date and time stamp. Yesterday at four twelve p.m."

Cartwright didn't look happy that Damon had taken matters into his own hands, but turned his attention to the screen. The shot was of the Myers' front yard, but Nash's house and empty driveway were plainly visible, as well.

Nash rubbed his hands on the legs of his jeans—he knew full well what would play out in the next couple of minutes. The other three men leaned closer to the screen when Valerie's car pulled in the driveway.

"Who's that?" Cartwright asked.

Nash clenched his teeth, his gut in knots.

"That looks like…" Myles squinted at the screen. "Is that Valerie?"

"Valerie?" Cartwright repeated. "She have a last name?"

"Valerie Yates. She's in town visiting her uncle, Rick Yates," Nash explained. "She was at the Yateses' home earlier this morning when you arrived."

Cartwright stared intently at the screen as Valerie walked to his door, knocked, then waved to a woman on the sidewalk with a baby stroller. "Oh, yeah. I remember her."

Then Nash's car appeared, pulling into his driveway behind Valerie's. Nash tensed as he watched himself and Valerie on screen, knowing the questions that would come.

"Why was Ms. Yates there? Had you been expecting her?" Cartwright asked.

"I hadn't. She came to talk." He wanted to leave it at that, but heard himself adding, "We were close as kids, and I hadn't seen her in a long time. We were catching up."

Nash felt more than saw Damon turn a querying gaze on him, but he kept his own eyes on the laptop screen. After a minute or two of nothing else happening in the camera angle, Damon hit fast-forward. Anytime a car or person appeared on the video, he stopped and replayed the footage. Several cars drove down the street as his neighbors returned home from work. Children and dogs ran down the sidewalk, the mother with the stroller returned from her walk the way she'd come. Night fell.

And Valerie's car remained in his driveway.

Patiently, without comment, as Damon continued fast-forwarding, stopping and rewinding, the four men watched and rewatched the security footage. Then when the time stamp read two twenty-six a.m., a vehicle stopped just past Nash's driveway.

"Hold the phone," Damon mumbled. "What's this?"

A large figure dressed in a dark jacket with the hood up stepped out of the driver's side and took something from the back seat. Opened Nash's trunk. Placed the object inside. Wiped Nash's car with a cloth. And hurried back to their car. The taillights of the pale sedan blinked as the car pulled quickly away.

Even knowing he had to have been set up, Nash's lungs squeezed as he saw the scene play out in the security video. While he'd been inside, making love to Valerie, some jerk had been in his driveway, framing him for his uncle's murder.

Damon hit a key on the laptop to pause the video playback. "There you go, Detective Cartwright. Someone planted that candleholder in my brother's car."

Cartwright leaned back in his chair, folding his hands behind his head as he exhaled a slow deep breath. "So it would seem." He chewed the inside of his cheek, his eyes unfocused and his forehead dented in consternation. Then, tapping his fist on the table, he said, "Play it back. What model car is that? Can you see the tag number? The person's face, even for a second?"

All four men leaned in to study the replay, and Nash's pulse bumped so hard, he could feel every throb in his throat, could hear the whoosh echoing in his ears.

They replayed that twenty-two seconds of video five times, but the angle was wrong for capturing the license plate. Between the poor light and the hood shielding the perpetrator's face, making a positive ID was impossible. But knowing the item used to kill his uncle had been placed in his trunk was compelling evidence in his favor.

That, and the fact that he had an alibi.

Once Cartwright was convinced they wouldn't get the license plate from that camera shot, he had Damon fast-forward through the footage until Nash and Valerie could be seen leaving his house in the morning and climbing in their respective vehicles. Without him saying a word, Myles and Damon were now fully aware of the fact that Valerie had spent the night with him.

As the men watched Valerie back out of Nash's driveway and her car disappear from view, Myles reached over and slapped the back of Nash's head.

"Hey! What the—"

"Why the hell didn't you say you had someone who could verify your whereabouts during the time the murder took place?" Myles asked, glaring at Nash.

"Same question." Cartwright nodded his head toward Myles, then narrowed his eyes on Nash.

"Because..." Clenching his fists, Nash sighed. Explaining the truth—that Val asked him to keep their liaison secret, because her mother's mental health was fragile, because Val was unsure of what she wanted—was as big a violation of trust and her confidence in him as their one-night stand. Half of the truth was out, but he still had a chance to protect some of the intimate details of what Val and he had shared, the full scope of their past.

Cartwright flattened both hands on the table and leaned toward Nash. "Do you need me to repeat the question, Mr. Colton?"

"No. I didn't say anything out of deference to Val's privacy, her reputation. I don't kiss and tell."

"Even when under suspicion of murder?" Cartwright arched an eyebrow.

"I knew I hadn't done anything wrong. I didn't kill Axel, and I had faith that *you*—" he paused briefly to give the word more weight "—would do your job correctly, and the evidence would clear me." He flipped a hand toward Damon's laptop. "Case in point. Video proof I was home all night and someone planted the murder weapon to frame me."

The detective grunted and scratched his chin. "Which

begs the question, why you? Why were you, specifically, singled out to frame?"

Nash gritted his back teeth and shook his head. "I wish I knew."

Chapter Ten

After the forensic team finished with Nash's car, a young police officer, whose name tag read *R. Tandy*, came to the Yateses' home to talk to the family. Everyone was clearly shell-shocked after having seen Nash put in handcuffs and shoved in the back of a cruiser. No one more so than Val herself. She knew with a simple few words—*he was with me*—she could clear Nash's name. But…

If he was innocent, wouldn't the evidence clear him?

Her stomach swam. *If* he was innocent?

Was she seriously doubting him? The man she'd made love to so gently and passionately couldn't possibly be guilty of murder. Nash had been genuinely stunned to find that marble piece in his trunk.

The truth was, if pressed on the matter, she had no idea what he'd done, how far the argument with Axel had reached before he'd gotten home and found her on his porch. And what was she supposed to do with these awful nagging doubts?

While she could keep quiet about her uncertainties, she knew she couldn't keep quiet about where she'd been last night—or rather, with whom—as much as she'd like to.

Nash's arrest suddenly made her one-night indulgence

relevant in a bigger theater. Uncle Rick and Vita already knew she'd been gone all night. They hadn't yet pressed her on her whereabouts, but suspicions were sure to rise soon. She exhaled slowly as she took a seat in the living room and followed the conversation in progress.

"He arrived around ten forty-five or so," Rick said. "Or that's when I first saw him here." Her uncle turned to her. "Val, did you see when Nash got here this morning?"

Valerie's breath snagged. "Uh, ten forty-five sounds about right." *Same as me.*

Did her guilt show?

"It's hard to say for sure. The whole family was here, Officer," Vita said. "It was very busy and confusing… in a good way. We were celebrating. Until the call came about Axel, at least."

"Are any of you aware of a beef of any sort between Nash and his uncle?" Officer Tandy asked.

Lila huffed loudly. "Look. I know you're just doing your job. But Nash did not kill my father. He wouldn't. It's ludicrous to even consider! This whole line of reasoning is a waste of time. The better question is who put that candleholder in his trunk? That's the path that will find the killer. Not these crazy rabbit trails!"

"Ma'am," the young officer said, addressing Lila, "we have to follow where the evidence takes us. The best way to clear your brother is to—"

"Cousin," Lila corrected, her tone reflecting her edgy mood. "We want to keep the facts straight, don't we?"

"Cousin, then. And yes, we do." Tandy used his pen to scratch his head, then asked, "Does anyone have anything to add? Any details or clarifications to what's been said? You never know what might be the tip that helps solve this case."

Valerie held her breath, knowing she needed to speak up. Keeping silent was tantamount to withholding key evidence in an investigation.

Admitting the truth, here and now, would mean she'd face many more questions from the family. Questions she wasn't prepared to answer. She hadn't fully processed for herself what her one-night stand with Nash meant. She'd let her emotions and memories lead her instead of keeping her head, keeping her distance. What had she been thinking? She'd worked too hard and too long to get over him, and then she'd fallen into bed with him again the first time they were alone together? So careless. An obvious mistake. A lapse in judgment she needed to keep quiet. To protect her privacy, to shield her mother, to sweep her recklessness under the proverbial rug.

When the young officer got no further comments or questions from the family, he tucked his pen in his shirt pocket and turned off the recording app on his phone. "Well, if that's all, I'll let you folks get back to—"

"Can—can I speak to you privately, officer?" Val asked.

Lila cut a curious glance toward her. "Val? If you know something about my father, I hope you would feel safe enough to share it with everyone."

Valerie felt her face heat, and her pulse thrummed. "No. It's not that. I just…" She fumbled and spread her hands, searching for the right words.

"If you prefer to speak in private, we can do that." Office Tandy waved a hand toward the foyer.

Well, she'd stuck her foot in it now. With an awkward smile to the room, she excused herself and stepped out on the front porch with the young officer.

The media members, of course, were still camped out

in Rick and Vita's yard, waiting for any morsel of information that they could dissect and cook into a story to feed their gossip-hungry audience. At Val's appearance on the porch with the officer, the cameras all swung toward her.

Giving the clustered reporters her back, Valerie scowled at Tandy. "Why do I feel like a tape of this conversation will be analyzed by a lip reader?"

"We could go downtown to the station. An interview room would be completely private."

And completely intimidating. She just wanted to confess her whereabouts, provide relevant details to Nash's defense as simply as possible. Going to the police station to be interviewed felt so...*real*. Significant. Terrifying.

Her expression must have reflected her thoughts, because Officer Tandy gave her a half smile. "It sounds scarier than it is. You're not in trouble. You'd be free to leave at any time. We can even go in separate vehicles if climbing in my squad car with the cameras watching bothers you."

She rubbed her arm as gooseflesh prickled her skin. "I guess..." A glance at the living-room window revealed faces watching her from inside the house, in addition to those out on the lawn. "Yes. The station will be fine. I'll follow you there."

Ten minutes later, she walked with Officer Tandy into the lobby of the police station nearest to Rick and Vita's house. Her nerves jangled, and she felt as if she could jump out of her skin if someone so much as whispered, "Boo."

"Wait here. I'll see which room is available, and be right back," Tandy said.

She nodded and watched him retreat down a long corridor, then stop as someone exited a door halfway down the hall.

Detective Cartwright.

On Cartwright's heels were Damon and Myles Colton. Valerie froze. She didn't want anyone else in the family to know she was here. What if they…?

Damon spotted her and nudged Myles with his elbow.

Damn it. So much for wanting to fade into the background.

Tandy spoke to Cartwright, and Cartwright to Damon and Myles. They all glanced her way before Damon and Myles were clearly dismissed and Cartwright disappeared into a different room with Tandy.

Myles and Damon approached her with knowing grins, and the anxiety inside her morphed into fury. Her disappointment and anger grew as Damon sang a quiet and off-key version of the refrain from Lionel Richie's "All Night Long" under his breath as he approached her. Now Myles poked his cousin with his elbow. "Cut it out."

Nash had promised to keep her secret, but not even six hours later he'd obviously spilled to his brother and cousin the truth about their night together. Sure, he'd had to provide an alibi, answer the detective's questions honestly, but why did he have to spill it all to Myles and Damon?

She wanted to cry. She wanted to scream. Even if she was at the police station to confess the truth, she wanted to rage in Nash's face and tell him how his faithlessness cut her.

In her head, she could hear her mother's voice saying, *I told you the Coltons weren't trustworthy. I told you so…*

Her hands balled in fists, she folded her arms over her

chest and tried to ignore the teasing grins as Damon and Myles reached her.

"So..." Damon began, his eyes full of light as he paused to speak to her. "What brings you to the station, Valerie?"

"Judging from your smirk, I'd say you know exactly why I'm here." She didn't even try to hide her annoyance.

Damon frowned. "You sound ticked? Why aren't you happy that Nash—"

"Ms. Yates?" Detective Cartwright approached them, and Damon said no more. "If you'll follow me, I have just a few questions for you."

Her jitters returned. As she fell in step behind Cartwright, she caught Myles's reassuring smile and the confident nod Damon gave her. Sure, they were happy for Nash to have an alibi, but what about the repercussions for her life? They didn't understand how precarious her mother's health was.

The detective directed her into a dingy room with a table and two chairs, then closed the door behind her. She shivered, despite the heat filling the stuffy room. The cubicle—it was really too small to even be called a room—smelled of body odor, mildew and stale food. The tight space was stark. Intimidating. No doubt intentionally so.

Cartwright must have seen the dismay in her expression because he said, "I apologize for the less-than-welcoming accommodations. I only have a couple of questions for you, so I went with expediency and privacy over comfort, but if you'd rather move—"

"No, I'm..." She considered the chair but decided to stand. The detective remained on his feet, as well. "Can we just get this over with?"

"Certainly. Can you tell me where you were last night between the hours of five p.m. and ten a.m. this morning?"

The specificity of the times left no doubt what Nash had told the detective. Acid puddled in her gut, and anger raised a sheen of sweat on her skin. Or maybe that was just the boiling heat in the small room. Valerie wiped the moisture from her brow and sighed. "I was at Nash Colton's house."

"The entire time?"

Her heart thumped a slow beat of defeat. "Yes."

"And was Nash Colton with you the entire time?"

"Yes."

"Can you tell me specifically where you were at two twenty-six a.m.?"

The oddly specific time surprised her. "At Nash's."

"Can you be more specific?"

She gave the detective a peeved look and huffed irritably. "In his bedroom. Is that what you wanted to hear? That I slept with him? I can't say whether we were making love at exactly two twenty-six a.m., but we were in bed together, and we did make love and took catnaps all night. Is that what you wanted to know?" Her voice cracked, and she was stunned to find that tears had leaked to her cheeks.

Cartwright had the decency to look apologetic. "Detail is helpful. I'm sorry if this is difficult. One last question. Did you hear or see anything in Nash's driveway at two twenty-six a.m.?"

Valerie stilled. There was something here she'd missed, being so wrapped up in her own anger with Nash and worry over how her spoiled secret would impact her mother. Nash's driveway. Where his car had been parked.

Has someone planted the murder weapon while they were inside asleep? Her stomach clenched. She struggled for the breath to speak. "I— No. I'm sorry, but I didn't… I don't…"

Cartwright sighed dejectedly. "Well, that's really all I needed from you. Thank you for your cooperation. If you'd stop at the front desk, I'll have your statement written up for you to sign."

She took a few steps toward the corridor before she faced Cartwright again. "What about Nash? He didn't do anything. Can't he be released?"

"Thanks to your statement and some other corroborating evidence, he'll be released within the hour, I'm sure. Just need to finish some paperwork."

The weight on Valerie's chest lifted like a pressure valve being opened to drain away the stress. Yet a lingering ache remained. News of their night together would spread like hot gossip at a beauty parlor…because Nash hadn't kept his promise.

VALERIE GOT BACK to Rick and Vita's with one goal in mind—holing up in the guest room and being alone with her thoughts, her heartache, her bone-deep fatigue. The roller-coaster emotions of the last twenty-four hours had wrung her out.

The family, however, had different ideas.

Lila met her at the door with Vita and Rick one step behind her. They immediately began lobbing questions in her direction as she took off her coat. Had she seen Nash? What did she tell the police? What evidence had they found in Nash's car? Has she seen Myles and Damon at the station? What was going on?

She raised a hand, trying to get a word in, and finally Carter loosed a shrill whistle that jolted them all into silence.

"Give her a chance!" Lila's fiancé led Valerie into the living room and the family clustered around her. She gave them the highlights. Nash would be released from custody soon. He had a confirmed alibi. She'd seen Myles and Damon, but had not had an opportunity to speak to them at length.

All true. If she felt a flicker of guilt for having left out certain bits of the whole story, she could deal with that compunction later. After a nap. After she ate. After she'd had time to talk to Nash and sort through her tangled emotions. But her desire for time to rest and think was thwarted within minutes as Damon arrived with Nash.

Nash's exhaustion was evident in the lines bracketing his mouth and the shadows under his eyes. Despite being released by the police, his slumped shoulders spoke of defeat and dejection.

The family, of course, swarmed Nash, expressing their relief that he'd been released and peppering him with questions. Like Val, Nash begged off answering more than a few cursory queries.

She tried to ease out of the room unnoticed, but Nash called to her as she reached the living-room door. "Val, hang on. I want to talk to you."

"Yeah, you do," Damon said with a lopsided smile and a knowing wink.

"What's that supposed to mean?" Lila asked.

Nash glared at his brother. "Can it."

Valerie avoided eye contact with the many curious

stares she felt boring into her as Nash made his way across the room.

"Let's go somewhere out of earshot, huh?" he said quietly.

Arms folded over her chest, she glowered at him, but knowing the family was watching, she finally nodded once and headed to the guest room, where she was staying. Once the door was closed behind her she whirled on him, poking his chest with a finger. "This is exactly what I wanted to avoid! It hasn't even been twenty-four hours, and the family already knows we spent the night together! Way to keep your word, Nash."

He gave her a chastened frown. "I'll talk to Damon and Myles, ask them for discretion."

"That's not the point!" she said in a fierce whisper. "I trusted you! You promised me not to say anything and you betrayed that trust!"

"That's not true." He stepped toward her and tried to place a hand on her arm.

She shook off his touch with a scoff. "Oh? So Detective Cartwright is psychic? He asked me specifically about the hours I was at your house last night."

"I can explain—"

"And I guess Myles and your brother just made a really good guess whom you bedded last night?"

"Val…"

"At least have the guts not to lie to me about it!" To her horror, she realized a tear had seeped past her eye and was tickling her cheek. She dashed it away with a brusque slash of her hand.

She fell silent, fighting for composure. She didn't want to fall apart in front of him, didn't want him to know how hurt she was. How much she cared.

Nash moved to the edge of her bed and sat down. "Are you done? Can I speak?"

She gave a petulant shrug.

"I didn't say anything. I did my best to protect your secret like you asked." His tone was calm and reasonable. "In the course of proving the candlestick used to kill Axel had been planted in my car to frame me, the truth came out about you."

"Meaning?"

"Damon acquired the security-camera footage from a neighbor that showed you arriving in my driveway and your car staying until this morning, when we left together."

She held his gaze, digesting what he'd said. Her anger dissipated, leaving her feeling all the more like a deflated balloon—wilted and flat. "Oh."

He nodded. "Oh." After a moment, he narrowed his eyes and tipped his head. "What did you say when Cartwright asked you about being at my house?"

Valerie's pulse spiked. She paced toward the window that looked over the backyard and licked her dry lips. "You were released, weren't you? Doesn't that tell you?"

"I was released because my neighbors' security camera recorded someone planting the candlestick in my car. But it also showed your car parked in front of mine all night. The security video proved my claim the murder weapon was planted and that I had an alibi."

She cut a sharp glance toward him, a surge of relief piercing her dark mood. "There's proof the candleholder was planted?"

He bobbed his head as he pushed off the bed to move toward her. "Yeah. But you haven't answered my question. What did you tell Cartwright?"

Valerie swallowed hard, trying to shove down the knot that swelled in her throat. "The truth. That you couldn't have killed Axel because you were with me all night."

One dark-blond eyebrow quirked. "So *you* told your secret?"

She squared her shoulders. "I couldn't lie to the cops. Besides..." Her throat tightened again, and she paused to take a slow breath. "I couldn't... I couldn't let you be arrested for a crime you didn't commit."

A slow, sexy smile spread across his face. "Well... thank you."

He reached for her, and when he tugged her into his arms, she went easily. Val melted against him, savoring the comfort his warm body offered. She curled her fingers into the soft fabric of his shirt, and a shuddering sigh rattled from her. "So now what? You've been cleared of murder, but your family knows about us. I'm not mad that you told Cartwright about us to clear your name, but why did you tell your brother and Myles?"

"Myles was there as my lawyer and Damon got the security video from my neighbor. They were in the room when Cartwright and I watched the recording."

Compunction for her castigation, for assuming he'd told their secret washed through her. "Oh. I thought..."

"Is that really such a bad thing, the family knowing?"

"You heard Damon..."

"He's my brother. Brothers tease. I'll talk to him. I promise." With strong fingers under her chin, he tilted her face up to his. He placed a gentle kiss on her lips, and ripples of sweet sensation flowed through her. His second kiss was deeper, and the third stole her breath and made her knees wobble. When he finally lifted his head and brushed his knuckles along her cheek, he whispered,

"Honestly, Val, what I want is to shout from the roof that you're my girl. I've waited for you, wanted you since I was twelve years old."

"Twelve? We didn't become a couple until you were sixteen. I was fifteen and—" The tender smile on his face stopped her. "Do you mean…?"

"Like I said. Twelve. You may not have caught on until later, but that summer we all went to the lake in Minnesota…" He pressed a hand to his heart. "I was a goner. There's a reason I wanted to play so much *Monopoly*. And it wasn't because I liked the tedious game you were obsessed with. No one else would play, so I had you to myself for hours on end."

She bit her lip and shook her head. "You let me win to keep me interested, didn't you?"

"Maybe."

Looping her arms around his neck, she snuggled close to him again. "All I've wanted, since I was old enough to realize my mother cared more about her next drink than she did me, was to have someone I could rely on, someone who'd have my back and love me for me. That's why it hurt so much when I thought you'd broken your promise about our night together. I thought you'd broken my trust."

Nash's brow dipped, and hurt clouded his eyes. "I thought we—"

The jangling notes of her cell phone interrupted Nash and jarred Valerie from the intimate moment. A small shudder of irritation chased through her at the interruption.

"Go ahead." Nash hitched his head toward her purse. "Take it. I'll give you some privacy. I need to call my boss, anyway, let him know what's happening. I had something like twelve messages from him when I got my phone back from the cops."

"Geez. Definitely. Go save your job." Her gaze followed him—she drank in the sight of his lean body and panther-like stride as he left the room. A flicker of heat spread in her belly as she retrieved her phone and remembered those long legs and his taut body wrapped around hers. Making love to her. Cradling her gently afterward. Comforting her when she'd shared her painful past with him.

What was she supposed to do with this complicated, sexy man?

"Hello," she said, answering her call distractedly, without checking her caller ID. Mistake.

"I told you those Coltons were no good!"

Acid pooled in her gut as her mother's sour tone spilled from her phone. She grimaced. "Mother."

"Have you seen the news?"

"No," she said honestly, not bothering to add she'd been living the tragic events with the Colton family.

"Erik's brother, Axel, was murdered! They arrested that boy—the one who got you pregnant—for it!"

Valerie gritted her teeth. Did she really want to hash this out with her mother? "Mother, calm down. It's not like that."

"Oh, it is exactly like that, Valerie Jane! I saw the footage of them putting him in a police cruiser and taking him in. I told you he was bad news, just like his father!"

"He didn't do anything, Mother. The evidence was planted, and he's already been released."

"I— My God, are you defending him? They wouldn't have questioned him without good reason!"

Dropping onto the bed, Valerie scrubbed her free hand

over her face. "You're an expert on police investigations now?"

"I know enough to know you need to come home. The sooner, the better."

"No."

Her mother sighed dramatically. "I know you feel a loyalty to your uncle and Vita, and you want to help. But this isn't your problem. If you stay down there around those Colton vipers, you will get bitten! No good can come of—"

"Mother, stop! You're wrong about the Coltons. Well, most of them. And especially about Nash."

"Oh, Valerie," her mother said, her tone heavy with sorrow. "They've brainwashed you. Don't be drawn in by their money and power. And please don't forget how that boy hurt you once."

Valerie's ire surged. It took a moment to catch her breath, but when she did, she snarled, "He's not a *boy*, Mother. He's a man. A good man. A successful architect and respected member of his family and the community."

Her mother snorted loudly. "And a Colton!"

"And for the record, you were far more responsible for hurting me than Nash ever was. You manipulated the situation and—"

"Me?" her mother shrieked. "All I've ever done is protect you!"

Val took a beat to shove down her frustration. Her mother's frantic tone was all too familiar, and a niggling suspicion poked Val. "Mother, are you taking your meds?"

"Don't start with me, Valerie Jane. I know what I'm talking about."

"Did you go to your doctor appointment yesterday?

To your AA meeting on Monday?" Maybe she should call her mother's counselor or ask her AA sponsor to check on her.

"I'm not a child, and I'll not have you speak to me that way. And don't change the subject! This is about you and that Colton boy. He's a criminal! A murderer and a liar and—"

"No, Mother. He's not! He didn't kill Axel. Please, take a breath. Calm down…"

"You don't know that. Clearly the police think he's guilty or they w—"

"I do know! Because I was with him! I am Nash's alibi. I was at his house last night. All night!"

Her mother gasped sharply. "What?"

Okay, that wasn't the way she'd intended to break the news to her mother that she and Nash had made a fresh start, but now that she'd lost her cool and blurted the truth, she needed to do damage control. "Mother, Nash is not like his father. He is a good—"

"No!" Her mother made a high-pitched noise, like a growl or whine. "No, no, no! Valerie, you need to come home! Don't do this to me!"

"Mother, I think you should call Dr. Richards. Or Nancy. You aren't alone—"

"No! You are dead to me!"

Valerie heard a clatter, as if the phone had been thrown. "Mother? Mother, are you there?"

Then a shuffling sound and silence. She checked her phone. The screen read, Call ended.

She tried calling her mother back but got no answer. Of course. Next she tried her mother's AA sponsor, Nancy Acree, and left a message. After a quick call to leave a message with Dr. Richards, her mother's psychiatrist, she contemplated returning to Ohio to check on her mother in person.

She'd come to Chicago to support the family she loved during one crisis, only to find herself the center of another. And she had unfinished business with Nash. How could she leave now? Valerie pinched the bridge of her nose and resolved to call her mother later that evening and to keep trying to reach Nancy until she was sure someone knew about her mother's episode.

Valerie bunched the bedspread in her hands and gritted her teeth, feeling a burning resentment bubble up in her. Her mother had been responsible for tearing her and Nash apart once before. She would not let that happen again.

Chapter Eleven

The next morning, having arranged for Nancy to check on her mother, Valerie walked over to the nursery to meet with Sara concerning the Yates' Yards winter advertising campaign, as she'd promised Rick she would. She found Vita on the sales floor, arranging the new shipment of poinsettias on circular shelves of decreasing width. The display looked like a Christmas tree of red, pink and white blooms with wide green foliage.

"Goodness, Vita! It's still three weeks until Thanksgiving."

"Not in the retail world, my dear." Vita aimed a finger at a pair of scissors. "Will you hand me those, please? I see a bit here that needs a trim."

After handing over the tool, Valerie paused to study the arrangement and wondered what it would be like to celebrate Christmas with Rick and Vita. And Nash.

As a child and teen, holidays with her parents had always been dismal affairs. Her father had been remote, tense, while her mother spoiled what few traditions they'd attempted with drinking and wild mood swings. Knowing the primary source of her mother's behavior had been undiagnosed mental illness did nothing to change the drab gray that colored her memories. A pang swelled in her chest, a longing to stay in Chicago with these people who knew how to love and celebrate and support one another through difficult times. She wanted a real Christmas, with color and warmth and a family that cared about her.

But that would leave her mother alone for the holiday. Vulnerable to her depression, her alcoholism, her isolation. Guilt bit hard. Valerie was the only family her mother had left. How could she abandon her for her own selfish wants?

With a smile to her aunt, she headed back to the small office in the back of the nursery, where Sara was already hunched over a desk, chewing the end of a pen as she studied a notepad. She looked up as Valerie entered, and a bright smile lit her face. “There’s my Florence Nightingale.”

Valerie snorted. “Hardly. I get queasy at the sight of blood.”

Sara shrugged. “Maybe, but I appreciate your help yesterday when I passed out.” Her cheeks flushed. “I’m not usually so flaky, but the one-two punch of no breakfast and the horrible news about Mr. Colton…”

Val placed a hand on her new friend’s shoulder. “You’re not flaky. And I think it’s sweet that you care enough about the Colton family to be shocked at Axel’s death.”

Sara opened her mouth as if to respond, then averted her gaze.

Valerie tipped her head. “Unless the Mr. Colton you mean is Nash and him being taken to the police station. In which case, never fear. He was released without charges. He had both an alibi and evidence the presumed murder weapon was planted.”

Sara's chin jerked up, and her eyes rounded. "Planted? Why would someone want to frame Nash?"

Valerie took a seat across from Sara and set the sketch pad she'd brought on the desk. "That is the question of the day. I don't know." She flipped open her pad to the last drawing she'd made. "Enough about all that trouble. Let's talk advertising. What do you think of this? I like the idea you had of focusing on how plants and flowers add a coziness to the holidays. The warm, family gathering theme."

Sara studied Valerie's sketch of a family together in a living room filled with Christmas greenery, poinsettias and amaryllis. "We can do another ad the following week that focuses on winter plants for the yard and the outdoor decorations we sell. Lights and wreaths and the like."

"Do you have a tag line in mind?" Valerie asked.

"I've been toying with a couple."

Excited by the campaign that took form as she and Sara collaborated, Valerie lost track of time. She loved being able to use her talents to help her uncle and Vita. Her artwork was more than a job to her. It was a passion. She'd been drawing, expressing her deepest thoughts and emotions with pencil and paper, for as long as she could remember. Her drawings were an extension of her soul, and sharing her talent to benefit her family filled her with joy.

She and Sara were buried in layouts and in the thick of a free flow of brainstorming when the office door opened with a thump that yanked Valerie from her thought stream.

"Soup's on!" Lila called as she breezed in with bags in her hands.

"Soup?" Valerie asked, peeking in the first bag Lila plunked down on the desk.

"I took the liberty of springing for lunch." She divided a look between Valerie and Sara. "Is now a convenient time for you two to take a break?"

"Sure. Good timing. My stomach's been embarrassing me for the last half an hour. Rumble, grumble." Sara grinned and clicked the mouse to save their work.

"What's the occasion?" Val asked as she pulled a paper-wrapped sandwich out of a bag with the logo *True* on it.

"Do I need a reason?" Lila asked with a coy shrug. "It's been such a long time since we had a chance to just…chat."

Valerie arched an eyebrow, grinning. "We've *chatted* several times since I arrived."

Lila grunted. "Too many of those conversations were tainted by the reigning glum topic of the moment. Kidnapping and murder and funeral plans. Bleh!" Lila unpacked paper bowls with lids from a second bag. "Besides, cumulatively speaking, we need to have many chats to make up for the years you were MIA."

Valerie gave Lila a nod of assent. "Touché."

Sara followed the back-and-forth of the exchange as if she were watching a tennis match, and an amused smile tugged at her lips. "I wish I'd had this growing up. Siblings. Cousins. A big family to share the hard times, the special days, the celebrations of life."

"You were an only child?" Valerie asked, and Sara nodded. "Me, too. I was often lonely. I was lucky to be able to adopt the Colton brood part-time from a young age thanks to my Uncle Rick marrying into the clan. I had many happy summers here." She reached for Lila's hand and gave it a squeeze.

Lila returned a squeeze but pinned a stern, inquiring look on Val. "Then why did you stop visiting? Why did you stay away for so long?"

Valerie paused in the middle of removing a lid from one of the steaming cups. "Oh. That is a long story. Complicated. Not one I want to dive into while we're eating." Seizing an inspiration to change the subject, she opened the container and glanced down at the bright orange puree inside. "Speaking of which, what are we eating?"

"That," Lila said, nodding to the cup Valerie lifted to sniff, "is pumpkin soup. Try it. It's amazing! Everything Tatum does at True is fantastic. And it's all farm-to-table."

"Two questions," Valerie said. "Tatum? True? And what's this?" She unfolded the paper wrapping from the sandwich and inhaled the savory aroma.

"That's three questions," Sara teased as she unwrapped what appeared to be a chicken salad sandwich.

"Tatum is one of the new cousins we learned about this summer," Lila said with a chuckle for Sara. "She's Alfred Colton's daughter and owner of True Restaurant, a local farm-to-table." She waved her hand to the spread. "You have a beef and cheese sandwich, but I'll trade if you'd rather have the veggie. They're both fantastic. The soups are pumpkin, cream of potato and tomato basil. I brought extra bowls and a knife so we can all sample everything."

"Good idea," Sara said. "It all looks wonderful."

"So," Lila said and shot Valerie a side glance as she divided the three sandwiches evenly. "You and Nash, huh? Do tell."

Valerie sighed heavily. "I was wondering when this

would come up. Nash swore Damon and Myles could keep it quiet, but families are too much like small towns. News travels fast."

"Why would you want to keep it a secret?" Sara asked. "Nash seems great."

Lila aimed her spoon at Sara. "Yeah. What she asked."

Valerie stirred the pumpkin soup and stalled. "We have a complicated history and… I'm not sure where things stand between us, where we're going. If we are going anywhere. I mean, my life, my job, my mother are all back in Ohio, and Nash is here. His family is here…"

Lila flashed a lopsided smile. "Geography. I get it. Things were a little tricky between Carter and me when we first got together. He travels for his job and I have my gallery here. But we decided we were worth the effort to work out a compromise. We will be together whatever and *wherever* that means."

An ache of longing tugged Valerie's chest. Had she ever had someone so loyal, so trustworthy, so devoted to her that she could lean on them unconditionally? She'd believed Nash was that someone when she was seventeen. And when that dream had shattered, the ache of loss and betrayal almost smothered her. But now her understanding of what had transpired all those years ago had been turned topsy-turvy, and even the jagged, painful beliefs she'd once stood on and clung to for a sense of stability shifted beneath her. The rootlessness was disconcerting.

Valerie smiled politely and took a bite of sandwich. If her issues with Nash were only about geography, things would be so much clearer. But her mother's obsession with the Coltons, her fragile mental health and the whole issue of trust. And commitment. And honesty. And forgiveness—they had a laundry list of baggage to deal with before she could see any future for them. "It's not just that we live in different states. Like I said, our history is messy and—"

"Wait. History?" Lila set down her sandwich and wiped her mouth with a napkin. "Did you and Nash have a thing before this trip? Like…as kids? All those summers you were here…?" Lila's eyes lit with excitement and fascination.

Valerie glanced to Sara as if her new friend could help her out of the awkward spot. But Sara grinned and leaned forward with eager anticipation bright in her gaze, as well.

"Um…"

Lila laughed and playfully swatted Valerie's arm. "Oh, my stars! You did! Your guilty blush is all the answer I need."

Valerie's shoulders drooped. "Okay, yes. But then there were misunderstandings, and broken promises, and disappointments, and—"

Lila took her by the wrist and drilled her with a green gaze so like Nash's it stole Valerie's breath. "The only question that matters is 'do you love him?'"

Once, she'd thought she did. She'd given her heart and soul to Nash, believing he was the one. Now, the honest answer she gave Lila was "I don't know."

NASH DIDN'T SEE much of Valerie over the next couple of days. He returned to work at Reed and Burdett, the architecture firm where he was rising through the ranks, hoping to make partner in a few years. He put in long hours, knowing he'd taken too much personal time of late. His bosses had, of course, seen the news footage showing him being hauled to the police station, but because they knew Nash, knew his character, they believed his explanation of what had happened. His bosses rallied behind him, even though Nash had to protect certain details of the case, both for the integrity of the ongoing investigation, and for his and Valerie's privacy.

Two days after he'd been hauled down to the police station, Detective Cartwright paid Nash a visit at work. The receptionist who ushered the detective to Nash's office lingered in the hall, pretending to decide whether a plant needed watering and checking her reflection in a decorative mirror.

Nash rounded his desk to shake the detective's hand and closed the door firmly. "What can I do for you, Detective?"

Cartwright pulled a file folder out of a messenger bag and tossed it on top of the blueprints spread on Nash's desk. "Tell me if you recognize this guy."

Picking up the folder, Nash returned to his seat and flipped to the photos inside. Some of the photos were fuzzy black-and-white shots, obviously taken from security-camera footage. Others were mug shots. Others were images likely lifted from social media and cropped to cut other people from the frame. The star of all of the photos was a hefty, middle-age guy with buzz-cut blond hair and a tattoo of barbed wire on his neck. The dude obviously lifted weights. Probably enhanced with one or more supplements that would disqualify him from professional sports. He had a pierced eyebrow and wore a grim expression on his square face.

Nash closed the file and tossed it back toward Detective Cartwright. "I give up. Who is he?"

"Nothing? You're sure?"

"That's not a face someone's likely to forget. No.

Never seen him before. Don't have any idea who he is." He lowered his eyebrows. "But I'm guessing you do and that you have good reason to ask me. So what gives?"

Cartwright grunted and slid the folder closer. He tapped the file against his knee before he returned it to his messenger bag. "His name is Simon Wilcox. We recovered a partial thumbprint from the trunk of your car that matched his."

"He's in the system?"

Cartwright nodded. "Yeah. Mostly minor stuff, but we've long suspected he's a…well, let's call him a thug for hire."

Nash arched an eyebrow. "As in 'dirty deeds done dirt cheap'?"

Cartwright tugged his cheek briefly in a fake grin, acknowledging the AC/DC reference. "As in he advertises his services on the dark web. For the right price, he'll do just about anything. Breaking and entering, terrorizing ex-wives, hiding bodies—"

"Planting evidence of murder?"

Rather than answer Nash's question directly, Cartwright said, "The suspect in the security video that your neighbor supplied has the same body type. We got two numbers off the license plate of the suspect's car. Three nine. Simon's wife has a light blue Cougar coupe. Tag number three-nine-five-G-R-two."

Nash spread his hands. "Sounds like you got the right guy."

"Except his wife swears, hand to heaven, he was with her all night."

Nash groaned. "And you really believe her?"

Cartwright shrugged. "Just saying. We brought him in to question him, as well, but got nothing. Not that we expected much. Not good for his business model if he squeals on the people who hire him."

"So you let him go?" Nash asked, aghast.

"For now. Until we have enough to build a more solid case. That's why I was hoping you had something to help us connect him to this."

Nash puffed out a breath and shook his head. "Man, I wish I did, but I never laid eyes on him until you showed me that picture. And I don't even know how to get on the dark web, much less how to hire a thug from a murky website or whatever."

Cartwright pulled a face and exhaled his obvious frustration. "Okay. Well, I'll get out of your way."

"Wait," Nash said, leaning forward and pinning the detective with narrow-eyed scrutiny. "That's it? You said you had a partial print. Isn't that enough to tag the guy?"

"It's certainly a start. But if that's all we have, his lawyer will claim he could've touched your car in a grocery-store parking lot. We need more that connects him to the candlestick. To Axel's residence. So..." Cartwright stood, ducked his chin in parting. "Thank you for your time."

Nash gritted his back teeth, knowing the cop wouldn't say more about an active investigation. The detective had made it to the door before Nash said, "One more thing."

Cartwright turned. "Yeah?"

"I understand from my Aunt Vita that you know Brad Howard, the FBI man that helped Myles when Jackson was taken."

"I do. We've worked together in the past."

"On the murders of Ernest and Alfred Colton?"

Cartwright pulled back his shoulders and raised his chin. His expression said he was weighing his response. Finally he said, "Yes. Why?"

"Turns out Alfred and Ernest were my half uncles. Dean Colton's legitimate children."

Cartwright nodded. "I'm aware."

"Axel was my uncle. Also Dean's son." Nash waved a hand as if the connection should be obvious. More likely, the detective was just being tight-lipped to see where Nash would go with his theory. "Doesn't that smell to you? Have you looked into a connection?"

"I've considered that angle, and, I assure you, we follow up every possible connection."

"So you don't think there's any link? Is that what you're saying?"

Cartwright hoisted the strap of the messenger bag on his shoulder and shook his head. "Your half uncles were random targets, killed by young sociopaths on a killing spree. One is dead, the other's in custody."

"Right. I know." Nash tried to keep the impatience from his tone. Failed. "We met our half cousins and heard the story. Followed the case on the news. I'm asking if it's possible there was a third guy involved in the killing spree, someone you haven't identified—"

Cartwright raised a hand, cutting him off. "I know you want answers. You're trying to help, but…no. That case is closed. We've not found any link or similarities."

Nash opened his mouth to further his argument, but closed it again with a sigh.

Cartwright reached for the doorknob and gave Nash a confident nod. "We will find the person responsible for killing Axel Colton. I give you my word."

LATER THAT NIGHT, Nash sat alone in his bungalow, turning the facts of the murder case and his conversation with Cartwright over in his head, feeling violated and angry over the cretin who'd planted the candlestick. Damon had stopped by earlier in the evening to renew his arguments to install a security system. For the first time, Nash was considering it, which also made him mad, because he hated feeling like he'd caved. But if Valerie was going to be spending more time here, he wanted her to be safe.

But that begged the question—would Valerie be here more often? Or even, at all? They hadn't really settled anything about what was between them. He couldn't say whether they were looking toward the future or simply glad to have some clarity on the past. He'd texted her once or twice, inviting her to come to dinner, to see where they stood now that they'd cleared the air. And gotten quick, if brief, replies putting him off for one reason or another. Already had plans. Migraine. Working late with Sara on ad campaign. Some part of him feared history was repeating itself.

Twelve years ago, she'd assumed the worst about him based on circumstantial evidence from her mother. She'd denied him the right to know about her pregnancy. She'd shut him out. And although she'd explained her side of events a few nights ago, the fact remained that, twelve years ago, she'd dismissed his needs, his feelings and his rights in order to protect herself. Was that what she was doing now, even after all his assurances to her?

Years ago, she'd easily bought into a lie that allowed her to justify her actions. She'd been hurting, yes. But she also hadn't given him a chance to defend himself, to speak the truth, to give her the love and support he'd wanted to give her.

And now? Could he trust her? She'd asked for time, for continued secrecy while she decided how to proceed.

But what was there to decide? Did she care about him and believe in him or didn't she?

Acid climbed Nash's throat as his irritation and resentment grew. He'd spent too many years waiting and hoping for his father's love and attention to repeat those mistakes with Valerie. Was it too much to ask for Valerie's unconditional love and faith? He refused to settle for anything less.

Stop it! He squeezed his eyes shut and shook his head as if to jar loose the negative track of his thoughts. He was letting his bad relationship with his father, the resentment over being framed for Axel's murder and a mistaken view of history between him and Valerie color his perception. He was an adult now and needed to view the situation without the warping lens of his emotions. He poured himself a drink at his wet bar and took a sip.

At least she hadn't shut him out, completely ghosted him, like last time. She'd told Cartwright the truth. That was something.

Nash carried his whiskey sour out to the front porch and sat in one of the rocking chairs that Nicole had insisted every front porch required. He sipped his drink and inhaled the cool crisp air and scent of fallen leaves. He blew out a slow, intentional breath and could feel the stress and negativity seep out of him like air from a leaky balloon. Yet a new, overriding sense of isolation and melancholy remained, and he tried to put his finger on the source.

A neighbor he recognized but didn't know by name strolled past on the sidewalk and waved. He returned a kind nod and smile.

His was a calm, quiet neighborhood. Safe. Friendly.

As if to echo that sentiment, the neighbor's calico,

who strangely seemed to prefer Nash's house to his own, sauntered up the porch steps and mewed as he rubbed against Nash's calves. Bending to scratch the cat's head, Nash snorted at the irony. "I don't feed you. I don't have a cat to be your buddy. I know your family takes care of you. Why are you always here?"

The cat's bland, even dorky, expression gave Nash a chuckle. "Why do I think you might not be too smart?"

The cat meowed as if to agree.

Nash opened his mouth to comment again and paused. Swore under his breath. He was talking to a cat. Geez, he really was lonely and pathetic if he'd stooped to conversations with his neighbor's feline for company. Taking another sip of whiskey, he realized living alone had never bothered him before. Until… *Valerie.*

One night of arguing, having dinner and making love to Valerie had him reassessing his whole life. Or was it because his siblings and cousins seemed to all be falling in love and finding life partners? He was the last of the family to be unattached, and having seen how happy Damon, Lila, Aaron and the rest were, maybe he was feeling a bit left out. Maybe seeing Valerie awoke old emotions he'd thought he'd safely archived. Memories of losing his mother, being pushed aside and neglected by his father… Valerie's disappearing act.

Dang, but he was maudlin tonight. Why?

A tomato-soup-red VW Beetle rolled past his house and pulled in the driveway two doors down. The cat moved to the edge of the porch, watching his owner get out and walk to the mailbox.

"Your mom's home."

The cat gave him a drowsy backward glance, then

moseyed down his porch steps and across his lawn toward home.

Nash tightened his grip on the cold highball glass in his hand. The pang that vibrated like a plucked string in his core was not—*was not*—loneliness over the cat leaving. That was pure nonsense. But…maybe the cat helped highlight to him what was missing from his life. He'd kept people at arm's length most of his life. Letting people get close was a recipe for pain. He'd learned that well enough.

Were surface, distanced relationships all he had to look forward to the rest of his life? Without trusting someone to see his heart, without letting someone into his life and lowering his guard enough for an intimate relationship, all he saw in the years to come was this empty house, this hollow ache and, if he was lucky, visits from someone else's cat.

"Well, that sucks." He needed to make a change. And that change just might start with Valerie.

Chapter Twelve

Two days later, as Valerie dressed for Axel's funeral, she battled the butterflies that flapped to life whenever she realized that she'd see Nash again. He'd have ample opportunities both at the service and the reception of family here at Vita and Rick's to corner her and demand answers.

She both wanted to see him and didn't. She'd put him off the last several days when he'd asked to see her with excuses as transparent as wet tissue paper. But she'd needed the time to process her feelings. She wanted to be sure she could keep her composure, deflect the gush of emotions that flooded her whenever they were together. She'd been honest when she told Lila and Sara she didn't know what she felt for Nash. The night they'd spent together had cleared up some misconceptions and buried some old anger, but dragged new puzzling feelings and questions into the spotlight, too.

Her mother's calls and texts, begging her to come home, warning her that Nash would hurt her and vilifying the Colton family every way imaginable, only complicated things for Valerie. So many of her mother's theories were clearly rooted in wild speculation and her mother's paranoia. She didn't really give them credence, but she was torn between duty and loyalty to her mother and the love and trust she had for the Coltons. Specifically, the relationship she couldn't stop daydreaming about with Nash. If her mother weren't a factor, would she step over the impediments and shoulder past the roadblocks that kept her from racing to Nash's house and promising him her all? Could she risk that kind of pain again? Did she want to?

After surviving the kind of breath-stealing pain and loss she had at seventeen, had the kind of root-deep suspicion her mother had planted pounded into her for years, a change of heart—going back to the beginning, putting her heart on the line—was so difficult.

She sighed as she looked at her reflection in the full-length mirror. The wide black belt she wore with the navy blue dress she'd borrowed from Lila for the funeral emphasized how much weight she'd lost in just the few weeks she'd been in Chicago. Despite the ample leftovers of Nicole's baking, Vita's generous portions at their family dinners and the discovery of Tatum's restaurant, True, Valerie couldn't be tempted to eat more than a few bites per meal. The stress of murders, kidnappings, arrests and emotional reunions had wrung her out and squelched her appetite.

She applied a little extra blush and chose a lipstick color that wouldn't wash her out, then hurried downstairs to join Vita and Rick for the drive to the church.

"Nash said to tell you he'd save you a seat," Vita said as Rick parked in the crowded lot behind the church.

Valerie snapped her gaze from the horde of journalists camped on the front lawn to her aunt. "Oh?" Then, after a breath… "Oh."

"Good thing," Rick said. "Looks like ol' Axel drew a crowd."

Vita shook her head and frowned. "Nosy Nellies, most of them, I bet."

Rick cut the engine and shrugged. "Don't be so sure. Axel had plenty of business associates and his children certainly had plenty of friends who would be here out of respect."

Vita straightened the stylish hat she wore and checked her lipstick in the visor mirror one last time. "Well, one way to find out. Myles said we'd have seats up front, but not that they'd hold the service so…let's go, huh?"

Valerie opened the back door of Rick's car, deciding Vita was gathering her courage to face the past as much as she was. Vita may have moved on, may have divorced Axel and built a far better life with Rick, but…well, funerals had a way of stirring up the past. Buried memories. Old hurts.

She linked her arm with Vita's as they headed inside. She offered her support to the woman who'd been so kind to her through the years as much as she drew strength from Vita's example.

Chin up. Shoulders square. No regrets. Only dignity and grace.

A few heads turned as they entered, but Vita didn't falter. Her aunt gave her a cheek kiss before slipping her arm free and striding confidently with her husband to the rows down front, where Lila, Carter, Myles and Faith waited.

With a quick scan of the pews, she located Nash, Damon and their half brother, Aaron. Both Aaron and Damon had their girlfriends beside them, and Ruby had Maya tucked close to her side. Nash motioned to the empty seat. For her. Taking a deep breath, she whispered apologies to Damon, Ruby and Maya as she sidled between the next pew and their knees.

Valerie settled on the cushioned seat next to Nash and smiled a silent greeting to Aaron and his girlfriend, Felicia. She glanced around the crowded church then leaned in to whisper to Nash. "Vita, Rick and I were debating. Friends or curious spectators?"

Nash glanced casually over his shoulder as if only noticing the full pews for the first time. "I'm not sure. Most are strangers to me. Some could be here out of respect for the Colton name. Not that Axel did anything to preserve the family's good name. The rest? They're probably busybodies hoping to witness a scandalous scene they can gossip about."

She gave Nash a wry smile. "Careful there. Your bitterness is showing. The man is dead now. Maybe for your own health you should think about letting bygones be bygones and let him rest in peace?"

Nash grunted. "I know." He took her hand in his and squeezed her fingers. "I wish it were that easy."

A loud wailing sound came from the back of the church, and Valerie joined the many other congregants who turned to see what—or more precisely *who*—the disturbance was. She spotted an older woman being led down the aisle by members of the funeral-home staff. The woman was dressed in black from head to toe, and alternately dabbed her eyes and pressed her hand to her breast as she sobbed loudly. Even to Valerie, the wails of distress sounded stiff. Forced. Lugubrious.

Beside Valerie, Damon groaned under his breath, "Good grief."

Val cut another look to Nash—his brow was creased

and his mouth was clamped in a taut line. “Who’s that?” she whispered.

He leaned close, his aftershave surrounding her and distracting her. “My grandmother. Carin Pedersen.”

“That’s her fake-mourning cry. Her oh-woe-is-me, everyone-pay-attention-to-me, I’ve-been-so-wronged tears. What a crock,” Damon added, earning an elbow jab and warning glance from Ruby.

“Pedersen? Not Colton?” Val whispered to Nash.

“She never married our grandfather, Dean Colton,” Nash explained quietly. “She’d been an affair, and he belatedly gave our dad and Axel the Colton name at the same time he paid Carin some hush money. She’s currently trying to claim her sons were Dean’s real heirs.”

In deference to the public nature of the event, Valerie tried hard to school her face, but a whispered “Wow!” slipped out. “How so?”

The organ music ended, and as the minister appeared at the altar, he motioned for all to rise.

“Later,” Nash promised.

Valerie nodded and stood with the rest of the mourners as the prayer of invocation was given. The service was somber, if a bit over-the-top for Valerie’s taste. By its conclusion, the ostentatious service felt more like a Broadway show than a funeral, with choirs, speeches and slide shows, concluding with a release of white doves from the front steps of the church as Axel’s casket was wheeled out to the hearse.

“Seriously?” Aaron muttered, one eyebrow arched. “Doves?”

“A vulture would have been more appropriate,” someone behind Valerie said. She didn’t see who, as her attention had snagged on Nash. His eyes were locked on someone across the lawn, and his jaw had grown granite-hard.

Before she could determine who had caught Nash's eye, however, Lila said loudly enough for her siblings and cousins to hear, "Heads up. Incoming." She groaned then added, "I'm not in the mood for this. Come on, babe. Let's make a run for it." Lila grabbed Carter's hand and made a hasty exit toward the parking lot with her fiancé in tow.

Nash gave a muffled groan and fixed a stiff smile on his face as Carin Pedersen marched up to them.

"You!" She aimed a bony finger with a long fuchsia-painted fingernail at Nash. "You have a lot of nerve coming here today!"

Valerie sidled a bit closer to Nash as if for protection—or maybe to protect him from the venomous vibe spewing from the older woman. His family seemed of a similar mindset. Several of them drew closer to Nash, forming a half circle around him, while others, notably Ruby and Faith, led their children away from what they clearly sensed could be an ugly confrontation.

Valerie felt the tension that coiled in Nash when she touched his arm in support. His eyes were cool as he forced a smile. "Carin. A touching service. My sympathies to you."

"Your sympathies?" she snapped at him, her tone shrill and her face screwing up with haughty indignation. "Your sympathies! You should be ashamed of yourself for showing your face here!"

"Oh?" he said in a surprisingly calm tone. "Why is that?"

"You killed him!" She shook the finger aimed at Nash, and Valerie had to battle the urge to slap away the woman's offensive finger. "I saw the news reports! The police had you in custody, had proof you'd killed my son. But thanks to some sort of favoritism or police corruption or other underhanded tactics, you wiggled off the hook."

"Because he didn't do it!" Valerie blurted before she could stop herself. "The evidence against him was planted."

Now the arthritic finger waved toward the other Coltons as Carin's eyes narrowed. "Who said that? Hmm? My son was murdered! And in the last conversation I had with my son—" she paused and squeezed her eyes shut, as if battling a sharp onslaught of emotion "—he told me how Nash accosted him. Threatened him." She squared her shoulders, her sour expression back in place. "I'll find proof you did this and see you pay!"

"What proof?" Valerie asked, unable to stay silent when someone she cared about was being attacked.

Nash wrapped his fingers around her wrist and silently shook his head, as if to say "Don't bother arguing with her."

Carin shifted her narrowed gaze to Val. "Who are you, anyway? What do you know about any of it?"

"This is Valerie Yates, Rick's niece from Ohio," Nash said, as if making introductions at a society soiree. "Valerie, my grandmother."

Shoving down the bitterness at the back of her throat, Valerie held out a hand to shake Carin's, but it went ignored.

"Rick's niece?" Carin grumbled. "Humph. That man has relatives coming out of the walls like roaches."

Valerie coughed to cover her dismay at the characterization of her father and Rick's relations, but recovered quickly. "Yes, we've been blessed with a large family.

Much like the Coltons. Just roaches everywhere!" Behind her she heard a muffled laugh.

Carin angled her chin up and sent an encompassing gaze around to the Colton cousins gathered on the church lawn. Now her focus stopped on Sara Sandoval. "You're new, too. Another of Rick's nieces?"

Sara shifted her feet nervously, clearly awkward with having been singled out. "I, uh…no."

Aaron moved forward and put an arm around Sara's shoulders. "She's a new hire at Yates' Yards. No relation. So back off."

Carin lifted one eyebrow, clearly miffed by Aaron's tone, then gave Sara another narrow look. "Are you sure she's not another one of Dean and Anna's brood? She certainly has the look of a Colton. Those eyes…"

While Aaron replied to Carin's badgering of Sara, Valerie leaned toward Nash again. "So Axel and your father were illegitimate," she said, trying to sort out the details of the family tree that seemed to grow new branches every day.

"Yeah."

As a kid visiting Uncle Rick and Vita's Colton clan, she'd never once considered the legitimacy of various family connections. Why would she? That was hardly the stuff a ten-year-old, or even a teenager, cared about. But now, given the discussions at Vita's dinner table or at other family gatherings, she was beginning to see the tangled web in a new light. "But he gave them the Colton name?"

"A bargain struck between Grandfather Dean and Carin, apparently. We only learned about Anna and her children and grandchildren recently ourselves. Carin hates that side of the family for obvious reasons. It gets rather messy, all the…roaches."

She snickered. "So it seems."

Carin was still wagging a disdainful finger at Aaron when a man with stooped shoulders and graying brown hair appeared at Carin's arm. He tugged her pointed finger down. "Careful, Mother. The cameras are watching."

Carin seemed ready to bark at the man beside her, then his words apparently sank in. She straightened a bit and put her grieving-mother face back in place as she turned slowly to face the gathering news media.

"For God's sake, why didn't you tell me sooner?" she hissed under her breath to the man.

When the man glanced toward Damon and Nash, Valerie saw the resemblance in his square jaw and green eyes, recognized who he must be even before he said, "Hello, boys."

Nash jerked a perfunctory nod. "Dad."

"Hi." Damon shoved his hands in his pockets, his stare flat.

The greetings were so stiff and cool that Valerie felt a prickle at her nape. Or maybe it was just the discomfort of meeting Erik Colton, the man who'd so cruelly rejected her mother that, years later, her mother still nurtured a bone-deep resentment. What would Erik say if she introduced herself as Carol Smith's daughter? Would he make the connection? Would he even remember her mother and the events of that summer thirty years ago?

"Ms. Pedersen! Ms. Pedersen!" the members of the media called as Carin turned toward the assembled cameras and dabbed at her eyes.

"Does Axel's death change anything regarding your lawsuit over Dean Colton's will?" one reporter called.

"Are there any new developments in your son's murder?" another asked.

"Can you confirm that—?"

"Please," Carin said, acting as if the barrage of questions was wearing down her already distressed condition. "One at a time."

"Where does Axel Colton's death leave the lawsuit against Dean Colton's estate?"

Carin lifted her chin. "The lawsuit is unchanged. My sons are—" She paused and clutched at Erik's arm.

Even if the older woman's actions were theater for the reporters, Valerie sympathized with Carin, at least in part. She remembered how difficult losing Nash's baby had been. She'd loved the unborn child immediately, even without ever seeing or holding the baby. Carin had shared decades of life experiences with Axel. She'd seen him take his first steps and learn to ride a bike, and shared dozens of holidays with him. Losing her son had to have left a mark.

"My son Erik is Dean Colton's legal heir," Carin insisted. "We will continue to vigorously pursue our claim to our rightful share of Dean Colton's fortune."

Valerie had heard mentions of the lawsuit that claimed Dean Colton's illegitimate sons were heirs to half of the Colton Connections fortune. Erik and Axel stood to inherit thirty million dollars if Nash's grandmother Carin won her lawsuit claiming her copy of Dean Colton's will was authentic. Valerie's head swam. She couldn't even fathom that much money.

"Are there any new leads in Axel Colton's murder?" another reporter shouted.

Carin's lips pinched, and she sent a baleful glance toward Nash.

Valerie's skin prickled, as if she sensed a predator breathing down her neck. The impulse to step between Carin and Nash and let the woman know, in no uncertain terms, that Nash was innocent and had done nothing to earn her scorn raced through her blood.

"No. The police had in their custody the most likely suspect and saw fit to release him. To say I am dismayed and displeased with the police department's willful disregard for the obvious would be an understatement."

Beside her, Nash sighed and muttered under his breath, "Thanks, Granny."

"Want to leave?" Valerie asked him.

"Not yet." Nash's gaze narrowed on the scene before them, but it seemed to Valerie that Carin wasn't his focal point.

"Mr. Colton, do you have a theory about who killed your brother?"

Valerie didn't see who asked the question, but she felt the tension that jerked Nash's body taut and saw Erik flinch before he firmed his thin shoulders and called back, "No comment."

"Surely you have some idea who might have wanted your brother dead," a different voice asked.

"Some might say you stand to gain the most with your brother's murder, if the lawsuit moves forward," a reporter near the front of the mob added.

Erik's fists balled, and he scowled at the man who'd made the last bold assertion. "I said 'no comment.'" He nudged Carin's arm and took a step away. "Come on, Mother. Don't give these vultures any more fodder."

With a loud *harrumph*, Carin turned to walk toward the waiting funeral home limousine.

"Carin?" Vita called from behind Valerie, then rushed forward when Carin paused.

Nash groaned quietly and whispered, "Oh, don't do it. Don't do it."

"The rest of the family is gathering back at our house. Would you like to come join us?" Vita asked, and Carin arched a thin eyebrow as if she'd been threatened instead of politely invited to break bread with her grandchildren.

Damon gave an equally dismayed and hushed groan. "Ugh. She did it."

Valerie covered an amused grin as she eyed Carin and Erik.

"Really?" Carin cast a suspicious glance at the huddle of Colton grandchildren and spouses. "You want me at your gathering? In your house?"

"You, too, Erik. You are family, after all." How Vita maintained a pleasant expression, Valerie didn't know. But for as long as Valerie had known Vita, Uncle Rick's wife had always shown grace under pressure and unconditional warmth.

"I, um—" Carin began, and then Erik spoke over her.

"No. Mother needs to rest. Today has been very trying for her."

Carin shot Erik a look as if to say "don't answer for me," but added, "I'll pass. I doubt I'd be welcomed by even your dog, and I have better things to do than make nice with people who don't want me around."

"Make nice?" Myles said under his breath. "When has she ever—?" He let out an *oof* as Faith elbowed him.

Vita managed a smile and gave a nod. "All right then. Take care."

As Erik escorted Carin toward the limo, the assembled Coltons gave a collective sigh of relief.

"Whew. That was close," Lila said.

"Yeah," Myles agreed, then said to Vita, "Mom, you're a saint. But don't ever do that again."

Damon chuckled wryly. "Amen."

Valerie turned to walk to the parking lot with the rest of the family, but paused when she realized Nash wasn't with her. She moved back to his side and followed his line of sight. "Nash?"

"Does my dad look…*old* to you?"

Valerie studied Erik a bit closer as the man circled the back end of the limo to climb in the opposite side. "He *is* getting old, Nash. Maybe not ancient, but…how specifically do you mean?"

"Just…worn down. Frailer somehow. I've always thought of him as this larger-than-life, indomitable figure. A Goliath among men."

"Goliath was beaten by a boy with a slingshot, Nash."

He gave her a brief side glance. "You know what I mean."

"Hmm. Seems to me dealing with your grandmother every day would be enough to wear down even a Navy SEAL."

Nash laughed. "There is that." He exhaled through pursed lips, then placed a hand at the small of her back to guide her out to his car.

"See you at Vita's?" Damon called as he held the door for Ruby.

Nash waved. "You bet."

THE FAMILY GATHERING after the funeral was a respectfully somber affair, but the love and support of the Colton children and their respective new love interests was on full display. For Valerie's part, she stayed close to Vita and

Rick, helping out wherever she could. She talked with Aaron and Felicia, entertained Maya by signing stories about her visits with the family as a youth and kept Sara company as she watched the Coltons from the sidelines.

But the confrontation with Carin Pedersen at the church had stirred a fresh line of inquiry for Valerie, namely how much Uncle Rick knew about her mother's history with Erik Colton. Did he know the whole story about her parents' past, her mother's hatred for the Coltons and Val's true paternity? The idea that Rick had kept secrets from her stung Valerie, and yet she, of all people, knew that keeping secrets was sometimes done to protect people one loved.

She mulled over the notion of how much Rick knew, had kept from her, throughout the afternoon. Finally, that evening, after helping Vita put away leftovers and clean the kitchen, she found herself alone with Rick as he locked the front door and turned off the downstairs lights.

"Well, good night, my dear. Thank you again for your help today," he said as he turned to climb the stairs.

"Uncle Rick, did you know my dad wasn't my real father?"

Rick stiffened and jerked his head around. "Good Lord, Valerie. Where is that coming from?"

"I've known for about twelve years now. My mother told me. Along with the whole story of my real father… and Erik Colton."

Rick's hand tightened on the banister as he turned slowly to face her. "Is that why you've avoided coming here to visit for so many years?"

Valerie hugged herself as a chilly draft swept over her and left goose bumps in its wake. "Not…directly. I had my own baggage to deal with."

Rick inclined his head and said softly, "With Nash?"

Valerie blinked hard, dropped her arms to her sides as her back straightened. "I— Wha—?"

Rick chuckled warmly. "Don't act so surprised. Vita and I weren't blind. You tried to hide your relationship, but we saw how you looked at each other. Knew you slipped away from the group at the same time for longer than needed to get a drink or use the bathroom."

Valerie gave a short laugh. "Wow. We thought we were so careful."

Rick lifted a corner of his mouth. "I'm guessing that's where you were the other night when you stayed out until morning. Hmm?"

Valerie rolled her eyes, and a you-caught-me sound rolled from her throat. "So that secret is out. Which brings me back to my mother and what you know. What you knew all along."

He raised a palm and twisted his mouth. "I knew enough. I saw most of it firsthand. My brother's infatuation with your mother. Her fascination with Erik Colton. The ruckus when she announced she was pregnant." His expression crumpled. "Are you angry with me for not telling you? I didn't see that it was my place to expose things your mother and father had decided to keep quiet. And you were always considered real family by Vita and me, regardless of who fathered you."

She gave him a smile. "Ditto."

"My brother—" he began and his voice cracked. "He loved you, Val. Even if he did a poor job of showing it. He was flawed, as we all are. Brokenhearted over your mother's drinking, and his own inability to cope with her behavior. He took the easy way out. Avoidance. He wasn't proud of his choices. But…he did love you."

Valerie kept a tight rein on her emotions as she listened to Rick. Until he added, "I tried my best to be the father he wasn't."

Val's breath caught, and tears filled her eyes. She rushed to him and wrapped him in a firm embrace. "You were. You absolutely were. I love you, Uncle Rick."

"What was your word? Ditto? Ditto, Val." He squeezed her back and kissed the top of her head. As he released her, he cast a glance toward the rear of the house. "Oh. I missed the light on the back porch. Will you get it before you come up?"

She nodded and caught him dabbing his eyes as he made his way upstairs.

When Valerie finally climbed in bed, she was physically exhausted and emotionally spent. She replayed the conversations of the day as she searched for sleep, her mind active even though her body was worn out.

Even though the younger Coltons had distant, often complicated relationships with Axel, it was clear his death had shaken the family deeply. His murder was an attack on the family—one more in a growing list of aggressions against them in recent months. The trend was alarming, to say the least, and Nash's family had circled their proverbial wagons and looked to one another for comfort, protection and support in a way Valerie's family never had. Other than Uncle Rick, Valerie had no one she could depend on for that kind of familial support. Was it any wonder she'd adopted the Chicago Coltons as the family of her heart?

She'd just gotten comfortable, the covers tucked under her chin and her pillow just so, when her phone jangled. She groaned and considered ignoring it. But she didn't dare, not with all the crazy twists and turns in recent days.

Clicking on the bedside lamp, she checked the caller ID and groaned again. Now she *really* wanted to ignore the call. And *really* dared not.

Chapter Thirteen

"Hello, Mother. It's rather late to be calling. Is something wrong?"

"Yes, something is wrong! Something is very wrong."

Valerie raked the hair back from her face, bracing. "What—?"

"I was sitting here, after a terrible day of being harangued by people time and again—your doing no doubt, but we'll get to that later—when what should come on the late news but a story about Axel Colton's funeral."

"Mother—"

"That was hard enough to watch, but then the camera panned the crowd and I saw *you* huddled up with…*them*."

"I went to the funeral with Vita and Rick, yes."

"And—and Erik." She heard her mother take a few shallow breaths. "I saw Erik. They interviewed him and his mother, and he—"

"Yes, he was there. Axel was his brother, but I didn't—"

"How could you do this to me?" Her mother's voice broke. "I've told you what those miserable people did to me. I've asked you to come home. But you… You're still down there. With Erik. With—"

"I'm not with Erik, Mother. I don't think I even spoke to him today. I saw him, but he's not—"

"You're with his son. I saw how close you were standing to him. I couldn't believe it when I saw it, but I rewound the report, and there you were. That boy's hand was on you. You had Coltons all around."

Valerie took a deep breath. "Mother, it's late. I'm tired. Is there a point to this call besides chewing me out for attending a funeral?"

"Honestly, Valerie! It's that kind of flippant attitude that tells me they are turning you against me."

Her heart sank. That kind of paranoia was more evidence her mother wasn't taking her medication. She'd call the doctor's office *again* in the morning. She didn't want to go back to Ohio yet, but if her mother was in a downward spiral…

"You have nothing to worry about, Mother. I'm not turning against you."

"You told Nancy to check up on me, didn't you? She called today. Twice. And so did the nurse from Dr. Richards's office."

"I was worried—"

"Come home, Valerie. I warned you that those people are poisonous. Why won't you listen to me? You need to get away from that boy. He'll hurt you. I can't let him hurt you again. They'll destroy us. They want to destroy us!"

"Mother! Take a breath. Everything is okay." She pinched the bridge of her nose. She'd have to ask Nancy to go by her mother's house tonight. Stay with her. Nancy had volunteered to be her mother's sponsor, because she'd had a family member with similar mental-health issues. She knew the routine. Knew the importance of keeping her mother on her medication.

Quiet sobs filtered over the phone connection, and Valerie sighed. "Mother, I'm going to call Nancy for you. You shouldn't be alone tonight."

"I don't want Nancy. I don't need— I'm not—"

Valerie's heart twisted, knowing what she had to do and knowing it meant letting Nash down, just when they were starting to rebuild their relationship. "Talk to Nancy tonight, Mother. Take your medicines and get some rest, and… I'll drive home tomorrow."

"You're going home?" Nash's grip tightened on his phone, and he grimaced as Valerie's announcement settled in his gut like a rock. Through his open door, the quiet hum of colleagues' conversations and laughter, ringing phones and the ding of elevator bells wafted into his work space. He rose from his desk to close the door, then asked, "For good? We had plans tonight. I thought…"

Never mind what he thought. He'd clearly been wrong. Disappointment made it hard to breathe.

"I know, Nash. I'm sorry. But when my mother called last night it was clear she was off her meds, and I knew I needed to go check on her. Handle things there. In person."

Nash's desk chair creaked as he sat down and rocked back. "Well, you gotta do what you gotta do. Huh?" He knew he hadn't done enough to modulate his tone, to cover his frustration. But knowing he needed to be understanding of Valerie's situation with her mother and not letting it open old wounds were two different things.

"Depending on what I find, how cooperative Mother is, what her doctor says, I could be back by tonight. Toledo is only a four-hour drive. I'm about an hour outside of town now, and my mother's appointment to see the doctor is at eleven."

Nash checked the time on his computer screen. Nine forty-five. Val had been up and on the road early if she was already an hour outside of Toledo. He respected Val for her commitment to her mother, despite the pain and strife she had caused through the years. But he also saw how taking care of her mother wore Val down. "We can reschedule. Don't drive if you're worn out."

"Nash, I'm okay. I have every Starbucks between Toledo and Chicago highlighted on my driving app."

He wished he could do something to help ease her burden. Wished he didn't feel the tug of resentment toward her mother for her part in ripping Val away from him years ago. Wish he didn't feel as if he was on the losing end of a tug-of-war with Val's mother for her loyalty, her time. Her heart. "Be careful, Val. And keep me posted."

"I will."

When Nash disconnected the call, he tried to concentrate on the blueprints for the business complex that were needed for the meeting with their client tomorrow, but Valerie pervaded his thoughts all day. He was about to pack it in for the day and head home, hoping she might be joining him for a late dinner, when she texted him.

Sorry to cancel on you. Spending the night in Ohio. Rain check on dinner? Back in Chicago by lunchtime tomorrow.

He texted back, Sure thing. Tomorrow night then?

Sounds good. Thx.

How's your mom?

Resting. Back on her meds. Still hates the Coltons.

Nash resisted the urge to send a glib reply. Instead he typed, CU Tm. Be careful. Love you.

Then, before he could hit Send, he frowned. His heart rolled. Did he love her? He had once. And they clearly still had sexual chemistry. But love—deep, true, lasting love—required trust and honesty. He wasn't sure they were there yet.

Before sending his reply, he backspaced. And deleted the last two words.

THE NEXT DAY being a Saturday, Nash spent the day at home, culling dead plants from his back garden, straightening his living room, putting clean sheets on his bed… and trying to convince himself he wasn't "house preening" for Val. He tried to distract himself with the Ohio State football game on TV, but every time the announcers mentioned Ohio, his thoughts returned to Val, her emergency trip to Toledo, her torn loyalties. And his agitation and ill ease would return.

He knew that Carol Yates's behavior was rooted in mental illness, knew that resenting Val's mother wasn't a good way to start a relationship with Valerie, knew Valerie needed his patience, understanding and support. And that was what he'd give her, damn it. He would not be the reason this second chance they'd been given failed. He cared about her enough to work at rebuilding their faith in, and their love for, each other.

Groaning his restlessness, Nash clicked off the football game and tossed the remote on the coffee table. An hour later, he put the salmon steaks on the counter to finish thawing and headed to the back of the house to start getting ready.

When he finished showering, Nash returned to the kitchen to start the salmon fillets sautéing. He checked the clock. Maybe it was too soon. Valerie should be arriving in about fifteen minutes, so he should wait a few more—

He stopped short when he discovered his neighbor's cat on his kitchen counter, nibbling the fish he'd left on the counter thawing. "Hey! You son of a— Get down!" He waved his arms at the cat. "Leave that— How the hell did you even get in here?" He snatched a towel from the oven handle and flapped it at the calico. "Go home!"

The cat meowed at him and sat down, licking his lips. Nash picked up the cat and headed to the front door. But it was firmly shut. Angling his head, he glimpsed the multipaned French door to the backyard standing ajar. One pane in the glass was broken. The one by the doorknob.

He put down the cat and crept forward, staying close to the wall. Across his living room, he saw a shadow move.

A wiry man with his face covered by a ski mask surged from behind the couch.

"Hey! What are you—?"

The man's arm swung up. He had a gun. And he squeezed the trigger.

The gun jammed. With a snarl of disgust, the man turned and ran toward the door.

Adrenaline spiked in Nash's blood. He leaped over the couch, knocking over a lamp. As the cat sprinted back outside, tail puffed, Nash chased the intruder to his backyard. "Stop!"

The trespasser grabbed one of the rocks that lined Nash's landscaping and spun to face Nash.

Balling his fist, Nash swung at the man. Caught him across the jaw. The man staggered back a step then charged again. This time Nash grabbed for the mask, wanting a look at the face of his attacker. The man ducked, as he spun out of Nash's reach, but the mask was unseated enough for Nash to catch sight of wiry, graying brown hair.

He surged forward again, leading with an uppercut that his intruder avoided. Then the man made his move, lifting the rock in his hand. Though Nash raised an arm to block the blow, the large stone cracked against his head with a force that rattled his teeth. The edges of his vision blurred, and his knees buckled. Then…nothing.

Chapter Fourteen

Valerie had just reached Nash's porch and raised her hand to knock, when she heard an angry shout from inside. A loud crash. More yelling. Was it the television?

She leaned close and pressed her ear to the door. No telltale music that would indicate he was watching a movie. A strange sense of alarm skittered through her, a sixth sense that told her the noises inside were signals of danger. She knocked harder. "Nash?"

No answer. Again. Still no response.

She tested the door. The knob turned, and, with her breath stalled in her throat, she opened the door a crack. "Hello? Nash? It's me."

No answer. Her nerves jangling, she entered the house and slowly checked each room as she moved deeper inside. The dining-room table had been set, but the room was otherwise empty. From the kitchen, she could smell raw fish, and with a glance found one salmon fillet on the floor. Odd.

"Nash?"

As she stepped into the living room, a chill autumn breeze reached her through the open back door. Was he in his backyard then? That'd explain why he hadn't heard her knock or call out. She crossed to the open French door, and her foot crunched on something hard.

Broken glass. A fresh spurt of concern swirled through her. "Nash?"

Stepping onto his back patio, she moved quickly, past the low hedge of boxwood, to the point where the yard opened…and found Nash sprawled, facedown, on the grass.

"Nash!" She raced to his side and dropped to her knees. "Nash, can you hear me? Are you all right?"

When he didn't respond, she conducted a cautious search for any injuries. Had he fallen from somewhere? Had a stroke? She didn't dare move him, in case he had a broken neck or—

She gasped as her fingers encountered a bloody gash on the back of his head. She parted his hair gently to examine the wound closer, and he groaned. "Nash?"

He lifted a hand to his injured head as he rolled to his back. "What happened?"

"I was hoping you could tell me. I just got here, but I heard shouting, a loud thump and found broken glass on your living room floor by the door. Now you're here, laid out on the yard with a busted head…"

He jerked his chin up with a sharply inhaled breath. "Where'd he go?"

"Who?"

Turning his head, he searched his yard. "There was a man—" He cut his explanation short, grabbing his head. "Ow!"

A tingle of alarm chasing down her spine, Valerie stood and surveyed the yard. Saw nothing. No one. "I don't see anyone."

"Damn. He got away," Nash muttered as he drew his

fingers back and stared at the red smears on his fingers. He blinked hard, squinted, then shielded his eyes as if the early evening twilight hurt his eyes. "I, um…"

"Can you stand? Walk?"

He waved her off. "I'm fine. I just…" He wobbled when he tried to rise, and she caught him as he stumbled.

"You are not fine. You hit your head."

"No, the intruder hit it for me."

The idea of an intruder attacking Nash sent a chill to her core. Axel had been attacked in his home. His head bashed. Now Nash…

Quashing the anxiety that thumped in her chest, she helped steady Nash. "Either way, we're going to the ER." She placed a firm hand at the small of his back and guided him inside. She let him sit on the couch for a minute while she got a rag to clean his wound and an ice pack to hold against his head in the car. As he hobbled to her car, she took out her phone, scrolled through her contacts and called Damon. "We're headed to the hospital now, but I think you should come take a look at his door and yard. Meet the police. Someone broke in and attacked him."

After assuring Damon that Nash was likely only suffering from a concussion, but that she'd keep him apprised if anything else became evident during the exam, she helped Nash climb into the car and headed to the closest hospital.

On the drive, Nash held the kitchen towel full of ice to his head and recounted the moments leading up to his injury. "I found the cat in the kitchen. He was eating our salmon."

"What cat?"

"Remember my neighbor's calico?" He explained how

he'd searched for the open door or window that the cat had used to get inside, seen the back door ajar…

His breathing grew ragged, stressed. "The guy had a gun. It misfired, or else I'd be—"

"What!" She cut a sharp look to him as she navigated the busy street.

Nash seemed to struggle to recall what happened next. "I guess I chased him, then—"

"My God, Nash! Did you recognize him? Could he be connected to all the stuff happening to the rest of your family? To Axel's—" Her throat clogged with terror, clamping down on the hideous word—*murder*. Could Axel's murderer have come for Nash? Had Nash drawn unwanted attention to himself at the funeral? Or when he challenged Axel at the racket club? When news of his questioning by the police leaked to the media? Geez! What was happening in the Colton family? Who could be behind all the bad luck and tragedy?

Once at the hospital, the ER doctor confirmed Nash had a concussion and stitched up the gash on his scalp. Though Nash couldn't remember past chasing the stranger out of his house, the logical conclusion was the stranger had hit him over the head with something before escaping. No further injuries were found, and the doctor released Nash to go home to rest. They were just getting his discharge papers and about to return to his house when Damon called.

Nash, who was going over the discharge papers and signing multiple releases, handed her his phone. "Tell my brother I'm fine."

She did, with caveats. Then, putting Damon on speaker so Nash could hear, she said, "We think the intruder hit him with something. Did you or the cops find anything when you searched his house?"

"Besides my brother's continued stubborn refusal to put in a security system?" Damon growled. "Yeah, I, uh…found a rock in the middle of his yard with blood on it. No doubt what was used to bash him in the head."

The contents of Valerie's stomach—a pack of crackers she'd gotten from the hospital vending machine an hour ago—soured. "So it's true. Someone tried to kill him," she muttered numbly, horrified.

"Maybe. Where are you headed? He's welcome to convalesce at my place, you know. Or I'm sure Nicole or Vita—"

"No. I can look after him. I'm sure he'd rather be in his own bed."

Nash nodded his agreement, then raised a hand to his temple, wincing.

"All right. I'm still here at Nash's place," Damon said. "My brother is getting a new security system whether he wants it or not. I'm taking measurements and checking his wiring now. I intend to have his system up and operational by this time tomorrow."

"Good. Thanks, Damon."

Nash handed the clipboard back to the discharge nurse and shot her a disgruntled look. From the phone, Damon said, "I've been telling him since he bought his house he needed one. This isn't Mayberry."

"Right," she said, holding Nash's gaze. "In Mayberry, no one tried to murder Opie. Speaking of which…won't he need to give a statement to the police?"

Damon chuckled without humor. "Way ahead of you. They'll be waiting to talk to Nash when you get here."

NASH GROANED AND put his arm over his eyes. The jackhammer in his skull was not being helped by the drilling outside his window. Damon had shown up at Nash's house bright and early the next morning and had been creating a ruckus ever since.

"Poor Nash," Valerie said. "Want me to tell him to knock it off?"

He moved his arm and found her standing at the door of his bedroom with a glass of grape juice in one hand and an orange pill bottle in the other. She'd stayed with him, waking him every hour to check on him throughout the night.

"Naw. The sooner he finishes, the sooner I can get some sleep."

She sat on the edge of his bed and offered him the juice. "I know juice is more for colds, but I figured it couldn't hurt for a concussion, so..."

"Thanks." He sat up in the bed, feeling his head swim and throb, and took a minute to let things stop spinning before he took the glass from her.

Val rattled the bottle in her other hand. "Painkiller? The doctor said you could have one of these every four to six hours."

"Mmm. I'll stick with Tylenol for now." He sipped the grape juice while she fetched the bottle of acetaminophen from his bathroom cabinet. "Have the police called with any updates?"

"Sorry. No."

Despite his injured head, he'd given the local police a full account of the intruder's attack as the bits and pieces of the incident slowly returned to him. He'd sat across from the uniformed officer that had come to his house last night and remembered being the subject of suspicion days earlier as questions were asked. Axel's murderer hadn't been caught yet, either. Was this attack on him linked to Axel's killer? Simon Wilcox, the man suspected of planting the candleholder in Nash's trunk, had been described as having short blond hair, but Nash had recovered a distinct memory of his attacker's shaggy, graying brown hair.

Was the break-in connected to Jackson's kidnapping? Were other members of his family at risk while this rogue assailant remained free? Nash gritted his teeth. There were far too many questions, too many assaults on his family and far too few answers.

While he popped a couple capsules in his mouth and washed them down with the juice, Valerie settled on the edge of his bed and placed a warm hand on his leg. "Can I get you anything else?"

He set the juice on his bedside table. "A kiss?"

A dimple puckered her cheek as she grinned at him. "Of course."

She leaned in to brush her lips against his. A teasing, light kiss. And not nearly enough. He caught the back of her head, deepened the connection, angling his head to more fully capture her mouth with his. The kiss woke every cell in his body, made his blood hum with desire. He pulled her closer, tracing the seam of her lips with his tongue and—

"Aha! I knew it!" Damon called from the bedroom window with a laugh. "I've always suspected there was more between you two than you claimed."

Val pulled away, turning to the window with color filling her cheeks. "I— It's not what it looks like. We just—"

Nash's chest tightened. Why was she denying the obvious? Didn't she know that if part of the Colton family already knew about them, then the whole family knew? The Coltons were a bit like a small town in that way. News traveled fast.

"It's exactly like that," Nash said, his focus drilling Val before he turned his attention to his brother. "Stop leering, Damon. You were perfectly aware that Val and I were…" What? A couple? Hooking up? In a committed relationship? What exactly did he and Val have? If she was still trying to dismiss and hide their link, did she even truly have feelings for him?

Val gave a nervous chuckle before pushing off the bed and hesitating awkwardly, as if deciding how much to claim or deny. Finally, without saying anything, she left the room with the rest of the Tylenol and didn't return.

"Was it something I said?" Damon asked.

Nash sighed, the constriction in his chest balling like a rock. He knew these sensations of rejection, disappointment and confusion all too well. From his earliest days of being ignored by his father to the painful months after Valerie shut him out of her life at eighteen, he'd experienced many moments where he felt deserted. Unwanted. Unloved.

"Save the comedy, bro. Just…finish the drilling out there and let me rest, huh?"

Damon's expression shifted from smug to concerned. "Hey, sorry if I stuck my foot in something just now. I thought, well…"

"Yeah. I thought so, too." Nash sank back into his pillow and pinched the bridge of his nose. The attack last night had preempted his dinner, his heart-to-heart with Val. But he wouldn't be put off again. The time had come for he and Val to have a reckoning. If she wasn't committed to a full, honest and open relationship with him, he was out.

What had just happened?

Valerie dropped on Nash's couch, the bottle of Tylenol still in her hand, and stared blankly at the wall. Why had she balked like that when Damon caught her kissing Nash?

She'd already told Uncle Rick and Vita the truth about her budding relationship with Nash. She'd confided her feelings to Sara and Lila. She even confessed the truth to her mother, for Pete's sake! And her mother was the one she'd been trying to keep in the dark all those years, the reason she'd begged Nash for secrecy. So why had she reacted with such reticence, confusion…and fear? Were denial and secrecy just ingrained default settings for her? Or had Damon's teasing called up some aspect of her relationship with Nash she hadn't acknowledged? Some deeper truth about her feelings regarding her rekindled first love?

As she sat there, trying to make sense of her reaction, sort through her thoughts, her unfocused gaze sharpened, and she realized she was staring at the sketch she and Nash had made together, years ago. Of a bungalow with flowers and trees adorning the yard. Of a peaceful home. The utopia she and Nash had imagined together.

A sharp ache pierced her heart. *Together…*

A quiet rattle drew her attention to the pill bottle. Her hands were shaking. In fact, a subtle trembling swamped her limbs, and a disconcerting jangle gripped her core.

She sucked in a breath, trying to fill her lungs, but only managed a shallow gasp. Her instinct was to shy away from the raw emotions. Hadn't she shoved down anything too painful and too difficult for most of her life? Wasn't that the coping technique she'd learned from her father, the reason it had taken so long for her family to get the BPD diagnosis for her mother? But where had hiding from pain, denying truth and ignoring hurt gotten her? It was only in recent years, since Nancy recognized Carol's illness and helped get her to a doctor, that life had begun to approach balance.

Val had glimpsed real joy last week when she and Nash had shared the night together. Even with the heart-rending confessions, the arguing, the painful memories, she'd come through the experience feeling freer, happier. And hopeful.

She stood and walked closer to the colorful bungalow drawing on Nash's wall. He'd kept it. A simple, silly drawing two teenagers had made together. It shouldn't have mattered. He should have tossed it in the trash the first time he'd straightened his room in high school, or when he'd relocated for college, or moved to this house. So many opportunities to discard the drawing. But he hadn't. He'd framed it. Hung it on his wall. Cherished it.

Her tears came fast and hard. That drawing of a landscaped and decorated house was their relationship. Youthful love that she'd hidden, denied, discounted. Because it shouldn't have been as important and meaningful as it was. Nash had seen all along how valuable and true their love was…and he'd treasured it. He'd honored the relationship, kept it close, even though living with his memories had hurt.

She'd run. Denied. Buried. Tried to smother the embers that still smoldered in her core. She lowered her face to her hands as her shoulders shook and tears flowed. She saw now that every bit of hurt and loneliness she'd suffered had been her own fault. Nash had been here, waiting, hoping, the whole time. Loving her despite her rejection, her denial, her silence. She had one last chance to regain his trust and save their love. She meant to make it count.

LATER THAT EVENING, after a full day of drills and wires and technological trial and error, Damon had Nash's home security system up and running. Nash, his head still throbbing, followed his brother around the premises as Damon explained the main control pad, codes, camera locations and the phone app to view the camera feed.

"The main one is back there and has an angle that encompasses the whole porch." Damon pointed out the small hidden lens. "That's the primary one. The camera over the door is secondary."

"Wait. Two cameras?"

Damon grinned. "Not in reality. Thieves these days are pretty much expecting there to be a security camera somewhere and know how to take them out. When they see this more obvious dummy camera, an intruder might disable it and think they're in the clear. But the more hidden camera, the one that's really monitoring the property, is still recording. I've done the same in the back and side yards."

"Clever. And thorough."

Damon raised his palms. "Do it right or why bother at all?" He flashed a cocky grin, then his expression faltered. "Considering all the sh—" Damon caught himself, glanced at Valerie and twisted his mouth. "Sorry, Val."

"I've heard it all. Don't sweat it."

"Yeah, but I'm trying to clean up my language. For Maya. She's getting good at reading lips." Damon squared his shoulders, looked back at Nash and said, "Considering all the stuff that's been happening to our family, I have to say, my gut is telling me this was a personal attack. And if this wasn't random, whoever jumped you will likely be back to finish the job."

"That's a cheery thought," Nash intoned.

"Are you sure you wouldn't rather come stay with me and Ruby?"

"And bring the danger to your house? To Maya?" Nash shook his head, then gestured to the new equipment. "All this buys me forewarning. Forewarned is forearmed. Let the bastard try again." He clenched his fists and gritted his teeth, relishing the idea of tearing into the man who'd attacked him. "I'll be ready for him."

SIMON WILCOX PACED his living room, a burner cell to his ear, and waited for his call to be answered. When it was, he said, without preamble, "I want my money. I did your job, now pay me what I'm owed."

"Who is this?"

He snorted. "Don't play games with me. You know damn well who it is. Why don't I have my money?"

He heard a huff, nervous breathing. Then… "I heard you were questioned by the police."

Simon scoffed. "A minor thing. My old lady covered for me. If they really had anything, I'd be sitting in jail instead of waiting over here for my effing money."

"Did you mention me? Can they connect you to me?"

Simon swiped a hand over his face and tried not to lose his cool. If the client freaked out, the whole gig could be blown. "I didn't say nothing. That's part of the service. The service you now owe twenty-five grand for."

"What? No. We agreed on twenty thousand."

"The price keeps going up until I get paid."

"You'll get your money. I swear. But I can't pay you yet!"

Cold fury filled his veins. "You told me you could pay. Do I need to explain to you what happens to people when they don't pay their debts?"

"No. I… Think about it! The cops are watching you. If you get a huge bank draft suddenly, they can trace it back to—"

"That's why I said *cash*, idiot! Put it in a paper sack and take it to the bus station. At exactly nine p.m. tonight, use the restroom and leave the bag in your stall. Someone will be there to collect the bag."

"I can't… What if I can't do that?"

He squeezed the phone and gritted his teeth. "I will come for you. I'll take fingers, ears and teeth as interest, bit by bit until you cough up my cash. The price goes up to thirty grand tomorrow, and I'll take my first interest payment. Understood?"

Through the connection, Simon heard only angry breathing.

"Understood?"

"This is extortion. I will not be ordered around by the likes of y—"

Simon hung up. "Fine. If that's how you want to play this."

He took the burner cell outside, into a cold drizzly rain, and smashed the phone to pieces.

That night at exactly nine p.m., Simon and his wife were at the bus station. The client was not.

"Come on, honey," he told his wife as he rose to head back to his car. He opened his umbrella and held it over them both. "We have another stop to make before we go home."

As Simon pulled out of the bus station parking lot, he

didn't pay any attention to the black SUV that entered the street behind him, one block later. He didn't pay attention to the SUV when it merged on the interstate with him, either. When he did notice the SUV, it was too late.

Chapter Fifteen

Nash was brushing his teeth when the call came in. Lifting his cell, he glanced at the caller ID and frowned. Spit. Wiped his mouth on the hand towel and answered the call.

"Nash, this is Harry Cartwright. I have an update on your case…of a sort."

"Tell me you found something else to tie that Wilcox character to Axel's murder."

"Um, no. It's…"

Nash could hear shuffling papers. Voices in the background.

"I had something come across my desk tonight from the highway patrol. I thought I'd call you before you saw it on the eleven o'clock news."

Nash straightened the hand towel on the rack, trying to be patient, despite the strange buzz building in his ears. "Tell me."

"Simon Wilcox and his wife were both killed in a rather gruesome accident involving an eighteen-wheeler on the interstate. Witnesses say a dark SUV changed lanes without looking, Simon swerved, hit the brakes hard and skidded on the wet road. Ended up under the eighteen-wheeler."

Nash mumbled a curse word. "That's, um…horrible. Was—was anyone else hurt?"

"Truck driver had minor injuries. The SUV had no tag. It left the scene."

A shudder raced through Nash. Just when he thought the strange circumstances of his life couldn't get weirder, darker…

"So, seeing as Wilcox was our best lead regarding Axel's murder, the case just grew rather cold."

"Yeah."

Nash couldn't say what else Cartwright said as they hung up. His mind was already spinning off in a hundred directions. The first call he made was to Valerie. He just needed to hear her voice, know she was safe. The drowsy sweet tone of her "Nash?" when she answered poured a sweet relief through his blood.

After relaying a summary of Cartwright's call, he bid her goodnight and stared numbly at his phone for a moment before dialing another number.

"Hello?" a male voice answered brusquely.

"Hi, Dad. It's Nash."

A grunt. "Do you have any idea what time it is?"

"Late. Sorry if I woke you. I just—"

"What?" Erik asked, his timbre as impatient as ever.

Nash shoved down a spurt of irritation at his father's coldness and focused on the reason he'd called. Axel's death. The intruder in his own house. The murder of his half uncles. Jackson's kidnapping . The fire at Lila's gallery. And the list went on. Coltons under attack.

Nash drew a breath from tight lungs. "Watch your back."

Erik grunted. "Is that a threat?"

Nash's shoulders drooped. Did his father really know

so little about him, his character, that he'd truly believe that? The further evidence of his father's lack of faith in him stung.

"No... Dad. It's not a threat. It's...a plea. Be careful. Be smart. Hell, look both ways before you cross the road."

"Why? What's going on? What have you heard?"

"Nothing specific. I just don't like the recent trend of violence against members of our family." He paused then added bitterly, "And my head is healing well after I was attacked, thanks for asking."

"That's right. I did hear something about you and a concussion from Damon."

Nash rolled his eyes. Such deep paternal concern... "If there's nothing else..."

Why are you such a selfish, distant bastard? Damon and I needed you to be a father, a real father to us. Why was that so hard for you? Why is it still *so hard for you?*

"No. That's all. I just... Well, be careful out there. Okay?"

"Always am." Erik fell silent, and Nash had lowered the phone to tap the disconnect icon when his father added, "You watch yourself, too."

"HE TOLD YOU to watch yourself?" Valerie asked on Sunday that week as she and Nash walked through a neighborhood park, the squeals of playing children and the nip of the coming winter in the air. "How did he say it? Was he voicing concern for you or issuing a warning?"

Nash pulled a face. "That is the question, huh? I'd like to think it was concern but..." He blew a breath that buzzed his lips. "His tone was flat, no warmth to it. But I can't remember my dad every having a soft, fuzzy tone for me. Not his style."

"Well," Valerie said and stooped to pick up a particularly colorful leaf, "keep in mind, he never had an involved father, either. And his mother was Carin. Based on what I saw at the funeral, I don't imagine she was all that loving and fuzzy herself."

"Good point." He laced his fingers with hers, tugging her over to a bench beside the sidewalk. "So…where are we?"

She shot him a confused look and playfully glanced around them as if trying to orient herself. "Um…"

He draped his arm along the back of the bench and scooted closer to her. "You know what I mean. Where do *we* stand? It's been a couple weeks since we first talked, and… I guess I'm needing to know if this is going anywhere? Clearly your mother is still a factor. You dropped everything and left town for her last week. To be honest, I wasn't sure if you'd come back."

His admission shot her with a pang of disappointment. But when she thought about the twenty-four hours she'd spent in Toledo, dealing with her mother's issues and debating what needed to happen, she recognized the truth that caused her ache. And admitted it. "To be honest, I wasn't sure if I would, either. Then. I'm more sure of some things now, though. But to be even more honest…" She bent her head to look at the leaf she twirled as she toyed with the stem.

He placed a hand at her nape and gave the muscles there a gentle massage. "Honest is good. Go on. In fact, let's promise each other going forward that we'll always be truthful and fully forthcoming in everything. Deal?"

She nodded. "Of course. What do we have without honesty?" Then with a sigh, she finished her earlier thought. "The truth is my mother will always be a factor for me. If we're going to have a future, we're going to have to figure out how to do it knowing she's always going to be my family, always going to be one slip away from drinking again or going off her meds. But even with her medications, life with my mother will never be easy, and she may always resent you."

Nash grunted and rubbed the back of his neck. "Hate me, you mean."

She slanted her mouth in rueful agreement.

"Okay," Nash said, spreading his hands. "So tell me what I'm signing up for. What should I expect?"

Val grunted and took a deep breath. "Extreme mood swings. Big emotions. She has medications that help stabilize her volatile mood swings and her anxiety, but she'll always have…a struggle with perspective. People with BPD have trouble processing emotions. Her brain literally works differently. Emotions for her trigger the innate fight-or-flight response, so Mother struggles with the idea that every situation and conversation has a hidden vendetta or danger for her. Paranoia is a problem for her."

"Like her belief that the Coltons are evil and I will destroy you?"

"Among others." Valerie tore a piece of the leaf and let it flutter to the ground as she expounded. "It's likely her drinking started as a means to cope with her mental stress, her extreme emotions."

Nash nodded. "Makes sense. But you said she's sober now."

"She was." Val puffed out an exasperated breath. "Now? Not sure. She's been really stressed out over me being down here. I've alerted her sponsor. But in addition to AA to keep her on the right track for her alcohol issues and medications for her emotional issues, she attends regular psychotherapy sessions. She has to keep up with all three or…" She lifted a hand. "It's easy for her to falter. She walks a tightrope every day."

Nash scrubbed a hand over his face and shifted to look directly at her. "So she's had this disorder your whole life, but only started getting treatment in the last few years?"

"Yeah. My dad was completely checked out and washed his hands of her when I was in elementary school. He got fed up with her bitter accusations, wild spending sprees and unpredictability—again all symptoms of her BPD we didn't recognize. Dad blamed her alcohol abuse, and I was a kid. What did I know?" She shredded the rest of the leaf and tossed the bits on the sidewalk. "Between them there was lots of denial and not much real understanding. If not for her AA sponsor Nancy and an astute therapist at a rehab clinic six years ago, we might still be in the dark about it."

"Damn, Val. That's— I never realized…"

"Of course not. Why would you? We weren't talking. Rick only knows a little bit. Not the whole story, but he's too discrete to air our family issues."

Nash nodded, processing it all.

Valerie bit her bottom lip, then added, "She…had a fit when I told her I was coming to support Faith and Myles during their crisis. She, naturally, accused me of abandoning her, siding with the enemy—all typical BPD anxieties. Learning I was seeing you again made things worse, made her—" She frowned and waved off the rest of the thought. "The point is whenever I come down here, it stirs up all her ill will toward your family, the trauma and abandonment she went through when she was a teenager. Her hatred for Coltons is deeply ingrained. So…you have to ask yourself if that's what you want to get into.

Because I can't abandon my mentally ill mother. I'm all she has. Her illness is not her fault. And while she's responsible for her actions, her drinking, her self-care—" she angled her body to face him "—she's always going to need my support, someone to monitor her, a guardian for her best interests if she ever needs…"

She couldn't bring herself to finish the sentence. Damn, this was hard.

"I suppose if you can live with the fact you'd be taking on the dreaded Coltons if you were with me, I can live with your mother's disdain."

Turning a dubious grin toward him, she caught his hand in hers. "Hardly the same thing. Your family is great. Well, most of them are." She chuckled wryly. "Will you trust me in regard to my mother? It won't be easy. Life with her can be…complicated. But I won't let her change how I feel about you. I won't let her hurt us again."

"I will trust you. Trust in *us*." He leaned over to kiss her temple. "So…we're officially a couple? We're going to see where this leads?"

A cool wind swept past them, and she shivered.

"Really?" he said, giving her an up-and-down look. "Being with me is that scary?"

She laughed. "What if I said yes?"

He tugged her close for a quick kiss. "Don't be scared. I'm here for you."

His promise and his touch spread warmth through her, chasing away the chill of the late autumn afternoon. After several days of steely skies and icy rain, the sun had peeked out this morning, and Valerie was glad they'd seized the chance to spend some time outdoors before the harsh cold of winter settled over the Great Lakes.

A stiff wind ruffled Nash's hair, and she couldn't resist the urge to comb it back into place with her fingers. Then, looping her arms around his neck, she grew reflective. If she and Nash were going to try again for a relationship, he had to truly understand her dynamic with her mother.

She bit her bottom lip, musing a moment, then said, "I know I've probably given you the impression that life with my mother was always bad. It wasn't. The thing about BPD is that her emotions are all so…big. Just as her criticism and fear can be really out of proportion, her highs—her good moods—can be really good. There were moments where I could pretend everything was normal. Her illness wasn't as bad when I was little…or else I was too young to recognize the reality behind her bad moods. But sometimes, we'd bake cookies together and laugh, or we'd shop for school clothes and go for frozen yogurt afterward." She wrinkled her brow. "Remembering those moments gave me hope as her condition, her drinking, worsened."

She ducked her head, staring at the zipper of his jacket, as a melancholy ache swelled in her chest.

With a gloved hand, Nash nudged up her chin. "But hope is a double-edged sword, huh? It can brighten one moment, lifting you, and crush you the next when it disappears."

"Hmm. Yeah." An odd sensation tripped through her, as if she was being seen for the first time. Truly understood. She tightened her grip on his sleeves. "Sometimes I thought it would be easier to never have those moments of hope, what I came to call her false rainbows. The downs hurt more, the farther you fell."

"I know. When I was small I used to get so excited when my dad stopped by the apartment, only to be disappointed when he'd brush us boys off or only stay long enough to give Mom money and a hard time."

"So…can you see why it was easier for me to believe the bad about you all those years ago, rather than clinging to a hope that had failed me so many times in the past?"

He took a deep breath, his eyes bright. "And you see why I have a hard time trusting people's commitment?"

She bobbed her head.

"Well—" He kissed her nose and splayed his hand low on her back. "Maybe now we have a starting place. A mutual understanding. I want to be with you, Valerie. I want to make you happy. I want to share more sunny Sunday afternoons with you and find joy in all the simple things life together can offer."

The warmth that his words filled her with was undeniable. Mesmerizing. "That sounds…wonderful."

He cast his gaze around them, then stood, tugging her hand. "Come here." He led her away from the more populated part of the park to a quiet trail, where he found an evergreen shrub that offered some privacy. Drawing her into his arms, he framed her face with his hands and captured her lips.

A half sigh, half moan slipped from her throat as she canted into him, savoring the heat of his body, the caress of his mouth, the security of his embrace. That dangerous hope they talked about moments ago flared deep inside her. Dangerous, but oh, so sweet. She wanted to get lost in the daydream of a future with Nash, where every day held the promise of treasured moments, security and an inner peace.

She angled her head to kiss him more fully, and he whispered seductive words to her. She let herself get lost in his lips, his embrace. His lean body wrapped around her…until a soccer ball crashed through the evergreen branches and landed beside them.

Valerie pulled back from Nash's kiss as a dark-haired girl with cheeks red from the cold and her exertion darted around the bush to collect her ball. The girl gave Val and Nash a shocked look and mumbled, "Um, sorry."

"Hmm," Nash grunted and tucked Val's hair behind her ear. "Enough PDA. What I really want to do with you requires privacy. Shall we head home?"

"Lead on."

"Hungry? I think I still owe you dinner. Between my neighbor's cat eating our fish and the attacker in my house changing our plans, I never made good on the home-cooked meal I promised you last week. What do you say we run by the market and pick up some steaks and a bottle of wi—" He stopped himself, gave her a considering look, then said, "Sparkling cider, and I'll fire up the grill in honor of this refreshing glimpse of fall sun?"

She gave him a smile of appreciation. Maybe his remembering her stance on drinking alcohol seemed a small thing, but to her it represented his cooperation, his attention to detail, to her preferences and choices.

"Sounds perfect."

AFTER A QUICK stop at the market and a favorite bakery, they arrived back at Nash's house in the late afternoon with enough time for…*privacy*, before they prepared their steaks for dinner.

Nash greeted the calico, which was sunning itself on the front porch—again—with a light scratch behind the ear. The feline answered with a rumbling purr.

"You know, this cat is going to keep showing up here

if you keeping rewarding it with attention," Valerie said, chuckling. But then she, too, bent to pat his furry friend.

Nash shrugged. "I don't mind him. He's not bothering anything. And he is pretty charming." He keyed open his front door and stood back to let Val go inside first. As he stepped into his foyer, an odd prickling nipped his neck. Why hadn't his new alarm sounded?

But even without the failed alarm, he sensed something was off. The house was too dark, for one thing. He typically left a lamp on in the entry hall, so that he never came home to a completely dark house. And he smelled something…

"What is that odor?" Val asked as she walked ahead of him into the kitchen. She set the bag of groceries on the counter and reached for the light switch on the wall.

His heart rate jumping, he took a long quick stride and slapped his hand over hers before she could flip the switch. "Don't!"

She clearly sensed the alarm in his tone and raised anxious eyes to his. "What—?"

But then her nose wiggled, and she inhaled deeply. Her brown eyes darkened to nearly black. "It's gas, isn't it?"

He nodded. "Get out."

"But—"

"Get out! And don't turn anything on. Leave the front door open." He cast his attention to his stove, where, sure enough, all four burners had been turned to the on position. The pilot light had been extinguished, and the burners gave a low hiss, like a warning from a deadly viper, as the gas leaked into the room, uncombusted. He bit out a curse and turned the gas jets off.

He pulled his phone from his pocket to call the fire station or gas company or—

His grip tightened on the cell phone as he stopped himself before he woke the home screen. Cell phones could create a spark, same as a light switch could. He exhaled heavily and hurried out to the front yard to join Valerie.

At his front door, the neighbor's calico cat was trying to invite himself inside. Nash scooped up the feline on his way out the door. "No you don't, buddy. Especially not now. It's dangerous in there."

He joined Valerie at the curb, where she leaned against the hood of his car with the phone to her ear. "Yes, we've gone outside. We will. Thank you." Once she'd disconnected the call, she reached out to scratch the calico on the head. "I've reported the gas leak to the gas company. They're sending a guy out. They suggest opening all doors and windows. Airing the place out as much as possible."

Nash nodded and set the cat on the ground. "Right." He scowled and dusted cat fur from his hands. "Val, that was no regular leak. Every burner on my stove was turned on and the pilot light put out."

Her expression darkened. "Excuse me? You're saying it was intentional? Someone was trying to—"

He lifted both eyebrows in answer.

"If Simon Wilcox is dead, then this—"

"Unrelated to Axel's murder, or someone has depth on their roster of criminals for hire."

At her confused look, he clarified the sports phrasing. "More than one skilled person to use if your number one goes down."

"And the money to pay for multiple hits."

"Unless you take out the hitman before you pay them. Dead men don't talk or require payment."

She frowned darkly. "Cold."

"Colder than hiring someone to frame or kill me?"

She wrapped him in a hug. "All of it. Sum total. Cold and scary as hell. Nash…"

He placed a kiss on her forehead. "Wait here. I'm going to open the back door."

Nash made his way through the wrought-iron side gate to his enclosed patio and the flower garden Vita had insisted on building for him when he moved in. A housewarming gift, she'd called it. *Because nothing warms a house like plants and blooms.*

He gave the small backyard and flower beds an encompassing glance, but saw nothing suspicious. He moved carefully to the back door, keyed it open, and left it gaping.

As he retraced his steps to the front of the house, the calico appeared at the gate and wound around his legs asking for attention. He nudged the cat away with his foot, then cut at an angle across his lawn. The cat followed him. "Val, will you report this to the police? I'm going to take Mr. Kitty here back to his house. It's about to get rather busy around here, and he'll just be underfoot."

"Of course." Valerie rubbed her arms, and he guessed it wasn't really the cool day that sent the chill through her. A similar icy sensation crawled through him as the meaning of this incident took root. Someone had intentionally tried to hurt him. Moreover, they could have hurt Val.

When he'd learned Simon Wilcox didn't match the description of the intruder in his house, he'd hoped the attack in his back garden had been random. An interrupted burglary. But a second aggression against him, unrelated to Simon Wilcox, sent a quiver down his spine. What the hell?

Nash leaned in to give Val a kiss, then scooped Kitty back into his arms and chuckled wryly as the feline gave a low purr. "Some watch cat you are. You could have at least tripped the intruder for me."

The calico grew cooperatively limp and looked about as he was carried like they were on a sightseeing adventure. Kitty's owner was in her yard, raking leaves. She set aside her rake and met him at the sidewalk. "I'm sorry. Was he bothering you? He does like to explore."

"No bother, really, but we've had something of an emergency come up, and I thought he'd be safer back home."

"Oh, no! Anything I can help with?" she said, taking Kitty from his arms.

"No. But thanks." He turned to go then paused. "Unless… Did you happen to see anyone, a strange car maybe, at my house in the last few hours?"

His neighbor scrunched her nose in thought, shook her head. "No. I don't recall anything. But… I was inside baking before I came out here. And the Tillsons' trees block my view of your house from inside."

Nash shrugged. "Worth a shot. Thanks, anyway."

As he headed back down the sidewalk toward home, Nash considered knocking on the Tillsons' front door and asking if they'd seen anything suspicious. And then he remembered. He could access the video feed from his security system Damon had installed from the app on his phone. Of course!

He thumbed through his apps until he found the right one and opened it as he hurried back to join Val.

"The police are on the way," she said.

He nodded distractedly. "Thanks."

He propped against the car beside her as the black-and-white image of his front door filled his phone screen.

"You know, you keep calling that calico 'he,' but genetically, all calicos are female," she said, sidling closer to him.

He fast-forwarded through footage from earlier in the day—him leaving this morning, Kitty crossing the porch to flop in the sun and nap. "Not all. Kitty is a rare exception. Happens like once in three thousand."

"Really?" she said with interest.

He glanced up at her startled expression. She blinked, pulled a what-do-you-know? face. Shifting her gaze to his phone, she asked, "What are you doing?"

"Checking the security camera footage."

He heard her breath catch, and she leaned closer, her floral scent distracting him for a moment. He moved on to the backdoor camera and was soon rewarded with the images he sought. A man with wiry dark hair, liberally threaded with gray or blond—hard to tell which from the black-and-white picture—entered his backyard by climbing his fence.

"There he is," Val said. "Do you recognize him?"

"No. You?"

"Nope. I think I'd remember that messy hair. Geez, man, buy a comb."

A memory teased the edges of Nash's brain. Grabbing his attacker's ski mask…shaggy graying hair…

Maybe…

The man stayed at the edge of the yard, and the camera angle, as he approached the back door. He blasted the dummy camera with spray paint, then donned gloves and turned to survey the back door. He apparently spotted the wires of the alarm system and pulled something indistinguishable from his back pocket.

"What's he doing?" Valerie asked.

"Bypassing the alarm. I couldn't even tell he'd been there just now when I opened the back door." He huffed his frustration. "This isn't his first rodeo." Nash watched as the man fiddled with the door's sensor then slipped inside. "That'd be why the alarm didn't sound when we got back."

She cut a sharp look to him. "That's right. It didn't. Oh, my God. I didn't even realize…"

A few moments later, the man left again the same way he'd come in.

"So not a thief," Valerie said. "He stayed only long enough to turn on the stove burners."

"So it seems."

Valerie snuggled closer to him, a shudder passing through her. "Someone wants you dead. Or at least seriously maimed. Or to send a message. But why?"

"No idea."

"You were cleared in Axel's murder. Surely whoever's behind this knows that!"

"Not necessarily."

Her grip tightened on his arm. "Nash, what if the person who killed Axel is working his way through the Colton family, and you were just the next on the list. Don't forget, the person who took Jackson hasn't been found. Damon and Aaron and Lila have had their share of dangerous encounters lately."

"Or the family is jinxed. I guess I was due."

Valerie gripped the front of his shirt and gave him a slight shake. "Don't say that! That's defeatist talk."

"Oh, I'm not giving up the ship. I'm going to find the

person behind this and make him pay, even if only for having put you in harm's way today." He faced her, taking her into his arms and kissing her deeply. "If anything had happened to you…if we hadn't smelled the gas in time and gotten out…" He rested his forehead against hers and sighed. "I've become rather fond of you, Val."

She levered back and shot him a wry grin. "Fond? Oh, you sweet talker! Stop or I'll swoon!"

"What I mean is—"

But before he could explain himself or expand on how much he'd come to care for Valerie, a truck with the emblem of the local gas company painted on the door pulled to the curb in front of them. He pulled free of Valerie's grasp and met the arriving service men with a handshake.

The gas company men ventured into Nash's house with a device to measure and detect the presence of natural gas, and Nash and Valerie settled in to wait. Soon the fire department and a police car were parked in front of the house, as well. Neighbors assembled on their lawns or walked down to watch the spectacle from the sidewalk across the street. A regular circus. Lookie-loos anxious to see what the hubbub was about.

The responding policeman, Officer Jim Hagan, according to his name tag, was an older man with a paunch. He greeted Nash and Valerie congenially, and when Nash introduced himself, the officer arched one bushy white eyebrow. "Colton?"

"Yes, sir. Why?"

"Nothing really. Just that we've been hearing that name a lot recently around the precinct."

"Yeah. My family's had a run of bad luck lately." Nash filled him in on the current situation and pulled up the security-camera footage. He put his arm around Valerie and handed over his phone to show Hagan the images of the intruder.

Hagan moved his glasses to the top of his head and squinted at the phone screen. "Well, we'll file a report, of course, and I'll call a forensic team out to look for fingerprints or hairs, any source of DNA the guy left behind, but it looks like the fella wore gloves. Quick in-and-out. Don't know that they'll find much of anything."

"That was my take, too, but just in case…"

Beside him, Valerie stiffened. Her fingers curled into his forearm, and she gasped quietly. With a low, urgent tone, she whispered, "Nash, he's here!"

"What?"

Hagan and Nash both glanced at her.

She angled her face toward Nash, but used her eyes to direct his attention across the street. "Over there. Be discrete. We don't want to spook him, but isn't that the guy? He's wearing a hat now, but I swear it's—"

"I see him," Nash said, then grumbled. "How bold. Returning to the scene of the crime to watch the fallout."

"Not unusual," Hagan said, handing Nash back his phone. Hagan's glance across the street required him to twist his body, turn his head.

The officer's movement clearly alarmed the intruder, and he took a step back from the gathered crowd and strode down the block at a quick pace.

Nash took one glance at Hagan and knew the older man would never be able to catch up to the intruder on foot. Without overthinking his choice, he shoved his phone into Valerie's hands and sprinted after the fleeing man.

Chapter Sixteen

"Out of the way!" Nash shouted to the milling onlookers as he raced after the intruder. He darted past family clusters and around baby strollers and tricycles, all while trying to keep his sights on his prey. Arms pumping, feet pounding, he pushed himself to eat up ground. His target had a lead on him, but Nash was younger, stronger, faster.

When the intruder cut across lawns, Nash followed.

When the man scrambled over low fences, Nash jumped and swung over with minimal effort.

As the intruder knocked over trash cans, Nash reacted quickly and skillfully negotiated the obstacles with fleet feet.

The man lost his hat, but Nash ignored it, taking mental note where it had fallen.

Within a few blocks, he'd gained ground on the man and waited for the best chance to tackle the cretin. Better to take him down on a grassy yard than the unforgiving sidewalk concrete. Sure enough, his target soon cut sharply to the left to cross a yard, headed for a side alley. Nash pounced. He flung himself forward, grabbing the man's shoulders and using his momentum to knock him off balance.

But, as if he'd expected the move, the intruder rolled as

he landed. With a twist, he freed himself of Nash's grasp and lurched to his knees, his breath sawing.

"No, you don't, you jerk!" Nash crawled forward, grabbed one of the man's ankles and tackled him again. He wrestled the intruder to the ground, grappling with the man's arms and dodging knee thrusts aimed at Nash's groin. Nash smashed his fist into the man's face, and blood sprayed from the intruder's nose. When his opponent tried to head-butt him in the nose in return, Nash jerked aside, avoiding the blow. They continued to exchange jabs, until Nash finally caught the man's wrists and worked to pin him to the ground. He almost had the man subdued when his prey bucked hard, shifting Nash's balance just enough that the cretin landed one of his knee jabs in Nash's crotch.

Pain exploded through Nash's belly, fiery hot and breath-stealing. Even so, he made a grab for the intruder as the man shoved free of Nash's grip and scuttled aside. With surprising alacrity, the man sprang to his feet, landed a kick in Nash's ribs and spun to stagger toward the side yard of the homeowner whose grass they'd wrestled in. All Nash could do was writhe in pain and groan as the man disappeared from his view.

"Nash!" Valerie rushed to him, out of breath and her face dented with worry. Officer Hagan was several strides behind her, his face flushed from exertion.

She dropped to her knees beside him, cradling his cheek with her palm. "Are you all right?"

"No," he wheezed. He dragged in a breath. "But I will be. Give me a moment."

Hagan stood over him, gasping slightly.

Aiming a finger toward the corner of the house

where the intruder had disappeared, Nash said, "He went that way."

Hagan glanced toward the side of the home, with its rose bushes and tall fence, and shook his head. "He's gone."

"But—" Valerie began, when Officer Hagan keyed the button on his shoulder radio and panted a radio code.

"Please advise units…to be on the lookout for…a Caucasian male in his…mid-fifties, five ten, weight…one-sixty. Black sweatshirt and khaki pants. Graying dark brown hair." He gave their location and more numeric codes, then signed off.

When he turned back toward Nash, his expression was dour. "What the hell did you think you were doing just then?"

Nash blinked. "What?"

"I should arrest you for assault and interfering with an investigation."

Nash had gained more of his breath and managed to sit up. He gaped at Hagan. "What!"

"Are you a policeman?" Hagan asked in the tone of an angry father lecturing an errant teen. "Did I ask you to pursue the suspect?"

"I—"

"I oughta take you down to the station, take your mug shot. Let your pretty gal pal bail you out," Hagan growled, glaring at Nash.

Nash gave Valerie a look that said, "Are you hearing him? Can you believe this crap?"

"Officer Hagan, Nash was only trying to stop the suspect that invaded his home from escaping. He was trying to help—"

"Pbbt," Hagan said, with a dismissive wave of his

hand. “I know what he was doing. But he needs to leave police work to policemen. He had no right to tackle that man.”

Nash sighed. The officer had a point. At the moment he’d raced after and jumped the intruder—the *suspected* intruder, Damon and Myles would be sure to specify—he hadn’t feared for his life or been protecting another’s. He’d seen an opportunity to catch the *suspected* intruder. His personal sense of violation, indignation and thirst for revenge had overruled what he had a legal right to do.

Valerie offered Nash a hand and helped him to his feet. She narrowed her eyes on his swollen lip and soiled shirt. Concern dented her brow. “You’re bleeding!”

Nash glanced down at the stains and flicked his hands uselessly at the crimson spatter. “No. That’s his blood. I think I busted his nose.” A tingle shimmied through Nash, and he faced the officer. “This is his blood. I’m sure of it.”

Officer Hagan seemed to see where Nash was going. His jaw clenched.

Nash whipped his shirt over his head and held it out. “You can take it in and get a sample of his DNA. Match his blood type. Work whatever forensic magic you need to and track him down.”

Officer Hagan held both hands up, palms toward Nash. “I can’t touch it, put my prints on it. There are chain-of-evidence rules.”

Nash nodded. “Right. Of course.”

“Um…” Valerie winced and twisted to pick up something she’d dropped beside her. “I touched his hat. Sorry. I saw him lose it and thought…”

Hagan sighed. “Look, I won’t take you in this time.

But consider yourself warned. Both of you. Leave the police work to the police. Got it?"

Nash dusted grass from his clothes and jerked a nod. "Got it."

But as they walked back toward his house, he knew he'd lied to Hagan. Because if anyone came within a breath of Valerie, so much as sent her a threatening glance, cop or not, he'd do whatever it took to protect her.

WHILE THE HOUSE finished airing out, with windows cracked and his doors locked, Nash took Valerie back to Rick and Vita's house. After explaining what had happened to her uncle and aunt, Nash and Valerie prepared dinner. The steaks, which a fireman had retrieved for them along with the other groceries, were diced, and Valerie added sautéed peppers and onions, turning the meal into fajitas, in order to stretch the dinner to serve four. They enjoyed the meal and conversation with Rick and Vita, even if it wasn't the romantic dinner for two Nash had envisioned.

"We can make up a bed for you to stay here tonight if you want," Vita offered.

"Thanks, but that's not necessary," Nash replied.

Vita blushed slightly and chuckled. "Oh, of course. You and Valerie would share..."

Nash covered an awkward chuckle with a cough. "I only mean that I plan to sleep at my house tonight."

"Are you sure that's safe?" Vita asked.

He nodded. "The air should be clear enough by then."

Vita exchanged a look with Rick. "I mean, what if this guy that's been sabotaging and attacking you comes back?"

Valerie raised a similarly worried gaze to him.

He covered Valerie's hand and gave it a reassuring squeeze. "Then he and I will finish what we started this afternoon."

"And if he has a weapon with him this time?" Valerie asked. "You said his gun misfired the first time he broke in. Don't you think after two failed attempts to harm you, he's going to be more certain of his means next time?"

"Assuming there's a next time." Nash wiped his mouth on his napkin and dropped it on his plate. "I'll be fine."

"But if you stayed he—" Valerie began, when the jangle of Nash's cell interrupted.

He glanced at the screen and recognized the number as the main switchboard at the police department. Had he really talked to cops that many times in the last few weeks? Sheesh.

"Sorry, I should take this," he said, pushing his chair back from the table. Valerie followed him into the next room.

When Nash answered the call, a male voice said, "Mr. Colton, this is Officer Hagan. I have an update on your B-and-E case."

Nash's gaze shot to Valerie, and he quickly switched to speakerphone so she could listen. "I'm all ears. Did you catch the guy?"

"We did. He was picked up a few blocks from your house by a patrol officer just after I sent out the BOLO. His name is Mickey Gorman. That name mean anything to you?"

"No."

Valerie shook her head, her expression void of recognition.

"Why?" Nash asked. "Should it? He saying he knows me?"

"Nah. He's not saying much of anything. He punched

the arresting officer, so we've got enough to keep him until his arraignment. Maybe a night behind bars will loosen his tongue. Just thought you might know something that would help us fill in some blanks."

"Sorry. Never heard of him. That's all you know about him? His name?"

"Well, no. He was in the system. He's got a rap sheet for some petty theft, public intoxication and drug possession from places as far away as Florida and Georgia and as close as Ohio. Current address listed as Toledo."

Valerie's breath caught, her eyes widening.

Nash's pulse kicked. *Toledo.*

He held her stare as Hagan continued, "Anyway, we've been in touch with his parole officer, but thought you might have something that might shed some light on why he was in Chicago. And why did he target you, your house?"

Valerie's eyes were bright as she shook her head again, and Nash's grip tightened on the phone. "Nothing now, but I have your card. If I think of anything, I'll let you know."

"You do that," Hagan said.

Nash thanked the man for calling and disconnected, his eyes still locked on Valerie.

"Toledo," he said simply.

She shook her head once again, more firmly. "No. I know what you're thinking but… I can't—" Val raked her fingers through her hair and got up to pace across the room. When she spun back to face him, her mouth was firm, her jaw set. "My mother is a lot of things, Nash, but she wouldn't—" He saw the doubt that flickered across her face. "It's just a horrible coincidence."

He pocketed his phone and strolled toward her. "Are you trying to convince me of that…or yourself?"

When she didn't reply, he pulled her into his arms and kissed her forehead. Her body was shaking, and he wished he could do something to ease her mind, take away the hurt and confusion she had to be feeling. Even if her mother was completely innocent of any involvement in the recent attacks, the simple fact that Val could even suspect her mother had to be tearing her up inside. She was conflicted enough because of her relationship with him and her torn loyalties.

She tipped up her face, and Nash's heart broke when he saw the tears in her eyes. Finally she whispered, "Give me twenty-four hours. Let me make a couple calls, check some things before you say anything to Hagan. Please?"

He gave her a soft kiss. "Okay."

"I'M COMING WITH YOU," Valerie said later that night as Nash was leaving. Snagging her coat from the front closet, she called over her shoulder to Vita, "We're gone. Good night!"

"Hold up." Nash sidestepped to block her path out of the Yateses' front door. "As much as I'd love your company, I think I'd feel better knowing you're safe here."

"Uh, Nash? Didn't you just spend the last five minutes convincing Vita your house was safe?"

He tugged her into his arms. "I'm willing to take any risk to show the person behind this I won't be cowed. But placing you in harm's way is a whole different story."

She tipped her head to the side as she gazed up at him. "What if I'm willing to assume the risk in order to be with you tonight?"

"Val…"

"Earlier today at the park, you said you'd be there for me. I believe you. I know you'll protect me, if needed." She kissed him gently, then added, "And I can help protect you. Be a second set of eyes and ears keeping guard..." She pressed her body fully against his and leaned in to whisper in his ear. "Besides, I've been waiting all day, weeks really, to get you alone and naked again."

He inhaled deeply as if preparing to offer another argument. She nipped his earlobe, and he half sighed, half groaned. Taking the sound as assent, she scooted around him and headed out to her car.

Back at Nash's bungalow, they checked the premises together for signs of intrusion, ventilation success and other mayhem before determining the house was clear, if chilly from having the windows open all day.

Nash pulled an extra blanket from the linen closet and wrapped it around Valerie's shoulders. "How's that?"

Looping her arms around his waist, she edged closer to him. "Good. But you know what's better? Body heat. Physical activity..."

"You don't need to ask me twice," he said with a low growl in his throat as he swooped in for a kiss.

Valerie stood on her toes, stretching to reach his lips and angling her head to allow him access to her throat. He trailed his kisses from her jaw to her neck. "You're beautiful, Val. You're all I've ever wanted."

The whispered words washed through her, a balm to her frayed nerves. Today had been upsetting and tiring in so many ways, but being here with Nash made it all seem worthwhile. She could block out the smell of the natural gas that lingered in her mind, push aside the concern of whether her mother was staying on track and mentally sound, and quell the fear of losing the man she'd come to realize she didn't want to live without. Nash truly made her feel safe. Anchored. Loved.

In a move that caught her daydreaming, he bent to catch her behind her legs and scooped her into his arms. He carried her across the bedroom and deposited her on the bed. He hesitated only long enough to kick off his shoes and shuck his blue jeans before following her down on the made bed.

"Come here, you," she said, folding the blanket he'd given her around them both as she hooked her legs around his. She met his kiss with equal passion and fervor. After their unexpected lovemaking weeks ago, the night of their overdue reckoning, she'd thought about being with Nash in so many stolen moments. While working with Sara. While driving. While showering…

An image, a scent, a word could carry her mind off to intimate moments she'd shared with Nash. As a teenager. On their recent night of passion. In her fantasies.

In truth, Nash hadn't been far from her mind in twelve years. And now he was in her arms. At last.

As he rolled with her, pulling her on top of him, she dragged the comforter with her, creating a warm cocoon around them. A dark nest that shut out the world. A snug cave where the woodsy scent of his body wash and the mint-toothpaste flavor of his kiss mingled and enticed her better than any aphrodisiac.

He helped her wiggle out of her slacks and pressed a line of toe-tingling kisses, nibbles and licks on her belly as he unbuttoned her blouse. Revealed her skin. One. Button. At. A. Time.

Slowly. Seductively. Maddeningly…

Her body was on fire by the time he inched the blouse off her shoulders and reached for her bra hooks. She writhed with pleasure as he freed her breasts from the satin bra and took her nipples in his mouth. She arched her back, wanting more, needing him…

"So sweet. Val, I—" He seized her mouth in another deep kiss, and she welcomed him with a lusty sigh, a plundering tongue and an open heart.

When he fought to get her arms free of the bra and blouse, she rolled with him, pedaled her legs to kick free the blanket…and found herself more tangled than before. A laugh escaped, and he raised his head to shoot her a quizzical look. "What's so funny?"

"Us. We're hopelessly tangled in covers and clothes and limbs. I think we need a reset."

He touched his forehead to hers, chuckling, then kissed her once more before fighting off the blanket and comforter that had become more mummy than cocoon.

Giggling like naughty children, they finished stripping, straightened the bedcovers and climbed between the cool sheets.

"Brr. Bring that hot bod back here, mister." She tugged his arm as he moved closer to her. "I miss your heat already."

"Likewise, love." He covered her, and with their bodies aligned, flesh to flesh, woman to man, teasing was set aside for hunger, for intimacy. For love.

She may not have spoken the words, but she told Nash with every touch and caress how much she cared for him, needed him, wanted him.

As he joined their bodies, whispering her name, she knew a soul-deep peace. The journey had taken years, carried her through deep valleys of sorrow and nearly broken her spirit, but with Nash, she'd finally found her way home.

Chapter Seventeen

Valerie waited until Nash went into work the next morning before making her inquiries concerning Mickey Gorman. She may have denied to him that her mother could have any involvement, but deep down, a terrible uncertainty nagged her. She sat on the bed where she and Nash had just made love, reconnecting, rebuilding the love and intimacy her mother had shattered years ago, and she steeled herself. With her back propped against the headboard and her knees drawn up to her chest, Val prepared herself.

The same red flags that had glared at her when Officer Hagan had called now replayed in her brain. Mickey Gorman. Toledo. Public intoxication. Drug use. Parole officer.

Could Mickey Gorman be a part of her mother's AA group as part of his parole requirement?

The one thing she knew for sure was she wouldn't get the answers she needed by stalling.

Taking a fortifying breath, she started with a call to Nancy, wanting to check on her mother's general condition before broaching a potentially dicey subject with her mother.

"She was actually much more upbeat the last time

I spoke with her," Nancy said. "Seemed to feel more in control, less harried. She went to AA with me a few nights ago and was much more relaxed after the meeting. I think your visit helped. She makes no secret that she's looking forward to you getting back home."

Valerie's chest constricted. *If she went back home.* How did she break the news to her mother if she did decide to stay in Chicago with Nash? She shoved aside that problem to focus on what Nancy was saying.

"—planning to call her or stop by tonight."

"Oh, good. Thank you." Taking a deep breath, Val asked, "Nancy, has my mother ever mentioned knowing someone named Mickey Gorman?"

Nancy took a beat longer than normal to respond. "Val, you know that the content of my conversations and counsel with your mother are confidential. I can't divulge anything your mother tells me and vice versa. Privacy is a cornerstone of the AA program. Without it, our members wouldn't feel the freedom to truly be open about their addiction and recovery struggles."

Val's shoulders drooped. "Yeah, I know. I just thought…well, never mind. Thanks for keeping an eye on her. You take care, too."

After disconnecting the call, Val slumped down on the bed. While it was encouraging to get a good report on her mother, Nancy's non-answer due to privacy concerns wasn't the decisive *no* that would have put her mind at ease.

She mulled how to approach her questions for her mother. Dread ticked in her gut like the timer on a bomb. She didn't want to set her mother off. According to Nancy, she was on a more stable track at the moment. Neither did she want to learn truths that could blow her world apart. But ignorance, or ignoring a potentially devastating truth, wouldn't resolve anything, didn't protect Nash from a threat that was within her power to stop.

Finally, she lifted her phone again and tapped the screen icons to call her mother. After basic salutations and inquiries of general well-being both ways, Val got to the heart of the issue at hand. "Mother, do you know a man by the name of Mickey Gorman?"

As Nancy had, her mother took a beat before responding. "Why? Where is this coming from?"

"Just…answer my question. Do you know Mickey Gorman?"

"It sounds to me like you're accusing me of something." Her mother's timbre began to tighten and rise in pitch. Caution lights flashed in Val's mind.

"No accusations. I just need to know if—"

"If you *are* accusing me of something, just say it!"

That her mother would jump to such a conclusion was common for her paranoia, but Valerie was uncomfortable with the bridge between the mention of the suspect's name and her mother's defensiveness.

"Why do you assume I'm making an accusation? Have you done something to be accused of?"

Her mother grunted loudly. "*He* put you up to this, didn't he?"

"If you mean Nash, then no. But when I learned that the man who broke into Nash's home and tried to create an explosion that could have killed both Nash and me is from Toledo, it just rang all sorts of warning bells."

"Nash and *you*?" Horror filled her mother's voice. "You're *still* hanging around with him? After everything I've told you? Valerie! I warned you to *stay away* from him!"

A prickle bit Valerie's nape. "Why should I stay away, Mother? What danger am I in if I'm with Nash? Something you set up?"

Carol's huff was loud and long. "He's turning you against me! He's lying to you and stealing you from me! He's no good, Val. All of those Coltons are cut from the same cloth and will hurt you, hurt *us*. You have to listen to me!" Panic was rising in her mother's tone.

"Mother, take a breath. I'm all right. Nothing is going to happen to either of us."

"You don't know that. You don't—"

Valerie bunched the bedspread in her hand, swallowing hard to fight the nausea that roiled in her gut. Pitching her own tone low and slow, she repeated, "Do you know Mickey Gorman?"

Silence answered her, and the anxiety and suspicion knotting her gut grew.

"Mother, did you hire Mickey Gorman to hurt Nash?"

"For God's sake, Valerie! I don't have to listen to this. If this is the only reason you called, then I'm hanging up."

"Mother, it's a simple enough question. If you didn't—"

"Goodbye." The line went silent.

"Mother?" But, as expected, no one was there.

A heaviness sat on Val's lungs, its crushing weight rooted in one awful truth. Despite her exclamations of dismay and indignation, her mother hadn't denied a relationship with, or her hiring of, the man suspected of trying to harm Nash.

VALERIE'S SUSPICIONS BREWED inside her over the next couple of hours, making her ill with worry. Her position, torn between her duty to her mother and her love for

Nash, was difficult enough without adding the question of whether her mother was behind the attacks on Nash.

She and Nash had been ripped apart years ago by innuendo, supposition and assumptions, and she wasn't about to leave their attempt at reconciliation to the mercy of doubts and impressions. As much as learning the truth terrified her, Valerie decided the best way to put the issue to rest was to go to the source.

After a distracted morning of trying—and failing—to work on the final art for the Yates' Yards winter advertising campaign, Valerie headed down to the police station where Officer Hagan worked. She had the front desk call him to the lobby, and she was told he was out on patrol.

Her shoulders drooped, and disappointment, all the more potent given the courage she'd had to muster to come down to the station, lanced her spirits.

She was turning to leave the station when another familiar face entered the lobby. She straightened and hurried to catch up with the man's long-legged strides. "Detective Cartwright?"

Cartwright glanced at her, then, clearly recognizing her, brightened with a polite smile. "Hi, uh, Ms. Yates, right?"

She nodded. "I need to talk to you, or…someone."

His expression modulated. One eyebrow lifted, an indication she had his full attention. "About?"

"Well, Officer Hagan has been working with Nash Colton concerning the break-ins and sabotage intended to cause a gas explosion at his house. I understand the chief suspect has been arrested and is being held here until his arraignment."

Cartwright squared his feet and folded his arms over his chest. "He was. But Mr. Gorman has been transferred to the county jail now. He just had his arraignment. In fact, that's where I just was. Considering it seems the repeated attacks on Mr. Colton were attempts on his life, I've been given the case."

"Oh. Um… I see. And what happened at the arraignment?"

"He pled not guilty. Of course. But considering he broke his parole in numerous ways, he'll likely be sent back to Ohio later this week. We're still working out those details."

Valerie wiped her sweaty hands on the legs of her gabardine pants. "Can I see him?"

Cartwright tipped his head. "Pardon?"

"I'd like to talk to him. Ask him a couple questions."

The detective's spine straightened. "Do you have information about the case, Ms. Yates?"

"Not exactly. Just questions. Something I really need answered."

The detective's incisive gaze bore into her, and she shivered. "What questions?"

She glanced around the lobby, her anxiety climbing. "It's probably nothing. I mean I can't imagine—"

He hitched his head toward a door that led deeper into the building. "Let's go to my office and talk."

Valerie's pulse scampered. She couldn't tell the detective anything that would implicate her mother. That would be a complete betrayal.

And yet…if her mother was complicit, how could she *not* tell the detective what she knew. She had to think about Nash, his safety. And what was morally right. She wasn't responsible for her mother's bad choices. If she had done the unthinkable, hired a man to hurt Nash, she had to be stopped.

Her feet felt leaden as she followed Cartwright to his desk and perched on the edge of the chair opposite him.

"So...what is weighing on you in the case against Mr. Gorman?"

Even as he asked the question, Valerie sensed that the detective already knew what she suspected. The man was no dummy. If he'd done his research on the case, if he remembered anything she'd told him when she'd been interviewed after Axel's death, he'd put two and two together the same as she had. The keen look in his eyes told her he was two steps ahead of her.

Perspiration popped out on her lip, and she knew a moment of regret, of guilt. Swallowing hard, she said, "I understand Mickey Gorman is from Toledo."

Cartwright nodded. "Yes. That's his current home address."

She twisted her fingers in the strap of her purse. "I think... I mean there's a chance..."

The detective said nothing, waiting patiently, his gray-green gaze fixed on her.

"My mother lives in Toledo. She doesn't like Nash." Valerie had to pause and take a calming breath to keep her gorge from rising. Blood rushed past her ears in a whoosh that drowned out all the other noises from the police station. "In fact, she hates him. And all of the Coltons. She's under a doctor's care for mental illness, but recently, she hasn't been taking her medicines properly. So I'm concerned that, in a moment of irrationality..." Her throat clogged. She couldn't say the words. It was too awful. Tears stung her eyes.

Cartwright's expression shifted. The same compassion he'd displayed when Sara had fainted filled his face as he leaned forward and reached to cover her hand.

"Take all the time you need. But I need to hear you say the words. Officially."

When she sniffed and wiped her cheek with her sleeve, he handed her a facial tissue from a box on the corner of his desk.

After she blew her nose and gulped oxygen, she blurted, "I think my mother, Carol Yates, hired Mickey Gorman to come after Nash."

Cartwright sat back in his chair, his expression calm and sympathetic. "Why do you think so?"

With nausea roiling in her gut, Valerie outlined her mother's history with the Coltons, her mental illness, her continued insistence that Nash would hurt her. "I know it's largely speculation and circumstantial, but when I heard Gorman was from Toledo, and was previously arrested for drug- and alcohol-related charges, and knowing my mother attends AA meetings and..."

Valerie paused, exhaled, squeezed the chair's armrests until her fingers blanched.

Cartwright lifted the receiver of his desk phone and pressed an extension. "Yeah, hi, Sally. Cartwright in Homicide. Can you bring Mickey Gorman up to an interrogation room for me, please. Yeah. I know. Yes, now. Thanks." When he hung up, he twisted his mouth and regarded Valerie with an intense scrutiny.

Valerie rubbed a hand on her chest where she thought her heart might crash through her ribs. Part of her wished she could take back her words, rewind and erase her traitorous suggestion to the detective.

"I can't imagine how hard it must have been to come in today, Ms. Yates." He pushed to his feet, signaling an end to the conversation. "But you did the right thing."

Valerie stood, too, although her legs were weak and

her knees buckled. She squared her shoulders with more bravado than she felt. "I still don't have the answers I need."

Cartwright sighed. "Ms. Yates—"

"Detective," she interrupted, her stomach swooping. "I want to come with you. Be in the room when you question him. I want to hear what Mickey Gorman has to say."

Cartwright shook his head. "That's not—"

"Please. I won't say anything or interfere in any way."

Hands on his hips, his mouth pressed in a grim line, Cartwright stared at her silently for a moment. Finally, his eyes narrowing, he said, "If I let you watch from an observation room, you have to understand that if you divulge anything we learn, to anyone, including Nash Colton, I can have you arrested for impeding an investigation. If Gorman gives up your mother and you tip her off, I'll charge you with aiding and abetting. Your complete silence and discretion is imperative. Understood?"

Including Nash Colton. Valerie's lungs struggled for air. If she agreed, if she got the answers she needed, she was promising to keep secrets from Nash again, just when they had reached a turning point in their relationship.

"I—"

"I mean it, Ms. Yates. Letting you observe is outside normal procedure. I can sell it as you being an informant, already being privy to the information gathered, but I need your sworn word it goes no further."

Her insides were being ripped in a hundred directions, her loyalties torn, and guilt chewed her soul. But she'd come too far to turn back. She'd set a boulder in motion that couldn't be stopped. Releasing a shuddering sigh, she gave Cartwright a nod. "I promise."

Chapter Eighteen

"Hey, where are you?" Nash asked, when he finally reached Valerie on her phone that afternoon. "I left work, thinking we'd steal away for a long lunch, and when I went by the house to get you, the only one I found home was that dang calico. Why haven't you been answering your phone?"

"I, um, had it turned off." She laughed stiffly. "I didn't realize it until a little while ago. Duh!"

"Okay, well, I'm back at work now and already ate without you when I couldn't find you, so… I guess I'll just see you back at the house later?"

"Well, maybe. I… I'm not sure what—" Valerie stopped abruptly, and in the background, Nash heard a male voice that said, "We're ready."

"Who was that? What's ready?"

"Sorry, Nash. I have to go."

"Val, what's going on?" Silence answered him. She was already gone.

Nash hung up his office phone and leaned back in his desk chair, puzzling over her abrupt departure, her unwillingness to answer his simplest questions. Old familiar doubt demons nipped at him, and he shook his head, wanting with all his heart to confidently dismiss the nagging suspicions. But Hagan's call wouldn't leave him alone. The fear in Valerie's eyes, even as he'd promised to give her twenty-four hours to answer her own questions, haunted him. Now she was shutting him out again. Like before, when they'd been teens.

He wanted to quash the niggling suspicions, but his gut told him plainly that something was up and Valerie was keeping it from him. After promising to be open with him. Candid and faithful.

Already she'd broken her promise.

But he'd given her twenty-four hours to learn the whole truth and bring it to him. He needed to wait. To trust.

His chest squeezed, and he began the painful, tedious wait. He didn't care what the truth she'd discovered was. No matter how bleak the news might be, his first and only concern was that she keep faith with him. They could face any challenge together. But if Valerie chose deception, distance and doubt again, how could he believe they had a future?

He refused to go down that dark path again.

VALERIE FOLLOWED THE uniformed officer who'd been assigned to sit with her in the observation booth next to the interrogation room while Cartwright questioned Gorman. They'd had to wait for the public defender assigned to Gorman's case to be called and arrive at the station. The PD, a woman named Jill Russell, had been at court, delaying matters. Valerie had spent the time pacing, second-guessing her choice and avoiding calls from Nash. Her white lie about having her phone off was only partly false. She had turned off her phone when he continued calling.

She'd only turned the phone on five minutes before

getting his most recent call, because she'd wanted to listen to her voicemail. His increasingly concerned messages broke her heart, especially knowing she couldn't tell him the whole truth about what she'd been doing, what she'd learned. She prayed that Nash had enough faith in her to let a generic answer stand. Enough trust to let "I can't say more" stand.

The uniformed officer motioned to a chair from which Val could watch the interview. She shook her head, too hyped on adrenaline and nervous energy to sit still. When the lanky, wiry-haired man was ushered into the small, drab interview room, Valerie's stomach lurched. Regardless of whether her mother was behind the attacks, this man was undoubtedly the face she and Nash had watched on surveillance footage breaking into Nash's home. This man had tried to kill, or at a minimum, maim Nash with a gas explosion. Acid crept up her throat, and she thought she might throw up.

"Mr. Gorman," Detective Cartwright began, his deep voice resonating through the speakers in the observation booth. "We've received new information regarding your case and have—"

Gorman leaned toward Cartwright with a snarl. "I told you before, I don't got nothing to say."

"Do you know a woman in Toledo by the name of Carol Yates?"

Gorman's flinch was tiny, almost imperceptible, but Valerie caught it. And she was certain Cartwright had, as well, because now he leaned forward, almost touching noses with Gorman, and said in a low, stern tone, "Don't take the fall for her. If Carol Yates put you up to this, paid you, blackmailed you, whatever, now is your chance to come clean."

Valerie held her breath. *Please deny it. Please...*

She held her breath. But any hope Valerie had that she'd misinterpreted Gorman's twitch as guilt or surprise evaporated when, after a few tense beats, the wiry-haired man sat back, his pale skin reddening. Gorman's mouth tightened, then he leaned toward Jill Russell, and whispered to his lawyer. Russell conferred with him, too quietly for Valerie to hear anything. But she didn't have to hear to know what they had to be discussing.

When both Gorman and Russell straightened in their chairs, the public defender faced Cartwright, placing her hands, fingers laced, on the table. "We'd like to discuss a plea. Mr. Gorman will answer all of your questions, in full, for immunity."

Valerie's knees gave out. Staggering backward, she slumped into the chair she'd refused earlier.

"Immunity?" Cartwright scoffed. "No way that flies with the DA. But we can see about a reduced sentence. We'll work with Mr. Gorman's parole officer and the courts in Ohio to get leniency."

As the negotiations in the interrogation room continued, Valerie's head swam, and a loud buzzing filled her ears. Gorman may not have said the words yet, but his turnabout, when faced with the truth, spoke for him.

Her breathing sawed from her in quick, shallow pants. Lifting a trembling hand, she covered her mouth, thinking she might be sick.

The uniformed officer squatted beside her. "Are you all right, ma'am?"

She lifted a blurred gaze to the policeman and shook her head. "No."

She'd defended her mother to Nash. Given her mother

chance after chance. But her loyalty to her mother had been ill-placed.

Her mother was behind the attacks on Nash. Valerie didn't think she'd ever be all right again.

VITA ANSWERED THE door when Nash arrived at the Yateses' early that evening. He'd worried about Valerie and her lack of communication throughout the afternoon, and, having not found her at his house when he left work and unable to reach her on her phone, he'd driven straight to the Yateses'.

"Oh, Nash, I'm so glad to see you." Vita ushered him inside, wiping her hands on her skirt. "Val's been upstairs in her room for the last two hours. She's clearly upset over something, but she wouldn't talk to us about it. Maybe she'll tell you what's wrong."

"Thanks." He took the steps two at a time and hurried to the closed guest room door. After knocking lightly, he called, "Val, can I come in? It's Nash."

He heard footsteps, then the door flew open, and she launched herself into his arms.

"Hey, hey," he crooned softly, rubbing her back as he held her. "It's okay. What's going on?"

Though she clutched him, her body shuddering as she nestled against him, she said nothing. He allowed her a few minutes to simply hug him and gather herself. When the trembling of her limbs calmed, he eased her back and guided her to the bed. She sank on the edge of the mattress, and he joined her. Angling his body to face her, he lifted her chin, trying to bring her eyes to his. "Tell me. What's going on? What happened today?"

She met his gaze only briefly before jerking her chin away and shaking her head. "I can't."

His stomach lurched. Were they over before they'd really started? He swallowed hard, working to rein in his gut reaction. "Can't what? What are you saying?"

She scooted closer, reaching for him. "Can you just… hold me?"

The fear that had gripped him eased. He wrapped her in his embrace again and leaned back against the stacked pillows, cradling her close. "Val, please talk to me. I hate seeing you like this." When she remained silent, he asked, "Did you talk to your mother?"

He felt her stiffen. Of course, her mood was about her mother. Val's mission this morning had been to find out if her mother was connected to the Gorman guy the police had in custody. She was always agitated after talking to her mother, so that explained a lot. But not all. Not the extent of her current distress. A different sort of tension curled in a hard ball inside him.

"What did your mom say when you talked to her? When you asked her about Mickey Gorman?"

Valerie buried her face deeper into the crook of his neck. Sighed brokenly. "She…never gave me a straight answer. She got hostile and defensive when she realized I suspected her of wrongdoing."

"Huh." He understood the subtle difference that Val had to be debating. "Do you think she was being deliberately evasive, as in she didn't want to admit the truth? Or was she so hurt by your assumption that she didn't want to dignify the question with a response?"

"I—" Her fingers curled into his shirt. "I also called her sponsor, Nancy. I asked her about Gorman, too. If my mother knew him, had mentioned him."

Nash noticed Valerie hadn't answered his question, but let it slide for the moment. "What did Nancy tell you?"

"Not much. She reminded me that privacy and discretion are cornerstones of the AA program."

"So if she knew something she was honor-bound to keep your mother's confidence?"

"Yeah."

Nash meditated on that briefly, then asked, "Even if she had knowledge of a crime?"

Val hesitated, then said, "Nancy did say that the last time she talked to my mother, she seemed in a calmer frame of mind. But otherwise, I—I really didn't learn anything else…from her."

Every time Valerie paused, as if carefully choosing her words, every time she avoided his questions, Nash grew more edgy. Coupled with her obvious distress over… *something*, he concluded she was withholding critical information.

"What aren't you telling me?" he asked, testing his theory.

Valerie was still, silent. Wouldn't look at him.

"You know you can trust me, don't you? If something has happened, if you learned something important—"

"Nash," she began, and he waited for her to continue. And waited.

"Valerie?"

"Just…stay with me tonight. Here. Hold me and… trust me. Please?"

He knew it was a leap of faith, but he nodded, pulled her close, kissed her head. "All right."

VALERIE SLEPT LITTLE that night. Her conscience plagued her for having kept Nash in the dark about her mother's involvement in the attacks. Guilt chewed her gut for having directed the police to her mother, and questions racked her about what was happening with the case. She'd wanted to go to Ohio, be with her mother when the police came for her, but Cartwright warned her not to. He wanted nothing to tip Carol off. Besides, Cartwright had contacted the police in Ohio about an arrest warrant for Carol, and Val couldn't have gotten to Toledo before it was executed. He had advised her simply to go to Rick's and wait.

But waiting was torture. Had her mother been taken into custody? Had she resisted arrest? Valerie had told Cartwright about her mother's mental illness, but too many things could have gone wrong.

And Nash. Dancing around his questions last night had torn her up. When Nash learned the truth, understood how much she'd kept from him, would it change his feelings toward her? At first light, afraid her tossing and turning would wake Nash, she finally tucked her cell phone in her pocket, slipped from the bed and went downstairs.

Vita was already awake and had coffee brewing.

"Good morning, dear," Vita chirped brightly. "You're up early. I hope that means you're feeling better."

Valerie didn't want to worry her aunt, so she forced the brightest smile she could manage. "Some better. Thanks. Have I had any calls?" she asked, knowing it was a long shot.

"At this hour?" Vita handed Val a mug of steaming coffee. "No. Are you expecting a call on the house phone?"

"I guess not." If there was news, both Cartwright and her mother had her cell number, and her phone hadn't been out of her sight since she left the police station yesterday. Just in case, she checked the home screen again for any indication she'd somehow missed a text or had a message.

Nothing. She wilted in one of the chairs at the kitchen table and raised her mug for a sip of fortification.

She heard the soft padding of feet behind her and turned, expecting to find Rick. Instead, Nash stood there, barefoot, hair rumpled and his clothes from yesterday wrinkled from being slept in. To Valerie, he looked sexier than any movie star or cologne model. Her heart swelled, and a bittersweet pang filled her chest. She wanted to wake up to groggy, rumpled Nash every morning for the rest of her life. But had her mother made that impossible?

He yawned widely and scratched his chin. "Does this house always get up so early?"

Vita filled another coffee cup and handed it to Nash. "Not always. Can I get you two breakfast?"

Even though she hadn't eaten dinner the night before, Valerie's stomach churned at the thought of food. "No, thank you."

Clearly her answer nettled Vita's maternal instincts, because she sent her a dubious look and sighed.

"Just coffee for me. I'll get a bite at home before I go into the office. I have to shower and change clothes—"

Valerie's phone jangled, sounding especially loud and harsh considering the early hour. Adrenaline charged through her and left her trembling, with dread close on its heels.

"Oh," Vita said, setting down her mug. "Maybe that's the call you were waiting for."

Nash frowned. "What call?"

Her caller ID read, *Chicago Police Department*.

Her mouth dried, but mustering her courage, Valerie rose from the table on wobbly legs and hurried out of the room to answer the call. It took two tries to scrape out a response. "Hello?"

"Ms. Yates? Detective Cartwright."

Her breath left her in a quavering exhale. "Yes?" she rasped.

"Have you been in touch with your mother since we spoke yesterday?"

Valerie hadn't a destination in mind when she'd left the kitchen to take the call in private, but she found herself on the back screened porch, the icy wind cutting through her thin sleep shirt. "I— No. You told me not to."

Cartwright grunted.

"Why?" She could barely hear herself over the thumping of her pulse in her ears. "What's happened?"

"Nothing. That's the problem. Officers in Ohio went to your mother's home, but she wasn't there. They waited all night for her to return, but she didn't."

A fresh kind of panic swept through her. Had her mother harmed herself? Had she overdosed on booze and pills? Given in to paranoia and despair? "Did—did they go inside? Are you sure she wasn't there?"

"They checked the premises. The house was empty. I just thought maybe she'd contacted you, given you some indication where she was?"

"M-maybe at her friend's house? Nancy, her sponsor?" Valerie forced her thoughts to settle enough to conjure Nancy's address from memory.

"Okay. We'll check it out. It should go without saying—if you hear from her, call me. Immediately."

"Right. Yes." She stood staring out at Rick and Vita's frozen backyard, shivering from the cold and her concern.

The early morning sun glinted off the frost like shards

of broken glass. The metallic scent of snow hung in the air. In the icy breeze, a random flake or two wandered down from the pale sky, swirling haphazardly like Valerie's thoughts. Untethered. Spinning recklessly. Leaving her cold.

Her mother was missing. Wanted for hiring an assassin. Determined to destroy the one relationship where Valerie had found deep abiding love and joy. Set on tearing her from the family where she'd felt happy and supported.

With a keening moan, she bent at the waist, lashed by pain and wrenched internally. Because she still felt a duty to her mother because of Carol's illness. She wanted so desperately to break free of the millstone of chaos and hatred that was her mother's hold on her.

"Val, my God!"

She gasped her surprise, not having heard Nash's approach until he spoke. He placed something around her shoulders. Her coat, she realized as she straightened and caught the edges of it to pull around her.

"Love, it's freezing out here. Why don't you come in?"

She nodded but couldn't speak. Didn't move. Soon his arms were around her along with the coat.

"I wish you'd tell me what's going on. It's obviously tearing you up." He smoothed a hand along her cold cheek. "How can I help you, if you won't talk to me?"

"Just…stay here. Be with me." She reflected on all that would likely come down in the following days, hours, and added, "And give me grace."

"Grace?" Nash frowned, the dark tug of his mouth reflecting confusion over her odd word choice. And suspicion. He had to understand that something bad was coming. She saw the hurt in his eyes when she dodged answering his questions and put emotional distance between them with her lack of candor.

But grace was what she'd need most when the police found her mother, when Nash learned the whole truth about what she was keeping from him, when her reckoning came and she had to choose a way forward, inevitably betraying someone she loved…

She couldn't live like this, with divided loyalties. It was too much…

Eventually, if she didn't make a choice, it would break her.

EVEN IF NASH hadn't been aware of how restless Valerie had been through the night, watching her across Vita's breakfast table left little doubt. She looked miserable. At the start of their reconciliation, her misery was not reassuring.

When he'd heard her plaintive wail, chills had sketched down his spine. Seeing her doubled over, crumpled with whatever pain tormented her, a rock had lodged in his chest. Not just because he hurt for her, but because she wouldn't share the source of her pain with him. Because she seemed to be moving away from him instead of closer. He was losing her, and he didn't know why. Or how to reverse course.

He could guess *who* easily enough, but her mother was a volatile subject. The big red danger button of their relationship.

He'd guided her back inside to Vita's breakfast table, but Valerie was clearly somewhere else. Though she held a mug between her hands, she stared silently into space. Nash studied the dark circles under Val's eyes, the worry lines etched between her brows, her faraway expression.

He was due at work in an hour, but every minute that passed made it more obvious he should take another personal day to stay with Val. If he still had a job with Reed and Burdett Architecture when all the Colton family drama was resolved, he'd owe it all to his understanding boss, and the fact that he'd accumulated six weeks of sick leave and vacation days since starting at the firm.

He battled down the frustration of not knowing how to help her and said quietly, "Val, if you don't want to talk to me…fine. But I think you should talk to someone. Vita or Nicole? Rick? Maybe Faith?"

She blinked slowly and finally met his gaze. "No. I…can't."

"Well, I'm not leaving you like this, so… I'll call my office and tell them I'll be out today—"

She roused a bit then. He mug thunked to the table. "No. That's not… I don't…"

Gathering her hand in his, he kissed her knuckles. "We'll go somewhere together. Leave town. Maybe a change of scenery to distract us is what we both need."

She shook her head. "Not today. I need to be—"

Drawing a slow breath, his heart in his throat, he ventured, "What about Ohio? Do you want me to take you to Toledo?"

Her chin jerked up, her gaze bright with alarm.

Cautiously, he continued, "I'll go with you, if you feel you're needed there."

Tears bloomed in her eyes, and her hand squeezed his. "Thank you…for offering. But…no. That's not…" Putting an arm on the table, she buried her face in the crook of her elbow and groaned. "I hate this, Nash. I hate it!"

He clenched his back teeth and struggled to calm his internal battle between frustration and concern for her.

Finally, he shoved back his chair and pushed to his feet. "Come on. We're at least going for a walk. Get your coat—"

Now it was Nash's phone that rang. As odd as it was to get a call at this early hour, the panic that filled Valerie's face set Nash's pulse on edge, even before he pulled the cell from his jeans pocket. The name on the caller ID was his second shock.

He scowled, hesitated.

"What is it?" Val asked.

"Not what. Who. It's my dad. He never calls me."

When he continued to stare at the phone, Valerie took his hand. He could feel her trembling, heard the note of dread when she asked, "Are you going to answer it?"

He didn't want to. Something in his bones told him not to, warned him it would be bad.

"It could be an emergency," she said, rising from her own chair to move closer to him, her face pale.

He arched one light brown eyebrow and grumbled, "That's no selling point." But he stabbed the screen before the call could go to voicemail. With a deep breath, he said, "Hi, Dad. What's up?"

He heard his father clear his throat, then in a tight voice, Erik said, "Nash, we have a…situation."

Of course they did. Because the Coltons couldn't catch a break this year.

Nash gripped the phone tighter, his gut tight with dread. "What kind of situation?"

"Do you remember a girl named Valerie Yates? Used to visit Rick and Vita years ago as a kid? In the summers, I think." Nash's heart seemed to still as he shot a worried look to Val. He put the call on speaker.

"Of course, I know her. Dad, she was at Axel's funeral

with me. Are you so self-absorbed that you don't even remember that? In fact, I'm dating her."

"You're what?" Through the phone connection, he heard a groan, some shuffling, a muffled second voice.

"She was my girlfriend years ago, too. You might have known that if you'd paid attention to anyone but yourself." But when had his father ever cared about his sons or anything that mattered to them?

Erik's voice remained strangely flat, yet with a thread of strain. "You may remember I had my hands full with your grandmother and the media at my brother's funeral."

"Yeah. Whatever. Your point?"

"My point is…right now, I'm with her mother," his father said slowly. The tension in his voice was more obvious now.

Valerie slapped a hand over her mouth, muffling a gasp, but her eyes were wide with confusion and alarm.

"You're…what?"

Erik sighed, his voice dipping lower. "You heard me. And she has a gun…pointed at my head."

Chapter Nineteen

A shudder rolled through Valerie as Nash's face paled, and he muttered, "What the hell?"

"She is requesting your presence…here at my house," Erik continued. "Or she will— Ow, easy there, woman! I'm cooperating! No need to be—"

They heard a quiet *oof*, then Erik said, "She wants us both here. She says she'll kill me if you don't come. Right now."

Nash met Valerie's eyes with a pained expression. No words needed to be spoken to realize the danger of the situation, the reason behind her mother's drastic actions, or the consequences of handling the situation the wrong way. Valerie held out a trembling hand for the phone. She knew, perhaps better than anyone, how explosive the situation could become. Or maybe it was already teetering near DEFCON 1.

She wiggled her fingers, asking for the phone. "Let me talk to her. Maybe I can get her to stand down. Use my phone to call the police."

"Dad…" Nash held up a finger, silently saying hang on.

"Who was that?" Erik sounded more panicked now. "I— Tell her no cops! Carol is adamant."

Valerie's hand shook as she brought up the number pad on her cell. Cartwright's number should be in her recent calls…

Muffled voices could be heard, then Erik came back on the line. "She says…if the cops show up, she swears she'll kill us both, no questions asked." His father growled under his breath, then whispered, "Nash, she's not right in the head. She— Ow!"

Valerie waved her hand again, silently begging for him to turn over the phone.

"Dad, put Carol on the phone. Valerie is here. Maybe she can clear this up."

"I— Okay. But you're coming? Right? She's serious, Nash. She wants you here. With me. She says it's the only way—"

Nash pressed the phone to his chest to cover their whispers. "We need to go. No matter how this plays out, we gotta at least try to—"

Val snatched the phone from him and said, "Mr. Colton, tell my mother to talk to me. Please!" But she nodded to Nash and picked up her purse as they headed out the door. She was still in her nightshirt, but they had no time for her to change. Vita's garden shoes by the door would have to do for her feet.

She followed Nash down the porch steps, tossing him the keys to her car as she waited for her mother to come on the line. She knew she needed to let Cartwright know where her mother was, what was happening. But she also knew what Cartwright would say about Val and Nash hurrying over to the scene, trying to handle the standoff between Erik and her mother themselves. But without help from the detective or some law enforcement, how—?

"Val'rie? S'that you?"

Valerie's pulse spiked as she climbed in the passenger seat. Her mother's voice sounded strangely high-pitched, slightly slurred. "Yes. Mother, please, you can't—"

"Are you with that Colton boy again after ev'rything I've said?"

Valerie closed her eyes. Took a beat to breathe in. Released it. Her mother had been drinking. She knew it in her bones, even without hearing her slurred speech—which made the situation all the more difficult to manage. Alcohol skewed everything. Despair stabbed her. She could imagine the familiar smell of alcohol fumes wafting off her mother. As with so many times as a little girl and a teenager, Valerie felt the roil of bile and acid in her stomach and climbing her throat. Fear, loathing and fury stirred in her core like a lethal cocktail.

Lethal. Poor choice of words. Or perhaps exactly right. Erik was convinced her mother intended to kill him. "Mother, you can't hurt Erik Colton. You need to walk away. Everything will be fine, but you have to put the gun down and—"

"No. No, no, no-o-o! I can't do that, Val'rie. It's all 'is fault. Ev'rythin'...started with him. He has to pay for what he did to us."

Valerie wanted to scream her frustration. The last few years of psychiatric counseling, drug therapy and rehab went out the window in an instant when her mother drank. She reverted to old thought patterns, paranoia and obsessions.

Nash cut a dark look toward her that showed his deep concern. He took Valerie's phone from her other hand, and when they stopped at the first red traffic light, he thumbed in a number. Indicating his phone in her hand, he mouthed, "Mute. I don't want her to hear me."

"Mother, I'm on my way. We'll figure this out together. Like always. Just...don't do anything rash. Take a breath. You're all right. Hang on." After that last encouragement, she tapped the screen to mute her end of the connection. "Nash, wait! She doesn't want police. They'll set her off, Nash. You can't—"

The call Nash had made on her cell phone connected, and she heard a chipper male voice that said, "Hi, Valerie! What can I do for you, gorgeous?"

With the phone on speaker in Nash's lap, he continued pushing the speed limit and weaving through traffic. "It's Nash. I need your help, bro. Get over to Dad's ASAP."

"Why?" Damon asked. "What's wrong?"

Nash gave his brother a bullet-point explanation, while Valerie could hear her mother and Erik over the line from the phone she held.

"You lied to me! Cheated on me. You used me and threw me away like trash!" her mother ranted.

"I don't know what you're talking about! I never met you before—"

Val cringed, knowing how Erik's denial, his memory lapse, would go over with her mother. In a word, disaster.

"What!" Carol shrieked.

"Look, I'm at least thirty minutes out. You gotta call the police, a negotiator or someone in," Damon said. "This could turn ugly quick."

"Uglier, you mean." Nash sighed heavily and pounded his fist on the steering wheel when they got trapped behind traffic at a stop light.

"I'll handle the law enforcement, get us some backup," Damon said. "You need to stay away, Nash. We need Val's mom to calm down. Stand down. Your presence isn't likely to do that."

Nash nodded as if his brother could see the response. "Maybe. But Val's with me, and she might be able to help de-escalate things."

"Maybe. But it's still risky. Don't do anything rash, bro. I'm on my way."

Once Damon disconnected, Valerie took her phone back from Nash and unmuted her mother. Taking a fortifying breath, she said, "I'm still here, Mother. Talk to me."

"The bastard says he doesn't even know me! Thirty years ago he had his hand up my dress, and now he doesn't know me!"

Normally, when her mother had a high-emotion episode, Valerie had been counseled to firmly and calmly disengage. For both her mother's sake and her own, she'd been advised to take herself out of her mother's emotional spiral, not to feed into a cycle of delusion and uncontrolled emotion. But how did she do that when her mother had a gun to Erik's head?

"I've had my hand up a lot of dresses, lady," Erik said in the background.

Valerie gritted her teeth. *Oh, geez! Not helpful, Erik!*

"Mother, let me talk to Erik. Hand him back the phone, okay?"

"Why? Are you plotting with him against me? Don't you understand how—?" More muffled noises interrupted her mother, then the line went quiet.

"Mother? Mother?" When she got no reply, Valerie sent a terrified look to Nash. "She hung up."

He angled a sharp glance toward her and the silent phone. "We'll be there in two minutes. Get them back on the line if you can."

Valerie nodded, but instead of calling Erik's phone,

she switched to her own phone and called the last number she'd entered in her speed dial. She cut a glance to Nash, who was fully occupied negotiating traffic. Still, when Cartwright came on the line, she kept her voice low. "It's Valerie. She's at Erik Colton's house. Please hurry! She's holding him hostage."

Chapter Twenty

Nash wheeled into the driveway of his father's home moments later. A gray sedan with bumper stickers and a license plate identifying it as an Ohio rental had been left on the grass near the front door, not even in the driveway.

Val climbed out of the passenger side with her heart in her throat, studying the haphazard parking of the rental vehicle on the lawn. Of course, her mother had driven here. Drunk. And highly upset, which was bad enough. Her heart thrashed in her chest, and she fought to rein in the adrenaline coursing through her. She needed to think clearly and focus if she had any chance of righting this crisis.

She circled the front fender of the car and reached for Nash's hand, stopping him as he charged toward the front door. "Promise me you'll let me handle my mother my way."

He scowled as he laced his fingers with hers. "I'm having a hard enough time not telling you to wait outside. I don't like the idea of you being around an unstable woman who's waving a gun around."

"I don't like it for you, either. But she's my mother. I know her best and how to handle her moods." They stopped at the bottom step to the stoop, and she tugged his arm to make him face her. The burn of acid in her throat made it difficult to speak, but she whispered, "She's more likely to listen to me than anyone else. Especially anyone with the last name Colton. Please, Nash."

A muscle in his cheek jumped as he considered her point. "Maybe we could stall until Damon comes? He has training with hostage—"

But before he finished his sentence, the front door flew open.

Erik Colton stood at the threshold with Carol inches behind him. Erik's stiff expression and the irritation bright in his green eyes told Valerie her mother still had her weapon trained on him, even though it wasn't visible.

After flicking her eyes over Nash with clear disdain, Carol's gaze went to Valerie. "Valerie, you need to leave. This is between me and the Coltons. This is their own fault."

Valerie raised both hands and took a cautious step toward the door. "Let's not talk about blame. Before we go any further, you need to put away the gun."

"No blame? Valerie, you know what they did to me! He has to pay!"

Beside her, Nash stiffened, and she squeezed his wrist, silently telling him to stay calm.

"Please, Mother. Put your weapon on the ground, and let us talk this through. Erik will apologize, and we'll—"

"Apologize?" Erik scoffed, and despite her dismay at the man's lack of cooperation, Valerie maintained eye contact with her mother.

"Dad," Nash said in a warning tone. "We all want to settle this without bloodshed or scandal. Right?"

Valerie took another slow step toward the door, with Nash on her heels. Could she use distraction to buy them time until Cartwright or Damon arrived? She was afraid of what might happen if she didn't defuse things before Cartwright arrived. "Mother, please. Talk to me. Let's resolve this peacefully."

Carol shook her head. "No. Th's is long overdue. I won' have peace 'til he pays for e'rything, he—"

Knocking Val aside, Nash lunged toward the door.

Carol startled, stumbled. The gun fired.

Nash landed on his hands and knees on the stoop, and Carol jerked Erik back by his shirt collar as she tried to slam the door.

"No!" Valerie threw herself against the closing door and wedged her shoulder inside. "Mother, don't! Let me in…" She heard scuffling and a crash inside.

Twisting, she glanced down at Nash. "Are you all—?"

He waved one hand at her as he got to his feet. "I'm fine. Go."

She shoved hard on the door, and it swung open. The foyer was littered with coats and umbrellas from the fallen coatrack. She prayed that was the crash she'd heard and stepped over the debris as she hurried deeper in the house. "Mother!"

She found Carol and Erik standing in the center of the living room. She still had his collar fisted in her hand, the gun at his temple. Erik's cheek was now bleeding from a short gash.

"Damn it, Mother!" Valerie growled. "This is not the answer to anything! You'll only make things worse for yourself if you hurt anyone."

Carol blinked, frowned. "Why d' you call me 'Mother?' You used to call me 'Mommy.' Are you trying to wound me, being so formal, so distant?"

Her response caught Valerie completely off guard.

"I—I don't know. It's not—" Maybe it was a subconscious way of distancing herself. She hadn't felt warm fuzzies toward her mother in a long time, and the more formal moniker just…fit. Valerie waved a hand, as if batting away the distracting comment. "Mother, focus. Put the gun down, and then we can talk about anything you want."

Carol grimaced and shook her head slowly, wearily. "I'm tired of talking. That's all I've done for the last few years. It doesn't help. It doesn't change things."

Val's heart twisted. She knew the fatigue, the relentless ache her mother meant. "Mother, you've been doing better. Things were going okay. You can do it again."

"So tired of it—"

Deep down, Val knew it would always be this way. Her mother would never be "cured." Carol would be fighting this battle against her mental illness for the rest of her life. Every day would be the same battle to retrain her thinking, fight the temptation of alcohol and fight the negative thoughts that taunted her. "I'm going to help you. You're not alone."

"Liar! You left me! You're on their side!" Carol swung the gun toward Valerie. "This is your fault!"

"No!" Nash shouted.

A strong, hard body tackled her from behind. Another ear-shattering blast echoed through the house.

The seconds that followed stretched like minutes.

Erik grappled loose from her mother's grip.

Nash shifted his body in front of Val's.

Carol panicked and sent another wild shot over their heads.

"Mother, stop!" Valerie shouted, her own panic rising.

No. Not good. She quickly put a lid on her emotions.

The key to getting through this was keeping everyone, her mother especially, from giving in to extreme emotion.

"We have to get that gun away from her," Nash mumbled under his breath.

"I know. I'm trying," Valerie whispered back.

"Well, your way is not working," Nash said tightly, "and I'm not going to sit back and let her kill—"

They heard a scuffling, a grunt, and Valerie whipped her head around to find Erik fighting Carol for the gun. The weapon discharged again, and Nash shoved from the floor and charged toward Erik. "Dad!"

A cry of frustration ripped from Val's throat. This was exactly the kind of chaos that would feed her mother's paranoia and spiraling anxiety. "Please, stop!"

Somehow, Carol managed to wrest control of the gun again, just as Nash inserted himself between the pistol and his father.

Erik swiped sweat from his face, aiming a finger at Carol, and yelled, "You are batshit crazy, lady!"

"Dad, can it!" Nash growled.

Seeing the ire rise in her mother's eyes, Valerie staggered to her feet and rushed forward, hands raised. She had to do something that would make a difference. Fast. "Mother, stop this now, and I'll come home with you!"

"What?" Nash barked. The hurt and shock in his voice reverberated to her marrow, but she had to focus on her mother. On saving them all from potential disaster.

"What do you say, Mother? You and I walk out of here now. Everyone safe?"

"It's too late," Carol whined, the gun still waving precariously in her hands. "It won't end until *he's* gone." She aimed the weapon at Erik, then moved it to Nash. "And him. You went back to him. Just like I knew you would."

"Mother..." She took a breath, searching for that something to make a connection. "*Mommy*, I need you to stop. Please."

"I h've to." Carol's face crumpled with anger and grief. "If that idiot Mickey hadn't botched things up..."

She sensed more than saw Nash tense. Her gut pitched, but Valerie kept her gaze locked on her mother. "No one needs to get hurt, Mommy."

"I hav'ta set things right, Val. They stole you fr'm me."

"You hired Mickey Gorman to kill me, didn't you?" Nash asked, his voice hard.

Val shot him a quelling look.

"You sh' be dead. But Mickey screwed e'ry thing up."

"Mother, we can work this out. Just—"

"And you knew, didn't you?" Nash asked, the disappointment heavy in his tone.

Valerie faced Nash, her heart sinking. She knew her guilt was written on her face, but she didn't have the strength to hide it.

"What the hell's going on?" Erik demanded. "Are you saying that she hired a killer? Did she murder Axel?"

"I wish I had." Carol scoffed. "One less Colton t' plague th' world."

"That's what had you so upset last night and this morning, isn't it?" Nash asked.

"I—" Val's voice stuck in her throat.

"Why didn't you tell me?" The question carried a world of pain, accusation and frustration.

"I'm sorry, Nash. I couldn't..."

"Couldn't or wouldn't?" he snapped. "My God, Val! I thought we were past all the hiding and secrets."

"Hello? Could you two have your lovers' quarrel later?

There's still a crazy woman with a gun pointed at us!" Erik growled.

His father's chastening seemed to snap Nash back to the danger her mother posed, but Valerie knew the matter was far from settled.

"No." Carol swayed, and the gun drooped. "Let them argue. Let her see how treacherous and unfaithful her Colton is!"

Nash's green gaze darkened to deep jade as he narrowed his eyes on Carol. His body tensed, and Valerie read his intent in his expression the instant before he lunged.

"Nash, no!"

He seized her mother's wrist, shoving the hand that held the gun into the air. Shots fired and plaster rained down from the ceiling. Fear stole Valerie's breath. Then a sense of urgency, a need to protect, compelled her forward. She darted to the grappling pair and tried to insert herself between them. Reached for her mother's shoulder, trying to tear her attention away from Nash. "Mother! Mommy, don't! I'll come with you! Let's leave now!"

"Dad!" Nash shouted, "Get. Val. Out of here! Both of you go!"

Hands grabbed her around the waist, dragged her back, even as she fought and called to Carol. "Mother! Mother, please don't!"

As Erik bodily lifted her and carried her outside, Valerie's energy left in a wave. Defeat and despair drained her, and she went limp as a sense of failure crashed down on her. She was numb as Erik led her into the icy morning, past the parked cars and toward the street.

But the crunch of tires in dead leaves on the street

roused her. Detective Cartwright emerged from his vehicle, a squad car pulling in behind him.

A bittersweet bubble of hope swelled. Cartwright's arrival was both a godsend and the beginning of the end. She struggled free of Erik's grip and staggered to the detective. "They're in the living room. Please hurry! She's trying to kill Nash!"

Chapter Twenty-One

Nash kept a firm grip on Carol's wrist, holding her arm up and keeping the gun pointed at the ceiling. Now that his father and Valerie were out of harm's way, he looked for an opportunity to overpower her. It wouldn't be difficult. He could already feel Val's mother weakening. The trick would be in not hurting Carol in the process.

He hooked a leg around Carol's, hoping he could trip her, knock her off balance and then take her to the ground with a wrestler's move. But just as he made his move, Val's mother smacked her forehead into his face. Pain exploded behind his nose, and the warm leak of blood dripped onto his upper lip.

On some level he heard the new voices approaching, but his focus was on maintaining the upper hand with Carol. Disarming her…

"Police! Drop your weapon and get down on the ground. Hands behind your head!"

Relief flowed through Nash, an odd counterpoint to the adrenaline and anger that had fueled his struggle with Carol. On the heels of the relief came surprise. The man charging into the room, leading with his own weapon, was not Damon.

"Drop the gun and get down!" Harry Cartwright repeated, his tone commanding.

Carol turned a startled look toward the detective as if she'd only just noticed him, and Nash used that instant of Carol's distraction to wrestle her to the floor.

But she clung tenaciously to the pistol. Even as Cartwright continued barking orders, Carol struggled.

"Colton, damn it, move away from her and get on the ground!"

Raising a silent prayer, Nash released Carol's wrist, then eased to the floor and rolled behind the couch. He heard a wail, and as he righted himself and turned to watch, Carol lifted the gun to her own temple.

"Get away from me! I'll do it! Don't touch me!"

Heart thundering, Nash held his breath.

"I don't want to hurt you, Carol," Cartwright said. "Everything will be fine. I just need you to place the gun on the floor and lie on your stomach."

A movement at the other side of the living room caught his attention. A uniformed policeman moved into the room silently, weapon drawn.

Carol wept, her hand trembling, the gun shaking. "No… No, no, no…get away from me!"

Nash held perfectly still, not wanting to do anything to unbalance the precarious situation.

Cartwright stayed put, as well, speaking in a low soothing tone, clearly trying to keep Carol's attention on him as the uniformed officer inched forward behind her.

And then in a matter of seconds, a swift move that disarmed Carol and another that wrestled her to the floor, it was over. She continued to sob and snarl invectives about the Coltons, but Valerie's mother was in custody.

Cartwright stepped over to check Nash for weapons

before he allowed him to stand, then started firing questions at him. On the other side of the adrenaline rush, Nash shuddered.

"You're bleeding. What happened?" Cartwright said.

"She headbutted me. Don't think it's broken." When Nash raised a hand to his nose, it was his torso that protested with a sharp, stinging pain. He grunted and looked down to find a red stain around a tear in his shirt. "I'll be damned. She winged me. I didn't even realize."

"That happens sometimes, in the heat of the moment." Cartwright angled his head, appraising the wound, when Nash raised his shirt to examine it himself. "You need an ambulance?"

Nash pressed his hand to the bleeding gash, hissed at the pain the pressure caused. "Nah. I'll get my dad or Val to drive me."

"I have to get statements from both of them. You, too. But yours will wait until you've seen a doctor."

Across the room, the uniformed officer had Carol on her feet, her hands zip-tied behind her. With a firm hand on her arm, he led her from the room.

"What will happen to Valerie's mother?" he asked, knowing how this turn of events would devastate Val. He had only to think of her brokenness last night and this morning for confirmation of that, and he ached for her.

But remembering Val's mood also reminded him how she'd hidden the truth from him, how she'd promised her mother to leave the scene with her, how she'd had the opportunity to choose him and had sided with her mother. Again. Her mother, who'd hired a killer to murder him. Who'd taken his father hostage and held a gun to them all.

Bitterness and disappointment swirled in his gut. Even

after everything they'd shared and discussed, Valerie continued to deceived and forsake him. To shut him out.

"Nash!" Damon entered the room, his DEA shield out identifying him as law enforcement. He flashed the badge toward Cartwright, who must have remembered him, since he barely glanced at the ID. "Are you all right? Val said shots were fired!"

Nash lifted his hand from his side and Damon's face paled. "My God!"

"Flesh wound… I think." Nash raised a querying glance to the detective. "Permission for my brother to take me to the ER?"

Cartwright nodded. "Go on. I'll catch up with you later."

Holding his side, which had begun to throb, Nash walked outside with Damon, scanning the lawn for Valerie. His father was leaning against a squad car on the street, talking to another uniformed officer. Erik lifted his head as Nash came out and gave him an up-and-down look, and when his gaze went to the bloody stain on Nash's shirt, he frowned. He excused himself from the officer he was speaking to and started toward his sons.

Nash continued toward Damon's car, still looking for Valerie. He needed to know she was safe, that—

The screech of a female voice drew his attention to the police cruiser, where the policeman who'd taken Carol into custody was trying to put her in the back of his squad car. Valerie stood near her mother, watching as the officer tried to get cooperation from Carol.

Seeing Valerie across the yard, her attention focused on Carol rather than on him, spiked the churn of harsh emotions that gnawed his gut. Even when her mother had so clearly betrayed Valerie, she still gave her mother preference over him. He gritted his teeth, trying to quell the petty jealousy and irritation. But deep down, Val's choice spoke to a deeper uneasiness and uncertainty within him, a years-old sense of being discarded and devalued.

Clearly upset herself, Valerie said something to Carol that Nash couldn't hear. Val turned to the officer, motioning, and got a short answer from the uniformed man. With a nod, she closed the distance between herself and her mother, touched Carol's face tenderly, then gave her a hug. In response, Valerie's mother snarled something and jerked away.

"She's a piece of work, that one, huh?" Erik said as he approached.

"She's mentally ill, Dad. A little sensitivity, please?" Nash turned to his father and sized him up. "You're all right? You're gonna get that looked at?" He nodded his head toward the cut on Erik's cheek.

His dad waved him off. "I'm fine. How bad is that?" Erik pointed to Nash's wound.

"Headed to the ER now," Damon said, sidestepping toward his car in a not-too-subtle hurry-it-up gesture. "We'll let you know."

"Yeah. You do that." Erik's gaze stayed on Nash. He seemed…worried?

Nash hesitated, sensing Erik was about to say more. Erik pursed his mouth, making the frown lines etched in his face deeper. His complexion looked sallow. His hair grayer. His face thinner. The recent events in the family, losing his brother and Father Time had aged Erik.

"You comin', Nash?" Damon called.

As Nash turned to leave, he cut one last glance to Valerie. Her focus remained on Carol, who was finally being put in the police car. With a sigh, he fell in step with Damon. "Yeah, let's go."

"Nash."

He turned back to his father when he called to him.

Erik pulled back his stooped shoulders. "Thanks. For coming when I called. I—"

His dad didn't finish the sentence, but the stiff words of gratitude were more than Nash had expected. "Of course. That's what family does."

VALERIE STOOD SHIVERING in the cold Chicago morning, watching with a shattered heart as the police car with her mother inside drove away. Her efforts to defuse the situation hadn't been enough. Her years of trying to protect and defend her mother hadn't been enough. Nothing she'd sacrificed or offered her mother had been enough to prevent this tragedy. After all these years of trying, hoping and doing her best for her mother, Carol Yates still resented her, blamed her, didn't care enough to consider how her actions affected her daughter.

Valerie squeezed her eyes shout and inhaled the icy air deeply. *Stop.* That's ten-year-old Valerie thinking. Eighteen-year-old Valerie. Pre-counseling, pre-educating-herself-on-the-realities-of-borderline-personality-disorder-and-alcoholism thinking. She worked to push aside the raw hurt and conjure her counselor's voice, oft-repeated refrains, advice for coping.

Not your fault. Not your responsibility. Her choices. Tough love.

She heard footsteps crunching in the frosty grass and blinked away the moisture in her eyes.

"You okay?" Detective Cartwright asked as he stopped beside her.

Not Nash, as she'd expected. She twisted, glancing to the curb where she'd seen Nash talking to Erik earlier. He wasn't there. Disappointment plucked at her as she exhaled a cleansing breath that clouded in the November chill. Cartwright was waiting for an answer. "Um, yes and no."

"If it helps," he said, angling his body to face her, "you did the right thing."

Valerie hesitated, trying to believe him. "Did I?"

He nodded. "Look, I know it's hard now. I'm guessing you're feeling kinda guilty about turning her in. But she was a threat to herself and others. You know that, right?"

Valerie let her shoulders droop. Nodded.

"If it helps you deal with things, you can blame me for giving you no choice."

She sighed. "Shifting blame is just another way we lie to ourselves, Detective. My counselor tells me facing hard truths head-on is the only way to affect real change and healing."

"You have a counselor. Good. I was going to recommend that."

Valerie twisted her mouth in a thoughtful moue. "I haven't talked to her in a while, but…it looks like I will be again. Soon."

"You should. This is—" he waved a hand down the road in the direction the squad car had left "—a lot to process."

His expression reflected more than just concern for Val's well-being. It seemed to her he was processing his own dark pain, but she didn't feel she had the right to ask him about it. So she simply nodded and muttered, "Yeah."

"And…it's Harry."

She sent the detective a puzzled look.

"I will follow her case, advocate for her, make sure that her mental illness is accounted for throughout her time in custody, the legal process and any detention. She'll be given a psych eval, of course. But rest assured, I'll see that she's cared for properly."

She tried to form the words of appreciation that knotted in her throat, but was distracted when a warm coat, redolent with an expensive-smelling cologne, was draped around her shoulders.

She cut a startled glance to Erik, who flicked a dismissive hand and said only, "I figured you were cold. I could see you shaking from across the lawn."

The gesture, so reminiscent of Nash's earlier that morning, resonated in her core with a bittersweet pang. "Where's Nash?"

"Left."

"He left?" Confusion and sharp disappointment sliced through her. She'd expected Nash to be upset with her, expected she'd have to explain her actions to him, but she'd never imagined he'd leave her. He had to know she was struggling with the issues of her mother's actions. He'd promised to be there for her but had fled the scene at the first sign of disagreement. "But… I don't understand…"

Erik shoved his hands deep in the pockets of the bathrobe he wore. "Damon took him to the ER a couple of minutes ago."

Valerie stiffened with alarm, and she took an involuntary step closer to Erik, grasped his arm. "The ER? He was injured? How badly? Which hospital?"

Erik shrugged. "Didn't ask which one. But don't panic. It wasn't life-threatening. The bullet really only grazed him."

Erik's cavalier disregard for his son's injury stunned

Valerie. But it shouldn't have. Nash had told her for years how disengaged and disinterested his father had been throughout his life. They made quite the pair, she and Nash, each with their own distant and dysfunctional parents. But at least they had each other. Or did they?

A fresh wave of pain blindsided her. She had to find Nash and explain her recent actions.

As she turned to get clearance from Cartwright to leave the scene, she tuned in to what he and Erik were discussing…and was hit with another shock.

"She left no question she hated me and my son. All Coltons, she said. Why couldn't she be the one who killed Axel?"

A ripple of anxiety swept through Valerie. Was it possible?

Cartwright made a noncommittal motion with his hands. "We'll look into it, of course, but we're currently following other leads that seem more promising."

"Such as?" Erik asked.

Was it her imagination or did Erik seem jittery? He *had* just been held at gunpoint, but still…

Cartwright schooled his face and gave his head a small shake. "Not at liberty to divulge specifics in an active investigation, Mr. Colton." The detective shifted his gaze to Valerie. "I think I'm about done here. Can I do anything for you before I go?"

She pulled Erik's coat around her shoulders tighter, gripping the edges closed with one hand. "No. Thanks. Just…look out for my mother?"

He gave her a grim nod before returning to his car and driving away.

"I'm going to the emergency room to find Nash." She glanced at Erik, pausing, hoping he'd redeem himself by expressing a desire to accompany her to check on his son. When he didn't, she squelched a spark of irritation and added, "May I keep this coat for a little while? I'll return it later today."

Erik flicked a hand. "Sure. Now if you'll excuse me, I have calls to make. Lawyer, insurance, builder. Thanks to your…*mother*—" He paused, his grimace telling her he'd debated what derogatory adjective to use and finally curbed the notion. But his tone said what his words didn't. "I have bullet holes to repair in my home."

BY THE TIME Valerie got to the urgent care clinic where Damon had taken Nash, he had been treated for the bullet wound, given an antibiotic to prevent infection and released. She met them in the parking lot as they were leaving the clinic, which Damon had opted for instead of the ER since Nash's injuries weren't life-threatening. When she saw the bruise already darkening Nash's face where her mother had head-butted him, she winced. He didn't have a broken nose, thankfully, but he was clearly in pain and moving slowly, carefully. But more frightening to her was the cool look in his eyes when he spotted her. He was angry. Hurt. Understandably so. She had work to do to salvage the mess she'd made.

"I'll take him home," Val offered, trying to ease under Nash's arm to help him to her car.

He waved her off. "I got it. And Damon's already said he'd take me." When she opened her mouth to protest, he nodded at her dishabille. "Besides, don't you want to go home and dress?"

She glanced down at herself. She was still in her sleep shirt, Vita's garden shoes and Erik's coat. Hair uncombed. No makeup. She must look a mess. But none of that had mattered when she thought Nash was injured. It still didn't, compared with her need to heal the damage she had done to their relationship.

"It's not a problem for me. And we need to talk..."

He stiffened and avoided eye contact. "Yeah, we do."

The hard edge in his tone cut Valerie to the quick.

Damon sent her a sympathetic look and shrugged as Nash hobbled past her and out the door. "I'll get him settled at his house and have him call you." He took a step, then gave Val a feeble smile. "He cares about you, but he's stubborn. You may have to fight to get past his walls, but don't give up on him. You were meant to be together. Even I can see that."

Damon's reassurances buoyed her, but after twenty-four hours of calling and having him ignore her calls, she decided she had to employ the move she'd used three weeks earlier. She'd arrive at his house unannounced and confront him.

Chapter Twenty-Two

Nash wasn't surprised to find Valerie on his front porch late the next afternoon, but he was surprised how relieved he was to see her. Even so, his teeth still clenched, his chest still hurt and his thoughts still spun when he thought about what appeared to be another betrayal, another secret between them. Despite all that, knowing she hadn't ducked and run back to Ohio without hashing things out with him was encouraging.

He yanked open his door, wincing when the motion pulled the muscles in his side that had been damaged when he was shot. Grazed, really, but he still felt quite sore. And the stitches were beginning to itch.

"Hi," she said and exhaled heavily as if she'd been holding her breath. As if she'd been unsure whether he'd answer the door or not for her.

"Hi, yourself." He glanced past her when a movement caught his eye. The calico emerged from his bushes and meowed as if complaining about the cold. Returning his attention to Val, he appraised her mood—brow puckered, eyes wary, smile tremulous.

"Can I come in?"

He'd been staring. Nash blinked hard, cleared his throat and stepped back to let her in. He stuck his foot out to stop the cat when he tried to follow Valerie inside. “Go home, goofball. You don’t live here.”

“I tried calling,” she said. “Several times.”

“Right. I saw. I should have at least texted back. But I…” He scratched his cheek.

“Why didn’t you?” she asked when he faltered.

“Well, when I got home from the urgent care clinic, I took one of the pain pills they gave me. It made me real sleepy, and I ended up napping the rest of the day. Turned my phone off. I’ve kinda had night and day backward since then and…”

And he hadn’t had time between calls from all of his family checking on him to think, to process what he was feeling, what he wanted to say to Val.

“How are you feeling?” Valerie asked as she shucked her gloves and shoved them in her pockets. She turned, looking for an empty peg where she could hang her coat.

“Is this the small talk portion of your visit or are you diving right to the part where we talk about how you wounded me with your broken promise?”

She cut a guilty look over her shoulder, coat still in her hands. “I…meant your injuries. Your bullet wound. But…” Val finished hanging up her coat and turned back to him, her countenance reminding him of a scolded puppy. “If you’d rather cut to the chase…” She waved a hand, inviting him to elaborate on whatever he chose.

Nash closed his eyes. Sighed. “Sorry. That was… harsh.”

After rubbing his gritty eyes, he forced aside his gruffness. He hadn’t slept well and hadn’t taken a pain pill recently, but he shouldn’t let fatigue and discomfort color this discussion. He had a gut feeling his future happiness hung in the balance, and he needed to play fair or live with regrets the rest of his life.

"Yeah. It was." Valerie squared her shoulders. "For the record, I didn't set out to deceive you or break any promises. I was…cornered by circumstances. Caught in the middle."

Cornered by circumstances? Irritation niggled at the possibility she was trying to dismiss her actions with lame excuses. Swallowing the questions that stirred in him, he hitched his head to the living room. "You wanna sit?"

Valerie followed him to the couch and sat on the edge, leaning toward him as her fingers fidgeted. He took the opposite end of the couch, and, moving a pillow in deference to his injured side, he angled his body to face her. "You knew your mother had hired Gorman to come after me before we got the call from my dad, didn't you?"

"Nash, I couldn't—"

"Yes or no?"

She pressed her mouth in a taut line. Her eyes reflected pain as she lifted her chin. "Yes."

"So even though you promised, just a few days ago, to be forthcoming and honest and not to keep secrets from me, you did just that about something as important as an assassin hired to kill me. Is that about right?"

"It's not that simple. You make it sound like I wanted to hurt you. I hated keeping the truth from you!"

"But you did."

"I couldn't tell you! You haven't given me a chance to explain what happened!"

"Explain what? The bottom line is, when push came to shove, you picked your mother over me. You chose secrecy and undeserved loyalty to her over our relationship and the promises you made me!"

Val shook her head, her eyes bright with conviction. "That's not how it happened. I wanted to tell you, but Cartwright told me I *couldn't* say anything to anyone about what we'd found out. Including you."

Nash gritted his back teeth as he mulled that information. "Detective Cartwright?"

She nodded. "After I talked to my mother and Nancy by phone, asking them about Gorman, I was left with very uneasy feelings. I had to know the truth. The limbo was agony. And I wanted to *protect you*!" Her voice broke.

The half sob that snagged her words caused his own throat to tighten. A sharp ache crept through his chest like a growing fissure in a rock.

"Nash, I couldn't ignore the real possibility that my mother was trying to hurt you. I had to know, so I could stop her." She paused for a breath, wet her lips. "I went to the police and told Cartwright everything. He questioned Gorman, and Gorman gave my mother up in exchange for a plea deal."

"You should have told me all this that night when I asked you. You remember, I specifically asked you what you'd learned about Gorman!"

"Yes, I remember! But Detective Cartwright could have charged me with all kinds of things about messing up his investigation or aiding and abetting my mother or—" Clearly flustered and exasperated, she waved a dismissive hand. "Whatever it's called. But he told me, in no uncertain terms, that I couldn't say anything to anyone while he followed up with locating my mother. Including you."

"Not even when my dad called, and we rushed out to

handle that whole disaster? You don't think a little heads-up about what you knew would have been helpful? Even then you were trying to hide the truth about your mother! Protecting her. Putting her first."

Valerie's mouth opened, and she goggled at him. "I chose you over her when I called Detective Cartwright, giving up her location, on the way to your father's house!"

"Wait... You called Cartwright?" He frowned, shook his head. "No. We called *Damon*. And you had my dad and your mother on the other line."

"But after she hung up and I couldn't reach them again, I called Cartwright. I gave him your dad's address. Don't you remember? You were there, driving the car! You had to have heard me."

A vague memory of Val making a brief cryptic call flashed in his memory. "That was Cartwright you called?"

"Who did you think it was?"

"I don't... I was focused on getting through the traffic and worried about my dad. I guess I didn't..." He expelled a breath in a loud gush and raked fingers through his hair as he considered what she'd told him, let it mesh with blurry memories of the frantic moments.

"When I left the police station the day before, Cartwright told me to let him know if I heard from Mother. If I learned anything."

She wrapped her hand around his, refocusing his attention on what she was saying. When he met her eyes, his heart jumped.

Val held his gaze with a teary, but determined, stare. Her expression radiated intent, gravitas and pleading. "I could have disobeyed Cartwright's order. I could have tried to protect Mother or helped her escape justice, but *you* meant more to me than making more excuses for my mother. She made her choice when she came after you, after your dad. And I made mine. I turned her in because I choose you, Nash. I want you in my life, now and always."

I choose you. He'd spent most of his life waiting to hear those words, waiting to feel that he'd been wanted. Not discarded or ignored. Not taken in out of pity. Not ghosted or avoided.

Wanted.

He took a moment, flopping back against the cushion while the notion digested. Settled and filled him with a warmth and love.

"What about you?" she asked, jostling him from his inner thoughts.

Nash frowned. "What about me?"

"You promised to trust me. You said you'd give me twenty-four hours to work things out. To find answers and deal with my mother."

He sat taller, a wariness prickling him. "And I did. All you told me the night before your mom showed up in town was that she hadn't denied anything, had avoided your question with redirection and taking offense."

She turned up a palm. "But trust shouldn't have a time limit, Nash. Either you trust me, trust that I have your best interest at heart, or you don't."

Nash stilled. She had a point. One he needed to address. "I do! I—"

Realizing he'd answered reflexively, defensively, and that his answer was as key, as fundamental to their future happiness as anything she could promise, he paused. Nash swiped a hand down his face as he took a mental step back and thought, really thought, about his feelings for Val, their past, his reasons for doubting her in days gone by.

"If you don't trust me, then what are we doing?" she asked, heartache weighting her voice. "That day in the park, we said we wanted to build a future. We said we could let bygones be bygones, make a fresh start."

He shoved off the couch, and his rib muscles throbbed a protest. Nash ignored the pain as he paced toward his back window. He stared out at the yard Vita and Nicole had helped him plan and plant. Nicole, who'd become like a second mother to him over the years. He hadn't warmed to her immediately. Even that relationship, which was so much a part of his current sense of love and a familial foundation, had been built slowly. One day, one loving gesture, one forgiving mercy at a time. Nicole had stepped in where his father had failed and showed him what real family, faith and grace meant. It all started with a rooted love. And if the past weeks with Valerie had shown him anything, it was that he'd never stopped loving her. His love had changed, matured. And in the past days had grown with respect and admiration and understanding. And passion, born of more than teenage hormones.

Nash exhaled a breath that seemed to free him of demons that had chased him for years. His old feelings of rejection by his father didn't have to shape his days. He had more powerful, more permanent and stable relationships to sustain him. His brother. Nicole.

Valerie.

"Nash?"

When he faced her again, he saw more than just the beautiful face and frightened eyes that waited for his response. He saw a woman who'd shown immense strength, caring for a mentally ill mother. Determination, as she educated herself and pursued her love of art and graphic design. And courage, having been the one to take the first step to end the painful abyss and misunderstanding that had separated them for years. And today. Valerie had risked rejection coming here today to fight for the love they were building together.

A knot formed in his throat and choked the words he knew he needed to say. The anxiety and doubts filling Val's face spoke for the hurt she had to be suffering as she waited for his reply.

His first job was to ease her mind, calm her fears. He strode quickly back to the couch and pulled her into his arms. As he cradled her head against his chest and pressed kisses to the top of her head, he rasped, "I trust you. I do. I'm sorry. I let this business with your mom mess with my head and…"

She squirmed free of his embrace in order to look him in the eye. "My mother will not come between us again," she said with the firmness and solemnity of a person taking a vow.

He nodded. "I talked to Detective Cartwright earlier. He said she'd be charged with attempted murder and a variety of other felonies, but that based on her psych evaluation, pending a judge's ruling, she'd likely be going to one of the secure state mental health facilities."

She nodded. "That's right. But that's not what I mean." Her grip tightened on his arms. "I will not let my allegiances to her override my allegiances to you ever again. For years, I met weekly with a counselor in Toledo who helped me sort out all the confusion and guilt I had surrounding my mother's drinking and mental health. I'd let that slide lately, but not again. The number one take-away my counselor gave me, which I'd let myself forget in recent weeks, was that my own mental health has to be my first priority. So I'm going to find a therapist here in Chicago."

"Here?" he asked, hope swelling in his chest.

She smiled. "That's where I plan to be living." She sobered a bit, then added, "To be clear… I'm not cutting ties with my mother. I'll visit her wherever she's sent, keep tabs on her treatment, talk with her doctors. But my priority will be my life, finding my own happiness."

A smile spread across his face as he studied Val's countenance. "You are incredible, you know that?" He pressed a hand to his chest. "I really admire you. Your strength and wisdom."

Tears bloomed in her eyes. "Thanks. They're hard-earned." Dabbing the moisture clinging to her lashes, she whispered, "In case you were still wondering, you are what makes me happy. You are why I'm moving to Chicago, and you are the home I want to build for the future."

He cut his gaze to the wall where the drawing of a bungalow that they'd made together all those years ago hung. Her gaze followed.

Framing his face with her hands, she pressed a soft kiss to his lips. "Sorry, Mr. Architect. A house is just a building. Four walls with flowers out front. It's the people and love inside that make a home."

He hummed his agreement as he kissed her again, then something in her statement plucked his heart and caused a strange buzzing to fill his core. "You love me?"

Valerie's brow dipped as if she hadn't heard him correctly. "You don't know that?"

Her answer wasn't a straight *yes*, but her astonishment said what she didn't. He was searching for his voice when she plowed her fingers into his hair and let her tears flow. "Yes, I love you, Nash Colton. I have since I was a teenager, and I always will. Don't you ever doubt or forget that."

He cleared the constriction from his throat and cradled the back of her head with one hand while drying her tears with his other. "And I love you, Valerie Yates. Deeply and forever. I don't ever want to spend another day without you. Promise me you'll grow old with me? Do life with me?"

She canted back slightly and arched a delicate eyebrow in query.

He laughed. "Yes, I'm asking you to marry me."

"In that case, I promise. I'm yours, Nash. For life."

Epilogue

Four months later

Three minutes. Just three minutes.

Good God, who knew three minutes could last so long?

Valerie tried to clear her mind, shift her focus, but waiting was still not her strong suit.

She bent over the paper in front of her and resumed sketching. Since moving to Chicago, she'd shifted her talents toward freelance work and was already building an impressive client list thanks to her many connections through the Colton family. She'd done graphic-design work for True, Colton Connections, a local bakery, a temp agency and the Peoria Parks and Recreation department. She'd even had a call from a distant Colton cousin in Whisperwood, Texas, who wanted a new logo for his wife's expanding private detective agency.

As a face began to take shape on her sketch pad, she had a flash of the last time she'd waited for a test result. She'd used drawing to distract herself then, too. She smiled as she filled in the squarish oval she'd started. Eyes, nose, lips…

Soft, demanding lips. Skilled lips that still *made her breath catch and her toes curl.*

She glanced across the room to the man pacing the bedroom floor.

"How long has it been?" Nash asked.

Valerie checked the timer on her phone screen. "Minute and fifteen seconds."

Nash stopped and scowled at her. "That's all? You're sure?"

She showed him the screen, where the numbers glowed on her cell.

"I'm going to look. I can't take this..." He started for the bathroom and she rushed over to intercept him, laughing.

"Patience, my dear. We swore we'd wait it out together." She rose on her toes to press a kiss to his tense mouth. By the second kiss, his lips relaxed and he pulled her closer, hugging her tightly.

When he raised his head, he whispered, "Have I told you today how much I love you?"

"Three times, not counting the sweet nothings during our lovemaking this morning." Her grin reflected all the joy that had filled her heart the last four months.

Although seeing her mother committed to the mental health correctional facility had been painful, she also knew a sense of relief. Her mother would get the medical treatment and counseling she needed. Valerie could rest easy knowing her mother was safe. And because of that, Nash was safe. And with Nash, her future was safe...and certain.

"Good. I don't ever want you to doubt how I feel about

you again." He kissed her and angled his head to glance at her phone. "Geez! Still forty seconds."

"What if it says I'm not pregnant?" she asked.

"Then we have the pleasure of trying again until you are." He tapped a finger on her nose. "And then doing it all again. I'm thinking three kids is a good number."

She gave a quiet sigh, but kept smiling.

As usual, he read her mood despite her pretense. Lifting a dark blond eyebrow, he frowned. "Wait. Where is this coming from? Don't you want to start a family?"

"I do. But...because of the complications I had last time, when I miscarried at seventeen, my doctor warned me I could have trouble conceiving again. Scar tissue and—"

"We'll cross that bridge when—"

The soft jingle of her phone timer stopped Nash, midsentence. His eyes widened. He swallowed hard. His fingers gripped her arms a little firmer. "Oh, boy. This is it."

She laced her fingers in his and led him into the bathroom. When they were both standing at the sink, she gripped the edge of the facial tissue she'd placed over the test stick and counted, "One, two, three!"

She whipped the tissue away, and they bumped heads as they leaned over to read the indicator.

"Well..." she said.

"So..." he said.

She pivoted on her heel to face him. "Congratulations, Daddy."

He looked stunned. Then a wide grin split his face. "I'm going to be a father!"

She laughed and nodded.

Nash whooped and lifted her from her feet as he hugged her. "Have I told you today that I love you, Val?"

She nodded, happy tears blooming in her eyes. "Yes. And I love you, too."

* * * * *

JOIN US ON SOCIAL MEDIA!

Stay up to date with our latest releases, author news and gossip, special offers and discounts, and all the behind-the-scenes action from Mills & Boon...

millsandboon

millsandboonuk

millsandboon

It might just be true love...